SAY IT

SHADOWVERSE

RAELYNN ROSE

TWISTED HEART PRESS LLC

TRIGGER WARNINGS

*S*ay It includes kidnapping, violence, blood and gore, death, dub con, hunter/prey, family trauma, abuse (not by MMCs), risk to pregnancy. There might be others I have forgotten. You know your heart and mind - please take care of yourself. I try to approach any delicate matter with tact and respect.

Raeylynn Rose @2024
Published by Twisted Heart Press, LLC

sold, or otherwise transferred from your computer to another through upload, or for a fee.

CHAPTER ONE

<u>Corazon</u>

Like a fucking gift, I sat in the back of the town car in a white, frilly dress, a full veil not just adorning my head but covering my face. Yep. All wrapped up for my soon-to-be pack.

No. I hadn't chosen them. I didn't love them. I could barely stand to be in their vicinity for more than an hour at a time, and that was only when my fathers forced me to be sociable with their people.

Their precious little omega. The only of six children. Somehow, my alpha fathers and omega mother had managed to birth five beta kids before they'd hit the lottery with me. Their words, not mine.

To me, my designation was nothing more than a damn curse. Something that Pack Alvarez had used as leverage in nearly every negotiation since the moment I'd perfumed and presented.

Since that day, I hadn't known a moment of freedom. I had been locked in a gilded cage, guarded and escorted by my fathers' men any time I dared leave the house. Even something as simple as going for drinks with my friends required days of planning and approval from not one, but all five of my alpha fathers.

With my arms crossed, I turned my head and watched through the passenger window while two men flanked me on either side with two more up front in the passenger and driver's seat. My fathers and mother rode ahead of us, my siblings all in vehicles with their own packs trailing behind.

Of course my fathers would make my lowly beta siblings not only drive their own cars instead of riding in a limo, but follow behind this ridiculous caravan that was leading me to my enslavement.

And how the hell else could I think of my bonding ceremony? This was not my choice. And I highly doubted the three alphas who'd been chosen to bond me had had a choice, either. We were all pawns in our family packs' games. We were prizes, tools to be used, to be sold and traded for more power.

It hadn't mattered how much I'd screamed and cried and begged. When I'd attempted to pack a small duffel bag and sneak out of the house with the intention of disappearing, my fathers' men found me before I hit the next town and dragged me back home.

And that had been the last night I'd slept without someone outside my door.

Twenty-three years old and I had no control over my own life. Twenty-three years old and I was being traded as a favor, as payment for whatever new deal my fathers and Pack Garcia had worked out.

Leo, Julian, and Roman. Those were to be my alphas. Those were to be the men with whom I would spend the rest of my life. Those were the men I would be forced to fuck and bare children for. Because that was part of the deal. Neither pack were content with simply bonding the four of us; I was to be impregnated within the year.

And then what? What if I was like my own parents and bore only betas? Would we then be discarded as easily as my own siblings had been? Would we be left alone?

Did that mean I might be able to build a life of my own, separated from the violence and power that followed my family's name every-where we went?

The man to my left uttered a curse under his breath and moved into my space to look around the front seat.

"What the fuck is this?" he asked.

"Construction," the guard in the passenger seat answered.

"Bullshit," my left side guard spit out. "I put in enough calls ahead of time. There shouldn't be a single roadblock from the house to the hall."

My heart began to thunder as all four men pulled firearms from the holsters hidden under their jackets.

"Stay alert," Raul – my father's most trusted guard and the front passenger – barked out. "Eyes open, necks on a swivel."

With shaky hands, I yanked the gauzy film from over my face so I could see my surroundings better, turning to look for my siblings behind us. But their cars were no longer visible. Instead, there were two black SUVs and what looked like a construction truck following a couple cars' length back.

As I opened my mouth to question how my brothers and sister had been separated from the caravan, Raul cursed and turned in his seat.

"Get her down!" he barked, shoving my head until it was practi-cally wedged between my knees, the tight bodice of my dress nearly cutting off my air supply.

"What? What is it?" I wheezed out as my head was held down.

No more did I get the words out of my mouth that the familiar sounds of gunfire began to pop around me, the loud dings of the car being hit causing me to squeak as panic squeezed my heart.

Between the fear and this awkward position, I was going to end up passing out if I didn't get some more air into my lungs.

The gunfire sounded as though it was coming from all around us, and I was a sitting duck trapped between the four guards. Eventually, they might have to step out to aid in protecting the trophy – me. Then what? Not as though any of them would give me a firearm to protect myself. Especially not after my one and only escape attempt.

A scream tore from my lips and I wrenched away from whoever was restraining me as an explosion shook the vehicle and shattered the windows.

"Get us the fuck out of here!" Raul ordered.

"Where the fuck do you want me to go?"

My parents' limo was nowhere to be seen. In front of us was the construction crew and vehicles. Only they weren't wearing orange vests and hardhats or holding jackhammers – they were holding semi and fully automatic rifles and had them pointed in our direction.

Was this some kind of an assassination attempt? Take out the princess of Pack Alvarez in hopes of crumbling the empire?

There were members of my fathers' guard shooting back, but they were far outnumbered and outmanned.

Shit. Shit shit shit.

"Give me a gun!" I demanded.

"Just keep your head down!" Raul ordered.

"And what happens if you four die? You're just going to leave me here with nothing but my garter to fight them off with?"

Someone huffed what almost sounded like a surprised laugh, but the sound was buried by more gunfire.

The pops slowed. Taking another quick peek around, I realized those who had blocked our path were the only ones standing and had surrounded the vehicle.

"We're okay, right? This vehicle is bullet proof…right?" I hated the tremor in my voice. Hated the looks in the eyes of the men who wore balaclavas to hide their identity.

"No," Raul growled.

"Oh god," I cried out.

They were waiting us out. They weren't firing into the vehicle. That might have boded well for me since they obviously didn't want to risk hitting me. But they weren't walking away, either. Would they simply…

A scream tore from my lips as four pistols rose, aimed at my guards, and fired. Blood sprayed my face, covered my silk and lace gown and veil, some even saturating my hair.

This couldn't be happening. I didn't exactly want to be sold off like I was nothing more than livestock, but…the devil I knew and all that. I had no idea what these men had in mind, whether they simply planned to take me to hold as ransom…

Or whether they'd planned to steal the jewel of Pack Alvarez, to fill me with pups, to end the reign of my fathers by killing off their possibility of any more alphas or omegas coming from their bloodline.

The door was yanked open and one of the men reached for me. Nope. No way in hell was I going willingly.

Kicking and screaming, I tried to scramble to the other side of the sedan, gagging when the guard on the right slumped forward and more blood coated my dress until I felt the sticky warmth seep through the fabric to cover my skin.

Hands hooked under my armpits and dragged me out with me struggling and fighting the whole way.

But really – how fucking hard could I fight when I'd been dressed to look like a big cupcake and my feet had been shoved into ridiculously high and sparkly shoes.

They weren't just high; they were fucking stilettos. And the moment any of these assholes got close enough, I started kicking, hoping to disable at least one of them. If the tip pierced one of their chests – and their hearts – all the better.

As easily as I'd been pulled from the backseat, someone gripped my legs and clamped their arms around my shins, leaving only my hands free. And my mouth. I cursed and screamed while clawing at any bare flesh I could find, leaving gouges on someone's hands, more on another man's arm.

Whether I died today or not, I refused to go down without a fucking fight. I hated growing up as the Alvarez jewel, but at least I'd learned enough through the years of watching my fathers torture and kill enemies to inflict damage to another person. If just one of these assholes would get close enough, I'd gouge out their eyes with my fingernails. Hell, I would even use my teeth to rip out their throats if given the chance.

None of the above happened. A cloth was slapped over my face until I feared they were going to suffocate me.

Then the world went black.

WHEN REALITY BEGAN to seep back in, my senses were assailed with the coppery tang of blood. It settled in my nose, even on my tongue.

Forcing my lids open, I moved only my eyes, taking in my surroundings, focusing on the softness below me, the warm, fragrant glow from a fireplace crackling somewhere nearby, a combination of unfamiliar scents that, oddly, lent me some comfort.

Memories of what happened slammed into my mind. Sitting straight up, I looked down at my blood-soaked bonding gown and gagged as my stomach turned and the contents of my meager breakfast threatened to make a reappearance.

Where the hell was I? I had never seen this room before. And the obvious scents of alpha weren't any I remembered encountering. These weren't men I'd met. At least I couldn't remember meeting them. Then again, because of my family's empire, I tended to meet a lot of new people I never saw past that one night.

Rolling from the side of the bed, I began to frantically claw at the fabric, trying my best to rip it away from me.

When the door opened and a man who stood a good foot taller than me stalked inside, my hands froze at the halter neckline that dipped and showcased more cleavage than should have been considered acceptable for a bonding ceremony for my family's place in society.

A balaclava still covered his face, leaving only pale blue eyes staring at me with zero emotion behind them. As he stalked closer, I began to back up until my knees hit something and I dropped onto a couch situated in...a bedroom. I was in a bedroom. There was a humongous bed, a couch that would fit several people, and a fireplace.

Who the hell were these people?

As he loomed over me, I refused to avert my gaze. I had no idea what his plans were, but just like when they'd attacked the caravan, killed my fathers' guards, and dragged me away, I would put up one hell of a fight in hopes he would give up and leave me be.

Then I would find a way out of this place, figure out where we were located, and get back to my family. I might not have approved of the planning of my future, but at least there I knew what to expect. I knew my fathers would never willingly let anyone hurt me. Or hoped they wouldn't.

The scent of gunpowder and charcoal swirled around me, sending my heart into a painful gallop as I waited.

"What the fuck are you staring at? Are you waiting for me to cry? To beg? You must feel like such a big man. Stealing away an omega, hiding your face like a fucking coward."

A big hand lifted and I fought the urge to recoil. But he grabbed the face covering and yanked it over his head a moment before he tossed a pile of clothing onto the couch beside me.

Coal black hair. Pale blue eyes that felt as though they were seeing through me. A jaw like it had been chiseled from stone complete with a damn dimple in his chin.

And zero emotion to be found as he watched me for a few more seconds before nodding his head toward an open door.

"Bathroom's through there. You can wear these until we find you new clothes. Toss that shit in the trash when you're done," he said, nodding at my dress before turning on his heel and leaving me watching after him.

The second the door shut with a soft snick, I lunged to my feet and ran as fast as my rubbery legs would allow, turning and yanking on the doorknob to find it locked. Over and over, I slammed my fists against it, screaming to be let out.

And was completely ignored.

Running to the windows, I tried each of them to find they were not only locked and nailed shut but barred from the outside and equipped with alarms. If by some miracle I was able to get them open, the house would be made aware. And what good would that do when there was no way to squeeze my round ass through the thick bars?

Twenty-three years of being watched like a hawk. Twenty-three years of being locked away like some damsel in a Disney movie.

And I had been kidnapped on the day my parents were giving me to a rival pack in order to form an alliance and increase their power and territory.

CHAPTER TWO

<u>Bain</u>

*L*eaning against the wall beside the door, I listened as the little omega pounded her fists against the thick wood of the door before running around the room. I didn't have to watch the cameras to know she was checking the windows, looking for another avenue of escape.

She wouldn't find one.

Even if she somehow managed to pick the lock to get out of that room, every inch of this house was covered by cameras. Every entry and exit were armed with alarms that would not only send alerts to each of our phones but to our men as well. She wouldn't make it two steps out of the house before she would be dragged right back in.

After a while, she'd fallen silent. Then I heard the bathroom door close a few moments before the pipes hummed as she started the shower.

And I refused to picture how that petite and curvy little body would look covered in suds, her small hands running across every dip and valley.

This was nothing more than a job. A mark. A step in bringing down the Alvarez and Garcia empires. And if we could kill two birds with one stone…

"What's she doing?" Valen asked as he stepped from his room, showered and changed into his regular attire of jeans and a navy blue Henley. I swore the man owned every color of those fucking shirts. When it was warm enough, he tended to walk around in nothing but boxers or swim shorts. At least when we weren't on one job or another.

"Showering," I answered as I neared the stairs and descended, heading to join my packmates.

"Why does that whole thing feel as though it was too easy?" Ford asked.

He sat at the kitchen island in a pair of sweats and a tee shirt with a flannel open over top, his hair damp, as well.

Once we'd all gotten home and deposited our prize onto the bed to let her sleep off the chloroform, we'd all showered off the blood spatters and gunpowder and waited.

I'd been the one who'd grown tired of waiting and headed to her room to check in on her. She'd looked like she had stepped straight off the set of Carrie, her poofy white dress drenched in the blood of the men who were supposed to have been her guardians.

"Because it was," Cohl said as he popped the top off a beer. "Her parents took off the moment we brandished the guns. Shouldn't that limo have been filled with guards? And why the fuck were there so few people in that procession? The whole thing was far too easy."

"I highly doubt Miguel or Vance Alvarez or any of those fucking alphas willingly let us take their precious omega daughter. That was nothing short of cowardice. Trying to save their own asses," I said as I grabbed my own beer and dropped onto a stool beside Ford.

"They had to know there was no benefit to us killing her. Doesn't matter they didn't know who was behind the attack; what would killing the omega daughter of a powerful family serve anyone?" Ford said.

"Which means they'll be waiting for a ransom offer," Cohl said. He pushed his hand through his auburn hair and turned to me. "She was awake?"

"Yeah. Gave her some clothes so she could get out of that goofy ass dress. Wash the blood off."

Valen chuckled darkly. "She was doing her best to beat through the fucking door first." He pulled his phone free and tapped on the screen a few times before turning it toward us. "She checked the windows, too."

"I figured she would," I said.

All the windows in our estate were equipped with alarms and barred from the outside. We were all more worried about the enemy finding their way in than we were about struggling to get out in case of a fire.

Besides, men in our line of work rarely died of something as simple as smoke inhalation. Our deaths tended to be bloody and violent and something all four of us anticipated coming for us one day.

"She'll need some shit," Ford said.

"Like what?" Cohl asked.

"Girl shit. Flowery shampoo or whatever. And scent blockers. Even past the guards' blood, her scent..."

Yeah. I'd caught that same scent when I'd stepped into the room. Lily of the Valley. Sweet and tempting. And like the flower, the girl could end up being deadly to us if we didn't leave our dicks and hindbrains out of the planning.

"There's shampoo and soap in that bathroom," Cohl said.

"Clothes," Ford pointed out. "Unless we want her walking around wearing our shit all day."

The thought of my t-shirt hanging almost to her knees made my dick twitch and I did everything in my power to ignore the incessant thump of it against the back of my zipper.

I wasn't blind. None of us were. Corazon Alvarez was fucking beautiful. And her scent was…well, mouthwatering. And I had the urge to be waiting outside the bathroom door to catch a whiff of it without the blood tainting it.

"It'll look suspicious if one of us heads out and buys a butt load of chick shit. We'll just get a delivery. Who wants to be the brave one and ask her size?" Ford offered.

I chuckled darkly. "I'll find out later. Told her to throw that dress away. If the size isn't on a label somewhere, I'll ask her outright."

"And you think she'll just offer up some personal information?"

Honestly…I hoped not. Because now that the idea had been put in my head, I'd rather see her traipsing around in my boxers, tanks, and tees. Especially without a bra or panties.

Fuck.

I'd known being around a beautiful omega would be a feat. I just hadn't planned on her scent calling to my baser need so strongly.

Digging through the fridge, I grabbed a half a sandwich someone had left wrapped and a can of soda. Maybe if I plied her with some food and water after she'd showered, she might be more willing to hear me out. We had no intention of hurting her. She wasn't going to end up as a sacrifice, her head on a pike outside her family's estate.

But until we could bring both Pack Alvarez and Pack Garcia to heel, she would become a long-term guest.

"You're not giving her free reign of the house, are you?" Ford asked as I headed for the stairway.

"At what point did I come across as a fucking idiot?" I shot over my shoulder as I climbed the steps slowly, partially dreading coming face to face with Corazon again, partially elated at the thought of walking away with her scent clinging to my skin.

Hesitating outside the room, I moved my ear closer to the door, listening to see if she was still under the shower spray or was once again attempting to find an escape route from the room.

No sound came through the door. The shower no longer hummed, and it no longer sounded as though she was trying to break her way through the door to her room.

Turning the lock, I pushed my way in, sandwich in hand, to find Corazon inspecting the windows closely.

"Every window in the house is barred and wired with alarms," I said, startling her.

She whirled around, hand to her chest, and glared at me.

And as my eyes traveled the length of her body encased in my t-shirt that hung to her knees, showing off her smooth, tanned legs, my dick once again thumped the back of my zipper as though trying to get my attention.

Yeah. I see her. Not ours. Like my dick ever listened to my brain.

Corazon moved around the room, keeping space between us as I stepped forward, the sandwich and soda in my hand. "I'm Bain. Figured you might be hungry since you missed the whole bonding ceremony and reception. Sorry it's not crepes and champagne."

She continued to inch away from me as I approached, my hand outstretched with my offerings while I fought the urge to drink in her appearance from her wet, dark hair waving around her shoulders to her braless tits swaying with each step.

Her scent was harder to ignore as the floral hints wafted from her, tinted with a sharper tang of her anger and fear tainting her signature.

"It's just fucking food," I growled out when she continued to glare at me with so much fire in her pretty brown eyes I was surprised I hadn't already burst into flames.

"And what kind of drug is in there this time? You think I'm stupid? You killed my family, killed my guards, and now I'm supposed to just take food from you like you're doing me a favor?"

Anger started to coil in my gut. Tossing the sandwich and can of soda on the bed, I inhaled deeply through my nose.

"We didn't kill your parents. They tucked tail and ran the moment they realized they weren't alone. They left you, princess." She winced at the title, and I made a mental note to use it as much as possible. That petty part of me refused to acknowledge the fact this tiny omega was probably terrified. But if she wanted to push, I could push back. "The sandwich isn't drugged. The can of soda hasn't been opened. Eat. Don't eat. I don't give a shit."

Turning on my heel, I started to leave the room. Until something wet hit the back of my head.

Slowly, I turned back to face her, then tilted my chin to examine the remains of the sub that now littered the hardwood floor and throw rug, lifting my hand to run my fingers over my hair, knocking lettuce and a pickle loose.

Her hand was still raised, this time with the soda clenched as though she was preparing to launch it at me. Hell no.

Eating the space between us in three long strides, I wrapped my fingers around her wrist, grabbed the can, and wrenched it from her hand. Rage simmered just below the surface, but I had never and would never take my anger out on a woman, especially not an omega as petite as Corazon Alvarez.

I struggled to refrain from squeezing her tiny wrist too hard and hated that she trembled under my touch.

I hated even more that my alpha was reacting to her scent and that her omega apparently liked the way I smelled if the hint of arousal lifting on the air was anything to go by.

"Let...go," she snarled at me, tugging on her wrist.

Instead, I crowded her more, stepping into her space until we were almost touching, and looked down my nose at her.

So many thoughts whirled through my brain, but I couldn't grasp onto any single one as she stared up at me with those big doe eyes and her bottom lip trembled.

She was struggling not to cry. But she was also full of so much hate and so much fire I knew she refused to show me an ounce of weakness. She could pretend all she wanted. Her body was giving her away with or without the fucking tears.

Finally dropping her wrist, I took a few steps away and set the can on the coffee table set before the couch. If she got hungry later, she could eat the ruined sandwich from the floor.

Fuck her. Tried to do something nice and ended up with the ingredients splattered across the back of my head and neck.

Just before I pulled the door closed behind me, something heavy crashed against it, the sound of glass tinkling against the ground letting me know she'd heaved one of the goofy ass knickknacks that decorated the room at my head but hadn't been quick enough.

"Let me out!" she screamed as something else smashed against the closed door.

My heart raced, my veins burned with a combination of adrenaline and lust, and confusion clouded my thoughts as I stomped to my bedroom directly next door to hers and slammed the door shut behind me.

So many thoughts...so much confusion. Anger. Lust. Determination.

My alpha wanted the little omega, something I hadn't expected even though we'd met in the past. Though she didn't appear to remember me. The Alvarez princess had met hundreds of people through her lifetime – why would she remember someone as inconsequential as me?

Anger pulsed through my veins as I dragged my now sauce covered shirt over my head and stormed toward the bathroom. The tiny woman had dared throw a fucking sandwich at my head. Seriously? I'd brought her food. I was trying to make her as comfortable as possible for the time she was here. If she'd just calmed down and listened for half a second, I might even have told her she had nothing to fear, that no one in the house would hurt her, that she would be returned to her family once they received and accepted the deal we were going to lay out.

But what if they didn't? Her fathers had fled the moment my pack and guards had brandished firearms. No one had lunged from the limo to defend their daughter. No one but the guards who'd been crammed into the town car with her had seemed as though they'd cared at all. Even the short procession that we'd cut off with SUVs and construction vehicles had immediately turned and fled in the opposite direction, leaving the omega to the enemy.

What kind of fucking alphas didn't protect their omega daughter?

As I twisted the handle to start the shower spray – again – I tried and failed to ignore the way my dick was still rock hard after my little encounter with Corazon. Yeah, she was hot as fuck. And she smelled amazing. But that was where any attraction should have ended. There was no reason my body should be this hard after she *threw a fucking sandwich at my head* and was planning to do the same with a full can of soda.

Stripping from my pants, I stepped under the spray and dropped my head back, letting the hot water rinse the sauce and remnants of the sub from my hair, neck, and back. Once I was clean, I put both hands on the tile and lowered my head, breathing deeply through my nose and blowing it through my mouth to control my growing anger.

Honestly, the more I thought about the whole situation, the more pissed for the omega I was growing. I'd wanted the plan to go without a hitch. Of course I did. But other than the guards in the car, not a single person had lifted a finger to protect her. I would have used my own fucking body as a shield to protect her if she were mine.

"Fuck," I ground out between my teeth, giving in and fisting my cock, pulling on it hard and fast until I spilled onto the shower pan and let it swirl down the drain.

Didn't help. Even after coming, my dick was once more rising as I fought the urge to knock the door down and force her to listen.

Bullshit. I wanted to shove her against the wall and cut off any of her protests with my lips, to taste her, to feel her curves under my hand.

Which meant from here out, one of the others would have to be responsible for her care. Because I had a feeling the next time she attacked me, I might not be able to control my alpha and would end up forcing a claim on her out of spite.

CHAPTER THREE

Corazon

Maybe breaking everything I could get my hands on hadn't been the greatest idea, especially since the only shoes I currently had in my possession were the stiletto heels I'd worn for my ceremony.

My choices now were to either stay curled up on the couch or bed or to walk around wearing Bain's shirt – and I could tell it was his by the heady, warm charcoal and gun powder scent – with heels. Great combination.

But seriously not my biggest problem at the moment.

I still couldn't believe I'd thrown the sandwich at the giant alpha's head. When he'd turned and stormed in my direction, I'd wondered if he would hit me. Maybe toss me around the room to prove how big and strong he was. Even when I stood there with the full can in my clenched fist, my arm cocked and ready to whip that in his direction, he'd done nothing more than restrain my arm and confiscate my makeshift weapon.

They left you, princess.

According to my captor, my parents had hauled ass away from the scene when Bain and his gang had pulled their firearms and started shooting. Meaning my fathers hadn't even attempted to help me. When I'd glanced back and hadn't seen my siblings' vehicles, I'd thought they'd merely been cut off by the pretend construction crew.

But had they run away, too? Had they left me to be killed or taken?

I wasn't stupid. I'd known my whole life my fathers didn't exactly love me. My mom tended to act as though she was jealous of me, or like I was a burden to her life. But being as I was the key to increasing the size of their empire, I would have thought they would have at least found a way to safely get me away from all the bullets that had been whizzing around the town car.

I could only assume Bain and the other men had taken me for a similar reason, that they hoped to use me as a pawn in their own game or to ask for a ransom. Would my fathers pay up? Would they negotiate for my release?

Or would they leave me to the fucking wolves as they had back on the highway?

My eyes fell on the ruined sandwich scattered on the floor among glass and wood and whatever else I had managed to destroy. Why, of all things, had I thrown the sandwich?

Bain had been right. I was starving. I hadn't eaten anything since… shit. Since last night. I'd had zero appetite today knowing I was being marched to the gallows by my own family.

The soda sat on the coffee table in front of me. At least I hadn't thrown that.

Popping the top, I tilted the can and took a long swig, then covered my mouth when a burp rumbled up my chest. Actually, maybe I'd force a big ol' belch in hopes of turning Bain off next time he dared to step into this room.

Who else was in the house? I'd heard male voices rumbling through the walls and had heard steps moving up and down the hall outside my room, but it had been over an hour since Bain had appeared as though bringing me a half-eaten sandwich would make up for the fact he'd killed four men right in front of me, shot at the vehicle I'd been riding in, and dragged me away from my family and future mates.

Okay. So the last part wasn't all that bad. If anything, they had saved me from something I had been dreading for months. But that didn't mean this situation was any better. I still had no idea what they hoped to achieve by taking me. And if Bain or any of his guards thought they could touch me without me gouging out their eyes or ripping off their dicks, they were in for a fucking surprise.

Time continued to tick by, but being as I was stuck on the couch while my stilettos were…shit…somewhere among the wreckage, I had no idea how much time had actually passed. But the sky was growing grayer outside as the day stretched into early evening. I hated this time of year when the days were short and the nights were long. I would much rather be laying out in the sun and heat over being locked inside for months on end.

Shit. What if I was locked in this place for months? What if they never released me? What if my parents did nothing to get me back?

Nope. Wasn't going to entertain all the worst-case scenarios. One way or another, I would find my own way out of this house and away from these guys. And then…I would disappear. I would find some suppressants and live my life as a beta and be free for the first time ever.

Staring at the darkening sky while the undrunk half of my soda grew warm on the coffee table, I steeled myself when the telltale sounds of the lock being turned out of place met my ears.

The door swung open silently and an unfamiliar face peered inside, gray eyes finding me on the couch before surveying the mess on the floor. He filled the space of the doorframe, his big body almost fully blocking the view of the hall.

Pulling his phone from a pocket, he tapped on the screen a few times, then stepped further into the room, kicking shit out of his way as he carried a few bags toward me.

"Figured you might need something other than our clothes to wear," he said, setting the bags on the coffee table in front of me.

He dug inside the bag then pulled out a pair of what reminded me of Ugg house booties and offered them to me.

"What?" I said, my arms crossed over my chest as I glared at him.

"You plan on sitting there all night? I assume you don't feel like walking on glass."

My nostrils flared as I took a deep breath then snatched the shoes from his hands, popping the tag between them before tugging them on my feet.

Slowly, I pushed to my feet and sidled around him, keeping my eyes on his face and waiting for him to grab me or stop me. I needed to pee. I'd been holding it for far too long.

But the door to the hallway was still open. What were the chances I could get out of this room and out of the house before anyone caught me?

"There are guards outside, the doors and windows are all locked, there are cameras and alarms everywhere. I wouldn't suggest attempting it," he said as he turned only his head to watch me.

Shrugging and feigning innocence, I said, "I'm just going to the bathroom."

He grunted a sound of disbelief but didn't exactly move as though to block my exit.

But I knew he was right. Even if he didn't catch me as I ran from the room, I had no idea how many people were inside, how many patrolled outside, had no idea whether there was a gate I would have to climb, and had no idea where this house was even located. Being as I had no idea how long I'd been out after they'd pulled me from the town car, we could very well be in another state.

Once I was behind the bathroom door, I slammed it shut and turned the lock in place. I had every intention of hiding out in here until the new guy left. But I really did have to pee.

After relieving my poor overly full bladder and washing my hands, I shuffled to the door and pressed my ear against the cool wood. There was a soft commotion and lowered voices, but I had no idea which voice belonged to who.

Hell, Bain was the only name I'd been offered thus far. But as far as

I was concerned, the sexy blue-eyed alpha could keep his ass as far from me as possible.

Shit. I'd just thought of him as sexy. It was nothing more than alpha pheromones. It was my hindbrain trying to push to the forefront.

My parents had intentionally scheduled the bonding ceremony as close to my cycle as possible. They and my betrothed pack had hoped I would get knocked up during my first heat with my new alphas.

Looked as though that was no longer a concern.

Nope. Now, I had a bigger concern. I was locked in the house with a bunch of murderous alphas. I'd noted two other closed doors in the room where I was locked and assumed one of them was a nest. Did it have a lock from the inside? Because no way would I let Bain or the gray eyed alpha or any other members of that pack anywhere near me or my body, no matter how painful it grew.

Noise outside the bathroom grew, new voices rumbled. I could stay in here until they left, but I really was getting hungry.

If they were going to keep me locked up, if Bain thought it was funny to call me princess, maybe I would just become a royal pain in their asses until they either tossed me out the door...or killed me.

Because, honestly, being dead would be far better than being tortured or raped.

Pulling the door open, I peeked through the crack to find four enormous men studiously cleaning the mess I'd made, sweeping and tossing pieces of broken crap into a trash can.

So many scents wafted in through the crack and my traitorous body grew warm as slick dampened the borrowed boxers.

Charcoal and gunpowder. That was Bain's. But his scent was joined by pumpkin, vanilla frosting, and saffron. I'd noted the spicy scent of saffron when the gray eyed alpha had appeared, so at least I could identify two of them.

As I let my eyes roam their bodies, my omega appreciating the sights and smells, four heads raised and four sets of eyes whipped in my direction as their nostrils flared.

Well, damn. They'd caught my perfume on the air.

As tempted as I was to slam the door and lock it again, I was the daughter of Pack Alvarez, daughter of some of the most ruthless and powerful alphas this side of the river. I refused to cower for anyone.

Stepping out, I crossed my arms, raised my head, and tried to appear as though the mere presence of the alphas was nothing short of a nuisance.

The gray eyed alpha who'd brought me clothes and shoes jerked his head toward the couch. I opened my mouth to tell him to kiss my ass, thinking he was ordering me to sit, before my eyes landed on a tray filled with food that wasn't wrapped in soggy paper.

Instead of diving for the food and shoving it into my mouth, I walked over slowly, keeping my eyes on the four, and lowered onto the couch, checking everything out.

"Is any of this drugged?"

"No," the gray eyed alpha said.

I snorted a sound of derision. "And I'm supposed to believe such upstanding citizens."

"You know what–" Bain started, taking a step toward me.

But the gray eyed alpha stopped him, slapping a hand in the center of his chest and pushing him back.

"I'm Ford. You've met Bain," he said, glancing at the alpha who was glaring at me as his chest rose and fell with angry breaths. "That's Valen," he said, nodding at the giant alpha with olive skin and pretty blue/green eyes. "And the ginger is Cohl."

I wouldn't have called him a ginger. His hair was auburn, only the lights shining from overhead highlighting hints of red.

"I assume you know my name." And if they didn't, I wouldn't be offering up a single thing about myself.

"Corazon Alvarez, princess of pack Alvarez," Bain said with a smirk. A fucking smirk. "Age twenty-three. Bonding ceremony planned today for three to pack Garcia."

"Great. You know all about me. Now what?"

I wanted them to leave so I could shovel the food down my throat. I was so freaking hungry I was getting a little woozy. The fact they'd knocked me out with chemicals didn't exactly help.

"Now we wait to see if your fathers will play ball," Bain answered.

The others watched me and I wondered if Bain was pack lead. It would make sense being as he was the only one really talking to me.

"And if they don't?"

He released a deep, dark chuckle and shook his head. "Guess we'll just have to wait and see."

And then he left me alone with the other three. They finally stopped staring at me and finished cleaning up the mess I'd made.

"Eat," Ford said, nodding toward the tray.

"Let me leave," I countered.

"It's up to your pack," Cohl said.

I pulled up the memories of a few hours ago, of the men who'd attacked the town car with their faces covered, tried to remember anything about the men who'd murdered my guards. I remembered seeing Bain's eyes. His pale blue eyes would be seared into my mind for the rest of my life. But I couldn't remember whether I'd noted any of these men.

They were there. I had no doubt. Had they killed my fathers' men? Had they killed people simply to get to me?

Had they realized how close they'd come to actually hitting me with those fucking bullets?

After a few more minutes, they finished up and Cohl carried the trash can from the room.

"Eat. Let me know if the clothes don't fit and I'll find something else," Ford said, carrying his broom with him as he stepped through the door.

"Wait!" I called out, lunging to my feet and chasing after him.

I skid to a stop, almost slipping when the bottoms of the knock off Uggs didn't grip the hardwood floor.

Ford stopped and raised his brows.

"What if they don't...play ball? Are you going to kill me? I'm not fucking any of you. And I'm not bonding with any of you, either."

Ford glanced down the hall, then stepped back in my room, closing the door behind him.

"You'd rather fuck and bond Pack Garcia?" he asked, his voice no longer open and friendly and warm. For some reason, I'd wondered if I couldn't turn Ford into an ally, maybe use him to find an escape.

But as he stared down at me, he looked almost as scary and deadly as Bain.

"No," I finally squeaked out as my throat threatened to close.

"Then maybe stop acting like we didn't just do you a favor," he said, sounding as cocky and mean hearted as Bain had.

"A favor?" I growled out. "A fucking favor?!" I screamed at him, closing the space to jab a finger into his broad chest. "How the hell is almost killing me, kidnapping me, then holding me as a prisoner a fucking favor?" I couldn't force my voice to lower as my temper came to the surface.

I shoved at him, trying to move him away from the door, still somewhat determined to run right through the front door and take my chances with outrunning the alphas and their men.

But he barely moved. It was like trying to shove a mountain out of my way.

As he stared down at me, I refused to acknowledge the way my body warmed under his attention, the way his spicy scent wrapped around me like a blanket, or the fact his eyes on me felt like a caress.

When he lowered his head and inhaled deeply, drawing my scent into his lungs, I suppressed a shiver.

"Don't touch me," I growled out when his nose nuzzled against my throat, as though he was trying to rub against my scent glands.

"You can say the words all you want. Your body won't let you lie. You didn't want that fucking pack. And I'm sure you're not happy you're here, either. But your omega definitely wants my touch."

Fear collided with want as my heart began to thunder behind my ribs. I refused to step away, refused to cower, refused to show any weakness.

So when Ford straightened with a quirk of his lips and stepped out of the room, I nearly collapsed with both relief, frustration, and brain scrambling confusion.

Because he was right – I didn't want to be here. I hated these men. But my omega wanted each of them to cover me in their scents so I could wallow in them, drown in them, wrap their signatures around me like the softest blanket.

I needed to keep my distance. I needed to stop goading them. I needed them to stay away from me.

I needed to get the fuck out of here before my heat hit and I ended up in a puddle of slick, begging for the closest knot when my hindbrain took over and I was no longer coherent or cognizant of what I was doing or saying.

CHAPTER FOUR

<u>Ford</u>

Feisty ass omega. Sexy as fuck omega.

She was going to be trouble. It might be time to have a few of the beta guards be in charge of bringing her what she needed like food and shit.

I don't know why I'd thought I could disarm her by bringing her a few supplies. Yeah. She was currently a prisoner, but not like we were keeping her in a dark dungeon or some shit. She was in the omega wing we'd had designed when we'd built this house years ago. We'd just never bothered actually looking for an omega to join the pack.

Why the fuck would we? Look what having an omega in the pack caused. Her simple designation put a big ol' dollar sign over her head and a bull's eye on her back. It was easy as fuck to destroy a pack simply by stealing or killing their omega.

Not that I was on board with executing innocent people, regardless of who we were trying to take down.

I'd brought Corazon clothes and shoes, had had food brought up for her, had even called in my packmates to help me clean up the mess she'd made. Yet she still thought she could talk to me like I was some common lowlife?

Made sense. She was used to her pack, used to watching her fathers treat people like shit. She didn't know me or my pack and had no idea we were as high up the food chain as the Alvarez pack.

Not for long. Once Bain contacted one of her daddy dearests and a deal was struck, we would control a majority of imports and exports in the area. Anything coming in or out of the area would have to go through us.

For a few minutes, I simply leaned against the door on the other side, willing my heartrate to a normal pace and tried to talk my dick down. I wouldn't admit this to my pack, but there was a good fucking chance the daughter of our enemy was our fucking scent match.

Didn't mean shit. Chemistry. Nothing more than our hindbrains trying to take control. And I sure as fuck wouldn't be a slave to my hormones.

She'd tried to hide it, but I'd smelled the sweet slick pooling between her legs. What really pissed me off was it was Bain's clothing she was wearing. It would be his clothing that would be saturated with her Lily of the Valley floral sweetness. His fucking boxers that had been so close to the place I wanted to bury my fucking face. I wanted to wear her thighs as earmuffs and suck on her clit until she screamed my name.

Shit.

I had to get out of here. Heading to my room, I shoved the sweats down my legs and dragged on a pair of jeans before shoving my feet into a pair of boots.

Cohl, Valen, and Bain were seated around the living room as I descended the stairs, snatching my keys from the hook.

"Where you going?" Bain called after me.

"Out. I need a beer."

"We have beer in the fridge," Cohl said.

"And we have a gorgeous omega with a sweet-smelling cunt in the house, too," Valen said. So he'd smelled her, too. Which meant I wouldn't be the only one struggling with her presence.

The sooner Bain made the deal with her fathers the better. Then we could return her to her spoiled ass life, let her go pop out a bunch of kids by the Garcia pricks, and we would make a shit load of money from the export game.

Three sets of feet were suddenly following me through the house and into the garage. Bain climbed into the front passenger seat while Cohl and Valen took the back.

As the garage door rumbled up and I backed out of my spot, I hit the button to roll down Bain's window as one of our guards jogged up to that side.

"The omega's locked in her room. No one but betas in the house. She does not leave, and no one goes inside her room," Bain barked.

"Yes, sir," the guard said, backing away and giving me room to maneuver my vehicle up the driveway and onto the main road.

No one said a word as I aimed the vehicle for one of the strip clubs we owned. Not all our money came from criminal activities. We had to own a few legit businesses to clean the money we brought in through the less savory means.

This particular business just happened to be my favorite because of all the tits and hot chicks.

Four doors *thunked* closed and then we all sauntered our way up to the doors, bypassing the rope holding back the crowd lined up to get inside. I nodded at the bouncer and pulled open the door.

We could have easily parked in the back and used the employee entry, but I wanted a look at the crowd, already searching for someone to ease my blue balls and erase the scent of floral sweetness from my senses.

"We could send her to another house. Keep her locked down with betas," Valen offered once we were in our private section where others wouldn't be able to hear us over the heavy thump of the bass.

I nodded toward a waitress, beckoning her over. We each put in our orders and settled against the red leather booth.

"No," Bain said, a heavy dose of possessive growl around that one word.

And I hated to admit even to myself I'd felt that same possessive urge at the mere mention.

"She's going to fuck all this up," Cohl said.

"Take it your dick's still hard, too," I blurted. What was the point of hiding it? I'd walked around with a bulge in my pants since I'd stepped in to find the destroyed room.

"Dude," Cohl said, shifting in his seat and shooting a disgruntled glare in my direction. "Stop looking at my dick."

Huffing a laugh, I shook my head.

"She's our scent match," Bain said, eying a dancer as she walked by, winking in our direction as her bare tits swayed and her ass cheeks jiggled. She must have just finished her set if she was walking around in nothing but her thong.

"Yep," I agreed, still shopping for someone to wet my dick in hopes of convincing my alpha that we were all wrong and I was just horny. It had been a few days since I'd had any pussy. It could simply be a case of sexual frustration.

"We mark her, we're fucked," Cohl said.

"Thanks, Captain fucking Obvious," Bain said as the waitress set our drinks on the table and scurried away.

I turned my attention to Bain. Fuck. With the way he was clenching his jaw, he must have fought himself to keep from doing exactly that and claiming the Alvarez omega. That would do nothing short of starting a fucking war. And while our numbers weren't low, we'd be fucked if we had to come up against both packs Garcia and Alvarez.

Even as it stood, we were still at risk because of Corazon. We'd taken away their bargaining chip to use as our own.

This would either be the best plan Bain and I had ever come up with or it would blow up in our faces.

Nah. I refused to believe this wouldn't end in success.

A dancer approached and waited for permission to enter our section. Bain raised a hand and beckoned her forward, spreading his knees when she moved forward and began dancing on him. She wasn't exactly naked, but there wasn't much between her tits and cunt and the rest of the world.

Throwing her head, her hair spun and wafted a hint of coconut shampoo in my direction. All our dancers were to wash with scent blockers before their shifts and we'd ensured the filtration system worked nonstop. The last thing we needed was an omega to perfume in a room full of horny alphas and cause a fucking riot when they tore into each other while trying to rut the poor man or woman.

The scent of coconut did nothing for me. In fact, the dancer, even as hot and curvy as she was, didn't so much as make my dick twitch with desire to be buried in her mouth. Or any other part of her body.

All I'd wanted was to get away from the omega, to drink to a black out state, have a pair of lips wrapped around my cock so I could empty my balls, then fall face first into my mattress.

Instead, I found myself comparing every woman who walked by to the dark-haired omega locked in the room two doors down from my own.

Bain was a lucky mother fucker. His bedroom was directly next door to hers. He would be able to smell her clearly. And she was wearing his clothes.

I should have forgone the new clothes and brought her a stack of my own. Then, when she soaked the boxers with slick, I could have used them to rub myself off while covering my cock in her scent.

When we'd approached the town car, she'd been dressed like a freaking cupcake or some shit, layers and layers of silk and tulle pooled around her. Her lips had been painted red, and makeup had coated her eyes.

Since she'd showered, her hair was no longer curled and braided and pinned by the goofy veil and hung almost to her waist. There were smudges of the mascara below her eyes, but her face was bereft of makeup. I hadn't wanted to notice the light smatter of freckles across her nose. I hadn't wanted to notice the way her full lips were set in almost a permanent pout and looked soft as fuck. I hadn't wanted to notice the way her nipples were pebbled and strained against Bain's t-shirt or the way they'd swayed and bounced with her every move.

A growl rumbled from my chest, catching the attention of the redhead grinding on Bain. Even with the dancer's ass rubbing along his crotch, my pack brother looked as distracted as I felt.

Glancing around the table, I realized Cohl and Valen were primarily focused on their drinks or their phones. We were so fucked.

"How many betas do we have in our employ?" I asked Bain, leaning forward and resting my forearms on the table.

He gently guided the dancer away, pulling a hundred from his pocket and handing it to her before dismissing her with a jerk of his chin.

The fact there weren't currently women hanging on each of us was telling enough. None of us were leaning back while one of our girls or someone we'd chosen from the crowd knelt between our thighs and swallowed our cocks.

Hell. I'd barely touched my fucking Scotch.

"No idea. And not happening," Bain said.

"I'm with Ford," Cohl said, nodding his head in my direction. "We all caught the same scent. We got to keep our fucking distance, make the deal, and send her packing. We don't have enough firepower or men to hold off an attack from both packs and their buddies. For now, they don't know where we're located. Let's keep it that way. Have the betas tend to her needs. Then let her go play omega queen with Garcia's men."

Cohl glanced at each of us, but no one said a word. Yeah. It had been my idea. So why did I have the urge to punch my packmate in the mouth for voicing it?

"She's our scent match," Valen grumbled after a long silence.

"And she hates us," Bain said.

"She thinks we killed her parents," I said.

Bain chuckled. "Nah. I told her how her fathers ran off like a bunch of little bitches."

It took a second, but the rest of us joined in the chuckles. We'd turned toward the limo, ready for guards to pour out in defense of the pack and the omega. But the tires had turned so quickly they'd left skid marks on the asphalt.

The vehicles that had been following behind had done a quick U-turn the second our men had climbed out donning balaclavas. I had no idea whether those following had been members of the bonding ceremony, family, or hired guards.

Either way, they'd all left Corazon alone with only four guards. Four guards who hadn't gotten a single shot off before we'd put bullets directly between their eyes.

Shame the poor omega had been coated in their blood and brains chunks. But she'd grown up around the same kind of men as us. By now, she more than likely had seen her share of violence and gore. She sure as fuck didn't show any fear when she'd been face to face with me, even if I could see the fluttering of her heart at the pulse point in her neck, the same place where I'd pressed my nose to inhale her scent deep into my lungs.

She could deny it all she wanted. But her body had reacted to my proximity. She'd reacted to my scent.

So now we had to decide whether we wanted to risk one of us fucking up and fucking her...or handing her care over to the beta guards.

When a long, deep possessive growl rumbled from my chest, I knew I had my answer without ever fully discussing it with my pack.

This was supposed to be temporary. She was simply a piece on the chess board. A pawn. A bargaining chip to get what we wanted.

Yet...my alpha wanted her permanently.

She was mine.

CHAPTER FIVE

Corazon

I'd stood at the window and watched as the big, black SUV pulled down the driveway and out of view. Someone had left. Or someone*s*. What were the chances I might have been left alone?

Rifling through the bag that Ford had brought, I found a pair of leggings. After removing the boxers that smelled heavily of Bain – and were now damp with the slick that had developed by the influx of so many alpha hormones – I pulled on the leggings, then redonned the faux Uggs.

Please let it be unlocked. Please let it be unlocked, I chanted as I jogged to the bedroom door.

Locked. Of course.

Okay. I was the daughter of five of the most ruthless and powerful criminals in the state. Surely I could pick a lock. With what, though? I'd broken nearly everything that had decorated the room.

Ohh. My hairpins. I'd taken them out before climbing into the shower to wash the blood and bits of skull and brains from my skin and hair. Could I possibly succeed at picking a door lock with a hairpin?

Only one way to find out.

Grabbing a handful, I tiptoed to the door, lowered to my knees, and started shoving the tip of first one then the another into the small hole of the door.

After several failed attempts, the click of the lock being removed sounded and I lunged to my feet and backed away quickly.

But I didn't recognize the man who stood before me and his scent said he was a beta. At least my body wouldn't betray me and react to his nearness.

"Stop," he said with a shake his head. "It's a fucking deadbolt out here. Not a door lock. Go watch some TV or whatever."

And then he pulled the door shut. Didn't introduce himself. Didn't ask if I needed anything. Just...pulled the door shut in my face.

A deadbolt? Seriously? From the looks of the room, this was intended to be an omega's quarter. I still hadn't checked to see if my suspicion was accurate and one of the closed doors led to a nest. So... why the deadbolt?

Because they were monsters who stole omegas on the day of their bonding ceremony.

Honestly, had things not happened the way they had, you know, with my guards being slaughtered in front of me and the masks and guns and all that stuff, I might have actually been thankful. Not that I would ever admit that to the four alphas or their thug guards.

But at this point, I would have been bonded to Leo, Julian, and Roman from Pack Garcia. I would have had to have sex with them. I would have gone into heat within a week or two and one or all of them would have done their best to knock me up per our fathers' orders.

Whether or not I was off the hook with the Garcia pack, it wouldn't last forever. Eventually, my fathers would negotiate something with these alphas and I would be set free. And then...

I groaned as I began to pace the length of the bedroom, my eyes repeatedly going to the closed doors.

Screw it.

Walking quickly, I yanked the door closest to the bathroom opened and peered inside. It was an empty but humongous walk-in closet.

The second was exactly as I'd guessed; a nest with a cushioned floor and walls, and stacks of pillows and blankets lining the far side of the room. It smelled of chemical cleaner and scent blockers. And I hated the surge of jealousy that slithered through my gut when I wondered if it had been cleaned of the scent of another omega or whether the lack of smell was due to the lack of use.

I shouldn't have been jealous. I shouldn't have given two shits if they entertained a whole bachelorette party in there at one time. This was temporary. Those men were nothing to me.

Stepping further in, I found a switch on the wall and flipped it, an unbidden smile pulling up the corner of my lips at the soft glow from the fairy lights strung along the ceiling like stars.

The room was well stocked, but impersonal and a little cold. My omega bristled at the white cushioned floor and pale colored pillows and blankets. While I might not have had the choice in how my bedroom had been decorated back at home, my mother knew my omega would be unsettled without a more personalized nest. The room had been covered in jewel tones and so many textures of the softest fabrics.

If this didn't all end soon, I would end up in a slick covered, pain filled puddle on the floor within a couple weeks. And locked in a house full of alphas, two of whom had stared down at me like predators and I was their prey.

Checking the doorknob, I sighed with relief to find it locked from inside. If I was still here when my cycle hit, I could lock them out and ride it out on my own. Shame I didn't have my vibrators or silicon knot with me to get through the worst of the pain.

Although...nothing would soothe that pain nearly as much as my inner walls being coated with the hot cum of an alpha.

Nope. Shut that shit down now.

Those were not thoughts I would allow to bounce around my damn skull. It might only be preheat that had caused my body to react to the four alphas who'd crowded inside my room while they'd cleaned up my mess or the fact slick had coated my pussy and upper thighs when first Bain then Ford had crowded me, but I didn't have to allow my designation to control my every fucking action.

Stepping from the room, I swung the door shut and sauntered back to the windows. I was so fucking bored. I might have been under constant guard when I'd been with my family, but at least I was able to leave my damn room. Even the house with my guards.

A large TV hung above the fireplace that had burned to nothing but embers since I'd woken here. And Ford had brought a bag of clothes, but nothing more than leggings and tees. I needed soft and cozy. I wanted my fuzzy socks with the unicorns printed all over them. I wanted my plush hoodie with the soft fleece lining.

Instead, I had to settle for dragging the duvet from the bed and wrapping it around my shoulders while I curled up on the couch and pointed the remote at the TV.

Holy crap. I swore these alphas had a subscription to every damn streaming service out there. When did they have enough time to watch so much TV? Even my housebound ass couldn't have gotten through so many selections.

Settling on a series I'd seen a dozen times already with the hottest Scottish man in history, I wrapped the duvet around myself as much as possible until I resembled a human burrito. It was probably late enough to go to bed, but the fact they'd locked me in without the ability to lock them out made me feel entirely too vulnerable.

These men were the enemy. Sure, they were hot and made my omega want to rub all over them until I was drenched in their scents, but they were still the fucking enemy. They were murderers. Criminals.

Just like every other damn alpha in my life.

As each episode ended and another began, my lids grew heavier and heavier. Had this day gone as my family had planned, I would have been back at the pack house with Leo, Julian, and Roman. I would officially be Omega Garcia. And I would have been knotted over and over, whether I wanted it or not.

And I didn't. I wouldn't have. Not that the three alphas were unattractive. But nothing about them appealed to me or my omega. Even growing up the way I had, even watching the complete and utter lack of passion and romance from my parents, I'd always hoped when I finally found my pack and we would have at least some kind of connection, even if it was initially based on friendship.

But yeah…love and attraction would have been ideal.

Thing was, Bain could act as though he and his buddies had done me a favor today. But the moment I was released, everything would go forward as planned. My life had already been planned out for me. My fathers had made a deal with the Garcias with me as the final bargaining chip, the hefty payment that ensured there was a truce, that the two empires would combine to become unstoppable.

I knew something everyone else didn't know, though. I knew the moment my fathers received enough control, they would find a way to end the Garcia line, leaving only me and my alphas. And who knew – the pack they'd sold me to could end up falling under the ax, as well.

What would my fathers do if I ended up pregnant within a year the way they'd all agreed? Would I be killed, too? Or would they simply demand I end the pregnancy to end the Garcia bloodline?

My hand slid under the plush duvet to rest on my stomach as though protecting a child that hadn't even been conceived yet. As much as I'd like to pretend my fathers weren't that cold or evil…I'd seen them do far worse.

Hand still protectively guarding my empty womb, I let my eyes fall closed and listened to the sounds coming from the TV while keeping an ear out for anyone entering the room. Issue was, I was kind of a heavy sleeper. If I succumbed to sleep, any of those men could saunter right into the room and I would be none the wiser.

Although I would like to think I'd wake if they were to touch me. I might be half their size and they might be big, strong men, but that didn't mean I wouldn't fight back.

My dreams began to form around the show, and I was the woman who'd been sent back in time, falling in love with a big, gorgeous redheaded Scot. I was the one who was building a life with someone who actually cared for me.

For as long as I could remember, I'd always dreamed I was born a beta and raised by parents who gave a shit about me. I used to fantasize about a mom and dad who would beam with pride when I accomplished things like graduating from high school instead of receiving care boxes when I'd been sent to prep school for omegas where they focused more on training us to serve our alphas rather than teaching us things that could actually aid us in building a career.

But all of those fantasies were exactly that – fantasies. Pipe dreams. Something I would never have. I'd accepted that long ago.

I didn't want to be bonded to pack Garcia, but I was an omega who'd been trained to do as I was told by my fathers.

My dreams continued to shift as I tried to stay awake, somehow staying in between waking and sleeping. At some point, the Scot in the TV show morphed into Bain. It was his pale blue eyes peering down at me, his hands pushing the hair from my face, his big strong arms protecting me.

At some point, I'd lost the fight and fallen fully asleep, my dreams changing to nightmares of the shootout while wearing a bonding gown. Instead of men wearing balaclavas, I saw the faces of the four alphas who'd set this whole thing into motion, the four men who had dragged me away from my family.

Even in my dreams, I knew I had to find a way out of this place. I would have to play ball, pretend I trusted them, pretend to be the soft, subservient, obedient omega I'd been trained to be.

Then, when their guard was down, I would make my move.

I just hoped it was sooner rather than later. Because my omega was far too interested in two of those fucking alphas and the last thing I wanted was to lose myself to my hindbrain.

CHAPTER SIX

<u>Cohl</u>

She was asleep. For the first time since she'd woken after we'd pulled her from that town car, Corazon was peaceful and relaxed.

Not like I could blame her for her outburst, but some of that shit she'd broken had been expensive and antiques we'd collected through the years for our future omega.

We would have to have this room completely cleaned once she was returned to her family. We'd designed this room when we'd built the house with the plan to one day add an omega in hopes of increasing our bloodline. Not that we shared a bloodline, but if each of us could knock up our omega, that would mean our pack name would live on for generations.

But it had been close to ten years since we'd filled this room with furniture and stocked the nest and we'd yet to meet anyone who made us feel...

Fuck. We'd yet to meet an omega who called to the four of us the way Corazon did. And wasn't that fucked up. She was the daughter of our enemy, our rival. This was supposed to be nothing more than a business transaction that, hopefully, would have ended quickly with all parties getting something out of it.

As I watched her breathing deeply, her eyes moving behind her lids as though she were dreaming, I started to feel like a bit of an asshole. How were we any better than her fathers? They were more or less selling her off to inherit some of the power that came from pack Garcia. And we had taken her to use her as ransom to take power from both packs Garcia and Alvarez.

We'd used her just like they had.

At least we weren't expecting her to fuck anyone.

Not that I would turn her down if she were to wrap her lips around my cock or straddle my hips. The omega was smoking hot with full pouty lips, big, brown doe eyes, and a curvy body that made my hands itch to explore.

Yeah. I'd been the one tasked with tracking her movements, watching for any repetition in routines, taking pictures of her with her guards so we could get a count of how many watched over her at any given time when she was away from her family's pack house.

I'd seen her in tight fitted dresses that dipped low in the front and highlighted enough cleavage to tempt me to see how long I could bury my face between her tits before I suffocated. I'd seen her in jeans that cupped her round ass beautifully. I'd seen her in flouncy dresses that made her look as though she was ready for a day at the beach.

But my favorite had been the skimpy ass bikinis she tended to wear around the pool on her family's property.

Their security sucked ass. The fact I'd been able to get so close undetected was a failure on their part. I could have just as easily hoisted a long-range rifle and started picking off the guard one by one and been long gone before anyone discovered where the shots were coming from.

Bain and Ford were convinced they were scent matched to the

curvy, petite woman wrapped in the duvet with the TV playing softly in the background, the glow flashing light across her features.

They'd only just met her. I'd had the joy of becoming obsessed with her over the weeks of surveillance, of following her around, of filling my phone and the camera's memory card with images of her. And none of my packmates were aware of how many times I'd jerked off to those pictures.

But I'd been a good boy and kept my hands to myself. I'd kept my distance. I'd only stolen a few pieces of her clothing and kept them stashed when I needed a hit of her sweet, floral scent.

I should leave. I should turn on my heel and leave her to sleep where she was. The couch was plenty comfortable enough, big enough for more than one person to snuggle and sleep comfortably.

There was plenty of room for me to wrap myself around her and hold her while she slept.

Suppressing the growl in my chest, I decided to leave her where she slept, lifting the remote to turn off the TV so she could sleep in dark and silence.

My packmates had all split off to their areas of the house when we'd arrived back from *Roxy's* and would be dealing with their own demons.

Or *demon* in the singular. In one way or another, we were all going to have to come to terms with the fact Corazon was ours. Yet...the day would come when we would have to deliver her back to the hands of the enemy.

Unless...

We could win her over. We could treat her like an omega, shower her with pretty shit, gifts and all that. Make her fall for us. Then we could keep her.

That would also mean admitting to my pack I felt the same way. They didn't know about my obsession – I could simply pretend it was nothing more than what they felt, the scent match connection.

As my eyes adjusted to the dark, I continued to stare down at the beauty unaware of my presence as the moonlight cast a silver glow across her face.

The temptation to wrap myself around her, to run my fingers through her hair, to bury my face between her thighs and draw in a strong hit of her sweet-smelling cunt was almost more than I could resist.

Almost. Because I would. And I did. *After* leaning over and running my nose along her throat, breathing in her Lily of the Valley sweetness. How poetic – beautiful, deadly woman who carried the beautiful scent of a poisonous flower.

Palming my cock through my pants, I tiptoed from the room, pulling her door closed behind me and resecuring the locks to keep her from bolting and making a run for it.

Not that she would get very far with our security.

Maybe I should let her run. And I would be the one to chase her. I'd let her think she had a head start then hunt her, take her to the ground before fucking her until she could think of no other alpha but me, until any memory of any alpha who'd touched her in the past was nothing more than that…a fading memory.

My room was at the end of the hallway, yet her scent grew no less enticing with the distance. I'd ensured I'd drawn enough into my lungs to get me through the next few hours.

And I still had my trophies that belonged to her, even if her scent was beginning to fade from the fabric.

Stripping down to my birthday suit, I dragged out one of the bikini bottoms I'd swiped from the Alvarez compound and held it to my nose, inhaling deeply as I wrapped my fist around my cock and pretended it was her lips slowly stroking my length.

I'd fantasized about her full lips and plump ass so many times, jerked off to fantasies I'd weaved around her so many times I was surprised I wasn't sore.

Shoving the bottoms between my teeth, I began to stroke myself harder and used my free hand to squeeze my knot to the point of pain until the tingles started at the base of my spine and pearly white ropes shot across my abs, my moan stifled by the fabric in my mouth.

The Alvarez princess would be the death of me. Of us. One day and we were all fighting our alpha instincts. One day and we were all contemplating risking the empire we'd built simply to keep her in our lives.

And wasn't that all kinds of fucked up. We had worked too hard, spilled too much blood to willingly give it all up for one woman whose pussy smelled like paradise.

CHAPTER SEVEN

<u>Corazon</u>

*I*t had been three days since my failed bonding ceremony, three days since this group had attacked the caravan heading to what would have been one of my fathers' greatest achievements, three days of looking at the same four fucking walls.

Bain and Ford hadn't returned, but the auburn-haired alpha, Cohl, and the pumpkin scented alpha, Valen, took turns bringing meals, water bottles, even wine. And I'd yet to find myself drugged or sick from anything they were feeding me. So I assumed they hadn't lied when they'd said they wouldn't hurt me.

But what about the rest? Had they contacted my family yet? Had they called Pack Garcia to barter for my release? And what exactly was their end goal?

My guess was still the same as it had been – power. They took me for the same reason my fathers were trading me to the Garcias – power. Maybe money. More than likely both.

The meager collection of clothing Ford had delivered was down to a few more pairs of clean panties and t-shirts. He'd only provided one pair of leggings. And being as no one had bothered to ask whether I wanted them washed, I was now on day three of wearing the same pants and was feeling just this side of gross.

What other choice did I have, though? It was the leggings, Bain's boxers, or my panties. And there was currently no wood in here to start a new fire in the fireplace to warm the room. I swore they kept this place cool enough for fucking penguins.

My current state was the aforementioned leggings, t-shirt, and the duvet wrapped around me like a cape.

When the locks clunked outside my room, I tugged the sides of the duvet around me tighter as though that would stop anyone from seeing or touching me.

Cohl. Again. The redhead was quiet, but he tended to stare when he was in here instead of actually, you know, speaking to me.

But any time he came close enough and set a tray of food on the coffee table, I craved cupcakes as his vanilla frosting scent seemed to float through the air and land directly on my tongue. The alpha smelled and looked downright edible.

Maybe he would be the one I could win to my side, get him to see me as a woman, a person, instead of a prisoner. And I wasn't above using my womanly wiles to earn my freedom, no matter how far I had to take it. If my fathers could sell me and my body for their gain, I could use it for my own, damn it.

"Cohl?" I called out, adding a little extra damsel into my tone.

He stopped on his way to the door, glancing at me over his shoulder with his russet brows raised slightly.

"Is there any chance I could get a hoodie or sweatshirt? And maybe some more clean clothes?"

I pulled the blanket away and pulled on the cotton of the leggings, letting them snap into place.

"I've been wearing these for three days and I'm feeling kind of dirty. And it's cold in here." Shit. Was I making too many demands? I didn't want to come off as demanding or entitled. "I just…I don't know how long I'll be here, and this room is kind of cold."

I all but batted my lashes at Cohl as he stood there watching me with emotionless brown eyes.

With a nod, he turned and hurried from the room, the sound of the stupid lock sliding into place far too loud in the quiet of my room.

Well...shit. For some reason, I'd hoped to get him talking. Even if it was something as simple as an agreement. Then I could start to look for a crack in his armor, find a way to manipulate him in a way only an omega could.

Huh. Guess all that training in prep school had actually been good for something after all.

Tugging the duvet back into place, I leaned forward and picked at the selection on the tray. It seemed when Cohl brought my food, there was always far more than I could eat and always included at least one kind of sweet like a brownie or cupcake.

Interesting. Either he was aware he smelled like the most delicious cupcake in the world or was trying to fatten me up. At this point, I wasn't sure I cared which of those motivated him to bring me the sugary treats. It was one of the few things I'd begun to look forward to as boredom made me antsy.

I had never been a couch potato and had grown tired of watching movies and shows nonstop...*yesterday*. And I had no idea how much longer this would drag on.

Nope. I needed to win at least one of them over so, if nothing else, I could at least leave this fucking room.

As I finished up the sandwich with several different kinds of meats and cheeses, the lock groaned as it was pulled out of place again.

Cohl reentered, his arms loaded with split wood. He dumped it onto the floor in front of the fireplace before stacking some strategically inside. Within seconds, a fire started, and the glow instantly made me feel warmer, even if the heat had yet to touch my skin.

And then he left me alone again.

Abandoning my dinner, I hugged the duvet around me and hurried to the fireplace, hovering close enough to warm up without catching the down filled blanket on fire.

I jumped with a squeak when the door swung open again and Cohl reentered, this time with his arms overflowing with various colors and textures of fabric.

Shit. Had that door been unlocked and I hadn't noticed? I might have had a few seconds to attempt an escape, consequences be damned.

"They'll be too big," he said as he stood there staring at me, the clothing almost spilling from his arms.

After a few seconds of staring at me, he carried them to the bed and set them all down, digging through until he found a thick gray sweatshirt.

He carried it to me and held it up, waiting for me to remove the duvet so he could gently tug it over my head. I was instantly drowning in vanilla frosting and slick began to dampen my panties and I feared it would soak through and dampen my one and only pair of leggings.

"I brought you some sweatpants, too, but they'll be long. I figured you could…I don't know. Roll them or something."

Yep. Cohl was going to be the one I won over, the one to help me earn my escape, the one I would literally do what I had to so I could get my ass out of this room, out of the house, and then…

Fuck my family. Fuck Pack Garcia. The moment I was free of these alphas, I would run. I would run and run until I found somewhere I could simply blend in, somewhere my fathers wouldn't think to look for me.

And then I would start a life of my own, take whatever was needed to pass myself off as a beta, and live a normal fucking life.

But as Cohl tugged on the hem until it settled at my thighs, I took a second to look into his eyes.

I didn't see a quiet, shy, easily manipulated alpha. What I found was another predator. What I found was a darkness I hadn't noticed before, like there was a sea of secrets swimming in the warm brown of his irises.

Yet…I wasn't afraid. Not of him.

Nope. I was afraid of the way his nearness made me want to tangle my fingers in his hair and shove his face between my thighs. I was afraid of the way, when his gaze dipped to my lips, I found myself hoping he would kiss me. I was afraid of the way my omega purred when his hands smoothed up my arms and settled on my shoulders, his thumb grazing the pulse point on my throat.

Damn it. I had *actually* purred. I'd purred for my fucking captor.

Stockholm syndrome. That had to be it.

Or...

Or worse – my omega had found her scent match.

CHAPTER EIGHT

<u>Cohl</u>

She was right here. And she'd asked me for help. Me. And it wasn't lost on me that one of the few things she'd eaten while I'd gathered firewood was the cupcake I'd given her, just like the one I'd brought every time it was my turn to bring her meal.

Now, she was wearing my clothes and staring up into my eyes with confusion, anger, and lust.

Oh, I wasn't a fool. I'd known exactly what she was doing when she batted her long lashes and all but stuck her bottom lip out while asking the big strong alpha to help the helpless little omega.

But what could I say? It fucking worked.

What she didn't know was, short of opening the door and letting her walk out of here, she could ask me for just about anything and I'd hand it to her on a silver fucking platter. Especially if she continued to look up at me like that, as long as she continued to fill my nostrils with her sweet perfume as her omega reacted to my nearness.

She wanted me. She could deny it and ignore it all she wanted, but she wanted me.

My hands were still on her shoulders, my thumb barely grazing her throat where I could feel the frenzied fluttering of her heart. Her eyes dipped to my mouth then back up.

Could this be another of her little ploys? Did she think she could kiss me, distract me, then dart from the room?

Fucked up thing? I was tempted to let her. She wouldn't get much farther than the hallway. And even if she made it to the front door, the alarm would blare and send dozens of our men sprinting in her direction. She wouldn't even make it to the sidewalk.

And I would still get to taste her lips. I would still get to feel her body pressed against mine.

But I would have to let her make the decision. Because no way in hell would I let her or my pack mates accuse me of forcing her to do shit.

Nor would I stop her if she pressed her lips to mine, if she shoved her hand down my pants and wrapped those soft fingers around my cock. If she dragged me on top of her, spread her thighs, and begged me to fuck her.

My cock was almost painfully hard as the silent moment stretched between us until I finally pulled my hands from her shoulders and took a step back.

She swayed and blinked a few times as though coming out of a dream or as though she'd been as lost to the moment as I had.

"Is there anything else you need?" I asked, a whole lot of growl lacing my words.

"No," she whispered, raising a hand to set it softly against her throat where my thumb had stroked.

Checking the fire to make sure it was big enough to warm the room, I nodded toward the pile of clothes. "I'll get you some more if you need."

As I reached for the door, I heard her move toward me. "Cohl," she blurted out.

I turned to find her reaching for me, but she pulled her hand away before she could touch me.

Watching her, I waited for her to speak.

Finally, she sighed and seemed to both snap out of her lust stupor and dropped a bit of the act. "I'm bored. I get that you guys can't let me go until you get whatever it is you're hoping my fathers will give you, but can I at least leave this room?"

I could bring her to my room. It would be a change of scenery. Wrap myself around her, hold her through the night, press my hard cock against her round ass as she nestled against my crotch while she slept.

"I'll talk to Bain."

He was our pack leader and had been the mastermind behind this whole plan. In the end, he decided what course of action would come next in nearly every operation, every transaction, every deal we made and with whom.

Her arms wrapped around her middle, her hands invisible inside the sleeves of my sweatshirt, and I didn't bother hiding the smile at the sight of her wrapped in my clothes. Covered in my scent. Her pupils still dilated from my presence and my scent.

With a nod, I stepped out and pushed the lock back into place, resting my forehead against the door a moment while I forced my heart to slow its painful cadence and tried to will some of the blood from my cock and back into my brain before I started thinking with the wrong damn head.

A hand wrapped around my bicep and jerked me away, then I was slammed against the far wall.

"What the fuck are you playing at?" Bain growled at me.

"I brought the omega clothes and made her a fire. The fuck is your problem? Jealous she won't smell like you anymore?"

I shoved him away and stomped off toward the stairs, jogging down them in search of something a little stronger than the wine I'd left for her alongside the fresh bottle of water.

Bain was hot on my heels, his anger palpable and turning his charcoal scent into an acrid smokey and burnt odor.

"You touched her," he said, doing his best to use his bark on me.

Sorry, fucker. Won't work.

"I touched her fucking shoulders."

Grabbing a bottle of whiskey from the bar, I carried it into the living room without grabbing a glass, and dropped onto the couch, ignoring the questioning looks from my packmates and the guard standing near the front door.

After unscrewing the top, I tossed it onto the coffee table then tipped back the bottle, savoring the burn of the liquor as it went down my throat.

"What's going on?" Ford asked, muting whatever they were watching and leaning forward with his elbows on his knees.

"He touched the omega," Bain said, jabbing a finger in my direction.

"For fuck's sake. I brought her food. She said she was cold. I gave her some clothes. Then I touched her shoulder. Better call the special victim's unit to come take a statement."

"We need to talk about this shit," Valen said, still relaxing in his armchair, a glass of his own sitting on the side table. "None of you fuckers can tell me you don't want her. So we–"

"We what? Trick her? Court her? She's the daughter of our enemy. She fucking hates us," Bain said.

"Daughter of our enemy but not our enemy," Valen corrected as he raised his glass to his lips.

"I want her," I said, ignoring the looks from both Bain and Ford.

The two were fully aware of my somewhat unorthodox taste in the more carnal side of life. If it were up to them, I would never have a chance to be alone with Corazon. But I wasn't some sick fucking monster. Yeah, I had jacked off to fantasies of chasing Corazon through the woods, of tackling her and holding her down while I took her hard and fast from behind, while I knotted her so deeply my cum would stay inside of her for weeks.

Didn't mean any of that would happen. Unless that was what she wanted, of course. Who was I to deny anyone of pleasure?

"We don't trick her. But we could show her who we really are. Show her we're not like her fathers," Valen said.

"How are we not like them other than not selling our daughter for our own benefit?"

"That. That's how we're not like them," Valen said, using his glass to point in Bain's direction as though it made any sense whatsoever.

"We court her. Buy her pretty shit. Let her out of that room. She said she's bored," I offered.

"She would drop to her knees and blow you if she thought it would get her out of this house," Bain growled.

My dick jumped at the possibility. Definitely wouldn't stop her if she wanted to try to manipulate me with a blowjob. I couldn't be manipulated. But she didn't know that.

Adjusting myself with no shame, I grinned up at Bain. "She's more than welcome to blow me."

"Stay the fuck away from her," Bain threatened.

Growing tired of his bullshit, I pushed to my feet and took the few steps that separated us until we were practically nose to nose.

"This was your idea, remember? Your idea to snatch her from the car, your idea to hold her here. I seem to remember someone suggesting we use betas to watch over her to keep our alphas calm. And I seem to remember you and Ford getting all growly and possessive. So which is it, asshole? 'Cause the longer she stays in this house, the harder it's going to get on all of us. Have you thought about what the fuck will happen if she goes into heat while she's here? You really think any of us can deny her if she starts whining and whimpering and begging for our knots?"

Because there wasn't a fucking chance in hell I would deny her anything.

At the mention of the inevitable, it was as though all the oxygen had been sucked from the room and no one moved a muscle for a solid five minutes.

"Fuck," Ford growled out.

"She won't ask for our help," Valen said with a shake of his head. "But we can order some shit to help her, at least. Something to ease her pain. They have toys and all that for omegas. The kind with artificial or silicon knots. There are plenty of blankets and pillows and all that in the nest, but we'll have to make sure someone keeps an eye on her, make sure she's eating and drinking. And I say that's where we bring in the betas."

Always the voice of fucking reason. I still wasn't sure how Valen had avoided becoming pack lead when he was usually the only one able to keep his emotions in check.

He was already tapping away on his phone, either searching sites for the various tools to help Corazon through her heat or maybe actually putting in an order.

That was all fine and dandy. But I had every intention of staying close to her, and fuck yeah, I would give her anything and everything she asked for, especially if that included tasting her cunt, of burying myself deep inside her heat, of knotting her over and over. All in the name of helping out the omega, of course.

I could feel Bain's eyes on me, could smell the anger turning his scent bitter. Not my fault Corazon was scared of him and felt comfortable around me. I didn't try to intimidate her, didn't crowd her. And I'd brought her clothes and shoes. And lots of food and treats every day.

And, yup, it was all to get her to trust me, to drop her defenses. But hey, she was obviously doing the same thing to me, batting her lashes and putting on the whole damsel voice when asking for a fire. I have never been naïve. I knew the hot omega was hoping I would relax enough she could either escape on her own or convince me to help get her out.

A smirk quirked up one side of my mouth as I wondered how else I could get her to relax around me, how I could get her comfortable enough to let me wrap my body around hers, how I could get her to ask me for a little one on one time and physical relief from her upcoming heat.

CHAPTER NINE

<u>Corazon</u>

After Cohl left, the sound of that lock sliding into place sending a mixture of dread and rage through my system, I picked through the large pile of clothing on the bed until I found a pair of sweats and a clean t-shirt. He and the others were far bigger than me so I would be drowning in his clothes. But at least they were clean.

And smelled like him.

Carrying the clothing into the bathroom with me, I closed and locked the door, then started the shower, stripping out of the leggings that I was tempted to toss into the trash, pulled the hoodie and t-shirt over my head, then stepped under the spray as steam began to fill the stall and spill over into the room.

Tilting my head back, I let the water saturate my hair and sluice down my body, the heat seeping into my bones and finally warming me up a bit. With the fire roaring in the bedroom, I would finally be comfy and cozy.

This was obviously an omega wing, yet they didn't have an omega. Nor did they know how to care for one, apparently, if the lack of comforts was anything to go by. Sure, there were pillows and blankets in the nest, but the room lacked their scents, the blankets I had seen were nothing like I would have chosen for comfort, and the room was way too cold.

Although, when my heat hit – fuck, would I still be here when my cycle came on – I would be thankful for the cooler air as my temperature raised to nearly dangerous temps.

But not now. Now I felt like I just couldn't warm up. And I had been so close to asking Cohl to snuggle me on the couch until I'd seen something a little darker in his eyes and realized how strongly my body was reacting to his nearness.

The last thing I needed was for him to smell my slick and think he could take advantage of me or my situation.

Then again, I had already decided I would use any and every means possible to earn my freedom. And if that meant sleeping with the enemy, so fucking be it.

Honestly, I was far more attracted to these alphas, even Bain and Ford, than I was to my betrothed pack. Leo, Julian, and Roman were attractive and had been nothing short of civil with me. But I hadn't felt the need to run my nose along their throats, to rub my cheek against their scent glands, to wrap my legs around their waists and grind myself against them the way I did with…well, shit, all four of my captors.

And didn't that make me a special kind of stupid? As in the too stupid to live character in movies and books I used to yell at for running up the stairs or into the basement instead of through the front door.

After washing and rinsing every inch of my body, I ended the spray and reached around the glass door for the fluffy white towel hanging on the other side. At least they got this part right. The towel was so freaking soft and felt like I was drying off with chinchilla fur instead of scratchy terry cloth.

Wrapping the towel around my torso sarong style, I then

wrapped another in my hair and stepped up to the vanity, wiping the steam away with my hand. There were only basics in this room, none of my skincare products, makeup, or anything for my hair more than a brush. While I might not have liked being the rare jewel of Pack Alvarez, I did like the luxuries my position had awarded me, the higher end skincare products and the soft as silk clothing.

Searching through the vanity, I could only find the generic body lotion that I'd discovered during my first venture into this room. Day three of smearing this crap on my face. I was scared it was going to end up causing me a breakout or even cause some kind of allergic reaction.

But it was better than nothing. I couldn't use the cheap stuff in the shower then walk around with dry, tight skin.

As much as I wanted out of this place, at the moment, I would have been satisfied with basic necessities past the toothbrush, generic lotion, and manly scented shower gel and soap.

Pulling the towel from my hair and hanging it to air dry, I carefully worked the knots from my hair from the sole brush in the room. Did they simply build and furnish the room without putting any thoughts into what an omega might need? Even if they'd somehow bonded with a male omega, he would have needed more than the bare basics that had been left in here.

Unless they'd simply planned to treat anyone they added to their pack as an ornament and baby maker. They wouldn't bother with anything else in that case.

Once my hair was as knot free as I could get it and my skin was a little greasy from the body lotion, I stepped from the room still wrapped in my towel and froze.

Cohl was sitting on the couch, his feet up on the coffee table, his eyes glued to the TV until he heard me step out.

He glanced at me, back at the TV, before his attention quickly whipped back to me. His attention roamed me from head to toe slowly, lingering on my legs, then the cleavage pushed up from the towel, before raising to my face.

"What…why are you in here?" I asked, trying not to sound too indignant or shitty. I was trying to win him over, after all.

He was quiet a few minutes, his hand raising to rub at his jaw and across his mouth, all the while his eyes went back to that slow perusal of my body.

This could be one of those moments, the time to start putting the first part of some kind of plan in action.

Taking a deep breath to steel my nerves, I sauntered to where he sat and stopped beside his knees. He dropped his feet to the ground and spread his knees while his arms stayed stretched along the back of the couch as though this was his room, as though he owned the space.

And honestly, as that sweet frosting tickled my senses and made my nipples pebble below the towel and slick to dampen my core and upper thighs, I couldn't help but think this man could own any space he entered.

All four of them were walking sex on a stick. But Cohl had a quiet sexiness to him, a darkness that drew me to him, a magnetism that made me want to crawl all over him and let his shadows sweep me under and hide me from the rest of the world.

In a word, I wanted this man to wreck me. I wanted him to destroy everything I thought I knew about alphas. I wanted him to…

Shit. Focus, Cora.

This was about manipulating *him*, not letting him drown me in his sex appeal.

Another deep breath and I raised a leg and swung it over his thighs, lowering until I was straddling his lap, my bare core directly over the hard length of his cock. Even through his sweats, I could feel how long and thick he was, could feel his knot beginning to inflate.

More slick coated my thighs until my hips began to rock against him before I could stop myself as my omega's need for touch took over and my preheat made me seek release.

"Tell me what you want, omega," Cohl said as he watched my face.

My lips parted but I couldn't find my voice, couldn't speak the words aloud. Because I was fighting both desire and shame, shame that I was more than willing to grind my pussy against him until I orgasmed, and it had nothing to do with manipulating him but finding my own pleasure by using his body.

When I didn't say anything, Cohl gently rested his hands on my hips and urged me to move.

"Take what you need. I'm all yours," he said quietly, his voice rough and husky with need.

And those words spurred me on.

Resting my hands against his chest, I began to rock, grinding my clit against his hardness as slick soaked the material of his sweats. He would have a noticeable mark but didn't appear to give a shit. In fact, the rise and fall of his chest told me he was enjoying himself as much as I was.

As much as I needed to feel those first tingles of release, I wanted to see him when he fell apart from me using his body for my own needs. I wanted to hear the deep growl or grunt as he came in his pants.

I wanted to feel his cum painting my inner walls so badly I was close to begging him to push his pants down so I could spear myself on his cock.

Before I could put any of my thoughts or fantasies into action, my core tightened, tingles started, then I exploded from the inside out, throwing my head back and moaning long and low as fireworks erupted behind my closed lids and pleasure rippled through me from my pussy straight to my fingers and toes.

His grip tightened on my hips and urged me to keep moving until he tensed below me and grunted, a deep guttural sound, as he came behind his sweats.

Holy shit. We hadn't had sex, yet that had been one of the most erotic moments of my life.

As my mind slowly became aware of what the hell I was doing and who I was sitting on, I opened my eyes and looked into his face, a new wave of arousal clenching everything south of my belly button as the vision of his blown pupils and parted lips greeted me.

When one hand released my hip and skimmed under the towel to swipe through my folds, I inhaled a sharp gasp. But when he brought his fingers to his mouth and sucked my release from them, I thought I would fucking pass out.

"You taste even better than you smell," he growled out after cleaning my slick and release from his fingertips.

Slowly and on shaky legs, I pulled away from him, tucking the towel around me to keep from flashing any part of my naked body at him. I'd just used his body to come and now I was feeling shy.

Of course I was. I had intended to seduce him, to turn him into an ally, to somehow convince him to help me escape.

Instead, my hindbrain had taken over and my omega had found a way to claim an alpha by not only covering myself in his scent but leaving mine on him.

Heat. Or rather *pre*heat. That was all it was. My cycle was close and my omega was becoming needy. It had nothing to do with the fact Cohl looked as though he could do exactly as I wanted and completely wring my body of every last drop of ecstasy or that he smelled as though every inch of his body and his hot cum would taste like the sweetest cupcake.

His eyes followed my every move, even when I grabbed a pair of the pants he'd left for me and dragged them up my legs and under the towel, then pulled the sweatshirt back over my head without bothering with a t-shirt.

Pulling the towel from under the hoodie, I carried it into the bathroom, closed and locked the door, then leaned against the wood, praying he would be gone by the next time I stepped out.

Because I wasn't fully convinced I wouldn't climb on top of him again. Only this time, I wanted to feel his skin against mine. I wanted to feel the heat of his hands on my breasts.

I wanted to feel every inch of him filling me until his knot was locked inside of me and I carried the scents of his skin and his cum.

What the hell just happened? What was happening to me?

While, yes, I could blame it on my hindbrain, I wasn't suffering any other symptoms, no emotional rollercoaster, no fever, no cramping.

So...could it simply have been what I feared, that my omega was reacting to her scent match?

And what the fuck would happen if the others began to hang around my room more? Or I was actually allowed to leave this room? Would I end up throwing myself at them, climbing them like trees and wrapping my legs around their waists while begging for their knots.

I had to get out of here. I had to leave before it was too late. I had to find a way out before I gave in to my baser needs, to my designation's need to bond with her chosen alphas. Because if they knotted and marked me, not only would I be tied to them for life, but my family and Pack Garcia would see it as an act of war.

And I would be helpless to stop it. I would be the cause.

Yet another moment when I wished I had been born different. Sliding down the door until I was sitting, tears pricked the backs of my eyes as I fantasized about the normal life I might have had had I been born a beta like my siblings.

CHAPTER TEN

<u>Valen</u>

The t-shirt was a little rough against my overheated skin as I wiped the ropes of cum from my belly and hand. Like a fucking perv, I'd pulled up the feed from the omega's room when Cohl didn't immediately step out after her shower.

And watched as she'd grinded her pussy against his sweats covered cock until she'd thrown her head back and come with a sexy as fuck moan, her long, dark hair hanging nearly to Cohl's knees.

I swore Cohl and I came at the same time as he'd urged her to keep rocking against him until he tensed and grunted. But, unlike me, he would be leaving the omega's room covered in the scent of her pussy, as well as soaked sweats from both his and her release.

Lucky bastard.

Well, he was lucky as long as Bain hadn't watched that footage. When I flipped through the various cameras, I didn't find him waiting outside Corazon's room. In fact, I didn't see him anywhere. The only bedroom with a camera was the omega wing and that was to keep her safe. The pack lead could be in his own bedroom spanking his own monkey and I wouldn't have a clue.

Actually, it was fine with me that I didn't have a view into my packmates' rooms. They were all good-looking guys, but I had never felt an ounce of attraction toward any of them. And really didn't feel like watching them jerk off.

What I wanted was to barge into the omega's room and to pull her down until she was sitting on my face, cutting off my air supply, suffocating me with her sweet-smelling pussy. What a fucking way to go.

Eyes still glued to the screen, I watched as Corazon hurriedly climbed from Cohl's lap and dressed. And shit…she was pulling on his clothes. Not only would he be covered in her scent, but now she would be covered in his. Why hadn't I thought of bringing her my own clothes so she would smell like me?

Right. Because we were supposed to be keeping our distance. Bain was supposed to be contacting her family pack as well as the pack of her future alphas. I had zero doubt this plan would work, that, by the end of all of this, we would control the majority of imports and exports in the area. If anyone wanted to travel through the area, they would have to pay us a tithe or they would lose their shipments in one freak accident or another.

And we would lose the first omega who had appealed to all four of us on a profound level. She called to my alpha. I wanted to tuck her against my side and protect her from the outside world. I wanted to run out and restock all the pretty shit we'd added to that room when we'd thought we would actually seek and add an omega. I wanted to bury myself so deep inside of her, to knot her, to fill her with my pups.

The thought of the beautiful woman with a belly rounded with my offspring made my dick twitch again.

Fuck Bain. Fuck Ford. Fuck Cohl. I wanted her.

Actually, I had a strong feeling Cohl wouldn't fight me on that. There was no doubt he wanted to spread her on the couch and devour every inch of her olive complected skin. It came down to convincing the pack lead. We had all admitted we were drawn to her. We had all admitted she was a scent match.

It was a matter of getting everyone on the same fucking page.

The moment we decided and were able to win her over – and fuck yes, I would do everything in my power to convince her we could make her happy – it was a matter of marking her without starting a war with two fucking packs.

We had the manpower. We had the firepower. But I wasn't sure Corazon would appreciate it if we slaughtered her fathers or any other members of her family. Not the best way to start a life together.

However…they were willing to trade her off for power. Surely, she couldn't be uber close to the fuckers if they were willing to treat her like a used car or livestock.

Cohl watched the closed bathroom door Corazon had stepped through. It was the only part of the omega wing that didn't have a camera. As awesome as it would have been to watch her run her soapy hands all over her body, everyone deserved a little privacy while using the toilet.

After a few minutes, he gave up on her coming back out and pushed to his feet and left the room, pulling the door closed behind him and, hopefully, slipping the locks back into place.

I smiled as the omega pulled the bathroom door open enough to peer out, then jogged to the bedroom door where she tried to open it. Yep. He'd locked it.

Honestly, I was a little surprised he hadn't left it unlocked. It would be the perfect reason for him to give chase. And the fucker loved nothing more than to chase his prey, to hunt them, to dominate them and make them submit to his darker desires.

Not quite my scene, but as long as both parties consented, who the fuck was I to judge?

My smile stretched wider when she slapped her hand against the door and released a string of curses that would make a sailor blush. For such a petite, beautiful omega, she had a mouth on her.

And fuck yes, even that made my dick perk up and pay attention.

After a few minutes of pacing the bedroom, she flopped onto the couch and laid back, an arm thrown above her head.

Her head rolled toward the door and then her eyes closed, her hand snaking slowly down her body.

"Oooh. You need more, don't you?" I whispered to the screen as her fingers dipped under her borrowed sweats.

Damn it. Now not only would she be covered in his scent, but those sweats would also be saturated with her slick. I could always wait until she fell asleep and steal them, hold them to my face and draw that scent deep into my lungs. But, unfortunately, I would also be scenting Cohl. Something about that combination wouldn't be nearly as delicious as getting it directly from the source.

My knot inflated again as precum wept from the slit of my dick. Her hand was moving below those sweats now as she closed her eyes, her lips parted, and soft panting sounds left her lips.

I had assumed she would be close to her heat. After all, if she was being used as a bargaining tool, what better way to combine the families than to make sure she was knocked up as soon as possible, that she would carry an heir to Pack Garcia immediately.

That meant our little omega would soon be insatiable.

Hell, she looked as though she was feeling that way already.

Unless it was simply because of Cohl. A green fog slithered through my gut at that thought. If we were to win her over, to convince her to join our pack, the four of us would have to share her time and body. But that didn't stop the urge to barge through that room, pull on my dick, and spill my cum all over her curvy body, branding her with my scent.

"Take those off. Let me see that pretty little pussy," I begged in a whisper barely above a breath as I stayed riveted to the scene playing out on my screen.

Were any of the others watching? Were they watching as the omega's back arched from the couch and a soft moan pulled from her lips.

Unfortunately, she didn't remove the pants or even pull the hoodie up so I could see those full tits. I'd seen the way her nipples had pebbled and strained against the borrowed t-shirt when we'd all helped clean up the mess she'd made when she'd woke that first day. But I had yet to see her traipse around her room naked. She tended to change in the bathroom as though she feared one of us would step in at any point.

Good thing she didn't know about the cameras.

With my hand pulling and jerking on my dick, I came a second before she did, once again shooting ropes of cum along my chest and stomach as a breathy whisper of a moan escaped her lips and the movement began to slow under the sweats.

To be in that room. To have my face pressed directly between her thighs. To taste everything her body had to offer.

Soon. Cohl had sat there and let her use him to get herself off. He'd somehow managed to get her to drop her guard. I could do the same. Shame I wouldn't come out and ask him exactly what he'd done other than delivering food and drinks to her every day.

Pretty shit. Omegas loved pretty shit. But we had to be careful. There were no women in our pack, none in our home. We had a housekeeper who came a couple times a week, but there would be no reason for us to buy her expensive and girly shit.

But I would find a way. I'd figure out what she liked and get it for her. Starting with that bathroom stuff. Surely, she didn't like the manly type products that had been left in there. Women liked flowery smelling crap. They liked pink and purple and shit like that.

And I had zero knowledge about any of it.

Fuck it. I'd figure it out. Even if I had to hand her a laptop and my debit card and let her online shop to her heart's desire. I'd have to sit beside her the whole time, though. Couldn't have her contacting anyone and letting them know where she was until we were ready, until every single piece of the plan was in place.

Yep. I was going to dote on this little omega, get her anything and everything she wanted, make her happy.

But I was definitely going to start with leaving some of my own fucking clothes in there. I needed her to carry my scent, as well. Even if it was only from my shirts or shorts. It had been my idea to send her somewhere else to be guarded by betas. And I had been the one to point out the obvious, that Corazon was our scent match.

Cohl was already as much a goner as I was. Now, we just needed to find a way to entice Ford and Bain, to break through their fucking barriers so they would accept the fact we'd not only found our omega, but we had kidnapped her...

And I had no intention of ever letting her go.

CHAPTER ELEVEN

<u>Corazon</u>

*D*ay six. Shame there wasn't a piece of chalk in this room so I could put marks on the wall as each day passed. If I had found something sharp enough, I might have scratched each day into the wall for no other reason than to be petty.

Then again, if I'd found a knife, I might have used it to earn my freedom, threatened one of the alphas or even myself if that was what it took.

Cohl hadn't returned since the night I'd rubbed myself on him like a cat in heat. Or rather an omega nearing her heat.

Damn it. For some stupid reason, I'd thought there might have been a possibility that this whole thing would be over before I hit my cycle.

But I had to wonder which scenario was better – being here with four hot as sin alphas who definitely looked as though they could deliver relief through the waves of my heat, being with three alphas I didn't feel drawn to, or being out in the world alone and fearing my perfume would send a stranger into rut when I begged and whimpered and whined for a knot.

I had also been stupid enough to think I might have earned some brownie points with Cohl after grinding against his dick until he blew his load. But I hadn't seen him. Now, every time my brain decided to draw that little memory to the forefront, shame washed over me and heat burned my cheeks.

Such an idiot. These were criminals. Thugs like my fathers and their men. They probably had women throwing themselves at their feet every time they turned around and I somehow thought simply rubbing on him would make Cohl betray his own pack.

Instead of watching TV yet again, I paced from one end of the room to the other, the faux Ugg shoes Cohl had brought me making soft whispers against the floor. Every once in a while, I would stop and peer outside as the sun began to set, noting the guards that patrolled the area, tried to memorize not just their faces but their rotating schedules, even tried – and failed – to memorize the license plate numbers of any vehicle that came and went.

The first time an SUV pulled onto the driveway, I'd slapped my hands against the glass while yelling and waving my arms to get their attention. The men merely glanced in my direction then looked away before heading toward the house.

I had no friends here. No allies. I was alone and cursing each day that passed that sent me closer and closer to my cycle.

There was a lock on the inside of the nest door. I could barricade myself in there and use my own fingers to bring me to release when the worst waves crashed over me. It wouldn't be enough and would cause the duration and severity to increase past the usual four days with an alpha's knot or silicon knot, but at least I wouldn't be begging these assholes to take me when I lost complete control over my thoughts or actions.

Resuming my pacing around the room, I glared at the pile of clothing resting on the bed. I had yet to sleep on the mattress, terrified of growing too comfortable and being so vulnerable while surrounded by the enemy. And no matter how my omega felt about them, my brain needed to remember they were exactly that – my enemy. Or at least my family's enemy. That was exactly why they'd attacked my bonding caravan, why they'd shot at my family, why they had killed my guards and dragged me from the backseat.

Another glare landed on the clothes left by Cohl. If I had any other option, I would leave that pile sitting there untouched. I had no option but to be surrounded by his sweetness every day when I pulled on clean clothing. I could practically taste him.

I *wanted* to taste him. All of him.

Damn it, Cora. You hate him.

At least I wanted to hate him. Or at least fear him the way I did Bain and Ford.

Ford had seemed sweet at first, kind, and then he'd crowded me and made my body sing with desire and caused slick to coat my thighs. And the flare of his nostrils told me he knew exactly what the hell he was doing, the smug bastard.

Did I fear them, though? Neither had reentered the room since they'd all filed in to clean up after I'd destroyed nearly everything I could get my hands on. Neither had barged in and demanded anything of me. And I assumed they had contacted my family or Pack Garcia by now.

Would my betrothed alphas bother agreeing to anything to get me back? They were powerful, wealthy men who came from an equally powerful and wealthy family. Surely, there were others who would be more than willing to gift their daughter for some form of business agreement. They didn't love me. I wasn't sure whether they even liked me. Like me, they'd been forced into this situation by their own fathers.

As I made yet another path across the floor, the groan of the lock pulled my glare in that direction. I had expected Cohl since he'd been my most regular visitor and the one who normally brought me food.

So when Bain stepped in, I felt my brows raise up my forehead and I slowed to a stop, crossing my arms over my chest and shooting him the same glare I'd been giving Cohl's clothes.

He held a tray full of food and a glass of wine. But there were no sweets like when the auburn haired alpha who'd made me come simply by sitting there while I grinded on his cock delivered my meals.

Bain's pale blue eyes landed on me briefly before he set the tray on the coffee table, then stepped away, shoving his hands in his pockets.

"Cohl said you asked to leave the room."

"Yeah. Days ago." I couldn't keep the attitude out of my voice. I might have been used to constantly having a shadow, but I had never been treated like a damn prisoner before. Sitting still for this long felt alien to me.

I wanted to feel the sun on my face, to feel the cool air brushing my hair back. I wanted my soft, pretty clothes. I wanted my Gucci heels and nightclubs and dancing.

He nodded but didn't approve nor deny my request.

"Well? Can I finally leave my room?"

One dark brow slowly rose, and my body heated under the look he shot me. Damn this man and his sex appeal. Damn him for making my body react when all I wanted to do was scratch his eyes from his skull.

His nostrils flared and his eyes made a slow perusal of my body, feeling like a caress of his fingers along every inch of my body.

When he looked back up into my face, his pupils ate up a majority of the icy blue of his irises.

"Do you realize you're perfuming? You did that last time we were in here, too." The sexiest – and cockiest – smirk was on his kissable lips and I wanted to cross the room to either kiss him until we were both starved for oxygen or slap the look off his stupidly handsome face.

Seriously. It should be illegal for anyone to look as good as these alphas. How the hell had four of the most delicious smelling, most ruggedly beautiful alphas end up in one fucking pack?

And how the hell had I ended up on their damn radar?

"How did you know about my bonding ceremony? I mean, how did you know which route we would take? Where the ceremony would be? Only a small circle was invited and privy to that information."

Because of the exact thing that had happened. It was bad enough being the child of men high in the mafia. But to be the omega daughter of one of the ruling families of the region resulted in me having around the clock guards no matter where I went. I wasn't allowed to pin my location on social media when I was out. Hell. I never even posted pics until the day after so my family's enemy couldn't learn of my location.

"We've had eyes on you for a while." That was the only answer he gave then went right back to staring at me. Nah. He was glaring. Trying to intimidate me.

But as I tilted my head and glared right back, I noted the increase in his hormones wafting on the air. He could pretend all he wanted, but he was attracted to me. He appreciated my scent. I might not have been able to manipulate Cohl, or even one single member of the pack. But perhaps I could convince them each that I could be trusted, find a gap in their defenses, and find my way to freedom.

"You've been watching me," I said, doing my best to add a little breathiness to my voice without overdoing it.

Who was I kidding? The longer he stared at me with those icy blue eyes and his warm yet deadly scent filling my senses, the warmer my body grew and slick coated my upper thighs.

Had my fathers chosen this pack, my omega would have been lost to them, to their scents. I might have actually been somewhat pleased by their selection.

Bain's thick arms were crossed over his broad chest. He nodded his head once. Cohl had been easier to seduce – or perhaps it had been me who'd been seduced – but Bain wasn't spread out on the couch and I wasn't wearing nothing but a towel.

"Have you called my family? Or Pack Garcia?"

When his head tilted and he watched me in silence for a few more moments, my heart began to race, and my perfume lifted on the air. Three of these men watched me as though they wanted to devour me, eat me alive.

And fuck if I wasn't starting to crave that very same thing.

"Do you want that pack?" he asked. Was his voice deeper?

"What do you mean?"

"Pack Garcia. We know it was arranged by your parents and theirs. So I'm asking you – do you want to be bonded to Pack Garcia?"

So many retorts ran through my mind, so many lies. But in the end, I deflated a little as I realized my tongue refused to voice anything other than, "No."

The moment the words left my lips, his arms dropped to his sides and he ate the space between us in three long strides. He stood so close a deep breath would push my chest against his. His body heat wrapped around me, his gunpowder and charcoal essence made me feel as though I had drank too much and fought the urge to lean closer, to rub my face along his neck, to jump up and wrap my legs around his hips so I could feel his length rubbing against me through our clothes.

"You want me," he uttered.

"What?" I said, a frown drawing my brows together.

"I can smell that sweet cunt crying for me. Just ask and I'll give you anything you want."

Oh, this arrogant son of a bitch. "I'm in preheat. Has nothing to do with you. My body would react the same way around any asshole with a knot."

He did close the space between us then, his fingers trailing from my cheek, down my neck, to my shoulders, before he slowly slid them past the waistband of my borrowed sweats. And for the life of me, I couldn't stop him, even when those long fingers slid through my folds and teased at my opening.

"We could test that theory. I could snatch one of those Garcia assholes. Leave them in here with you. See if you get this wet for them?"

A whimper left my throat when he dipped just the tip of his index finger into me.

The sexiest and most wicked smirk kicked up one corner of his mouth. Shit. I was rocking my hips, trying to fuck his hand, trying to force his finger deeper.

Lifting my chin, I glared up at him. "It's just preheat. I'm sure my body would react to anyone with a knot." I'd repeated the words, yet they felt as much a lie the second time as they had the first.

He slowly began to remove his hand. "Does that mean you want me to stop?"

My traitorous body took over before my brain had a second to catch up. I snatched his wrist and kept his hand buried in the sweats. Hell no, I didn't want him to stop. After just the slightest touch, I was ready to rip my clothes away and present for this alpha.

Although…honestly, I think I felt that way from the moment he'd removed his face covering. Or maybe it was the moment he'd stepped into the room and his scent had washed over me and tried to sweep me under.

No matter how many times I tried to convince myself this was nothing more than my body preparing for my cycle, I knew it was something deeper. And if I wasn't careful, I could end up screwing everything up for not just myself, but this pack, as well.

But why the hell should I care what happened to them? They'd killed guards I had known for years. They'd executed them while I was sitting inches away. Did they not think about the fact they could have easily struck me with one of those bullets they'd been spraying across the Town Car and the caravan?

When Bain slid a long finger into my core and bent it just right, all thoughts of why I should hate and fear this pack dissolved from my brain. The only thing my damn brain latched onto was the growing pressure low in my belly and the way my upper thighs were wet with slick.

He growled a pleased sound deep in his throat. "You're drenching my hand, little omega. Tell me again how it's not me you want, but anyone with a knot."

A part of me wanted to scream at him to shut up and fuck me. But that louder part, the part that refused to allow this alpha or any alpha to make me feel as though I didn't have control over my own life reared its head.

As his finger worked in and out of me, his thumb stroking my clit with the perfect amount of pleasure, I jutted my chin forward and stared him right in the eye.

Bain smirked down at me. "I want to hear you say it. I want to hear you say you want me."

I clamped my lips shut, even as that pressure built, and tingles heralded an oncoming release.

When I continued to glare up into his face, Bain pulled his hand from my pants, then put his fingers in his mouth, cleaning my arousal and slick from his fingers in achingly slow laps of his tongue, sucking the finger he'd used to fuck me clean.

Then he lowered his head until his lips were right next to my ear, grazing the shell. "From now on, if you want to come…you'll have to beg me."

He put space between us and I couldn't help but lower my attention to the obvious bulge in his pants. I wasn't the only one currently affected.

With a soft huff, I returned his smirk. "Looks like I won't be the only one suffering."

Bain backed away, nodding slowly as though he'd come to some conclusion in his head. "Your family has been contacted. So have your future alphas," he said, the last word wrapped with a deep growl. "And neither has responded."

"What happens if they refuse to give you what you're asking for?"

I didn't think these men would kill me, but I knew nothing about them. But I did know about men *like* them, alphas like them who would and could easily use an omega for their own gain. Just like my own fucking family.

Would they find someone willing to pay for an omega? Would they traffic me?

Or would they decide to keep me for themselves?

And why the hell did the thought of staying here with the four of them make my heart thump hard in my chest and force me to fight a purr from my omega?

He chuckled low and backed from the room, that stupid lock groaning back into place.

He'd never told me whether I would be allowed out of this room. He hadn't given me an answer as to my future if neither my family's pack nor Pack Garcia were willing to give in to their demands.

Bain was trying to intimidate me, scare me. Well, he could kiss my ass. He wasn't the first monster I'd encountered in my life. And he sure as hell wouldn't be the last.

CHAPTER TWELVE

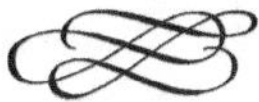

<u>Bain</u>

ell, that shit had backfired. I'd really thought she would say it, say she wanted me, admit that she wanted us.

Instead, the little spitfire had glared right at me and lied through her fucking teeth.

Yeah, she was nearing her heat, but her pupils dilated until her eyes were almost black any time one of us came near. Her perfume exploded from her the moment I'd stepped into the room and I'd smelled her cunt crying out for me.

Once her hindbrain took over, sure, then she wouldn't care whose knot she was riding, as long as she found relief. But that wasn't the case now. She was reacting to her alphas. Her true alphas. As in me, Cohl, Valen, and Ford.

Fuck. She'd gotten herself off by grinding on Cohl's covered cock. And I'd wanted nothing more than to feel her pussy clenching around my fingers. Instead, she was determined to be a stubborn omega and pretend as though it was her hindbrain taking over rather than the fact her omega recognized her scent matches.

I wasn't sure how long I stood outside her door after dipping my finger into her tight heat, but my cock had yet to go down and my knot was still swollen. Gripping myself through my pants, I was tempted to barge through that door, shove her onto the bed, pull my cock out, and jack off until she was covered in my scent. Let her fucking pretend she didn't feel the same pull the rest of us did when she was smothered in my essence.

A chuckle dragged my attention down the hall to find Cohl leaning against the frame of his door.

"Backfired, didn't it?"

"Fuck off." I stormed into my room. But before the door could swing closed, Cohl stopped it and invited himself inside. "What part of fuck off didn't you catch?"

I flopped onto my bed, throwing my arm over my eyes.

"You could try being nicer to her. I didn't have to say a thing and she straddled me and got us both off. I mean, I would have preferred her cunt wrapped around my cock, but still."

A growl tore from me.

"'S going on?" Valen asked.

I pulled my arm away enough to peek toward the door where Valen stood just inside.

"Why the fuck is everyone inviting themselves into my room all of a sudden?"

"Your room smells the strongest of Cora," Cohl said with a shrug.

"Cora? Giving her a nickname already?" Valen asked with a chuckle.

"Why the fuck are you both in here?" I pushed to a sitting position, grunting when my cock was practically strangled behind the constraints of my pants.

"We decided we're keeping her," Cohl announced, dropping onto the mattress.

Glaring at him, I growled. "You got a death wish? Get the fuck off my bed."

Of course the asshole just made himself more comfortable, scooting until it looked like he would try to cuddle up against me.

"I will break your fucking neck," I dead panned.

"We're keeping her," he repeated. "Valen agrees."

I turned my attention to the other alpha, who shrugged with his thick arms crossed over his chest. "I'm not up to forcing her, but... what he said. She's ours. And we were watching that shit. She totally wanted you. But then you had to open your fucking mouth and ruin it. Should have just bent her over and fucked her."

"Or you could have used your bark. Under that bristly exterior, I think is one hell of a submissive," Cohl said.

Jabbing a finger in his direction, I put the full weight of my alpha bark behind my warning. "Do not fuck with her."

He shrugged. "Eh. She'll come around. Mark my word. I can see it. She's just begging to choke on my cock. Can you image how pretty she'll look with tears and drool streaming down her face? With pinkened ass cheeks and a swollen pussy?"

"For fuck's sake," I grumbled, adjusting my cock in hopes of easing some of the discomfort. The mental images Cohl was putting out there weren't helping. And I wasn't even a natural Dom. Sure, I liked to fuck hard and fast, but I wasn't into the same primal kinks as my packmate.

"I ordered her some toys," Valen said as he leaned against the wall beside my door, his arms and ankles crossed.

"What kind of toys?" Cohl asked, shooting up to a sitting position with far too much interest in his eyes.

Valen shook his head with a roll of his eyes. "For her. Not for you. A silicon knot. Vibrators. That kind of shit. If she's telling the truth and is in preheat, she'll need them soon."

"Nah. My knot will fill that tight little pussy just fine," Cohl said, resting back on his elbows.

And fuck me, she *was* tight. She'd clenched around my finger as though trying to suck my entire hand inside her.

"Where's Ford?" I asked, surprised he hadn't joined our little party.

"He agrees with us," Cohl said.

"Not what I asked."

"And that's not what he said," Valen interjected.

I turned a frown to Valen. "He doesn't agree? Doesn't want her?"

"He said he wouldn't force her. Same thing we said," Cohl said.

"Not the same thing, dumbass," Valen muttered.

Cohl scooted closer and his nostrils flared. "Fuck, you smell like her."

I glared at him until he stopped trying to sniff me. "If you start dry humping me, I'll break your dick."

A maniacal grin spread across his face a second before he lunged from my bed. "I'm going to go hang out with our omega."

"Might want to stay away from her. Pretty sure I pissed her off," I said. But really, I didn't want him to be the one to smooth those sharp edges she'd revealed to me. My luck, she would pounce on him and ride him like a rabid cowgirl while I sat in here with an aching dick and the worst case of blue balls.

Just before he stepped into the hall, he turned and pointed at me. "*You* pissed her off. Not me."

Valen's head was tilted down, his eyes on his phone. His hand shot out and wrapped around Cohl's arm, tugging him until he was close enough to see his phone.

"Ho-ly fuck," Cohl ground out.

My brows lowered. Grabbing my phone from my nightstand, I pulled up the footage from Corazon's room, zooming in until I could see her clearly.

She was on the couch, her back arched, her hand down the front of her pants as she obviously pumped her fingers into her core. Her other hand had pushed the front of her shirt up, revealing one plump tit that she massaged before pinching and tugging on her nipple.

Her lips parted and she released the sexiest, throatiest moan.

"Fuck. Shouldn't have stopped me. I could have given her a hand," Cohl said, his voice holding a touch of disappointment as we all watched her hand slowly pull from her pants.

When she hesitantly brought them to her mouth, her tongue

darting out to taste herself, I nearly came in my pants with two of my packmates only feet away.

"Oh, I'm so going in there now," Cohl said, but was stopped by Valen's hand clamped around the back of his neck.

"Leave her alone. Let her grow more frustrated," Valen said, surprising the shit out of me.

He hadn't spent more than fleeting moments with Corazon, and only when he delivered a meal. But he seemed to be picking up something about her.

"I ordered her some other shit," he said, finally turning off his phone and shoving it into his back pocket.

"What kind of shit?" I asked, throwing my legs over the side of the bed. Watching her get herself off after I was the one who worked her up only served to make me that much hornier. Shame we'd never thought to add a beta to the mix, someone who would be interested in a physical relationship with us. At least then, I could ease the ache growing from my waist down.

But wasn't that a fucking lie? Because I had plenty of resources at my fingertips, plenty of people who'd be more than willing to kneel at my feet to swallow my cock or bend over and let me plow into them.

I wanted the omega next door. I wanted the woman whose slick was still sweet on my tongue. I wanted the daughter of the people who had run away at the first hint of danger and had yet to contact us back after we laid out our demands.

She'd asked whether we had made contact yet and I'd told her the truth. What I hadn't bothered to tell her was that it had been three days of radio silence. I wasn't sure whether they would simply throw their omega daughter away or if they were trying to rally others behind them in hopes of some form of rescue mission or attack.

They could attack all they wanted. There was no way anyone could get anywhere near the estate without our knowledge. And we had plenty of guards, plenty of firepower, and a few fun tricks around the perimeter that would stop anyone and anything short of a fucking tank from breaching the walls.

The reason I'd refrained from telling her that no one had responded in that period of time shocked the shit out of me – I didn't want to hurt her. I didn't want her to be reminded that she obviously meant nothing to her family or her future pack.

If she was mine, *ours*, we would have burned the fucking planet to the ground to find her within the first hour of her disappearance. At no point in my life would I have ever been considered the hero of the story. I would sacrifice just about anyone for those I loved.

Well…maybe not kids. They didn't deserve the darkness of the world we lived in, the world alphas like my pack, like Packs Garcia and Alvarez had built.

"Presents. Pretty shit. Some clothes. Perfume and jewelry. Shit like that."

I cocked a brow. Cohl stared at him with a mixture of jealousy and confusion.

"Are you trying to court our prisoner?" Cohl asked, a mischievous smirk pulling up his lips.

Valen shrugged up his shoulders.

Our phones all dinged one after another. Ford texted the three of us to meet in the office. I wasn't sure how much Corazon could hear through the walls, but it was best to discuss delicate information far away from where we kept her locked up.

Valen jogged down the steps first, Cohl and I following.

"You going to let her out of that room or what? I told her I'd ask you. Don't make me look like a liar."

"I told her you asked," I said, keeping my eyes aimed ahead as we descended the stairs and turned a few times until we entered the office where Ford was leaning back in his chair, his feet on the desk, his phone on speaker.

"And?" Cohl whispered.

When a man's voice filled the room from the phone, I held up my hand to cut him off. That shit could wait.

"What you're asking is far more than what the omega is worth."

Ford raised a brow at me. Valen shook his head. Cohl actually began to growl and stalk toward the phone as though he could throttle the person on the other line.

Ford quickly scribbled on a yellow legal pad then held it up. *Leo from Pack Garcia.*

The alpha who was supposed to have been bonded with Corazon had just declared she wasn't worth saving, wasn't worth paying every penny in his pocket to keep her safe. As far as that fucker knew, we'd had our way with her ten times over. He had no idea whether she'd gone into heat, whether we were stuffing her with our cum or passing her around to our guards like a living sex doll.

Just one more reason for the four of us to stake our claim and never return Corazon, regardless of whether the two packs followed our demands or not. They didn't deserve her. She was stubborn, maddeningly so. She was absolutely the princess I'd nicknamed her that first day but fuck me if she didn't deserve to be treated accordingly.

Now I was happy Valen had ordered that shit. Even if we didn't get the privilege of keeping her in our life – because, honestly, if her family didn't follow our demands, we would still let her go – at least she would be treated right while she was under our roof.

"You're kind of a piece of shit. Anyone ever tell you that?" Ford said, smirking at me when I huffed a silent laugh.

A very not intimidating growl rumbled over the line and Cohl actually pretended to tremble in fear, a grin on his face the whole time.

"Lower the price if you want us to consider the deal," Leo said.

"Or…and hear me out…we could just keep her a little longer. See which of us can fill that curvy little body with our pups first. We can turn it into a race."

The phone shuffled and another voice came over the line. "You realize who you're fucking with?"

"How the fuck would I? You rudely took the phone from our buddy Leo and didn't bother introducing yourself," Ford said, a shit eating grin stretching across his face.

"This mother – Roman."

"Well, Roman. Nice to meet you. This is Ford of Pack Rivera. Now look at that. We're friends."

"You sick mother fucker. You know what? Keep the Alvarez omega. Not the only bitch out there we can breed."

Something dark slithered through my gut and wrapped around my heart until I felt as though I was nothing but darkness, as though an evil presence had possessed my body. Crossing the room, I hovered until my face was only inches from the phone.

"Not only will we mark and breed the omega, we're coming for you. You hear that, you cock sucker? But we won't kill you. Nah. I'm going to castrate you. Make sure you can't fuck another day in your life. After, I'm going to peel your skin from your body, mutilate that face of yours, make sure you look like the monster you really are."

And then I ended the call before anyone could say another word.

I had zero control over my body as I stormed from the office, sprinted through the house, and practically took the door down as I charged into Corazon's room.

It wasn't dominance I was after, but possession. I wanted to punish that pack, but I wanted my claim so deep inside Corazon Alvarez there would never be a doubt as to whom she belonged.

Her lips popped open and her eyes widened. But I didn't slow my pace until I was able to reach down and grip her hair, tilting her head back so I could slam my mouth onto hers.

She only hesitated a half second before she opened for me, her tongue darting into my mouth as we fought for dominance.

My hands gripped the backs of her thighs and tugged her up until she wrapped her legs around my waist. I could have ripped her clothes away from her body, released my cock, and taken her like that, but I wanted to claim her in every way possible short of my bite.

I'd told her the next time she would have to beg me, beg me to fuck her, beg me to let her come.

But right now wasn't about chasing or giving pleasure. Right now was about leaving as much of my claim on her as possible.

My lips left her mouth as I carried her to the bed, nipping at her jaw and biting at her throat and shoulder hard enough to leave bruises without breaking the skin.

She moaned and tilted her head in the most beautiful show of submission, giving me full access, almost as if begging for my bite without voicing the words.

Dropping her onto the mattress, I immediately began tearing away the clothing that smelled heavily of Cohl. That was fine. She could carry both our scents. Mine more heavily by the time I was finished with her.

The moment her full tits were exposed, I wrapped my lips around one of her pebbled nipples and drew it into my mouth, biting down before soothing it with my tongue while her thin fingers fisted in my hair.

I smoothed my hands over every inch I could touch, sucked on her skin, bit with my teeth, leaving marks, hickeys, anything I could until the day I could sink my teeth into her flesh and open the bond between us. That time would come, of that I had no doubt. But not today. That would be something I truly would make her beg for so there would be no lingering doubts in her mind, no way for her to accuse us of taking advantage of her or coercing her in any way.

My fingers hitched into the sides of her sweats and dragged them down her legs with more force than I'd intended, but I needed her bare. I needed to taste her, to feast on her, to drown in her sweet-smelling cunt, to drown on her slick and release.

Shoving her thighs wide and pressing her knees until they were almost to her chest, I fucked her with my tongue, sucking on her clit, spearing her opening with my tongue before teasing her back hole.

She tried to grind against me, to ride my face, but I held her in place, dominating her and owning every moan that tore from her lips.

"This pussy is mine," I said, slapping it once before diving face first again, sucking and licking and driving her closer to the edge.

Slick pooled from her, soaking the comforter below her and soaking my face.

More. Fuck, I needed so much more. I wanted to drink her down, to taste nothing but her for the next fucking week.

"Bain," she cried out as her body tensed, her fingers tightening in my hair until it felt as though she would pull it loose from the roots, then came on my tongue.

And fuck...she tasted better than anything I'd experienced in this lifetime.

CHAPTER THIRTEEN

<u>Corazon</u>

I wasn't sure what had come over Bain, but the moment he'd barged into my room, my omega immediately recognized him for exactly what he was – mine. My alpha.

He'd left me aching and covered in my own slick, but I was a master at getting myself off. He'd said I would have to beg him next time.

There was no begging happening now.

The intense alpha continued to lick and suck my clit through the aftershocks, not bothering to give me time before he lunged up my body, his cock filling me to the hilt, his knot bumping against my opening as my inner walls still fluttered from my release.

"Fuuuck," he ground out, only waiting a moment while my body adjusted to the invasion of his rather impressive cock stretching me.

I didn't need a moment. I needed him to fuck me, to fill me, to stretch me around his knot.

When he'd stepped into my room there was nothing short of

ownership written all over his face, in his nearly black eyes as his pupils dilated, or the intense hormones exploding from him.

His teeth had constantly scraped along my skin, biting with the most delicious pressure without ever breaking the skin. He'd sucked on the flesh of my neck, my tits, and my stomach. Surely, there would be countless bruises and hickeys by morning. And I couldn't find a single fuck to give.

Later, I might wonder what had sent my alpha into rut, or how I was so willing to accept him as my alpha when I was supposed to hate him. But when he began to thrust into me the same time my senses were filled with his gunpowder and charcoal along with pumpkin, saffron, and the sweetest vanilla frosting, my omega pushed all those thoughts aside.

Pack. My pack. My alphas. I wanted them. Needed them. Preheat or not, I wanted to carry anything and everything they could give me so the world would know where I belonged, that I was no longer a pawn to be used on some fucking chess board of criminal activities.

Cohl climbed up the side of the bed until he was kneeling beside my head. My hands shot to his waist band, yanking it down until his cock was revealed, hard and veiny, precum glistening at the tip and begging to be tasted.

I shouldn't have wanted this. I should have been demanding all four of these assholes leave the room.

That's not what I did nor was it what my omega wanted.

Instead, I tugged him forward and opened my mouth, wrapping my lips around the head of his cock, moaning as the taste of vanilla icing exploded on my tongue. I was right – he tasted as sweet as he smelled.

His fingers gently threaded through my hair, tightening and pushing my head further onto his cock until I gagged. And holy shit, that one move made my body coil as tightly as a spring then explode, covering Bain's cock in my release, coating him until I felt it sliding down the crack of my ass.

"Fuck, you're squeezing my cock. You want my knot, omega? You want your alphas to fill you, to cover you in our cum?"

I moaned my answer, the only thing I could do when Cohl was roughly fucking my face, pushing forward periodically until he cut off my air flow before pulling back enough to let me suck in gulps of air.

The bed dipped on either side of me as saffron and pumpkin wrapped around me. From the corner of my eye, I could see both Valen and Ford pulling their cocks free, fisting them and jerking hard and fast.

Were they watching Cohl fuck my face, or was their attention on where Bain was tearing through my cunt?

"I'm going to knot you so deep you'll never forget who this pussy belongs to," the alpha said a second before he shoved forward hard, not giving my body time to adjust as he stretched my opening to the point of the most beautiful pain.

His hips didn't stop as he rutted into me until he roared out a release, his fingers digging into the flesh of my thighs as he painted my inner walls with his hot cum.

Cohl followed after a few minutes later, spraying the back of my throat and tongue. "Swallow it, omega. I want you filled with my cum," Cohl ordered, keeping his cock in my mouth so I had no other choice.

Wet heat splashed across my stomach, my tits, my throat, and chin as both Ford and Valen covered me with their release. Someone's hand smoothed over my skin, spreading and mixing the cum until my entire upper body was covered from chin to the top of my pussy.

"You're mine," Bain said when Cohl pulled back and I could look into his face. "You're ours. And we're going to remind you of that every day."

My heart began to thunder in my chest. For a moment, I thought it was fear, fear that these men who'd stolen me away from my family and my future plans had just staked their claim on me.

But when his hands slowly trailed up my body, smoothing through the cum glistening on my skin and swiping across my lips before dipping his fingers into my mouth as though to make sure I tasted all of them, a sense of rightness washed over me.

Something had happened from the time Bain had left my room

until he'd crashed through the door. Once I came down from the high and Bain was no longer locked inside my cunt, I would question him.

For now, I was content to enjoy the high of such an intense fuckfest with this pack.

Cohl climbed from the side of the bed and disappeared from view. Bain leaned forward until our chests were pressed together, then rolled so I was on top of him, straddling his hips.

When Cohl reentered, he chuckled. "Shit. Should have fucked her like that so one of us could have taken her ass."

Heat flared to life in my veins and my pussy clenched around Bain's cock.

He smirked up at me with a knowing look in his eyes. I didn't have to say a word – my body had just let all four alphas know exactly how good that had sounded with my slick and my perfume.

The redheaded alpha carefully and gently cleaned my torso with a damp towel. He wasn't using soap, so I would still smell like this pack, but at least I wouldn't be sticky until I could get in the shower.

"Want to tell me what just happened?" I asked.

When Bain continued to stare up into my face with an unreadable and slightly confused look in his eyes, I turned my attention to the others.

"We claimed you. That's what happened," Cohl said, flopping onto the bed near Bain's head.

"If your dick comes anywhere near my face..." Bain growled at the other alpha without pulling his eyes from my face.

I couldn't help the giggle. "Take it you four aren't involved that way?"

Cohl curled his nose. "Fuck no. Look at them. They're not pretty enough for a hot mother fucker like me."

"Dumb ass," Ford grumbled.

"You realize you can't claim me," I said, sitting up and wincing when Bain's knot tugged.

"The fuck we can't. Just did," Bain said, folding his hands behind his head and staring up at me.

His eyes were back to that icy blue, his pupils no longer completely swallowing the color.

I chewed on the inside of my cheek as I watched varying emotions cross over his face. Looking from Cohl to Ford then to Valen, something squeezed my chest.

"They're not coming for me," I said. I wasn't sure whether I should have been happy or devastated by that news.

"Haven't heard from your fathers yet," Ford said.

"Pack Garcia?"

Ford shook his head.

Okay. Definitely not devastated by that news, but it did piss me off a little. This was a pack that my fathers had promised my life to and they had no intentions of protecting me. Not that I needed to be protected from these alphas, but they didn't know that.

"They're not coming for me, so you decided to keep me for yourself?" Anger began to build in my chest.

The moment Bain's knot deflated enough, I stood and winced as the mixture of his and my release as well as a rush of slick puddled on his groin.

He reached for me, trying to stop me from climbing away from him, but I swatted at his hands.

"Why do all you alphas think I'm some toy that can be shared and passed around?"

Bain's dark as midnight brows slammed together. "I don't remember you complaining when you covered my face in your come or when you were swallowing Cohl's dick."

"It's just—"

"I dare you to blame it on preheat."

My mouth snapped shut and I turned my back on the pack, grabbing the shirt I'd been wearing and tugging it over my body. I felt far too exposed standing in front of them all naked while they'd merely tugged their cocks out. None of them had even bothered taking off their shirts before having their way with me.

You enjoyed it, my omega reminded me.

Shut up.

I needed to focus and remembering the way I'd fallen apart around Bain's cock or the way I could still taste Cohl on my tongue wouldn't help.

All four alphas were watching me closely now. Bain and Ford looked pissed. Valen looked confused. Cohl...that alpha leaned forward as though anticipating my next move, that same look of a predator in his brown eyes. What would he do if I did try to run? Would he chase me? Was he one of those people who got off on the hunt?

And why the hell did testing my theory send a fresh wave of slick spilling from me until I had to clench my thighs to avoid embarrassing myself?

Glancing over my shoulder, my heartrate kicked up at the opened door.

"Don't even think about it," Bain warned.

"I wasn't," I lied. Because I totally was. But they'd already warned me of the alarms and guards. Even if they hadn't, I'd seen the men clad in black wandering the grounds every time I looked through the windows of my current prison. "But looks like you can't lock me in here anymore."

The door was half hanging off the hinges and the deadbolt dangled from a single screw. How strong was this alpha that he'd managed to nearly smash the door down?

"If the Garcia pack isn't going to bother falling for your plan, then what? We wait for my fathers?"

A deep growl rumbled from Bain as he rolled from the side of the bed and prowled toward me. I stood my ground, fisting my hands and tilting my head back to look into his face.

"Did you miss the part where I said you belonged to me? To us?"

"It was dirty talk while you fucked me," I said through my closing throat. I tried to keep the tremble out of my voice, tried to keep my expression neutral. But saying the words felt false even to my own ears.

"Believe that all you want. But you're ours. Doesn't matter whether your fathers ever decide you're important enough to play ball, Princess. This is your home now."

"Princess? We're back to that bullshit?" I said, trying to look as intimidating as him while failing miserably. The fact my bare legs peeked out below Cohl's shirt was bad enough. But I was covered in this pack's scents and Bain's release was still inside me, still coating my pussy and easing from inside me.

Cohl had cleaned my chest but hadn't bothered with my core, I assumed because I was still locked around Bain.

"You can't just lay claim to a human being, asshole," I spit out. When his nostrils flared and his dark brows slammed together, I smirked. "What? Don't like your new nickname?"

He stormed away, stopping at the door. "Get the betas at the door until it's fixed."

"Wait! You're going to fuck me and still not let me out of this room?" I yelled.

He whirled and stalked toward me with the most intense look that I nearly backed up. But I still refused to show him or any asshole alpha an ounce of weakness. He could call me princess all he fucking wanted. I was raised around men as ruthless as him, had alphas try to force me into all types of situations my entire life.

No way would I let another attempt to dictate my life.

"Until you're ready to say you belong to me, to us, that you're our omega, you'll stay in this fucking room. Oh, and just because I know you're still thinking someone will rush in and rescue you like a damsel locked in the tower, your fathers haven't responded in the three days since we'd contacted them. Your betrothed let us know in no uncertain terms that you weren't worth the price we were asking, and they could find omega pussy anywhere. Actually, I believe his exact words were *keep the Alvarez omega. Not the only bitch out there we can breed.*"

With that, he stormed from the room, his heady, smokey, and charred scent lingering.

The others quietly made their exit, but not before Valen stopped and looked back at me. His eyes didn't hold the same heat or anger as

Bain's or Ford's. He didn't look at me like Cohl, like he wanted to tackle me to the floor and ravage me.

No. His look was a little sad. And there was a bit of longing there in the green-blue of his eyes, as well.

Before I could rush across the room and through the door, two men clad in black with pistols strapped to their thighs appeared, their backs turned toward me. They were obviously betas by the scents and their slightly smaller size. But they were by no means any less intimidating than the alphas.

The four had just covered me with their scents, fed me, and filled me with their cum. I would be covered in bruises from Bain's teeth and lips as he'd laid his claim while fucking me senseless.

And I was right back to being a prisoner to the men who'd committed murder inches from my face and stolen me from everything I had ever known.

Your betrothed let us know in no uncertain terms that you weren't worth the price we were asking, and they could find omega pussy anywhere. Actually, I believe his exact words were keep the Alvarez omega. Not the only bitch out there we can breed.

He'd said that to hurt me. And as much as I hated to admit it, it had worked. Not because I cared whether Pack Garcia would care whether I lived or died, but because Bain, the first alpha my omega felt safe around, had intentionally found a way to cut me.

And then left me to bleed out all alone.

CHAPTER FOURTEEN

Valen

Of the four of us, I had always been the most even tempered. Calm. I could talk my packmates down from whatever cliff they had climbed.

But now?

The moment my feet hit the bottom step, I lunged at Bain, taking him to the ground and holding him there with my forearm pressed against his threat.

"The fuck?" he growled out, trying to shove me away.

"You fucking hurt her," I said with a sneer.

Ford and Cohl each grabbed a shoulder and tried to pull me away from our pack lead. But the asshole waited until he was free and swung at me.

My head whipped to the side with the sucker punch and I smiled. Fuck yes. I needed to expel this energy and, being as he was the cause of it, Bain was about to get the full brunt of my rage.

Shaking off two of my pack brothers, I began to pummel Bain, relishing in the ache and tearing of my knuckles as I rained punch after punch against his face, his head, anywhere I could strike that he wasn't blocking.

I was pulled away again, giving Bain a chance to tackle me around the waist, taking me to the ground. He landed a few punches before we were once again torn apart.

"The fuck is wrong with you two?" Ford bellowed.

It took me a second to realize it took not just Ford and Cohl to pull us apart, but a few of our hired guards, as well. Several betas and alphas in matching black stood between us.

"He fucking hurt her!" I roared.

"We were there. She wasn't fucking hurt. She loved every minute of it," Ford bit back at me. He was more like Bain than even he would admit to himself.

"Did you not bother looking her in the eye after he threw in her face that the pack who was supposed to protect her saw her as nothing more than pussy? You really had to inflict as much damage as possible, didn't you? And all because your fucking ego was bruised."

"Fuck you," Bain growled out, spitting blood onto the hardwood floor. That mother fucker could clean up after himself. I would've stopped any staff who attempted to do it for him.

"Fuck you! We're supposed to protect her, win her over. Instead, you went all fucking caveman and littered her body with bruises then ripped her chest open with your bare hands and tore out her heart."

"She looked pretty with those bruises," Cohl, the unhinged mother fucker, said.

My nostrils flared as I glared from Bain, turned that fucking glare to Cohl, then swung it right back to our pack lead.

"She's ours and needs to fucking accept it," Bain said, each word growing louder until he was yelling.

"She doesn't fucking trust us. And I don't fucking blame her. We're no different than those fuckers she grew up with or the assholes she was promised to. If you'd taken more than a second to look at her before stomping out of the room like a petulant child, you would have seen how deep your fucking words cut her. We killed her guards right in front of her. Took her from everyone she knows. You fucked her and left bruises all over her. You really think she'll accept us now?"

Bain's mouth opened, then closed. His midnight black brows were pulled so low there was a shadow cast over his pale eyes.

After a few seconds, he turned and left the house, the front door closing so hard the windows shook.

The guards who'd stood between us waited a few minutes, looking to each of us as though waiting for confirmation that shit was cooled down.

As long as that cock sucker kept his distance from me – and especially Corazon – it would be fine.

"We're good. Get a new door ordered. Beta contractors only. No one in the omega's room without a member of the guard or one of us present," Ford told one of the guards, Keller, before turning and dropping onto a couch as though he was exhausted.

"Yes, sir," Keller said, pulling his phone free as he and the others filed from the room and retook their posts around the house and property.

Cohl looked as though he planned to bound back up the stairs. Grabbing him by the back of his neck, I shoved him toward the living room, but I couldn't sit. Not yet. There was still too much pent-up anger burning through my veins.

So close. We were so fucking close. She'd accepted us, accepted our presence, accepted Bain's knot and appeared to revel in being covered in our scents in the most intimate way possible.

And then Bain opened his fucking mouth and ruined everything within minutes.

I might have understood his desperation, might have understood the sentiment behind his words and actions, but he went about it the wrong way, especially with someone as strong as Corazon. She wasn't some submissive omega who lived to serve, who wanted nothing more than to dote on her alphas and earn our affection.

We might have saved her from a life of servitude with those assholes from Pack Garcia, but now she was living in yet another prison with another group of alphas she didn't know.

And her own fucking family had yet to make contact. Something Bain made sure to throw in her face, to make her feel as though no one cared about her.

I'd turned before the first tear had trailed down her cheek, but I'd seen them shimmering in her pretty brown eyes, had seen her bottom lip quiver as she'd tried and failed to hide her emotion.

Another urge to track down Bain and beat him to a pulp made trembles ripple through me.

"I'll be downstairs," I growled out, hurrying through the house to the home gym in the basement.

Punching the shit out of the hanging bag wouldn't be quite enough, but it was probably better than challenging our pack lead. Again.

Maybe that's exactly what needed to happen. I should challenge the asshole for pack lead.

Taping up my knuckles, I rolled my neck until it cracked then started pummeling the bag until it swung on the creaky chains holding it to the ceiling. Over and over, I slammed my fists against the leather until my knuckles tore beneath the tape and left bloody smears along the surface. I swung and punched until my muscles burned, until my body glistened with a sheen of sweat.

I'd ordered a bunch of girly crap for Corazon. It would be delivered today or tomorrow. Fuck Bain. I would take my time courting her in my own way, showing her she could trust me, trust us. I would win her over the way an omega like her deserved.

Stepping away from the bag and setting my hands on my hips, I dropped my head and sucked in deep gulps of air, the *squeak, squeak, squeak* of the bag swinging on the chain mixing with the sawing of my oxygen deprived lungs sucking in breaths.

Why the hell hadn't Ford stopped Bain? The two oftentimes acted like they were two halves of one brain, thought the same, plotted the same, had butted heads and fought on more occasions than was healthy for a pack.

Yet I'd been the one to attack our pack lead. Fuck that. I hadn't attacked him. I'd punished him for daring to make my omega cry.

As my heart thundered behind my ribs and my knuckles ached, I started to form a plan in my head, one that didn't involve anything to do with her family pack or the cowards who should have been leading the charge to find her.

By now, everyone knew exactly who'd been behind the attack, who held Corazon. They might not know where we were holed up with her or where she was being held, but there was nothing short of death that would keep me from finding her if she would just allow me to be her alpha.

Hell, even with Bain's stupidity and caveman behavior, I knew he would burn the planet to find her if someone were to somehow drag her away from us, regardless of whether she carried a mark from any of us yet.

Yet. She would. She would carry our marks, carry our bond in her soul. And one day, she would carry our pups. She would be the mother to any children we had. We would dote on her, cherish her, worship at her feet the way she deserved, the way any omega deserved.

First step was getting her out of that fucking room, no matter how much Bain was against it. Not like she could leave the property without one of us knowing. If she was in our presence, what exactly could she do? And, hypothetically, if she were to manage to escape through the front door, she'd end up face to face with one of our guards.

That was another matter. I sure as fuck didn't want any of the alpha guards anywhere near her. And I didn't want any of them to treat her as though she was truly a prisoner. They were to keep an eye on her, keep others off the property, keep her from disappearing into the night. But none of them better lay a fucking finger on her or intimidate her in any way.

Our guards might have been with us a long time, but I had no problem putting a bullet in their brain pan if they dared to touch her.

An alert of an incoming vehicle gave me a little peace. It couldn't be a contractor, not yet. Meaning some of the gifts I'd bought for Corazon had arrived.

Instead of piling them all in her room, I'd go through them, make sure they were on hangers or whatever, then present her with my gifts at one time. I would give her space, especially after Bain's fucking outburst, then do whatever she needed to see me as her alpha instead of one of the monsters who'd turned her life upside down.

CHAPTER FIFTEEN

<u>Corazon</u>

I had cried so much since the alphas left the room that my eyes were puffy and my nose was pink. At first, I'd locked myself in the bathroom. There were guards standing outside the door and I didn't want them to run to Bain or the others and tell them I'd broken down.

Eventually, I'd grown tired of sitting on the cool tile floor and shuffled back into the omega quarters and curled up on the couch, wrapping myself in a blanket that wasn't nearly as soft as what I would have chosen. Especially this close to my cycle.

My skin was sensitive and felt too tight. And after having all four alphas around me, after feeling Bain buried inside me, it felt as though my heat had been kicked up a notch and would be coming sooner than I'd planned.

I had maybe a day or two before I locked myself in the nest and did my best to keep the pain and fever at bay using nothing but my own damn hands.

Because no way in hell would I ask any of them for help. Not after Bain...

Fresh tears welled in my eyes as I watched a beta installing a new door to my bedroom. He never looked in my direction, never even acknowledged my presence.

Did he know I was being held here against my will? Did he know I was a prisoner to this pack?

Did he know I didn't have a person in my life who cared enough to do anything about it?

I knew Pack Garcia didn't love me. The bonding ceremony had been planned by our family packs. It hadn't been because we loved each other or because we wanted to form a family. So why the hell would they put themselves in danger for an omega who meant nothing to them?

My body felt heavier than normal and I barely had the energy to drag the blanket tighter around me until I resembled a human burrito.

After a while, the door was finished and the lock clicked back in place, locking me back in my prison. Sure, it was a beautiful room inside a beautiful house. But a gilded cage was still a cage.

But...why bother attempting to escape anymore? At one point, I'd contemplated finding a way out of here, procuring suppressants, and living my life as an anonymous beta. But after having the fact no one in this world gave a shit about me thrown in my face, I felt...hopeless.

What was the point? Assuming a thing and hearing it stated as fact were two different and powerful things.

For a moment, I'd thought I was actually forming something deeper with this pack. Especially after Bain crashed through the room and my omega instantly warmed at the sight of the possession and heat in his pale eyes. And then he'd cut me with his words, intentionally inflicting as much pain as he could without physically attacking me.

Hell. I would have rather he punched me square in the face. At least those bruises, those wounds would heal with time.

But the gash he'd ripped open in my heart felt more like a crater that could never be filled. There would forever be a scar left in my chest.

The longer I laid there, the heavier my body felt, the heavier my lids grew. The sun set, leaving the room in darkness, yet I never turned on a lamp, didn't bother flipping on the TV. And I sure as hell wouldn't climb into the bed that now smelled heavily of me and the pack.

I needed a shower. I needed to wash them off my skin. Yet I couldn't force myself off the couch. Couldn't even make myself sit up.

Closing my eyes, I let the tears that had welled roll down my temples and soak into my hair. This was my future. Unless by some miracle my fathers decided I was worth something, I was trapped with this pack, the pack I'd believed were my scent matches, that I had started to believe actually cared for me, that I had believed were my true alphas.

Until you're ready to say you belong to me, to us, that you're our omega, you'll stay in this fucking room. Oh, and just because I know you're still thinking someone will rush in and rescue like a damsel locked in the tower, your fathers haven't responded in the three days since we'd contacted them.

Another alpha laying claim to me, a human being, and solely because I was an omega. He'd made sure to remind me that I had no one.

Your betrothed let us know in no uncertain terms that you weren't worth the price we were asking, and they could find omega pussy anywhere. Actually, I believe his exact words were keep the Alvarez omega. Not the only bitch out there we can breed.

Bain's words had played on repeat in my head since the moment he'd stormed out of the room with the others hot on his heels. At least Valen had hesitated, had looked as though he'd felt bad about the events that had occurred after what I thought was a beautiful connection with the alphas.

Something had happened once they'd left my room. I'd heard the yelling, had heard several thumps and thuds and what sounded like a fight. But all I could focus on was the fact I was nothing.

I would never be anything to anyone because of my designation. I was a body to be used. A vessel to carry children. A pawn to be sold and traded for power.

Sleep eventually swept me into a fitful rest where I was plagued with nightmares and constantly woke to the sounds of phantom gunshots or the feeling of the guards' blood slapping me in the face and running down my neck.

Rustling sounds mixed with the nightmares until my lashes fluttered and my lids slowly raised. The room was lit with early morning sun. I was still on the couch, still wrapped in a blanket, but others had been draped over me, as well.

And I was no longer alone.

Valen and Cohl were tiptoeing around my room, sliding things into drawers and carrying armfuls of what looked like clothing into the closet.

Slowly, I pushed to a sitting position and watched them silently until Valen glanced in my direction then did a double take.

He froze on his way into the bathroom, a box in his hands. His eyes widened the slightest before they dropped to the floor as though he couldn't maintain eye contact with me.

Cohl stepped into the room with another armful of fabric. But unlike Valen, a grin stretched on his face and his brown eyes lit with something that looked like a combination of excitement and mischief.

"Good. You're awake. I'm not the greatest at being quiet. The big guy got you a bunch of stuff, so we were putting it away. Although… was this supposed to be a surprise?" he asked, turning to Valen, who still refused to look at me.

My eyes felt so heavy from all the crying and I had a headache. I was sore between my legs, my throat felt scratchy, and my stomach grumbled with hunger since no one had bothered to bring me dinner last night.

Not that I would have eaten it.

All my life, I'd fought to maintain my fire, had done my best to keep my spirits up even when I knew I would never have a choice in my own future.

And all it had taken was a few words from Bain to break me.

"I heard that. You're hungry. I'll be back." Cohl started to dart from the room, then quickly returned and dropped the clothing on hangers onto the bed before rushing from the room.

"What's going on?" I croaked out when Valen stood there awkwardly shuffling from foot to foot with that box still in his hands.

"I got you some stuff. Some clothes of your own. Girl...stuff. Like shampoo and body wash and...whatever. Stuff. For an omega. I got some more blankets and pillows, too. I didn't know what you..."

He trailed off, his eyes dropping back to the ground again before raising to my face. He looked...vulnerable. That was the only word I could put to the look in his eyes as he watched for my reaction.

"Thank you," I muttered, the words sounding hollow and emotionless in my own ears.

He nodded, and then carried the box into the bathroom. Drawers opened and closed; cabinets did the same.

When he stepped back out, the empty box hung from his fingers by his thigh.

"Can I..."

"What?" I asked when he didn't finish his sentence.

"Sit. With you. Can I sit with you?"

"Do I have a choice?"

I shuffled over, making plenty of space for the big alpha to lower onto the cushions without crowding me.

The closer he got, the more my omega begged me to snuggle into him, to press my nose to his throat and suck the warm scent of pumpkin deep into my lungs.

"I'm sorry about yesterday. None of that should have happened." His voice was soft, low. "Um, I know you're close to your heat. And I know you won't trust us after..." He inhaled a deep breath and blew it out in a rush. "I ordered a bunch of heat aids for you. They're in the nest whenever you need them. And I stocked the minifridge with bottles of water and left some easy to eat snacks in there."

I watched his profile as he spoke since he refused to look in my direction.

"Which part?" I asked after a few moments of silence.

He turned to look at me then, his dark brown brows pinching together in confusion. "What?"

"Which part shouldn't have happened? The part where I was knotted? The part where I was covered in my...in your scents? Or the part where I learned I mean absolutely nothing to anyone?"

Damn it. I'd truly believed I'd cried all my tears out last night, but they were welling in my eyes again.

When Valen scooted closer, wrapped an arm around my shoulders, and tugged me to his side, I couldn't find the energy to fight him or push him away. When the softest purr rattled from his chest, I didn't fight the urge to turn my face against his chest and let the tears fall.

"You mean something. You mean everything," he murmured, his lips pressing to the top of my head as he hugged me tighter to him. "I know you won't believe me, but Bain didn't mean that shit. He...the asshole lashes out when his feelings are hurt or when he's angry. He was trying to hurt you since he was hurting."

"He's an asshole," I mumbled against Valen's firm, muscular chest.

These alphas were all so big and I felt so small and protected in Valen's arms, even if I should have been pushing him away. But, for once, I wanted to let someone else carry the burden for me, even if just for a moment.

I was tired. I was tired of being strong, tired of holding my head high and fighting everyone around me. I was tired of being seen as nothing but a toy. I was tired of being seen as less because of my designation. I was tired of having absolutely no control or say over my own life.

But I could control this. I could allow this alpha to hold me. He might have been in the room last night, might have left his release on my skin, but he'd looked downright gutted by the way I'd reacted to Bain's words and his treatment.

"Hey," Cohl said as he stepped through my door. "I wanna cuddle."

"Leave her alone," Valen said, tightening his hold around me until it was almost hard to breathe. Almost. That didn't mean I wanted him to loosen his arms.

"But–"

"Just set the food down."

"Can I stay, too? Bain was the one who acted like a prick."

I felt more than saw Valen tilt his head down to look at me. Without pulling my head from his chest, I nodded.

"Yes! Finish snuggling. I made breakfast. Like, I actually cooked and shit. And I promise it's good."

A smile tugged at my lips. I couldn't help it. The alpha was... unhinged was the only word I could think of. He was different than alphas I'd known through my life. There was this dark gleam to his eyes that promised he could and would devour me if given the chance, but he always behaved as if the world was his playground, like he refused to take much seriously. He was scary and intimidating and endearing, all at once.

The couch dipped on the other side of me until Cohl was wedged so closely against me, I was practically on his lap.

"You didn't shower," he said. "You still smell like us."

A fresh wave of tears filled my eyes as a whine tore from my chest. This time it felt more like the emotional rollercoaster of my upcoming heat. Or maybe it was a reminder of what had happened – and how everything had crumbled – last night.

CHAPTER SIXTEEN

<u>Cohl</u>

$\mathcal{V}$alen could glare at me over Corazon's head all he wanted. I couldn't stop sniffing the beautiful omega. Her Lily of the Valley was still there, but now it mixed with the rest of our scents until it created the most delicious smell in the world.

I was so fucking tempted to start licking her from head to toe. While spending a lot more time between her thighs, of course.

Minutes ticked by with her crushed against Valen's chest. As tempted as I was to declare it was my turn and wrench her away from my packmate, she'd finally stopped crying. And I wouldn't be the one to upset her again.

"You want to eat?" Valen asked softly, dipping his head to whisper in her ear.

She nodded and slowly pulled away from him.

Reaching for the coffee table, I dragged it closer so she wouldn't have to reach for the food.

I'd made her bacon and eggs, some pancakes, toast, poured a glass of orange juice and a mug of coffee. I had no idea how she took her coffee since I'd never watched her in the morning, so I had creamer and sugar on the tray, too.

"What the fuck, Cohl?" Valen grumbled.

"What?" I asked, looking from him to the food, to Corazon, then back.

"The shit's burned."

I looked at everything on the tray again. "Looks fine to me."

A soft chuckle sounded from between us and stole my breath. Had she just laughed? Had I heard her laugh yet? The sound was so soft and a little throaty and made my dick instantly stand at attention.

"It's fine," she said, crossing her bare legs under her and rewrapping the blanket so she was wrapped up the way she had been when Valen and I had snuck in her with all the crap he'd ordered.

"It's inedible," Valen said with a look of disgust on his face.

Another soft chuckle was like music to my ears. And when she bent forward and snatched a piece of bacon from the plate and slipped it between her lips, my brain instantly went to how beautiful those lips had looked wrapped around my cock.

I bit back a groan at the sight, but Valen noted something in my face because he gave me a warning look and shook his head in the smallest movement.

My eyes returned to Corazon as her nose curled after taking a bite of toast. Okay, yeah. It was a little burned on the top, but it was edible. I'd even buttered it for her.

While her attention was on her breakfast, I let my eyes roam over her and wished she would drop that fucking blanket. I wanted to see the bruises Bain had left all over her, to see where he'd bitten her and sucked on her skin until purple hickeys bloomed.

Her ass would look amazing with my handprint pinkening her fleshy ass. Her face was so pretty last night when tears had welled as she'd choked on my cock, the way drool and cum had seeped from her lips when I'd spilled in her mouth. She'd barely missed but a few drops and Bain had swiped her lips clean and slipped his fingers into her mouth so she had all of my release in her mouth.

Valen could win her over with his gentle manner. He'd been smart as fuck with the whole smothering her with gifts thing. Personally, I'd make her mine in a whole other way. I had a feeling she would enjoy my games. I'd seen the way her chest had risen and fallen with heavy breaths, the way her nipples were hard enough to cut glass, the way her eyes stayed glued on my face as I'd fucked her throat.

Fuck. My dick was painfully hard, and it wasn't getting any better. I could excuse myself, wrap one of the things I'd stolen from her during my surveillance to jack off on, and relieve the pressure in my balls.

But that would mean leaving this room. And I didn't want to leave this room. There hadn't been a whole lot of space between her curvy bottom and the side of the couch, but I was determined to sit with her. So now, her warm body was pressed against mine and Valen's as she picked at the food I'd made her.

"You really don't have to eat that. I'll get you something else," Valen said, shooting a glare in my direction.

"It's fine," she said, pushing the tray forward. "I'm not really that hungry."

She grabbed the mug of coffee and cradled it between her hands before sitting back. She didn't sweeten it. She was drinking it black. My kind of girl.

"You want a shower? Try out some of your new stuff? Wear something that isn't four sizes too big?" Valen asked.

"I can wash your back."

Valen looked like he was ready to lunge across the couch and punch me square in the jaw. Until Corazon's lips quirked then she laughed. A real laugh. The sound was fucking amazingly beautiful.

"I can wash my back. But thank you."

She set her mug down and set her feet on the ground. It took her a minute to push to standing like her legs were weak or something.

"Can I at least carry you to the bathroom? I promise to turn around while you get naked. I mean, I'll probably sneak some peeks, but I won't outwardly ogle."

"For fuck's sake, asshole," Valen grumbled.

"I'm fine. And you're a weirdo."

Before she could fully move away from us, my hand shot out and wrapped around her wrist before I could stop it. Valen instantly started to growl.

Corazon turned a frown on me and I could see the moment when she prepared herself for a fight.

"Bain didn't mean any of that. I just want you to know he's sorry. He probably won't tell you that, but he is. And he was right when he said you were ours, because we want you to be ours. *I* want you to be ours. But...he was a dick. Don't blame us," I said, jerking my head toward Valen, "for him being an immature prick."

It took a few moments of her staring into my face while I stroked my thumb along her wrist, noting the way her heartrate had increased.

Was she scared of me? I wanted her scared, but not yet. And not in this scenario. I wanted her scared on my terms when she wasn't sure whether she would escape me or whether I would–

"Thank you," she said, cutting off my thoughts before they went too far.

Her tone was empty, like she'd spoken them because she wasn't sure what else to say. "Can I have my arm back?"

Valen punched me in the shoulder, that growl still rumbling in the air.

I released her, then rubbed my fingers together, reveling in the way they still tingled from where I'd held her dainty wrist between them.

She stepped into the bathroom and closed the door behind her, the lock clicking into place and shutting us out. Not that I couldn't smash it open with my shoulder. But Valen had told me his plan to make her trust us, to accept us as her pack. And breaking down the door when she obviously wanted some privacy wouldn't help that plan move forward at all.

Valen pushed to his feet and hurried to hang the clothes I'd left laying on the bed when I rushed to the kitchen to make her breakfast. Breakfast that she'd barely touched. At least she'd eaten a little.

Once we'd finished hanging clothes up and closing drawers, Valen grabbed the tray and jerked his head for me to follow. We had a plan and Bain could kiss both our asses if he had a problem with it.

I pulled her door closed but left enough of a gap for her to realize it wasn't locked and she could step out at will.

She still wouldn't be able to run away. Valen had instructed the guards to keep an eye on all exits from the house in case she decided to take the little taste of freedom and slip outside.

Her room smelled heavily of her signature, of the sweet, floral hints of Lily of the Valley. And now it also smelled of pack.

But I was dying to have her sweetness soaking into every surface of the rest of the house, as well. Especially my bed. Preferably after making her cum over and over until she drenched my sheets.

"Her perfume was stronger," I said to Valen as he carried the tray into the kitchen and proceeded to scrape the leftovers into the trash.

"She's going into heat. Day, maybe two."

My dick twitched as if to fist pump the air.

He turned and shook his head. "Don't expect to be invited in. Not after Bain's bullshit," he said, glaring at the pack lead, who was sitting at the table sipping coffee.

Our packmate looked like hell. He was sporting a few bruises from Valen's big fists and dark circles underlined his eyes from either stress or lack of sleep. His hair stood up in odd angles and he hadn't bothered to pull on anything more than sweats when he rolled out of bed.

I'd had every intention of walking around in the same state – I fucking hated clothes – until Valen let me in on his plan and let me help.

"Might want to get dressed," Valen muttered to Bain but didn't offer any explanation.

"She'll need us," I said, ignoring our pack lead and keeping my focus on my omega. "She'll need our knots. She'll need her pack."

"She hasn't accepted us as pack. And no fucking way will she let any of us near her now. I left toys and silicon knots in the nest for her."

"No way. I'm not fucking letting her go through that shit alone," I said, crossing my arms and glaring at Valen.

"You'll stay the fuck away from her," Bain said from his place at the table, doing his best to insert his alpha bark in his words as though that would affect me.

Jabbing a finger in his direction, I fought the urge to do exactly as Valen had and beat him to a pulp, especially after seeing her swollen eyes and the way she'd clung to Valen for comfort when she woke up to find us in her room. "You don't get to tell me shit when it comes to our omega. You're the one who fucked it all up. It was going great then you got your dainty little feelings hurt. Don't worry – we apologized for you, asshole."

I stomped from the room, not sure exactly where I was going until I ended up at the bottom of the stairs and lowering to sit on the first step. I wanted to be right here when she realized she was no longer a prisoner in that room. I wanted to be the first person she saw when she rounded the corner and finally got a look at the house where she would – hopefully – one day call home.

CHAPTER SEVENTEEN

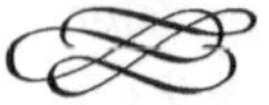

<u>Corazon</u>

alen and Cohl hadn't been kidding about stocking me with necessities. They'd also purchased a bunch of luxury things like bubble bath, bath bombs, oils, and even makeup. In the right shades, which made me wonder how the hell they knew anything about that kind of stuff.

There was a brush, curling iron, blow dryer, even products for my hair.

After finishing up and even applying a little makeup for the first time since the day I'd realized my life had been turned upside down, I opened the door with the towel wrapped around me and peeked through the gap. The alphas were gone, as was the terrible attempt at breakfast.

I had to give poor Cohl credit for trying. The two seemed as though they were trying their hardest to smooth over what Bain had done. I wasn't sure makeup and bath wash would be enough to erase the pain in my chest, but I supposed it didn't hurt to be comfortable until…

Until what?

That ache started in my chest again when I realized the first people to ever show me kindness for no other reason than because they wanted to were Valen and Cohl, my freaking captors, my prison wards.

I'd seen both Valen and Cohl putting things in the closet and the drawers of the antique dresser. After rummaging around, I found brand new panties and a bra – in my size. Which, of course, once again begged the question as to how they knew something as intimate as my bra size.

Ford had bought me clothes in the beginning, just plain t-shirts and leggings. But after stepping into the closet, it appeared Valen had taken his time in choosing a decent variety. There were slacks, jeans, skirts, tops, and dresses. Lining the bottom were flats, heels, sneakers, and a fluffy pair of house shoes.

And that was exactly what I wanted. I chose a pair of soft as silk leggings and a sweater that could have easily been mistaken for a cloud with its weightlessness and snuggly feeling against my skin. The rich burgundy would look good against my olive toned skin and mahogany hair. The alpha had good taste.

Stepping from the room with my feet shoved in the squishy, soft slippers, I froze in place when I noticed the door was open. Not all the way, but it was cracked open. Not locked.

I couldn't help but look around as though this was some kind of trick, like Bain or Ford would be hiding in wait for me to step out so they could treat me like crap again.

Tiptoeing across the room, I pulled the door open more and looked left to right. No guards positioned outside the room.

The sounds of the alphas talking filtered up the stairs. They were all still here, but they hadn't locked me in my room.

Or rather, Cohl and Valen hadn't locked me in my room. They were granting me at least a modicum of freedom, even if I wasn't allowed to actually leave the house.

Pulling the sleeves over my hands and clenching my fingers around them, I shuffled down the hall until I stood at the top of the stairs...

To find Cohl waiting on the bottom step. The moment my foot lowered to the first stair, he whipped around, a wide grin immediately stretching his handsome face. He had this dark yet boyishly sexiness to him that made me both want to cling to his back and run away in hopes he would chase me. It was confusing as hell.

"You're free!" he announced, lunging to his feet and running up the stairs to meet me halfway before extending his arm for me to loop my hand through.

I shook my head. "From the bedroom. Not the same thing."

"Are you still hungry?"

"I wasn't hungry to begin with," I said. Well, my stomach had grumbled, but I didn't have much of an appetite. I'd forced the little I had down my throat to keep from getting sick.

"Your skin is warm. Like...really warm." He was no longer grinning as he glanced down at where my hand rested on the crook of his elbow. "Are you in heat?"

"Not yet."

"Valen said it's a day or so. And he said you wouldn't want us to–"

"Leave her alone," Ford said as he turned the corner from another room.

Since I'd been brought here while unconscious, I had no idea about the layout. I could tell from the size of my room that it had to be a fairly large house. Men like these alphas lived the same way as my fathers. They liked to show off their money and always had staff on hand, guards and housekeepers. Apparently, they didn't have a cook on their payroll if Cohl's pitiful attempt at cooking was anything to go by.

I tensed at the sight of the dark blond alpha. Except when he moved closer and his warm, earthy saffron signature teased my senses, I fought the urge to lean closer, to wrap myself around him, to bury my face against him the way I had with Valen.

Coming down here where I would be consumed by the scents of

so many alphas – both from this pack and from their guards – wasn't the best idea when I was so close to my damn heat. Even as I stood glaring at Ford, trying to keep him from seeing the pain I still carried from Bain's actions and words last night, my brand-new panties were growing damp with slick.

"Want a tour?" Cohl asked, completely ignoring Ford's order.

He guided me past the blond alpha and down a hall to a humongous living room. It was as big as the one back home, except far less pretentiously decorated. It was obvious this pack had power and money, but they didn't decorate with gaudy accessories and the room felt homey and comfortable, the kind of space where I could see myself snuggling in a big puppy pile with my alphas.

Damn it. Not mine.

My omega refused to listen to reason no matter how many times I chastised, no matter how many times I reminded myself that I was no more to these alphas than I was to my family's pack or Pack Garcia.

There were three deep couches loaded with pillows and a couple recliners, all facing a stone fireplace with a TV almost twice as big as the one in my room hung over top. Shame, really. Personally, I would have put the TV in another room so the fireplace could be enjoyed without the monstrosity taking away from its beauty. I had always loved to sit in front of a crackling fireplace while reading during the colder months.

Valen entered the room, smiling softly at me. "You look pretty," he said.

"She doesn't smell like us anymore," Cohl grumbled as he continued to lead me through the living room and to a big, beautiful kitchen that would be a professional chef's fantasy.

I huffed a small sound and shook my head. That was kind of the point. I wanted their scent off me after Bain basically told me exactly what he thought of me, pointed out that I was nothing more than a possession to him, to my family, to this pack, and to any other alphas.

Honestly, I still wasn't sure whether it was the same anger I'd carried over the treatment of my designation, or whether hearing it from Bain after sharing what I'd thought was a beautiful moment we'd shared had hurt my feelings.

For some stupid – or maybe naïve – reason, I'd truly felt as though we'd formed some kind of connection last night. I had even begun to crave their bite, crave a bond with this pack.

And then everything had been turned on its head and my heart had been smashed under Bain's big foot.

As though I'd conjured the jerk, my eyes met his as we rounded the corner to fully enter the kitchen. He sat at the table, a mug between his hands as he leaned on his elbows and watched me closely, a look I couldn't decipher in the icy blue of his eyes.

What really pissed me off was the insane urge to rush across the room and throw myself at him, to wrap my arms and legs around him and cling to him like a baby koala or something.

He, however, continued to stare at me, his expression unchanging, only his eyes moving as they followed me through the room.

"Here," Ford said from the stove, setting a plate on the table.

I frowned at him then glanced at a plate of golden pancakes and crispy bacon.

"I already ate. But thank you," I said, not bothering to plaster a fake smile on my face.

Bain might have been the one to cut me with his words, but Ford had worn a similar expression as the pack lead when he'd followed him through the bedroom door. He apparently felt the same way.

"I saw what Cohl made you. That wasn't food. Eat."

My brows drew together at his order that was just short of a bark. "I'm not hungry. But again…thank you."

The smirk I shot him was nothing short of defiant.

Scents filtered into the room. Foreign scents. Alpha scents. Caramel corn. Papaya. Damp forest floor.

Too many delicious scents. Too many hormones. And I was too close to my heat to be fully surrounded by so many fucking alphas.

A whimper tore from my chest before I could swallow it down.

The alphas who'd stepped into the kitchen, fully clad in black and loaded with firearms strapped to their thighs and sides, froze in place and turned wide eyes to me as their nostrils flared.

My perfume exploded from me, snaring their attention. But those weren't the alphas I wanted. They'd merely caused my body to react as the primal need to breed arose with my quickly approaching heat.

Cohl slammed me to his side, his arm wrapping tightly around my shoulders as though he could wrap his entire body around me and shield me from the rest of the world.

Growls erupted and my now muddled brain couldn't discern who was growling. Were the newcomers challenging the pack? Were my alphas warning off their guards?

And why did my omega refuse to acknowledge the fact these alphas weren't mine and never would be? Never could be.

At the increased sound of growls, slick pooled in my panties and dampened my thighs. I clutched at Cohl, my fingers wrapping in his shirt in an attempt to pull him closer.

Bain slowly pushed to his feet, his eyes on me. "Out! Now!" he barked, sending the guards nearly tripping their own feet, whatever reason they'd entered forgotten in their haste to follow their boss's orders.

As the pack lead stalked around the table, his eyes burning into mine, I pulled from Cohl and launched myself at him before I was able to question my own fucking sanity.

Not *my* sanity. This was all primal need, my omega recognizing something I refused to accept.

Bain's strong arms wrapped around me, one of his hands cupping my ass and urging my legs around his waist. No urging was required. I was more than happy to feel his body against mine, to feel his hard length against my core through our clothes.

But it wasn't enough. The other three were too far away. I was still angry, but my hindbrain was quickly taking over and all I could focus on was the sweet vanilla frosting, warm pumpkin, earthy saffron, and smokey charcoal and gunpowder.

The hormones swirled around me, wrapped around me,

embedded themselves directly into every pore and cell in my body until I was intoxicated on these alphas.

My alphas.

His lips crashed on mine. Or maybe it was the other way around. Either way, we became a clash of lips and teeth and tongue as bodies pressed against me from every side. A purr rumbled from my chest, from Bain's, from someone behind me.

"She needs her nest. She's officially going into heat." Valen. That was Valen's voice, but it sounded strained. And a little far away.

Wind brushed against any exposed skin as I was jostled against Bain. We didn't pull apart, didn't stop kissing, even as he carried me up the stairs and practically kicked the bedroom door open.

It grew darker behind my closed lids as Bain stepped down into the nest's cushioned floor.

Not right. This isn't right.

I pulled away from my alpha and looked around, a whine steadily pulling from my chest. What was wrong with me? All four alphas were here, already removing their clothes as Bain struggled with mine.

But it wasn't right. I hadn't taken time to prepare for this. Part of me had believed I would leave this house before my heat arrived. The other part had been reluctant to accept the fact that this was my nest, my home, my pack.

It didn't smell right. It smelled of chemical cleaners. Even with the pack now touching me, helping Bain remove my clothes, it still didn't smell right.

"What's wrong with her?" Cohl asked as his hands grabbed my stretch pants and ripped them down the back, exposing my ass and core to the room.

"Not right," I whined, barely able to recognize my own voice.

"What, Princess? What's not right?" Bain asked.

Princess. Only this time, he didn't say it as though he was making fun of me, rather as a term of endearment.

I began to scrabble from his arms. After a few seconds, he released me and I dropped to my hands and knees to crawl when the first overwhelming, uterus crushing cramp hit me.

Someone touched me, pulled me upright, but I batted their hands away until I was at the side of the bed, hauling myself up and lying face first against the bedding.

Pack.

A purr rumbled forth even as my insides felt as though they were rebelling against me.

"Shit. The scents," Valen said.

"On it," Cohl announced.

I was still wearing my bra and ruined pants while the alphas were completely naked, their cocks hard, their knots full and engorged.

Cohl's feet thudded heavily against the floor as though he was sprinting around the house. Within less than a minute, he returned with both arms full of pieces of clothing that he carried to the nest.

Valen gently removed my bra, then tugged the torn leggings down my legs and tossed them both to the floor. One arm slid behind my back, the other under my knees until he was lifting me from the bed and carrying me back to the nest. Only, he'd made sure to cocoon some of the bedding around me, keeping that whine from pouring from my chest again.

The fairy lights overhead cast the room in a soft, warm glow. The room now smelled heavily of the pack with pieces of clothing littered around to join the blankets and pillows.

"Better?" Valen asked softly, his lips grazing over my temple then my cheek.

Tangling my fingers in his hair, I tugged his face closer to mine rather than speaking. It was much better. And I would analyze the fact my omega had grown unstable at the lack of this pack's scents in the nest while I was going into heat.

I'd had every intention of fighting through it alone, had planned to use the knotting aids Valen had ordered and placed in the small room for me.

But the moment those unknown alphas had invaded the space and my alphas had immediately grown possessive at the surge of my perfume…all logical plans fled and were replaced by raw, unadulterated need.

There was a desperation for these alphas I'd never felt in my life, and, if I were honest with myself, I wasn't sure it was solely because of my heat.

Valen knelt on the floor with me in his arms, the head of his cock bumping against my ass. And not where I needed it to be.

"Alpha," I whined against his lips.

I was pulled away from Valen and laid on my back. Hands smoothed through my hair, over my breasts, my thighs were urged apart.

A warm, wet tongue licked through my folds, the sensation increased from my heightened senses. My eyes rolled shut as that talented mouth began to lick and suck on my clit, moving lower to press into my hole, before sliding down to tease my back hole.

"So beautiful," Valen muttered softly, his fingers trailing over my collarbone and down between the valley of my breasts.

I stared up into his face, at the way his pupils were blown, almost completely hiding the pretty blue green of his irises. His lips were a little pink from our kissing.

But it was the absolute affection and admiration in his expression that urged me to reach for him. I would beg him to come closer if that was necessary. I needed more than the gentle touches. I needed a release from the pressure growing and growing in my lower half. I needed the stretch of a knot.

I needed the pain squeezing my ovaries and uterus and the fever causing my skin to feel tight and way too hot to go away.

"More. Please," I finally begged when Valen continued exploring my body with his gentle touch.

He could be gentle later. I needed release now. I needed this pack, my pack to knot me, to make me come, to make me scream. I needed their hands and mouths on me. I needed to be filled until I could barely breathe.

The mouth covering my core felt as though it became a vibrator against my clit as he growled, deep and long, his lips closing around the bundle of nerves, his tongue lashing and flicking against it until I threw my head back and cried out.

Within seconds of the aftershocks fading, another wave of need crashed through me, more intense than the first.

This was going to be a hell of a heat. More intense and far more pleasurable than I'd ever experienced when I'd used a silicon knot or checked into the heat clinic with some random alpha hired specifically to ease omegas through their cycle.

And it had everything to do with the four men who were moving closer, who were lifting me to straddle Valen's hips as he pushed his cock into my opening while someone pressed against my back hole, barely teasing the opening.

Ford knelt in front of me, his hand fisted around his cock as he pumped it slowly, offering it to me and waiting as I wrapped my lips around the head, greedily lapping at the addictive flavor of his precum.

This was a start...but I needed far more. And I knew deep inside my heart and soul, these alphas would take care of me while I was at my most vulnerable and was quickly losing all coherent thoughts to my hindbrain and need to be bred.

CHAPTER EIGHTEEN

<u>Ford</u>

Corazon was currently on her hands and knees, presented for me as I pounded into her slicked cunt from behind. We were on day three of her heat. The lulls between waves of pain and need were finally stretching into close to an hour, meaning we were each able to rest while we took turns tending to our omega.

And fuck me, I didn't give a shit how hard she fought against it, Corazon was ours. We had to find a way to get her to accept it, to accept us, and to accept a bonding bite from her four alphas.

Then, we would deal with the fallout from her fucking family of cowards. Pack Garcia apparently wasn't a risk being as they'd more or less told me to take the offer in return for their omega and shove it up our asses. In not so many words, of course.

She was ours. She would become the official and only omega of Pack Rivera. And as much as I was tempted to push her hair away from her shoulder and sink my teeth into her flesh now, I wanted her to be fully aware and able to give consent without her hindbrain muddying her thoughts.

Her soft moans filled the air, mixing with the erotic sound of my cock sliding through her wet, slicked heat and my hips slapping against her round ass. We needed mirrors in the nest, because no matter how far I craned my neck, I couldn't quite get a good enough glimpse of her full tits bouncing and swaying with each thrust of my hips.

Not that I hadn't been nearly hypnotized by watching them while my packmates took her, sometimes one at a time, two at a time, even three at a time while she would jack off the fourth in her hand. As much as I would love to use the word insatiable about our omega, I was finding it hard to keep my hands and dick to myself around her now, too.

Who the fuck was I kidding? It'd been a struggle since the moment she'd come into our home. It was only heightened now because she was willingly spreading her legs for us, begging for our cocks, begging to be stretched around our knots.

"You're taking me so well, omega," I purred, running my hand down her spine, then back up to wrap in her hair. Tugging on the handful, I urged her to lift onto her knees until her back was pressed to my front. "I want to take your ass. You think you can handle my knot back there?"

"Alpha. Please," she begged, although I had no idea exactly what she was begging for. I wasn't sure *she* knew what she was begging for other than more. More of everything. More touch and dicks and knots and orgasms.

I might knot her ass, but I'd make damn sure she got off and covered the cushioned floor of the nest with even more of her release.

"If you're taking her ass, I want her cunt wrapped around my cock. I want to feel how tight she gets," Cohl said, his voice gravelly with sleep and exhaustion.

Out of the four of us, he had taken her the most often, constantly rutting into her, painting her inner walls with his cum, covering her skin or shooting his release down her throat as though he needed to fill her as much as possible.

It was starting to piss me off. Whether he realized it or *she* realized it, Cohl's alpha was trying to breed the beautiful omega. She wasn't officially ours. If he succeeded and knocked her up, she would hate him – us – for the rest of her life. Hell, a pregnancy could very well put her life at risk when she wasn't bonded to our pack.

With a growl, I pulled from Corazon, soothing her with my hand around her throat as I grazed my teeth along her shoulder, while Cohl laid back and lifted her until she was hovering over his cock.

Holding his dick steady, he thrust upward, spearing Corazon hard without knotting her. She cried out, her head dropping against my shoulder, making my fucking gums ache with the urge to clamp down on the skin I was teasing.

"Fuuuck," Cohl groaned out, gripping her waist in both hands and tugging her down, setting a rhythm so she was riding his cock.

Reaching between us, I slid my fingers through her folds and gathered slick on my fingers before teasing her ass. She'd taken us perfectly over and over, but she hadn't been knotted in her back hole. An omega's body was capable of so much more than an alpha or even beta, but I didn't want to cause her any discomfort.

Slowly easing first one finger then another into her back hole, I fisted my dick with my other hand, stroking myself to the same pace I finger fucked her sweet little asshole.

Her whimpers and moans grew until I could no longer hold out. Shuffling forward, I teased her opening with the head of my cock, slowly pushing forward as her ass all but swallowed my length.

Every inch of her body was fucking bliss, but there was something so primal and sexy about her taking two of her alphas at once and fuck me if she didn't feel as though she was made for each and every one of us yet also for the pack as a whole, as well.

"Fuck, omega. You're so perfect. You're taking your alphas so beautifully," I growled in her ear, smiling to myself when goosebumps broke out along her back and arms.

She was so responsive to our touch. And, sure, I could have blamed that on her heat, but she hadn't thrown herself at the alpha guards who'd entered the kitchen, unaware that our omega was present.

No. She'd whimpered at the increase of our hormones, had clung to Cohl, then climbed Bain like a fucking tree as need overcame her and washed away all thoughts or fears or doubts she might have had about our pack.

Now, we had to find a way to make her feel this head over heels with us when her body and hormones were no longer in control.

"I need to knot you," Cohl said, his eyes on her face as he thrust upward while I pumped into her from behind.

"Not yet," I ground out. The moment he filled her and locked her onto his cock, it would milk my dick of my own orgasm and I wanted to enjoy the feeling of her tight little ass around me a little longer.

"Gonna fill you with my cum. Fill your belly with my pups."

I was almost too far gone to react, but I did lose my rhythm a bit as Cohl's statement startled me. Fuck. Was this where Corazon snapped out of it, where she ordered us all out of the nest, where she demanded we return her to her family?

"Yes, alpha. Please. Breed me. Mark me. Bite. Please bite," she cried out as her ass began to clench around me.

She was coming. And begging Cohl to bite her while he fucked her. She was begging him to fucking bond her and breed her.

"Don't you fucking dare," I growled out at Cohl.

But he didn't hear me. I wasn't sure he was aware there was anyone but Corazon in the room as his eyes stayed glued on her face, his pupils blown until his eyes were black.

"Need to fucking knot my omega," he ground out through clenched teeth. And I didn't have time to try to stop him before he gripped her hips in a bruising hold, pulled her down hard while he thrust up, his knot stretching her cunt and rubbing against my cock through the thin membrane separating us.

Fuck. Fuck me. That was it. That was the last sliver of my self-control. With my hands gripping her just above where Cohl still clung to her, I shoved forward, my knot stretching past the tight ring of her ass and locked myself deep inside of her as my dick twitched with each jet of my release.

I didn't stop rutting against her. Neither did Cohl. Moments later, we both came again with Corazon crying out so loudly it was nearly a scream, her voice scratchy and hoarse from days of moaning, whining, begging, and screaming.

And then she fell forward and collapsed onto Cohl's chest, forcing me to quickly lean forward to keep her from hurting either of us.

Her breathing was slow and steady. She was asleep.

Holy shit, that had been intense.

"Cohl," I muttered softly so as not to wake her. She needed her rest for the next round of fucking.

The redhead's attention was fully on the omega using his chest as a pillow.

"Cohl," I grunted out a little louder.

It was eerie the way his eyes slowly turned from Corazon to me, the way it felt more like he was looking through me than at me.

"We need to roll to the side or I'll end up crushing her."

It took some maneuvering, but we were finally able to lie on our sides with Corazon sandwiched between us.

After some time, my knot deflated, but I couldn't make myself pull free from her, even when my cock softened a bit. Not fully, though. I wasn't sure my cock had been fully soft since the moment this sexy ass and fiery omega came into our life.

Or rather when we'd forced her into our lives.

This hadn't been the plan. Like every other asshole alpha, we'd planned to use her against her family and future pack. We'd planned to use her as leverage to gain more control and power.

And then we'd all fallen for her like a bunch of lovesick teenagers.

It was her scent. She smelled so fucking good. And it didn't hurt that she was not only stunningly beautiful and had the most fuckable body, but she was also stubborn and strong and intelligent.

My muscles burned, my joints ached, and I was starving. We'd taken turns leaving the nest to retrieve small and easily eaten snacks, but none of us had eaten a full meal. Valen had been smart enough to stock the minifridge with bottles of water when he'd ordered her nearly everything an omega could need, and then some. She had a whole new wardrobe, blankets and pillows for the nest, undergarments, bathroom crap, and even makeup.

Valen had the right idea, but I wasn't sure that alone would be enough to win her over. And Bain's words the night before her cycle had hit hard and fast sure as fuck wouldn't help. I still couldn't believe Valen had tried to beat the shit out of our pack lead. I wouldn't have batted an eye had it been Cohl, but definitely not the even tempered, calm as fuck Valen.

What else could we do, could *I* do to convince her to stay with us, to let us take care of her, to bond her to us and make her our omega?

While I would never do anything against her will, there was a small part of me that wished I'd bitten her when she'd begged. Then the bond would open between us and she could feel how sincere we were when we told her how much we wanted her. And not because she was part of our fucked up plan.

At least not anymore.

CHAPTER NINETEEN

The five of us were currently half awake in the huge garden tub in the omega wing bathroom. Corazon was between my raised knees, her back against my chest, her head resting against my shoulder.

Cohl had poured far too much of the bubble bath stuff until the suds started to pour over the rim of the tub and onto the floor. At least that had gotten a sweet giggle from our omega as I'd carried her in to soak away the aches and pains we were all suffering after five days of being locked in the nest.

Not that I or any of my packmates were complaining. It was, hands down, the best five days of my life to date.

Bain was staring at Corazon and I could practically see the wheels turning in his head. He hoped that, since she'd allowed us to help her through her heat, since she'd thrown herself at him, that she would then easily accept us as her pack and a bond from us.

The moment his eyes rose to my face, I shook my head slowly, warning him off before he could open his mouth and ruin the peaceful moment.

She needed to learn she could trust us, and constantly pressuring her wouldn't help. She'd shown us from day one that she couldn't and wouldn't be bullied into shit. I was mildly surprised she'd allowed her family to cram her in that cupcake wannabe gown for a forced bonding with a pack she didn't choose.

Although, if she'd known nothing but her family, if she'd been raised the way so many omegas had, she would have done exactly as she was told.

She was the only omega from the children in Pack Alvarez. She would have been raised for the sole reason of increasing her fathers' power, their reign.

And, yeah, we'd taken her for that reason, as well. I wanted to believe we would have done things differently had we known what Corazon would have come to mean to us, but fuck…not like we could rewind time.

We might very well have never had the chance to get to know her had Bain not come up with the plan to attack the convoy with the intent of using their precious gem as a bargaining chip.

The decision hadn't been fully made, but I knew the others felt the same way I did – there wasn't a chance in fucking hell we would willingly hand her over to her family pack. For one thing, she was ours. Fuck me, she was mine. In such a short time, the tiny omega had dug her way into my heart and claimed it as her own. She held it in her tiny little hand without even knowing it.

A bigger issue with handing her over was the fact she would still either be gifted to Pack Garcia or another group of her fathers' choosing. They would promise her to some other group of alphas for power, money, another wrung on the criminal ladder.

"Corazon," Bain said, and I shook my head again.

But the fucker ignored me.

She raised her head slowly as though it was too heavy for her neck to hold. We'd been able to get her to drink periodically and nibble on a few things here and there, but she was definitely dehydrated and needed a few days of hot meals to get her strength back up. That and a lot of rest and pampering.

"I want to apologize for the shit I said. That night after we…"

Huh. Not what I'd expected him to say.

She grunted a soft response and let her head drop back against my shoulder.

The water swished and bubbles nearly covered her face as he scooted across the tub to get closer to her. Her hand weakly raised to push the mound away as a soft giggle shook her body and awakened my still semi-hard cock. What could I say? Hard not to be turned on with her cradled against my groin like this.

Corazon's head lolled against my shoulder as she focused on Bain, who was now within touching distance of her. He lifted one of her legs onto his lap and began to massage the muscles. She sighed and relaxed even further against me.

"I wanted to talk to you about…us. About the pack. And you."

Her body tensed against me, and it took everything in me not to kick Bain in the face. Seriously? This couldn't wait until later, like after she'd recovered from a week of pain and fever and fucking?

After the four of us had taken her over and over on the fifth day, she'd collapsed onto my chest and promptly fell asleep. Her heat was officially over. She'd slept for a full six hours, the longest she'd rested since it had begun, and I'd carried her to the bathroom for a quick shower to wash away the sweat, slick, and cum that covered nearly every inch of her body as Cohl filled the tub. We'd been in here since, even having to drain and add a little more hot water periodically to keep our girl from getting cold.

"What about you? And me?" she asked. Or rather croaked. She'd screamed and moaned and cried out so many times that her voice was scratchy. I was sure her throat was probably raw, too. And the pain would have been from the erotically beautiful sounds she'd made along with how many times she'd had one of our cocks shoved down her throat.

Bain continued to massage her foot, moving upward to her calf until she began to relax against me again.

I wrapped my arms around her shoulders, letting them cross over her chest as though blocking and protecting her from the world. Or maybe just from my stupid as fuck pack lead who was about to ruin fucking everything.

When Bain scooted closer, he managed to bump into my leg and I didn't bother resisting the urge, raised my foot, and shoved him back with a deep frown pulling my brows low.

Cohl had managed to scoot forward, as well, and was now toying with Corazon's foot as it rested against this chest. That alpha had become downright obsessed with our omega from the get-go and hadn't bothered to even try to hide it. He was and always would be an in-your-face mother fucker and gave zero fucks about anyone's opinions.

While Bain focused on massaging, Cohl raised her foot and began kissing each of her toes until she squirmed with a tinkling giggle.

"Fuck, I love your laugh," Cohl said, returning to kissing and licking her toes to make her squirm and giggle some more.

And of course, that made her rub her ass against my cock until my knot began to inflate.

"Damn it, Cohl," I muttered, gripping her hips to move her so she wouldn't think I was trying to take advantage of our cozy position.

"Can't help it. She has the cutest fucking toes."

Bain reached out to cuff the back of Cohl's head, but he ducked the blow.

"What did you want to talk about?" Corazon said around a giggle as she finally tugged her foot free from Cohl's grip.

Didn't stop the redhead. He scooted closer and began to mimic Bain, massaging her calves and moving further up to knead the muscles in her thigh, earning a throaty and satisfied groan. And a satisfied purr from Cohl.

"Joining our pack. Officially. You asked for the bite. But none of us...we wanted to make sure you knew what you were asking. Now that your cycle is over–"

"That was my hindbrain, not me," she said, the tension returning.

She even sat up and put a little space between us, something that caused a soft growl to rumble from my chest as anger at Bain and disappointment over losing contact with the curvy omega ruffled my alpha.

"Your omega recognizes her pack. You can't tell me you don't feel it. You can't tell me you haven't felt the same strong pull toward us that we feel toward you," Bain said, his voice growing angrier, his words clipped.

"Are you trying to fuck everything up?" I ground out between clenched teeth.

Bain's eyes flicked to mine then immediately returned to Corazon's face. "We fucked up when we took you from your family, but I can't say I regret it."

"You don't regret murdering four men whose only job was to protect me? You don't regret snatching me from my family, for endangering my siblings, my parents, even me? Do you know how close some of those bullets came to hitting me?" Now her voice was growing louder, and her scent was becoming sour with her simmering rage that was quickly hitting a boiling point.

"None of the bullets came anywhere near you. We're not fucking amateurs," Bain said.

Corazon's spine went ramrod straight as she tensed and glared at Bain. "I was covered in blood, brains, and pieces of skull from men I had known my entire life. Men who'd risked their lives for mine on so many occasions. And you just casually put bullets through their heads. And you didn't think that would affect me? Piss me off? Break my heart?"

Bain opened his mouth then shut it. His eyes shot to mine over her shoulder, then moved to Cohl and Ford.

Fuck. I honestly hadn't even thought about the fact Corazon might have actually cared about the men who were charged with her safety.

When we'd converged upon the Town Car, one of the guards had been holding her head down as though keeping her from the bullets flying while the other had crowded his own body over hers, creating a shield of skin, muscle, and bones.

And we'd callously shot through the windows and killed all four. In front of her. Covering her in their gore.

Of course she would be traumatized by that. Hell, even if she hadn't given two shits about the four men who'd been in that car with her, being covered in someone else's blood and brains would be enough to freak anyone out, whether they'd been raised by members of the mafia or not.

I reached for her, desperately craving her skin pressed against mine again, but she jerked away, glaring at me over her shoulder before returning her full attention to Bain again.

"I was in heat. My omega took over. My hindbrain took the steering wheel. *I* didn't ask for your bite. I would *never* ask for your bite. I am not your fucking omega."

And with that, she stood on shaky legs, batting Cohl's hands away when he reached for her to keep her steady, and stormed from the room with water and suds streaking down her body while all I could do was watch her go.

Sure, I could have chased after her. I could have used my bark to make her stay here in the tub with us while we argued our case, begged her to change her mind. But Bain was the dickhead of the group, not me. I would win her over the old-fashioned way.

That is, if Bain didn't affectively scare her away forever.

A slow grin started to creep across Cohl's face as he watched the open bathroom door, listening to her moving around the omega quarters. "She's going to run," he blurted as he climbed from the tub and prepared to chase.

Well, fuck. This situation was quickly turning from bad to catastrophic. Because hunter and prey was Cohl's favorite fucked up game.

CHAPTER TWENTY

<u>Corazon</u>

Who the hell did Bain think he was? Hell, who did any of them think they were?

Yeah, sure, I'd thrown myself at Bain like a starving woman who'd just found the last Twinkie on the planet. But that was nothing more than my baser needs taking over and shoving all logical thought into the trunk.

So now he thought because my omega had lost her shit and begged for a bite, that I belonged to them?

The look on his face, on Ford's and Cohl's faces, when I'd brought up the fact they'd killed men I'd known as long as I could remember right in front of me, covered me with so much gore, was nothing short of confusion. Seriously? That had never crossed their minds?

Violence wasn't new to me. I'd seen men killed only feet from me when they'd been stupid enough to try to kidnap me or when they somehow pissed off one of my fathers. But that was far different than simply doing their jobs and getting killed for it.

Did I love the guards who'd died? No. I wasn't even sure I knew what that word meant or how it felt. My mom had always been a bit distant, unaffectionate. My fathers treated me like I was...well, a tool in their arsenal to be used at will.

Just like these assholes. They'd taken me to get my family pack and my future...not my future alphas. Not my future pack. Because according to Bain, they didn't give a shit that I'd been taken, that I was being held by a rival group.

Hair and body dripping water everywhere, I grabbed a pair of sweats and a t-shirt from a drawer and dragged them over my body. They didn't get to see me naked anymore. I'd made it through the worst of my heat. I had months before I had to deal with all that again. And, hopefully by then, I would be free from here and back home.

And then that urge to disappear into society hit me like a ton of bricks. If I went back home, my fathers would simply shop for another pack, would put me back on the market to gain more control over their rivals or to merge the two for more power, more wealth. More control over everything and everyone who happened to be sucked into their orbit.

After shoving my feet into a pair of sneakers – forgoing the time it would take to don a pair of socks – I darted from the omega quarters, down the hall, and tried not to fall down the stairs as I ran as fast as my legs would allow.

A beta clad all in black with guns holstered under both arms and against his thigh stood near the front door, his blond brows pulled together as I rounded the corner, the soles of my shoes squeaking against the marble floor.

One exit blocked. But there would be more than one. I would find the back door or the garage door. I might not have the keys, but I could hotwire a car as well as any thief. Once I was in a vehicle, I would bust through the heavy gates I'd seen through my bedroom window and aim for the closest highway.

And wouldn't stop until I ran out of gas. Hell, even then, I might just get out and walk or catch a bus. Not that I had any money for a bus pass. Or a hotel to sleep and shower. Or, you know, food.

I'd seen only a few rooms in this house before the presence of the alpha guards had sent my hormones into overdrive and Bain had scooped me up and carried me upstairs. And I refused to acknowledge the fact my omega had been unsteady in the nest until Cohl had littered the flooring with the pack's dirty clothes, filling the small space with their scents.

Living room. Kitchen. I knew these rooms. But there were two other hallways that led from different spaces and I felt like I was running through a maze, like a fucking mouse trying to find the cheese.

If I didn't find a way out soon, I would end up trapped in this place forever. With this pack. With these alphas.

Mine.

My wet hair swung against my back as I shook my head to dispel that thought before it was able to fully take root. Because they weren't mine. They would never be mine. They were no different than my fathers. No different than the alphas from Pack Garcia. They'd intended to use me, didn't take my thoughts, feelings, or desires into consideration before they'd ambushed the caravan, before they'd murdered my guards, before my family had run away like cowards to leave me defenseless.

Why, when I was intent on trying to find an escape from this house, was that last thought the one that cut the worst? The moment Bain had thrown that into my face, my heart had hurt more than I'd known was possible. I'd never been under any illusion that my family loved me as their daughter but saw me as something they could exploit.

How long would it take for Bain, Ford, Cohl, and Valen to decide to do the same thing? How long would it take for them to drop the façade of wanting me as their omega before they started putting out feelers for someone willing to pay top dollar for the rare gem of Pack Alvarez. My fathers had made plenty of enemies through their business – what better way to get revenge than to hurt, kill, or breed their daughter?

Is that what this pack wanted? Revenge? To sell me? To breed me?

Gonna fill you with my cum. Fill your belly with my pups.

The hazy memory of Cohl's words, of my pleas for him to mark me, to breed me made me trip over my feet and almost face plant as I ran through what looked like a den. I grabbed the back of a couch to keep myself from hitting the ground, then kept my feet moving.

There. French doors that opened onto what appeared to be the backyard.

I nearly crashed into it in my haste to get outside…until two arms banded around me, locking my arms to my sides.

Sweet, sticky vanilla frosting coated my tongue as Cohl's face nuzzled the crook of my neck. "Caught you, little omega," he purred in my ear.

His hard cock nudged against my ass, and for the briefest moment, I caught myself pushing back against him in invitation. Until I remembered I was trying to escape him, escape his pack.

Escape this life of captivity. It didn't matter if I agreed to Bain's requests, his fucking demands. I would always be a prisoner to any pack I bonded with.

"Let…go," I ground out as I tried to wiggle my way out of his iron-clad grip around me.

"I like the way you feel in my arms. I like the way your ass feels against my cock when you wiggle like that," he said, his lips brushing the shell of my ear and sending unwanted – yet delicious – tingles down my spine.

What was it about these alphas that made me hate and want them at the same time? They should repulse me. It didn't matter how good they smelled. I'd met plenty of alphas who smelled like sex on a stick, but they didn't make me forget everything and fight the urge to dry hump the very air around them.

"I'll make you a deal," Cohl whispered in my ear. "I'll open the door. You run. If you make it to the gate, I'll get you out of this house and take you on a date. But if I catch you, I get to fuck you however I want for as long as I want."

My mouth opened to tell him to go fuck himself, but my body reacted strongly to his words. Slick pooled in my sweats and dampened my upper thighs as my nipples hardened until a darker part of me wished he would just rip the clothes away and take me right here against the door.

Nope. Not just nope but fuck no. I refused to allow my brain to turn to mush over this alpha or any of the rest of the pack.

Lowering my head slowly, I let it fly back like a slingshot, then winced at the pain when I succeeded in headbutting Cohl enough for him to release his hold.

My hand was around the knob and pulling it open, but he stopped it from opening by pushing his weight against mine, using us both as a barricade.

"Cohl!" Bain barked as Cohl began to rock his erection against my sweatpants covered ass.

Good thing I got dressed before attempting my poorly planned escape. More like fully unplanned. I should have waited until these four lowered their guards, until I'd learned the full layout of the house. Then I could have snuck out while they slept and been long gone before anyone noted my absence.

The weight pinning me to the door was pulled away and I whirled, raising my fists in preparation for a fight.

Cohl was the only one who hadn't bothered to pull on any pants. And now that I was looking at them without the foggy lens of heat... damn, they were attractive. Built like the most beautiful statues. Bain had a tattoo across his left pec. Valen had a scar down his right side that snaked over part of his stomach. Other than that, all four of them were the absolute epitome of physical and masculine perfection with their muscles and height and broad shoulders and slick inducing scents.

Ford had a hand wrapped around Cohl's neck, tugging him away from me. Bain's inky brows were pulled together forming a crease between them and shadowing the icy blue of his eyes. Valen looked... it was a combination of anger and concern, but I wasn't sure which emotion was for which person.

"The fuck is wrong with you?" Ford muttered to Cohl, shaking him once like a rag doll. That seemed to snap the auburn-haired alpha out of whatever trance he was in.

"She ran," he said with a shrug as though the explanation was plain as day.

"Go put on some pants," Ford said, turning and shoving Cohl toward the staircase before turning back to face me.

Ford looked as scary as Bain at the moment, but again, I wasn't sure whether that anger was aimed at me for attempting to run away or at Cohl for going all stalker/hunter on me. Maybe a little of both.

Valen's hand lifted, and I fought the urge to wince or back up, even with my fists still raised to defend myself.

But he wasn't reaching for me. He was holding a towel.

Raising my eyes to his face, I frowned.

"Your hair is dripping everywhere," he said with a shrug, still offering the towel in his outstretched hand.

Of course it was dripping. I hadn't dried off before pulling on my clothes and darting from the room. I hadn't planned a single second of the last ten minutes. Obviously. Because I was right back where I started.

Not true. They had yet to drag me back up to my quarters and lock me in the way I had been since I'd arrived.

Slowly relaxing my fists, I took the towel from Valen and squeezed it around my hair, wringing it of the bulk of water. If I didn't brush it soon, it would end up in knots. But that was the least of my concerns with four alphas staring me down and freedom just at my back.

As though reading my mind, Bain shook his head. "There are guards out there. You won't get more than a few feet."

"So this is how you court an omega? You murder her friends, drug her, lock her in a room, then hold her prisoner?"

"Do you have any fucking idea what would happen if you were out on the street alone? Or, hell, if we were to simply drop you off at your family's house? Just because Pack Garcia is full of a bunch of pussies who aren't willing to fight for you doesn't mean there aren't other packs who wouldn't barrel their way through any obstacle to have the Alvarez Omega in their pack," Bain growled out.

He'd apologized in the bathtub, had almost sounded genuine. Then had once again tried to talk me into joining his pack by telling me what I did and didn't want. Regardless of the whole part where I wasn't fully cognizant of my actions.

And now, he was back to throwing in my face that I had no one. That there wasn't a soul on this planet who gave two shits about me.

Without really thinking about my actions, I threw the towel at Bain's face. He reached up and slowly dragged it down, revealing a scowl etched so deeply he'd be lucky if they didn't leave permanent lines and wrinkles.

"I fucking get it. I'm nothing. I mean nothing. You can remind me as often as you want, but I've known that since I presented at the age of twelve and my parents sent me away to be trained to be the dutifully, well trained omega to my future alphas."

"I didn't mean–"

"I know exactly what you meant to say. You're trying to make it out like I have no choice but to choose you. Or like you're the lesser of two – or twelve – evils."

Valen stepped forward, his shoulder slightly blocking Bain from my view, and I wondered whether he was protecting his pack lead from me or keeping his pack lead from lunging for me.

I was half the size of all four of these alphas. They had at least fifty or more pounds of pure muscle over me. And I knew without a doubt I would lose miserably against them, but if Bain tried to attack me, I would fight with everything in me.

Bain and I stood there staring, seething, scowling at each other.

And then my fucking body once again betrayed me and released a plume of perfume into the room.

The answering growl from Bain sent shudders through me and a whimper escaped my lips before I could choke it back.

It only took half a heartbeat for Bain to shove Valen aside and crush me against his chest, his lips slamming onto mine, his arms tight around my back. He kissed me like he was trying to possess me, dominate me, sear himself into my very being. And I gave as much as I took.

Until conscious thought and my anger shoved forward again. Pulling away with a gasp, I raised a hand and slapped Bain across the cheek, the sound of my palm striking his cheek loud in the stunned silence.

His lips were parted and a little pink from our kisses. My chin burned from the way his stubble scraped against my sensitive flesh. And we were still pressed together so tightly that every inhale and exhale rubbed my hard nipples against the soft cotton of my shirt...or rather against the hardness of his broad chest.

"Why was that so hot?" Cohl asked somewhere from behind Bain.

But all I could focus on was the alpha still clutching me to his body, still staring at me with fire and lust and anger bright in his eyes. All I could focus on was the way my clit throbbed with need, the way my inner walls clenched around air as though craving the feeling of him – or any of the other three – filling me so completely.

This was wrong. So fucking wrong. My body craved these four like my lungs craved oxygen. And it was screwing with my brain.

I shouldn't want them. I should hate them. I should have been shoving at Bain, demanding he release his hold on me, demanding he move away from me.

Instead, I grabbed the back of his neck and tugged his mouth down to mine again, then hopped up to wrap my legs around his waist when his hands gripped the backs of my thighs.

CHAPTER TWENTY-ONE

<u>Corazon</u>

*H*ate fuck. Hormones. Primal need. That was all this was. All I would ever admit to as I shoved my hand between us to pull Bain's cock free from his pants.

Problem was I was fully dressed. Meaning Bain would have to set me on my feet so I could tug my clothes away before he could fuck me the way my body so desperately needed.

It didn't make sense. I was completely over my heat. Those cramps, the raw, dizzying lust, the fever, they had all faded sometime in the night. And then I'd finally gotten more than a few minutes of sleep. In fact, I'd slept the night through and woken to Valen gently running his fingers through my tangled hair.

Valen had been nothing but attentive and gentle, even went out of his way to order me some clothes that weren't four sizes too big or, you know, clothes that didn't belong to the pack. He'd also had plenty of luxury items delivered to make me more comfortable.

I would never admit it aloud, but he'd earned my trust merely by keeping a respectful distance and attending to my needs before they arose rather than demanding anything from me.

Cohl…it was hard not to like the crazy alpha. He said exactly what he was thinking when it crossed his mind. He didn't try to put on an act to disarm me in any way.

Ford…he was as confusing as Bain when it came to the way my body reacted to him, to his nearness, to his saffron scent.

Bain grunted against my lips as my hand wrapped around his hard shaft, his lips feasting on mine, his tongue wrapping around mine, dancing and dueling, fucking my mouth the way I needed his cock to fuck me.

The cool, hard wood of the kitchen table met my ass as he lowered me to its surface and tore his mouth from mine, pulling at my clothes as though he was in rut, yanking the sweater over my head, then dragging the pants down my legs. His hands were rough as they lifted both my knees over his shoulders and licked a line from my back hole to my clit with a flat tongue.

My fingers fisted in his hair as a long moan tore from me. My eyes rolled closed as he began to devour my core. And that was the only way to describe the way he worshipped my folds, my clit, teasing my entrance before wrapping his lips around the sensitive bundle of nerves and sucking hard.

"Bain," I moaned, tugging on his coal black hair until I was sure there would be loose strands in my hands by the time he was done.

His growl was like a vibrator directly against my clit and sent me spiraling over the edge so fast and hard I couldn't draw in a full breath.

Dizziness made my thoughts sluggish until he stood and positioned the head of his cock against my core.

"Open your eyes. Look at me," he barked, forcing my omega to twitch and obey immediately.

As I lifted my lids and looked into the crystalline blue of his irises, he leaned forward and gripped the nape of my neck as he shoved himself forward, sheathing his cock deep inside of me with one hard thrust.

My mouth opened on a soundless scream.

"Say it," he growled out as he started a punishing rhythm of his hips, the sound of our flesh hitting and the wet sounds of my slick and release mixing with the panting tearing from our lungs.

I shook my head. I knew what he wanted but refused to give it to him.

"Say you're mine. Say I'm yours," he growled out, fucking into me so hard I was scooting against the wood, my skin sliding along the surface causing a soft squeaking sound.

My lips parted, and the words were right there on the tip of my tongue. But I refused to let my baser side make permanent decisions for my logical side, no matter how much I wanted him, no matter how right if felt with these alphas.

Because the fact remained, I refused to allow anyone else to claim ownership over me, especially four alphas who planned to use me the exact same way my family had.

"Fuck you," I ground out between clenched teeth, fighting the instinct to allow this alpha to have all of me.

His deep growl reverberated through me and filled the room, sending the small hairs on my body standing on end.

I knew without a doubt that Bain could and would protect me. I knew they all would. But I was so fucking tired of being nothing more than a prize to alphas.

Bain's fingers dug into the skin at the back of my neck, his grip possessive as those bottomless pools of blue glared at me.

"You're mine, omega. I want to hear you say it. Say *yes, alpha. I'm yours.*"

"Fuck...you," I managed to force out, even as everything from my waist down began to tingle as wave after wave of pleasure made me clench around Bain's long, thick cock plowing into me.

Somewhere in the distance, I barely noticed the sound of a door opening and closing, the sound of heavy footfalls moving through the house.

And then a cacophony of growls mixed with the erotic sounds

Bain and I were making as scents of caramel, burnt popcorn, and clay mixed with the signatures of the pack.

There were a lot of thuds and curses before Bain pulled from me, lifted me to my feet, and shoved me behind his body. Before my brain could catch up, he'd grabbed my shirt and yanked it over my body. Not that it covered much more than my breasts. My lower half was still exposed since my leggings were in a pile on the floor.

"What the fuck is wrong with you?" a man asked.

Those growls didn't lessen. A scuffle came from somewhere down the hall.

"Fuck. Ford. The fuck is wrong with you?" I recognized the scent from the day the guards' presence had shoved me face first into my heat. But I didn't have any names for any of them. Didn't know any of them.

And apparently, my pack saw them as a threat. Did that mean I was standing there half naked and in danger from the people they paid to protect their empire?

"Ford!" Valen barked. Not that his alpha bark would have much power over his packmate.

"Stay here," Bain barked, and my muscles tightened under his order.

He tucked his cock into his pants, still doing up the button and zipper as he left me standing half naked in the kitchen.

He'd told me to stay here. He hadn't said a word about getting dressed. Because no way would I stand here so exposed if there was a threat in the house. Especially if it was something the four couldn't handle on their own. If some asshole got past them, I didn't want to be standing in the kitchen like a prize waiting to be claimed, my pussy and ass on full display.

As I hopped in place to pull the tight leggings up and over my ass, Bain's bark began to fade. So, I tiptoed from the kitchen and peered around the corner of the hall.

Ford was holding an alpha clad in all black against the wall by his throat. There was a bruise already forming on his cheek as though he'd been punched. The guard wasn't fighting against Ford, but he did have a hand wrapped around Ford's wrist as though trying to ease some of the pressure so he could breathe.

"What the fuck are you doing?" another guard asked, keeping his distance with his hands out in front of him as Cohl stalked closer.

Cohl's back was to me, but I could feel the raw power rippling from him and detected the rush of alpha hormones in the air.

"Would the two of you fucking stop and tell me what the fuck is going on?" Bain bellowed, causing everyone to freeze as though someone had hit the pause button.

"My omega," Cohl growled out, his voice more animal than man and pulled a whimper from my throat.

Six sets of eyes turned to me and the alpha hormones rose more as growls erupted again. But only from my pack. The guards were doing their best to remain neutral. Probably because both Ford and Cohl looked like they were ready to tear the alpha guards to pieces.

"Go upstairs," Bain barked.

And even though my muscles tightened and burned to obey, I crossed my arms over my chest and glared. First, he'd tried to use his alpha power to force me to let him claim me as his. Now he was ordering me around? I'd barely just had a chance to leave my room after being here for over two weeks. No way would I run upstairs to be locked away again.

Cohl was watching me, his nostrils flaring, his pupils fully eating up the warm brown of his irises until he looked downright scary.

Turning his back on the guard he'd cornered, he began to stalk toward me and my body countered on instinct, backing away, matching him step for step.

"For fuck's sake, do not run," Valen said, shoving past Ford and the guard he held, until he stood between me and Cohl. "Back the fuck off, Cohl."

"Mine," he growled.

Shit. That was the second time in less than thirty minutes one of these alphas tried to lay claim on me.

But unlike with Bain, Cohl seemed as though the world officially revolved around me. Bain made it sound as though he needed the words for himself. Cohl looked as though anything that came from my mouth would make or break every single part of the sexy redheaded alpha.

Do not run. That's all I wanted to do. Although…it wasn't out of fear. There was something in Cohl's eyes, a look of a predator that sent a buzz through my system, a strange excitement. I *wanted* to run. I wanted to dart outside to see how long it would take the slightly unhinged alpha to catch me.

And find out exactly what he would do when he tackled me to the ground and had me at his mercy.

With a hard shake of my head, I shook all those thoughts loose. All four alphas looked on the verge of killing someone. Not someone – their own guards. They weren't beating them to pulps or pulling any weapons, so I had to assume they weren't a threat to me.

So then why were Ford and Cohl acting so erratically?

Valen glanced at me over his shoulder, then focused back on the chaos playing out in the middle of the living room.

"Ford, let him go. The two of you need to get out of the house. Let the other alphas know to refrain from entering without letting one of us know until further notice." His words were calm, but they sounded growly, as though he was fighting against his own alpha urges to beat these two to death simply for being in the same room as me…their proclaimed omega.

Valen stood in front of Cohl, using his body as a shield to keep the alpha from stalking closer to me. Bain was muttering in Ford's ear, too low for me to hear, but I assumed trying to convince him to release the poor guard whose face was mottled, his lips turning blue.

The guard nearest the door backed up, reaching behind him and creating an exit without tearing his eyes from the pack. The same pack who happened to pay them and was now trying to kill them simply because they'd come into the house while I was downstairs.

There had been guards near my door after Bain had smashed it open, but they had been betas.

They had no right to be possessive over me. I could appreciate if they were trying to protect me from a known threat, but these were men the pack apparently trusted enough to watch over them and the estate.

Bain had told me to go upstairs, but Cohl was effectively blocking that exit. I could try to step out the back door through the kitchen, but that could cause more problems if there just happened to be another alpha guard outside. I had no desire to see anyone else killed because of me.

I didn't like this. I didn't like the feeling of being trapped. But what was worse was my omega preening over her alphas' need to protect and the possessive urges that caused Ford and Cohl to attack simply because the alphas had dared to step into the house while I was here. Or was it because I was naked in the kitchen, stuffed full by Bain's cock.

Ford finally released the guard he'd been strangling and let Bain pull him away. The poor guard rubbed at his throat as he gasped in deep breaths of air and stumbled toward the front door.

Cohl's eyes stayed narrowed on him as he passed, that guttural growl increasing in volume and power until it pulled another whimper from my chest before I could stop it.

"Fuck," Valen ground out a second before Cohl attacked.

Why the hell would these men want me – or any omega – in their home if they were going to freak out any time another alpha was nearby?

"Cohl!" I screamed before I had a second to actually think through my actions.

The memory of my fathers' men's blood slapping my bare skin was still vibrant in my mind. I couldn't watch someone else get hurt simply because I existed.

Cohl froze mid-step and turned his eerily unfocused eyes on me.

I took a step back. Then another.

"Fuck, Corazon. Do not fucking run!" Valen warned.

But that was exactly what I was planning with the sole purpose of distracting Cohl. He might not have a problem with fucking up one of the men under their employ, but I had a feeling he would regret it when his alpha was no longer pushing him into rut.

A squeal escaped my lips when Cohl darted for me. Turning on my heel, I ran down the hall, through the kitchen, and yanked the French doors open so I could run into the backyard.

I only had a moment to appreciate my first breath of fresh air in over two weeks before that deep, guttural growl sounded behind me, accompanied by thundering steps hitting the cold ground.

The alpha's legs were much longer than mine and he was eating the space between us quickly no matter how hard I ran, no matter how much I begged my shorter legs to move faster.

If I was trying so hard to get away…why was excitement skittering through me and a smile stretching across my face?

"Damn it, Cohl!" Bain yelled from behind us.

I didn't dare turn to look. This was already a lost cause; no way could I outrun any of these alphas, but especially when my flirty and sexy as hell alpha looked as though he was ready to dominate me in the most animalistic manner possible.

"You better not fucking hurt her!" Valen yelled.

Too late.

I hit the ground hard as Cohl tackled me from behind, knocking the wind from my lungs. I thrashed and bucked, trying to get him off my back, but…

Part of me was enjoying this if the fresh gush of slick pooling in my leggings and coating my thighs and the throbbing of my clit were anything to go by.

His hands were rough as he grabbed the fabric of my pants and tore them down the center, exposing me to him and the cool air that caused gooseflesh to raise across my body. Or maybe it was the power rolling from him and his scent drowning me in sweetness.

"Get him off her!" Ford yelled.

Feet hit the ground hard as the pack ran toward me. I caught sight of black clad bodies sprinting across the yard from the opposite end of the yard in their attempt to rescue me.

But I didn't need to be rescued. Everything about this moment felt right, felt monumental…

Felt like home.

I couldn't explain it, couldn't explain why I'd refused to acknowledge Bain's demands I call him my alpha or that I admit that I belonged to him when all I wanted was for Cohl to plunge his hard cock into my core while sinking his teeth into my shoulder.

His body stretched over mine and his cock slid between my thighs, nudging against my entrance. I lifted my ass, inviting him in, or maybe I was trying to force him into me. Because I needed his stretch.

I'd found release twice with Bain before all hell had broken loose at the mere presence of two alphas. Yet I needed more and I couldn't figure out why. I was far from a virgin, but I'd never thought of myself as insatiable.

I'd also never found four alphas who made me question every single aspect of my life, nor alphas who could so easily hurt me while putting me back together within a span of seconds.

Cohl grunted as he fully sheathed himself inside of me, his lips brushing the shell of my ear.

One of his hands slid around until he was cupping my throat right below my jaw and tilting my face up.

"Mine," he growled against the side of my face. "You're *my* omega."

"I'm yours, alpha," I breathed out before I could stop the words from escaping my mouth as he started a rough, punishing rhythm, pounding into my sensitive pussy and shoving my hips into the hard ground.

His hand left my jaw and yanked the fabric of my shirt away, then teeth scraped my skin then pierced the delicate flesh. The sting and ache quickly faded as his knot nudged my opening, stretching with each thrust as he tried to fully lock us together.

"Mother fucker!" someone yelled.

"Stay the fuck back!" someone else yelled.

I had no idea who was talking or who was being ordered to stay away, not with the overwhelming warmth that flooded from my shoulder to settle in my chest. The bond blew wide open until I could feel Cohl everywhere, inside my cunt, inside my heart, my soul, swimming through my veins as though he was the very thing keeping me alive.

Later, I would realize what I'd done, that I'd allowed this alpha to claim me, that I was now permanently tied to this pack.

But for now, I relished in every sensation buzzing through my system and overriding everything but mind-numbing pleasure…

And rightness.

CHAPTER TWENTY-TWO

<u>Bain</u>

She'd denied me. Or at least refused to my demands that she admit she belonged to me, to my pack.

To her fucking alphas.

Yet, she was spread out on the ground with Cohl's knot buried in her tight cunt as he lapped at the seeping wound he'd left on her shoulder.

I supposed I should have been ecstatic. She was officially the omega to Pack Rivera. Or rather, she was Cohl's omega.

But he was pack. That made her fucking pack. That made her ours.

They couldn't stay out here. It was too cold, and she was half fucking naked. Not to mention Cohl's bare ass was exposed. Definitely not something I wanted to stare at.

Yet, they couldn't move yet, not until Cohl's knot deflated, and being as he was still rutting into her after both of them had clearly gotten off a couple times, Cohl filling Corazon's pussy full of his cum, that wouldn't happen any time soon.

"You need to let your omega up," Valen said, kneeling beside their faces and speaking in a calm voice. Always the voice of reason. Which was why it shocked all of us – especially me – when he'd attacked me and accused me of hurting her.

Of course I'd hurt her, or at least hurt her feelings. But why the fuck would that cause him to try to throttle me? Yeah, I'd verbally lashed out when I'd felt as though she'd rejected me after we'd fucked the first time, but that didn't necessarily warrant getting pummeled by the bigger of the four of us.

Why the fuck wasn't he beating the shit out of Cohl right now? Not only had he taken Corazon to the ground hard, but he'd marked her while fucking her.

Although...she had told him she was his, had bared her neck in invitation.

The guards who watched the perimeter had heard the commotion and came running. Luckily, Valen had had enough forethought to order them back or there might have been a big, fucking problem. I still couldn't believe Ford had attacked Keller simply for walking in while I'd been buried balls deep inside of Corazon. I hadn't even had the chance to finish inside of her, damn it.

Cohl growled at Valen and continued his shallow thrusts into Corazon. But she looked exhausted. And, frankly, she looked as though she was being crushed by her alpha.

Fuck. Her alpha. Cohl was her fucking alpha. I was pack lead, yet she'd rejected me. Well, might be because I could be an overbearing asshole who tended to let my mouth run with the most hurtful shit possible when I didn't get my way, but still.

"You're hurting her, Cohl," Valen said.

Those words appeared to get through his brain. His hips stilled, his eyes widened, and he lifted up onto his hands, only their lower halves now touching.

Corazon took a deep breath as though she'd only been able to breathe shallowly before.

"Are you okay?" Valen asked, lowering his head further so he could stare directly into her eyes.

She nodded, but her eyes looked clouded with lust and a tad unfocused. Her perfume constantly lifted onto the wind, blowing around us and keeping my dick at its rock-hard state.

"Boss," a beta guard said from the French doors. I glanced back at him. He held up a blanket.

A beta wouldn't be seen as a threat, even with Cohl still in rut.

Once they were both covered, the beta quickly retreated, leaving the three of us staring down at Cohl and our new omega. She was ours. She only carried the mark of one of her alphas, but she was ours.

Would she regret it when the omega urges settled? Or, like us, would she realize we were meant to find each other, even if the four of us had only intended on using the daughter of our enemy?

I couldn't give a fuck about Pack Alvarez now. Fuck them and their tenuous hold on power. We didn't need to use our omega. We didn't need to use anything but our own fucking strength and strategy to overthrow their empire and take over the export/import game.

And the first thing we would do was put a fucking stop to the human trafficking game in our territory. Or at least we would do our fucking best to put down the actors behind that bullshit.

First and foremost was making sure Corazon's family knew that, not only were they never getting her back, but she had a pack and would no longer be a tool for them to use for their own benefit.

It took close to thirty minutes before Cohl's knot deflated enough to pull out of our omega. It was another thirty minutes of me, Valen, and Ford begging and threatening him to lift away from her so we could get her inside, clean her up, and redress her in something that hadn't been destroyed.

Cohl refused to allow any of us to touch Corazon, lifting her in his arms and carrying her through the house with his ass and cock still out for anyone to see. It was like he didn't even notice that his junk was flopping in the wind or feel the cold air on his bare ass.

"Take her to the tub," Valen said, passing the two of them and entering the omega quarters ahead, presumably to start another bath.

Problem with the tub was that all four of us would end up wanting to be in there with her. Which would result in either one or all of us fucking her again. And we really needed to have a civil conversation and find out whether she was aware of what had happened on the back lawn.

"Shower," I called up the stairs from behind Cohl.

After a few seconds, I followed Cohl into the bathroom with Ford right on my heel. The unhinged alpha started to step into the huge shower stall, our omega still partially dressed, but Valen stopped him and even talked him into passing Corazon over so they could both help her strip before the shower.

Yeah, a bath would have felt amazing on the omega's battered body, but she needed to get cleaned up and put to bed to rest, not have all four of us pawing at her, vying for her attention. Because, if the other three were feeling even a sliver of what I felt at the moment, they had the same insane urge to claim her body with their dicks and their teeth. My fucking gums ached with the urge to latch onto her throat and leave my mark for the world to see and tie her in the most irrevocable and permanent way possible.

Valen held onto Corazon's elbow after stripping her fully naked and helped her into the shower so she wouldn't slip. Cohl stepped in immediately after. But he looked and was acting a little more in control as he grabbed a shower sponge and poured some of the girly smelling body wash Valen had ordered onto it, then began to gently wash her from neck to toes.

Gaining Valen's and Ford's attention, I jerked my head for them to follow me out of the room, letting Cohl tend to his omega. *Our* omega. Soon she would be *ours*.

Fuck me, I hoped it was soon. I wasn't sure how much longer I could control the animalistic need to brand myself into every corner of her being, to imbed myself in her so deeply she could never escape me.

Ford paced to the windows overlooking the front of the house, both hands pushing through his dark blond hair. Valen glanced back at the bathroom door that we'd left open a few times then finally dropped onto the couch, leaning forward to rest his elbows on his spread knees.

"Fuck," he muttered with a shake of his head. "She's going to be fucking pissed."

"She claimed him, too," Ford said with his back still to us. He glanced at Valen over his shoulder. "Honestly? I thought you'd be the first one she accepted with all your sappy shit and buying her presents."

"You mean treating her like an omega or treating her the way she deserves to be treated?" Valen shot back.

Ford held up both hands. "Wasn't a barb, asshole. Just saying, she seemed pretty fucking comfortable around you."

"Cohl was the first one she fooled around with. I think she was trying to seduce him into letting her leave and got caught in his fucked up web," I said.

Ford huffed a laugh, but there was no smile on his face. "She begged for our bites during her heat. That might have been her hind-brain, but somewhere inside of her, she knew we were...*are* her pack."

"You going to call the Alvarez fuckers?" Valen asked me.

"Planned on it. Want to make sure she's okay first. Then I'll let that whole group of assholes know they can no longer use her. She's ours. We'll take care of her and protect her. Fuck the Alvarez alphas. Fuck the Garcia alphas."

A wicked smile stretched on Ford's face. "You realize we're going to have trouble on our hands. They'll use it to start a war."

"Good. It'll be easier to take out the whole lot if they're in one place."

"Right. Because her fathers are brave enough to come up against us face to face," Ford said with a sardonic snort.

Of course they weren't fucking brave enough for that or they wouldn't have left Corazon behind when we'd crashed their little bonding party. They would have climbed from the back of their limos and fired back. They would have made sure no one laid a single finger on their omega daughter. For all they knew, we were there to kill her and the only people who'd bothered to protect her...

Well, fuck. The only people who'd been willing to risk their own lives to protect her were killed by us. She'd thrown that back in our faces a couple times. Would she ever forgive us? Could she forgive us?

Had we known how important she would become to us, had we known how utterly fundamental she would be to our pack, we would have done things a whole hell of a lot differently.

There was no way to change shit now, though. We just had to hope the five of us could move past that little fuck up. Or rather, *huge* fuck up.

Valen pushed to his feet and opened drawers, pulling clothes out and carrying them to the bathroom. "Seriously? Let her fucking rest, Cohl," Valen barked before stomping out of the room.

A soft moan met my ears a second later. That asshole was taking her in the shower after fucking her in the yard.

Honestly, though, I couldn't really be mad. I'd been inside her wet heat and knew how addictive she was. I would never get enough of her, enough of her scent, her sass, her full tits, or her tight cunt.

Within two weeks, the presence of the tiny, smart mouthed, stubborn as fuck omega had turned our world upside down. And now, I wanted nothing more than to hand her every part of me on a silver platter...

And finally admit that she belonged to me.

CHAPTER TWENTY-THREE

<u>Ford</u>

Since I'd been the one to make first contact with Pack Alvarez, I took it upon myself to call them again, only this time with the news that their precious daughter was no longer available to be used and abused at their whim. She was officially the omega of Pack Rivera and would forever be under our protection.

Bain sat in a chair across from my desk, both of us doing our best to ignore the hormones and pheromones floating in the air or the occasional moans echoing down the stairs.

Since Cohl had marked Corazon's shoulder on the back lawn, he'd repeatedly fucked her, as though he couldn't knot her deep enough or fill her cunt with enough of his cum.

Valen was up there with them, too. She'd begged him to stay. Or rather enticed him by grabbing the waistband of his pants when he laid her in bed and tried to move away. When Bain and I forced our feet to carry us away from the room, she was being spit roasted between the two alphas, swallowing Valen's cock while Cohl plunged into her core hard and fast over and over like a junkie chasing that first high.

"You have no right," one of Corazon's fathers said, his whiny ass voice grating along my last nerve.

Bain smirked and leaned forward, resting his forearms on the top of my desk. "We have every right. You were offering your daughter up like a lamb for slaughter. The way we see it, we saved her from a fate worse than death."

"You kidnapped our only daughter," another of her fathers said.

"If I'm not mistaken, she's *not* your only daughter. She's your only *omega* daughter," Bain said, raising his brows as he met my eyes.

We'd done plenty of research on the entire family before we'd bothered with our little mission. In fact, Cohl had been the one tasked with surveillance, of learning the routines of the entire family and their guards, of monitoring Corazon's outings. She was never without at least two armed guards any time she left the Alvarez property.

But even with so much security, no one had been any wiser to the fact someone had been not only trespassing and taking pictures of the property – and of Corazon – but had been following her around.

Fuck. No wonder Cohl had been absolutely obsessed with her from the beginning. He'd seen her dozens of times before the day we'd ambushed the convoy. He had followed her and tracked her every movement for long enough to develop fantasies around the sexy omega.

"We gave you options. You chose to ignore those options. And that little pack you chose to gift Corazon to told us outright they have too many choices to waste on one person. Great parenting, there, by the way," Ford said, smirking at me. He was baiting the alphas of Pack Alvarez.

Honestly, they definitely deserved more than a little baiting for blatantly disregarding their daughter's safety and happiness.

"Did you honestly believe we would willingly give up half our profits?"

"For your daughter? Yes. Actually, we did." I wouldn't say it aloud, not to any of these fuckers, but I would give up just about anything for

Corazon and realized I would have even before I felt her wrapped around my cock.

It was more than merely sexual with Corazon. She'd seen utter horror the first day we'd met her, had woken in a bonding gown covered in blood, yet she hadn't cowered from us. She'd been strong and defiant from the first moment. She was intelligent, strong, stubborn as a fucking mule, and so fucking beautiful. Any alpha would be lucky to have someone like her in their life.

"The fact you had the balls to not only fire on us and our omega, but to–"

"We weren't calling to negotiate. This was merely to let you know your daughter – whom you were supposed to protect by the way – is officially claimed, bonded, and a member of Pack Rivera."

"You realize we will have to see this as an attack on our family," one of the alphas said, calmer than the first two.

"You can view it as you please. But we plan to treat Corazon the way she should be, treat her better than that piece of shit pack you'd chosen for her ever could."

"And you think she'll accept you after what you did?"

"She already has. She willingly asked for and accepted a bite from us." Technically, only from one of us. But that wasn't a piece of information I planned to share. "From here out, we will take control of the region's imports and exports."

"Or what? You'll send Corazon to us in pieces?" one of her fathers said. I supposed we should have bothered learning their names, but… nah. None of us gave two shits about the old codgers. We'd focused most of our attention on Pack Garcia being as they were next in line after bonding with Corazon.

Not to mention the old fuckers meant literally nothing to us other than the fact one of them fathered such an amazing woman.

A growl rumbled from Bain and he glared at the phone as though he could see the fuckers through the plastic.

"The fact your mind immediately went to hurting your daughter tells me all I need to know about you. As far as we're concerned, you're nothing in this game. We will take over, even if we have to execute every single one of you," I said, raising a brow at Bain. His growl still rumbled from his chest.

"You arrogant son of a–"

"We're done here. If anyone so much as looks at Corazon the wrong way, we will end their life. If you attempt to send someone for her, we will mow down your entire line, including the rest of your offspring."

And then I hung up as one of the alphas sputtered and cursed at me.

"That went well," I said with a sardonic chuckle.

"Fucking assholes," Bain grumbled. At least his growl had died off. "You know it's not over."

"Fuck no. I expect threats and a few attacks. But for now, they don't know about this house. We need to keep a low profile, or at least keep her under wraps for a bit."

"That'll piss her off," Bain said.

"More than the fact I just informed her fathers that she belongs to us now?" I said with a smirk.

While she did, indeed, belong to us, it was more that she belonged *with* us. We weren't of the mentality of ownership like her fathers or even the pack her family had tried to sell her to.

A fresh wave of her perfume floated through the air. "How is she still...could she still be in heat?" I asked, looking toward the door as though I could see upstairs and to where Valen and Cohl were no doubt tending to our girl.

"Nah. That broke. I think it's the bond."

The four of us knew barely the basics when it came to omegas. While we'd entertained the possibility of bringing one into the pack early on, those plans had gone up into flames as our lives grew more dangerous and we accrued more enemies.

We definitely needed to do more research to figure out what Corazon needed other than soft and pretty shit. And we definitely needed to up the security now that we'd let her family pack know she would be staying with us permanently.

And then there was the fun conversation that would be coming with Corazon, the one where we let her know about our talk with her fathers and how she was officially Corazon Rivera of Pack Rivera. From what I'd learned about the omega, she was going to fight us on that every step of the way, regardless of the mark on her shoulder or the bond that had been blown wide open between her and Cohl.

Of all fucking people, it had been the most unhinged alpha she'd allowed in, the alpha she'd chosen to tie herself to. I supposed I shouldn't have felt jealous, being as that meant she was ours. But fuck me…I wanted to be her first alpha. I wanted to feel her flesh give way under my teeth. I wanted to feel that thread in my chest tying us together so I could feel her with me every moment of the day, so I could feel her emotions.

"We need a grocery run," Bain said.

"I'm not fucking leaving. Not until whatever…that is," I said, waving my hand toward the ceiling, "is over. I don't exactly trust Cohl not to hurt her."

"He wouldn't fucking hurt her," Bain said.

I frowned at him. "Did you not see how hard he took her to the ground?"

"Did you not smell her pussy practically weeping for joy when he'd chased her and tackled her? She liked that shit."

Which could bode very well for me and Bain. We'd both kept ourselves in check thus far. But the two of us could be a little rough in the bedroom, especially when we were enjoying someone together.

That was something else we would have to broach with our omega at a later date. There was a whole hell of a lot that we all needed to figure out in the meantime.

"Send one of the betas with a list. Maybe ask Corazon if there's anything she needs. After she's done ravaging Cohl," Bain said.

I huffed a laugh. I was pretty sure it was the other way around and the alpha was ravaging our omega. Or maybe they were both giving as much as taking pleasure from each other. And Valen.

Fuck. The thicker the pheromones grew in the house, the harder it was to talk my dick down. It was like a fucking divining rod, guiding me to the woman I could lose myself in for days and forget the rest of the world existed.

Bain leaned back in his chair and reached down to adjust the bulge in his pants. Yeah. The pack lead was feeling the same fucking desperation I was. But, as much as I wanted to sprint up the stairs, shove the other two out of the way, and bury my cock in every single one of Corazon's holes, there was shit that needed to be done first. I could have always left it all up to Bain, but I'd been his right-hand man since the day we'd formed this pack and had all taken his surname as our own.

After, though. The moment I had a single spare moment, I planned to drag her under me and plow into her tiny cunt until neither of us could move for the rest of the day. Or the week.

CHAPTER TWENTY-FOUR

<u>Corazon</u>

My lashes fluttered as I struggled to open my eyes, blinking against the sun streaking in through the open curtains and beaming straight into my damn pupils. Every inch of my body was sore…but in a good way.

The past…however many hours since Bain had taken me on the kitchen table, then Cohl had taken me and marked me in the yard, had been a blur of fucking and coming. Bain and Ford hadn't made an appearance until after Cohl, Valen, and I finally separated and headed for the bathroom for a long soak to ease our sore muscles and joints.

This wasn't a heat cycle. I didn't have the cramps or fever that came with it. But I sure as hell felt as insatiable as I did during that time. Since the moment Cohl's teeth had latched onto my shoulder, it felt as though I couldn't be close enough to him, even when he was buried knot deep inside me. If I could have opened his chest and burrowed my way inside, I would have.

Now, though, I was in the gigantic bed in my designated room completely alone. The room still smelled heavily of the pack mixed with my perfume. And the sheets were…well, sticky. None of us had bothered changing them even after I'd soaked them with my slick and the three of us had come over and over again.

Rolling so I could throw my legs over the side, I smiled when I noted there was no tray of food waiting on the coffee table and the bedroom door was cracked open. They'd made sure I had privacy but wanted me to know I was no longer a prisoner to the omega quarters.

My quarters.

My toes curled into the plush rug beside my bed as I pushed to my feet. I took a second to stretch, humming with pleasure as bones cracked and popped. The skin at my shoulder burned a little and I touched my fingertips to it, a smile ghosting my lips as I shuffled into the bathroom to relieve my full bladder.

Teeth and hair brushed, I stepped back into my bedroom, the smile still tugging at the corners of my lips, and pulled a fresh pair of panties, sweats, and a t-shirt from the drawer, then pulled a hoodie over top to keep away the chill. The alphas tended to keep a fire burning in the fireplace in this room, but it had long since gone out, and I swore these alphas were part penguins with how chilly they tended to keep the house.

Spring was around the corner and a part of me was so ready for flowers and warmer weather and finally taking a swim in the pool I'd spotted yesterday when I'd distracted Cohl from beating the piss out of his guards by giving him a little of what he obviously needed – a chase.

I hadn't for a second thought that would have ended up in me giving myself freely to Cohl, but it had felt right, the entire moment had felt right, the bond that blossomed to life in my chest felt…it felt like everything I'd ever wanted, ever needed.

The scents of the pack clung to every surface of my quarters, even after they'd all left the room. Didn't hurt that the couch and bed had both been used for our…connection. I couldn't get enough of Cohl after he'd tied me to him, as though I was feeling both his and my arousal.

Where Cohl was primal and rough, Valen was sweet and gentle, kissing and stroking me, using my mouth and throat while Cohl was determined to fill my pussy and ass with his cum as often as possible.

There was a part of me that wondered whether or not I should have been worried about the fact that not only was I not on birth control – because my fathers and Pack Garcia's fathers were determined I get knocked up as soon as possible – but we hadn't used a single form of protection any time I'd slept with any of the alphas. While it would be unusual for me to get pregnant outside of my cycle, all four alphas had filled me to the brim while we'd been locked in the nest.

Those thoughts and fears were for another day. I was still riding the high of Cohl's bond. Or maybe I was simply feeling his high energy.

I had resisted my omega's urges to claim this pack, had refused to acknowledge the fact they were my scent matches, that the moment I'd woken in this room and caught their scents a sense of rightness had swept over me.

But now…today was the first time I'd woken with something in my heart other than dread.

Of course, I'd only bonded with Cohl. And there were four alphas in this pack. Bain had tried his damnedest since the first week to make me his, and there was still that part of me that wanted to make him work harder for it. After all, he'd hurt my feelings more than once.

I was damned near skipping down the hall to join the pack – *my* pack – for breakfast.

A beta stood at the top of the stairs, clad all in black as I'd noted all the guards wore. His eyes found me, he nodded, then looked away. It almost felt like a dismissal, but was more than likely due to what had happened yesterday when the two alphas had come into the house while Bain and I had been…

My cheeks burned at the memory. Who had I become? I had let that alpha fuck me on the kitchen table where anyone could see. How long had the other three watched before attacking their employees?

And had any of the guards seen what was happening through the glass of the French doors?

Male voices rumbled through the house as I descended the stairs, but a new scent tickled my senses. It reminded me of Bain, but had a different edge to it, something spicier.

My feet slowed as the words started to make their way to my ears.

"The Garcia fuckers upped the ante," a male said. I didn't recognize his voice, but I'd only seen a couple guards inside the house since I'd been brought here.

"They can fuck all the way off," Cohl said. "She's mine."

They were talking about me. Of course they were. Which meant the Garcia pack was using my bond with Pack Rivera as an excuse to start a war.

Could this pack possibly hold their own against both my family's pack and the Garcias? One on one, absolutely. My fathers never got their hands dirty. The most I'd ever seen from them was executing someone at gunpoint. Not once had I ever seen them actually go toe to toe with an enemy. They would simply send their enforcers to take out any competition.

Would they send people after my pack? Would Garcia have men out hunting for my pack?

And would I simply be locked in this house until further notice? Because I had a feeling none of the alphas would let me step into public as long as there was a possible threat to me. They wouldn't care whether someone threatened their lives, but I'd learned enough about them in the weeks we'd spent together to know they would hurt anyone they deemed as a threat to me...even their own fucking guards.

My socked feet barely whispered against the hardwood floor as I snuck closer. Okay, yeah, maybe eavesdropping on my pack wasn't cool, but I knew they would either stop talking the moment they spotted me or would go all possessive alpha again with their omega in the room.

"They're claiming you forced a bond on her. Trying to rally others behind them." That same guy from minutes ago.

"We didn't force shit," Cohl said.

"You kind of did when you kidnapped her," the guy said, humor in his voice.

"Everything else has been her choice," Bain said.

"You've given her the choice to leave?"

Silence.

"Fuck. She smells good."

Growls trickled down the hall then cut off abruptly about two seconds before Valen appeared around the corner, one brow raised at me.

"I wasn't technically eavesdropping," I said, stepping into his side when he raised an arm. His warmth wrapped around me, his scent calming my frayed nerves. "Are you guys going to freak out if I come in here?" I asked my alphas as I rounded the corner into the living room.

The newcomer snorted. There were actually three new men sitting on a couch, watching me closely as I was led to where Cohl was practically vibrating through the bond.

He tugged me down beside him, pulling me away from Valen a little roughly until I was tucked against his side.

"Share, asshole," Valen muttered.

"Mine," Cohl growled back.

Had anyone said those kinds of things a few weeks ago, I might have started throwing shit or cursing them out. But being as I could feel Cohl in my heart, he wasn't saying it as a sense of ownership, but rather a warning for the three alphas staring at me.

As I studied them, I realized one of them held a strong resemblance to Bain.

Turning to the pack lead, I raised my brows.

"Corazon, this is my brother Enzo," he pointed to the man on the far left with the same coal black hair but gunmetal gray eyes instead of the icy blue like Bain. "Cyrus." The man in the middle jerked his chin up in a greeting. "And the fucker on the end is Ax." A highly attractive man with dark blonde wavy hair that brushed his shoulders smirked and winked at me.

Ballsy. And for some reason, the action didn't make me uncomfortable, but kind of made me like him, like he was naturally a shit disturber.

"Nice to meet you, omega," Enzo said with a nod.

Then he turned his attention back to Bain and the others. It felt far too much as though I was being dismissed, as though I wasn't a part of the conversation.

Being as the entire conversation was all about me, no way would I let them shut me out.

"Corazon," I corrected him.

A smirk tugged up one corner of his lips, but it wasn't nearly as knee shaking as when Bain gave me the same look.

"Stop flirting with my omega," Cohl growled out.

Enzo chuckled softly and shook his head.

"So what's going on?" I asked, turning to look into my official alpha's face – who was steadily glaring at Enzo – before looking to each of my pack then the newcomers.

Cohl's arm tightened around me until I squirmed. "Too tight," I whispered, nuzzling my cheek against his neck to both scent mark him and grab a little of his essence.

A rusty purr rattled from his chest, and he returned the move, nuzzling his cheek against me.

My eyes met Enzo's in time to see him roll his and shake his head at his buddies who sat beside him.

"Your family and betrothed are none too happy about Ford's declaration of ownership," Enzo said.

"Excuse me?"

I jerked away from Cohl and was met with a displeased growl but ignored it as anger bubbled up in my chest.

"What the fuck is going on?" I asked, turning to glare at Ford.

"That's now exactly what happened." Ford turned his own glare on Bain's brother. "I contacted your family to let them know you were no longer at their disposal, that you'd been claimed and had a pack. And apparently, they promptly called Pack Garcia. They're treating it as a challenge for power."

"I don't have a fucking owner," I said, clinging to Enzo's choice of words.

"That's not what he meant," Valen said, shooting a glare at Enzo before glancing back down at me.

He attempted to wrap an arm around my shoulders, to pull me to his side, but I shrugged away like I had with Cohl.

"How else would you describe it?" Enzo asked. "You licked her, you claimed her." His broad shoulders shrugged up and that infuriating smirk stayed in place, his eyes locked on mine.

And a growl rumbled from my own chest, though not nearly as intimidating as my alphas'.

"Bain's brother or not, you're about to wear out your fucking welcome," Ford warned.

"We're here to give you a heads up. Word is making its way down the line and there are a lot of people chomping at the bit to get their hands on your business. Packs Alvarez and Garcia are making it sound like not only did you kidnap the omega and force a bond on her against her will, but you've become weak. The two packs won't be the only ones looking to issue a challenge," the one Bain introduced as Cyrus said, leaning forward with his elbows on his knees. Unlike Enzo and Ax, he barely ghosted glances in my direction, whether from apathy or respect, I didn't know.

"And where do you stand?" Ford asked, glancing at Bain briefly before returning his attention to the pack sitting across from us.

"We stand with you. And not because you're this fucker's brother. We'd have nothing if it weren't for you four assholes," Ax said.

My brows rose up my forehead. What did that mean? Were these guys into criminal activities, too? Had they somehow become partners with my pack? And since when did I so easily accept the fact that I was claimed and packed with a group of alphas I'd known for less than a month?

"We appreciate the heads up. Keep your ears to the ground and let us know if they plan an attack on our home," Bain said.

"I would keep the omega close. Wouldn't want to see her get hurt in some crossfire or snatched by your competition."

"My fucking name is Corazon," I growled out at Enzo.

His lips quirked at the corners and something that looked like respect flashed through his gunmetal gray eyes before they returned to the almost empty look. Now, he was back to looking like a soulless shell of a human being as he returned his attention to his brother.

Which of them was older? And how exactly had my pack helped them? I shouldn't have been curious about other alphas, especially since the scents of my alphas had all turned a little burned since the moment I'd stepped into the room, but being as Enzo was kind of my brother-in-law...

Then again, Bain wasn't technically my alpha. Not yet. I'd only allowed Cohl to mark me.

As though he could hear my train of thoughts, Bain looked in my direction, something dark and intense in the crystalline, icy blue of his eyes. They were like looking into the eyes of a wolf, just as haunting and deadly.

"I wasn't forced," I blurted out, finally turning to look back at Enzo.

"But you *were taken* by force," he said, one brow cocked as though waiting for me to challenge his words.

Okay, yeah. I was taken by force. I was, by all terms, kidnapped. But the rest...I had chosen this pack before I was even aware of it. I had welcomed Bain into my bed. More like I had thrown myself at him that night he'd crashed through my bedroom door, ripping it from its hinges. I had allowed them to help me through my heat, fucking every one of them over and over. I let them take care of me in a way no one had in my life.

I had claimed Cohl and exposed my neck in nothing short of submission, giving him full permission to mark me as his, to bring me into the pack and complete our bond.

Our beginning had been...rocky, to say the least. But beginnings weren't always pretty. Like in just about any fairy tale my nanny had read to me as a child, we had started with a butt load of challenges to hurdle.

It might take me a bit longer to fully trust Bain and Ford, to allow them as deeply into my heart as I had allowed Cohl and even Valen, but my omega was preening over the fact I was no longer Corazon Alvarez.

I was Corazon Rivera. Omega of Pack Rivera.

If only that title didn't come with so many fucking warning labels.

CHAPTER TWENTY-FIVE

Bain

Creaks and pops sounded as I rolled my neck. Anxiety burned through my veins, mixing with anger.

We'd had to leave our omega at home to be watched over by our guards to deal with this latest cluster fuck. The cluster fuck actually had a name – Garcia.

"How many dead?" Ford asked as he walked through the warehouse, his eyes taking in the puddles where bodies once laid, the dozens upon dozens of spent shells, and the missing inventory.

"Twelve. Seven of ours," one of our guards reported.

My nostrils flared on the inhale.

Pack Garcia hadn't exactly left a calling card or told us they'd stolen some of our inventory while killing seven of our fucking men, but this particular territory was one we had been fighting tooth and nail to take away from those cock suckers.

Valen walked through the remaining shipping containers, his head slowly wagging side to side. Cohl looked like he was ready to bolt from the metal sided warehouse, though I wasn't sure whether it was to chase down the perpetrators or rush back to our omega.

It had been four days since Cohl had sunk his teeth into her shoulder and officially tied her to our pack, three days since my brother and his pack had given us a heads up that word was already trickling down the vine about possible attacks on us.

Enzo and his pack hadn't had any specifics, but we were looking at the first of what I assumed would be many attacks on our business.

Fuck! Seven of our men were dead. I might not have been close to most of them, but we only hired those we trusted, those who were loyal to our pack and to our enterprise. They deserved better than being slaughtered by a bunch of trust fund babies.

And that was the only way I could see Pack Garcia. We had built everything we had from the ground up while the assholes Corazon had been practically sold to were merely working for their fathers, growing their families' business.

At least Corazon's fathers were self-made. That was literally the only thing I could possibly respect them for, because they sure as hell hadn't shown an ounce of anything that resembled loyalty or nobility. Especially after treating their daughter like livestock and then running away when there was a threat.

"I want to go back," Cohl said as he paced the length of the warehouse like a caged animal.

"Calm the fuck down. We have to finish up here," Ford said before refocusing on the guard he was speaking to.

"She's back there alone," Cohl said. "They could attack the house and take her."

"She's heavily guarded and my brother and his pack are hanging out until we get back," I said.

A growl echoed throughout the warehouse.

Cohl had become even more unhinged since he'd marked Corazon, attacking any unbonded alpha who happened to come anywhere near her. It had become a feat for the remaining three of us to so much as hold her without him getting possessive and trying to pull her from our arms.

"I want this shit secured. I want names. I want blood," Ford said as he stormed by to where I stood.

"You know who the fuck this was," Valen said, his hands on his hips as a muscle jumped in his cheek.

He hadn't marked Corazon but had stayed as glued to her side as Cohl since that day. The three of them had spent hours locked away in the omega quarters until they'd finally collapsed from exhaustion. A few hours later, Ford and I had made our way into the room and climbed into the pack bed, though we hadn't been able to actually cuddle against her since Valen and Cohl had their bodies wrapped around hers like they were her very own cocoon.

I glared at Valen a few minutes, swallowing back the growl that swelled in my chest. The last thing we needed to do was turn on each other. Yeah. I knew damn well who'd done this. They'd made sure anyone who would listen knew they planned to attack. We'd doubled the guards at each warehouse as well as around our own property.

Yet that hadn't stopped them from stealing half our shit and killing *seven of our fucking men.*

When my phone chirped with an incoming text, my packmates all froze and turned toward me.

Your omega is getting on my nerves.

FUCKING ENZO.

What's going on?

She won't stop pacing the floors. You almost done?

. . .

A SMIRK KICKED up one side of my mouth and I huffed a laugh. She was unsteady without her pack there. She would feel every moment of Cohl's emotions through their bond.

"What's going on? She okay?" Valen asked. He didn't need to say Corazon's name. She'd been on all our minds since the moment we'd stepped out of the house and into the vehicle. It was damned near obsession at this point, and we needed to get our shit together if we were going to be able to focus on our job and hunt down every single actor in this attack.

And then we'd take out the piss ants that not only hadn't bothered to fight for Corazon but had dared come after my empire.

"Enzo said she's climbing the walls," I said with another huff of laughter.

"We done? I want to go back," Cohl said as he continued to pace.

Another chuckle rattled forth as I wondered if the two were mimicking each other as they slowly became unraveled with the distance.

"We got it, boss," Keller, one of our most trusted guards, said. We should have left him behind to watch over Corazon, but I needed his clear head. And he was one of the alphas who'd sent our omega into heat that day. Cohl refused to allow him anywhere near her or even into the house. Part of me wondered if my packmate feared Corazon might have been attracted to him.

Cohl didn't bother waiting for me to agree or disagree with Keller, just turned on his heel and practically sprinted toward our SUV.

Would it be this bad when Corazon finally allowed me to leave my mark on her?

Who the fuck was I kidding? I might not have been as outwardly rattled as Cohl from our short time away from our omega, but she'd been on my mind nonstop. I feared for her safety, and I wanted to draw her scent deep into my lungs and feel her soft, curvy body pressed against mine. That is if I could pull her away from Cohl long enough.

"Idiot," Ford muttered, following Cohl. He could grumble all he wanted, but he wasn't exactly taking his time returning to the SUV where Cohl was already behind the wheel with the engine running.

Valen was beside me as we made our way to the vehicle, climbing in beside Ford while I took the passenger seat. I would have rather someone else drove because I already knew the redheaded alpha was going to drive like a bat out of hell to get back to the house and to our omega.

It took less than twenty minutes and way too many near misses before we were pulling into the garage beside our individual cars, trucks, and motorcycles parked in the extended space.

"At least turn off the fucking…idiot," I yelled as Cohl shoved open his door and darted for the entrance, the engine still rumbling and the key fob sitting on the console.

Pushing the button, I turned off the vehicle, grabbed the keys, and shoved from my own side. Yeah, I would have loved to rush inside, sweep Corazon into my arms, and leave my scent on every inch of her soft skin. But not only was my brother inside, I had some calls to make, some shit to put in order before I could call it a night.

Lily of the Valley smacked me in the face and hardened my dick the second I stepped through the door into the mud room that would lead into the kitchen. I could hear her sweet voice, could hear her giggles and half-hearted demands that Cohl put her down.

Enzo, Ax, and Cyrus sat outside on the balcony, the door wide open and the cool air filling the house.

"Why the hell did you leave the door open?" I growled out after grabbing a beer and joining them at the table.

"Couldn't hear if she needed us if it was closed," Enzo said with a shrug.

"Or you could have just kept your ass inside."

Ax shook his head. "Fuck no. Between her whining, pacing, and perfuming, I was about to lose my shit." His brow cocked and he jabbed a finger in my direction when a growl erupted from my chest. "And that right there is exactly why we're out here."

I cut the rumbling off and took a long pull from my beer. Ford stepped outside and pulled the door closed.

"Any issues?" he asked, his eyes bouncing from my brother to each of his pack, to me, then back again.

"Other than the fact your omega is either going into heat or knocked up?" Enzo said nonchalantly.

And my fucking heart stopped.

"What did you just say?" It felt like I was forcing the words through a roll of barbed wire stuck in my throat.

"There's no way she's pregnant," Ford said, leaning against the wall beside the door and crossing his arms over his chest.

"I can smell the five of you all over the house. Can't tell me you four haven't been knot deep in her–"

"You trying to get yourself killed?" Cyrus muttered, cutting my brother off before he could be his usual crass self and get a face full of my fucking fist.

"How would we even know if she was pregnant? It's only been a few weeks. Would her body even register the change that soon?" I asked, looking up to Ford as though he might have the answers.

But he looked as shell shocked as I felt.

"Fuck if I know. All I know is the way she was acting. She barely looked in our direction other than to ask whether we'd heard from you, so she wasn't perfuming for us," Cyrus said.

"It's too soon for another heat," Ford said. Or more like whispered. The words sounded strangled.

"Not necessarily. Stress and change can affect an omega in a shit load of ways, including either making her skip her heat or even go earlier than normal. And I would say being kidnapped on her bonding day, held captive by her family's enemies, then discovering that same enemy happened to be her pack is the definition of a stressor and change," Enzo said.

Always the asshole.

Ford and I stared at each other. He had to be thinking the same thing I was – someone needed to go get her a test. Or we could always call in a private doctor to draw her blood.

"You need us anymore or you good?" Enzo said, pushing to his feet before I answered.

"Unless you want to hang out with your big brother..."

He snorted a sound of dismissal, clapped me hard on the shoulder as he passed, and led his pack through the house to where their own SUV waited in the driveway.

"If she's pregnant..." Ford started, but let his thoughts trail off.

If she was pregnant, would she be pissed or happy? Would *we* be happy? It was yet another risk, something else our enemy could use to get to us, to punish us. Any child we had with Corazon could end up born with a bull's eye permanently tattooed on their back simply because of his or her parents.

"Could she simply have missed us?" I asked, turning and looking through the French door as if I could see through the walls to wherever Corazon was.

"She missed Cohl." Ford scowled as he took the seat across from me that Enzo had vacated. "We need to mark her. Bond her to us, too."

My head nodded up and down several times as I tried to work through the latest cluster fuck that we might have in our laps. Because dealing with dead guards and theft from an enemy pack wasn't enough. Why not just throw in a possible pregnancy with our new omega who'd yet to accept the bond from three of her alphas.

Thanks, Universe.

CHAPTER TWENTY-SIX

<u>Corazon</u>

Something was definitely up. Since the moment my alphas had returned home, someone had been in my line of sight at all times. Although not always a member of the pack. They'd been leaving a lot lately, always telling me not to worry when they left for the night.

And as much as it pissed me off, I *did* worry.

I hadn't wanted this. I hadn't wanted an alpha, hadn't wanted a pack. And I sure as hell hadn't wanted to feel anything for the alphas who'd ambushed the motorcade the day of my bonding ceremony.

I hated four men had been killed that day, would always feel their deaths weighing on my conscience since they'd died protecting me, but my life had been changed to the point I barely recognized it or myself anymore.

I didn't have to put on a front with them, didn't have to behave, as my fathers used to say. I swore it turned Bain on when I cursed him out as much as letting Cohl chase me turned him on. It was like each of us had discovered our own little games to play.

Yet I still only wore one of their marks. I was proud to carry the name Rivera, but I wasn't sure I was completely ready to hand myself over fully to Bain and Ford just yet. After the rocky beginning, part of me wanted to make them work for it, to grovel and beg, to walk over hot coals to show me they would never break my heart again.

But Valen...he hadn't so much as brought up the fact he hadn't yet sank his teeth into my skin yet. And I was this close to begging for his mark. I loved that I could feel Cohl in my heart every time we were apart. I could feel his emotions and knew he was safe. I couldn't feel the others and that was part of what scared the shit out of me.

Yet another fact that pissed me off. I didn't want to have to worry every single time a member of my pack left that it might be the last time I saw them. At least if I'd been bonded to Pack Garcia, it would have been nothing more than my duty. There would have been no love involved. So, if one of them happened to be killed...

What kind of person thought so little of a human life being lost? Oh. Right. The kind of woman who was raised by cutthroat, heartless, violent alphas who treated their own omega as though she was merely a roommate or a warm body to be used for their own pleasure, especially after my mother had passed the age of childbearing years.

My mom's emotionless eyes passed through my mind. I favored her the most. My fathers all had the same dark hair and dark eyes. Any of them could have fathered me. But I wasn't close to a single one of my parents.

But this pack...they were treating me like their very own princess. It had started with Valen buying anything and everything he thought I might need or want. None of them were comfortable with me leaving the house just yet, so they always made sure to have my favorite snacks on hand and hung out with me every free moment they had whether we watched movies, binged TV shows, or played games.

Although, our favorite activity tended to happen when we were all naked.

Since my heat, my body felt as though it was constantly primed. I constantly wanted one of them touching me, one of them filling me until I was a boneless puddle of slick, sweat, and release. If I hadn't already gone through my cycle, I would have wondered if I was in preheat with as often as I felt the need to be with one – or preferably all – of my alphas.

At the moment, I was curled up on the couch with a blanket draped over my legs, staring at the movie playing without actually seeing it.

No one would tell me what the hell was going on or why they came home so angry every time. Or why Bain's brother and his pack tended to hang out any time my pack left. All four of my alphas had declared they trusted their guards to not only keep their hands to themselves, but to protect me. So why bring in three more men?

Not like I could ask Enzo, Ax, or Cyrus. Every time I stepped into a room they occupied, they would all three lunge to their feet and leave. The first time, I'd raised my arms and sniffed at my armpits then my hair thinking maybe I stunk. All I'd smelled was my body wash and my alphas.

Valen finally admitted they were concerned Bain or Cohl would beat their asses simply for being in the same room with me. Which was stupid. I didn't want Enzo. I didn't want any of that pack. The first time I'd felt such a need to be near an alpha as often as possible was with the members of Pack Rivera.

Yep. That would probably piss me off for a while. The rational part of me knew I should hate them. But my heart and my omega craved them more than my next breath. I hadn't and wouldn't say anything aloud, but I was starting to fall hard for both Cohl and Valen. They were so opposite in personalities but called to every part of me in a way I hadn't known was possible.

"I'm bored!" I yelled, tilting my head back to make sure the sound would carry throughout the house and to the kitchen where I could hear Enzo and his buddies chatting.

"Find something to do," Enzo called back, amusement evident in his tone.

Head still thrown back, I stared up at the ceiling for a few minutes before tossing the blanket away and pushing to my feet. And if the three stooges thought they'd run to another room the second I stepped in, I would just follow them. I was not only bored, but lonely. And freaking worried about my pack. I could feel Cohl, but it almost felt as though he was muting the bond between us, like there was something he was trying to keep me from sensing.

Snatching the blanket from the couch, I wrapped it around my shoulders and stomped into the kitchen. The moment they started to rise from their seats, I held out both hands.

"Keep your asses in the chair or I'll go on a full omega freak out," I threatened.

All three froze, their asses a few inches from their chairs. Enzo raised one brow at me, his lips twitching as he tried to hold back a smile.

"What does a full omega freak out entail?"

"I don't know. But I'll figure something out."

"You're a bonded omega. We're unbonded alphas. Not trying to start a war with my brother and his pack," Enzo said. But he did lower back into his seat and wrap his hand around a beer bottle resting on the table in front of him.

"I have no intention of sitting on your lap. As long as I'm not covered in your scent, it'll be fine. I'm bored and worried. Keep me occupied."

Cyrus raised both brows and looked to Enzo. I'd gathered that he was their pack lead. Must have run in the family being as both brothers ended up leading their own packs as adults.

"How are we supposed to keep you occupied?" Cyrus asked.

"Ever hear of conversing? Tell me about yourselves. Or tell me what Bain was like as a kid. Was he always an overbearing, possessive ass?"

Enzo barked out a laugh. "Actually, he's calmed down since he met you."

"Bullshit," I huffed out around a chuckle.

"Yep. He almost seems normal."

"Nothing about any of you is normal," Ax said against the mouth of his beer, a grin stretching on his face. "All four of them are assholes," he said to me.

"How come you three don't have an omega? Or a beta?"

"We asking personal shit now?" Enzo asked. He pointed his bottle at me. "How about we go question for question?"

My shoulders shrugged up. "I've got nothing to hide. Answer mine and I'll answer yours."

"Ooooh. Kind of like show me yours and I'll show you mine?" Enzo teased.

"You really are trying to get your throat slit, aren't you?" Ax said with a wide grin and a shake of his head.

"We haven't found anyone we're interested in adding into the mix," Cyrus said with a roll of his eyes.

"What do you guys do for a living? Do you work for Enzo and the pack?"

"Uh uh. That's two questions. You have to answer one for us, first," Enzo teased.

"Fine. Ask." I hugged the blanket tighter around my shoulders and drew my feet up onto the chair until I could cross them beneath me.

"How come you haven't let my brother mark you yet?" Enzo asked.

Okay. He really meant it when he said we were asking personal questions.

"I...don't know. He hurt my feelings early on. No. That's not the right way to say it. He broke my heart and crushed my spirit. I guess.... I guess I'm waiting to make sure he won't verbally lash out at me every time I disappoint him or piss him off."

Enzo nodded. "Sounds legit. He's good at spouting off shit without thinking. Cutting with words. Especially since he'd never raise a hand to you or any woman. What did you do that made him–"

"Seriously?" I blurted out, cutting him off. "What makes you think I did anything? I acted out when they brought me here, but do you blame me? I didn't know them. All I knew was they'd attacked us, and I'd woken up in a house full of strangers. Alphas at that." He'd actually hurt my feelings again after that, but there was no need to bring up every single moment of our rocky pack life. "Your turn to answer."

"We own a couple clubs. Run them together. And he strips," Enzo said, nodding his head toward Ax.

"I don't strip, asshole."

"Wait." I held up my hands and leaned forward, a grin stretching across my face. "You strip? Like the whole Magic Mike, wearing a thong kind of thing?"

Ax pointed a finger in my direction, but his own smile mirrored mine. "First of all, how dare you. Magic Mike wishes he was as hot as me. And second, I absolutely do not wear a thong. I dance, not strip."

"You accept singles while you're gyrating your hips for horny people. You give private dances in the back. How is that any different than being a stripper?" Cyrus asked. All three were smiling now.

"Because I don't wear a thong," Ax said with a shrug before taking a drink from his beer.

These three were a trip. And it was obvious they were as close as brothers. Or…

"Are you three *mates*? Or just pack mates?"

"Are you asking if we fuck?" Enzo asked, leaning forward on his forearms.

My face flushed hot and my panties grew damp at the way he was leering at me.

Ax answered with another shake of his head. "Seriously, dude. Are you flirting with your sister-in-law?"

"Nah. Just like watching the omega squirm."

"The omega's name is Corazon," I said with an eye roll. I knew damn well Enzo knew my name.

But it wasn't lost on me that none of the three alphas had answered my question about whether or not they were simply pack-mates or romantically involved.

Cyrus smirked as he pushed his shoulder length hair away from his face and wrapped an elastic around it.

Eventually, the three alphas relaxed, and we fell into a fairly easy conversation without them darting into another room and avoiding me at every turn.

I decided to take a chance and see if I couldn't get them talking just a little more.

"I know you three know what's going on. Other than the usual with my family and Pack Garcia. Why have the guys been disappearing so often lately? They won't tell me shit."

All three alphas just looked at me, their faces devoid of a single hint of emotion.

"Seriously? Nothing?"

"If your alphas want you to know, they'll tell you," Enzo said before finishing his beer and pushing to his feet to grab another from the fridge.

I snatched the new bottle from his hand before he could sit, forcing him to get another.

With a smirk, I tipped it back and took a long pull, holding Enzo's eye contact until he shook his head and retrieved a new one.

"They haven't told you because it's nothing for an omega to worry about," Ax said.

Pointing the bottle at Ax, I shook my head. "See, that is the kind of thing that pisses me off. My designation means absolutely nothing when it comes to whether or not I'm told something that could be important. You know, like whether my pack is safe."

"*Are* they your pack?" Enzo asked with both brows raised.

"What the hell is that supposed to mean?" I set my beer on the table and leaned back in the chair, tugging the blanket tighter around me.

He shrugged. "You carry one mark. You've been here, what, over a month? Sounds to me like you have an alpha, not a pack."

"You're kind of a judgmental prick. Anyone ever tell you that?"

"All the time," Ax said with a chuckle.

"They're my pack. Period."

"And if they were to open the door and tell you you're free to return to your family? Would you stay?" Enzo asked.

"Yes," I blurted out then blinked.

Holy shit. Yes, I would. Enzo was right – I only carried the mark of one of my alphas. And, yes, I'd wanted nothing more than to leave this place and return to the life I knew before. But as time passed, I grew to realize that while Bain's words were cruel and meant to hurt my feelings – since I'd apparently hurt *his* delicate feelings – they weren't exactly a lie.

My fathers had tried to sell me off to a pack I hardly knew to expand their power, their empire. And when I was in danger, when I could have easily been killed, they hadn't hesitated to run away. They refused to acquiesce to my pack's demands in order to get me back home.

For the first time in my life, I'd found someone who cared about me, alphas who wanted nothing more than my happiness, to protect me. Hell, I knew they weren't exactly comfortable with unbonded alphas near me, yet Bain made sure his brother was here any time they had to leave as an extra layer of protection.

Enzo sat back in his chair and crossed his thick arms over his chest, a smirk pulling his lips until a wide grin stretched across his face.

His mouth opened but snapped shut at the sound of the garage door rumbling up. My pack was home.

Shoving to my feet, I let the blanket drop to the ground as I hurried to the mudroom to wait for their appearance. Yep. I'd become one of those needy omegas. But I never felt truly settled until all four of them were home and I knew without a doubt they were safe and in one piece.

My socked feet slid across the tiled floor as my four alphas stepped inside...covered in blood.

"What the hell happened?" I shrieked, grabbing Valen's face in both hands as he stepped through first.

His fingers wrapped around my wrists and pulled my hands away. "Let us clean up first."

"Are you hurt?" My eyes roamed over every single one of them. Their clothing was torn, blood was splattered across nearly every inch of their exposed skin, and there was bruising in various places.

"We're fine. Give us a second. I don't want you covered in this shit," Valen said, guiding me to the table with a hand on the small of my back.

He pulled the chair out as though he expected me to sit and wait when I had no idea how much of that blood was theirs and how much of it was the enemy's. And who was the enemy? What the fuck had happened to make my alphas come home to me looking like they'd just gone through a war?

My eyes were wide and my heart thundered behind my ribs as they filed through the kitchen, each of them barely grazing their fingers over my shoulder, my back, or my hair as they passed.

I tried to follow, but Enzo locked his hand around my wrist to hold me in place.

Glaring at him, I frowned. "Either let go or I'll scream, and every single member of my pack and the guard will run in here and kick your fucking ass."

He pulled back with a smile and raised brows, holding both hands up in surrender.

As I slipped and slid trying to follow my pack upstairs, I heard the three chuckling.

"They've got their hands full with that one," Ax muttered, followed by more chuckles.

All four of my alphas split off into their own rooms instead of heading into the omega quarters where the shower would have fit all four of them comfortably. I needed to check over all of them but wasn't sure which of them to follow first. They all moved stiffly; they all looked as bad as the other.

Damn it.

Running through Valen's door since his was the first in the row, I stopped short in the bathroom as he peeled away his clothes and tossed them onto the tiled floor. There was more blood beneath his clothes, but I still couldn't tell whether it was his or had soaked through his clothing.

But the bruising along his ribs and the left side of his face told me there was some kind of hand-to-hand combat. Someone had dared to touch my pack. Some assholes had hurt my alphas.

Valen wouldn't meet my eye, even when I started to peel my own clothes away to step into the shower behind him. I needed to see for myself that he was whole, that he hadn't been shot or stabbed. I wasn't exactly happy that someone had hurt him in any form, but bruises would heal.

His back was to me as he stood under the spray, the water sluicing in red streaks down his face and hair, his back, to swirl down the drain.

As his skin began to clear and I'd yet to see any life-threatening injuries, my heartrate slowed a little more.

Until he turned to face me and four scratches across his chest caught my attention. Scratches. And they looked as though they'd been formed by a small hand, as small as mine.

"What…who scratched you?" Moving closer, I put my hand up and moved in slow motion. "Were you with another fucking omega?" I all but screamed as a rush of possessive rage turned the blood to ice in my veins.

CHAPTER TWENTY-SEVEN

<u>Valen</u>

Earlier

I got that we had built this empire. I got that we had work to do if we wanted it to continue to grow. But I fucking hated being separated from Corazon, even for a few hours.

What the fuck did that say about me as an alpha that I needed to feel my omega pressed against me, that I needed to swim in her Lily of the Valley scent, that I needed to see her with my own two eyes?

Cohl was even worse. And that asshole could feel her through their bond. How much worse would it be when I finally gave in to my instincts to mark her, to bond her, to fully claim her as mine?

Honestly, mark or not, Corazon was my omega. Our omega. We would protect her with everything we had, including our own lives if necessary.

Instead of being home with our omega, instead of worshiping her beautiful body and listening to her moans and cries of pleasure, Ford had contacted Pack Garcia for a sit down. They had chosen a neutral location somewhere in public to avoid any trouble.

Bain had sent a couple guards ahead of time to check things out, check for any weapons hidden under tables or in the bathroom. Once we were sure we wouldn't drive up to an ambush or walk into a firing squad, we left our beautiful girl in the care of our guards and Bain's brother's pack.

I still didn't like leaving her with unbonded alphas, but Bain trusted his brother and I had to trust my pack lead. Besides, the three alphas had been in completely different rooms from our omega each time we'd left her to their care, and she'd never carried even a hint of their scents upon our return.

Turning toward Cohl, I shook my head at the look on his face. It was a mixture of anger and constipation. That was seriously the only way to describe the way his face was scrunched up as he attempted to keep the bond between him and our omega muted.

After the first few times of leaving her behind while we conducted business, we'd realized how distracted the unhinged alpha could get when he focused on the thread tying him to Corazon. As his anxiety grew, so did hers. Which would then make him even more volatile. An endless fucking cycle that had almost ended up in bloodshed during a meeting that hadn't required such.

Two SUVs filled with our guards pulled into the parking lot and along the curb of the restaurant. The moment they exited, their eyes scanning the parking lot to ensure once more there weren't any snipers lying in wait, the four of us pushed from our seats and headed inside.

The restaurant was closed during the afternoon, but we had been able to pull some strings and get the manager to let us in for this little meet and greet. Or rather a negotiation. I wasn't overly optimistic. Or optimistic at all. Being as we'd taken the woman who'd been designated as their pack's omega and they'd done nothing to get her back.

Bain led the way to a back room and took a seat facing the door where Pack Garcia would enter. The three of us followed suit, forming a semi-circle around the large table, and waited.

It was another thirty minutes before Leo, Julian, and Roman entered with a gaggle of guards. That was fine. We hadn't expected them to come in without their own entourage being we'd brought our own extra muscle.

I sat on the outer seat, leaned against the back, my knees spread, hands folded on the tabletop. Every one of us carried pistols at the backs of our pants and I had no doubt the three alphas of Pack Garcia did the same. Not to mention every single one the guards watching over both packs were heavily armed and ready for battle.

We'd picked a public place but had decided against business hours. Just because we'd hoped there would be no issues didn't mean we trusted these assholes.

As the last guard stepped through the door, a small bleached blonde omega sauntered in, lowering onto Leo's lap instead of claiming her own seat.

"That was fast," Ford said with a smirk that held zero humor.

Leo shrugged up one shoulder as he wrapped one of his arms around the woman's shoulders. "Like I said, plenty of omegas out there. No point in dwelling on one."

The blonde didn't so much as wince at his words. Did she not realize she meant literally nothing to this pack, that they would easily sacrifice her if necessary and simply claim another in her place?

As much as I wanted to blow it off, to pretend it wasn't my problem and had nothing to do with us, anger burned through my veins, both for Corazon and for this oblivious omega.

"You called this bullshit meeting. What do you want?" Leo asked, his attention solely on Bain.

"You killed seven of our men. You stole a portion of our merchandise. I wanted to offer a form of a truce since you so flagrantly disregarded your intended omega..." Bain pointedly looked at the blonde. "In return for a business arrangement."

"Your arrangement was utter and complete bullshit. In what world did you think giving up seventy percent of our profit would be acceptable?" Julian said, his face a mask of boredom.

"We could simply kill you now and take over your entire business," Cohl said, his voice barely sounding human as a growl laced around his words.

Both sets of guards tensed, their hands twitching toward their firearms.

But Pack Garcia didn't look the least bit phased. "You could try. But from what we've seen, you four are in way over your heads. Hell, you're down quite a few soldiers at my last count."

A growl rumbled up my chest.

"How's our omega, by the way? Have you knocked her up yet?" Roman asked, a smirk on his stupid fucking face. My hands itched with the urge to remove that look with my fist.

A deep rumbling growl filled the space as Cohl began to rise to his feet. Ford clamped a hand on his shoulder and forced him back into his seat.

"Mine," Cohl growled out.

"Eh. You were second choice," Leo said with a dismissive wave of his hand.

These assholes were baiting us, goading us, trying to get a rise so they had a reason for their guards to open fire.

I had no idea how many guards they'd brought other than those who were in the building, but I knew Cohl would become blood thirsty at the first chance at violence, especially after they'd been stupid enough to bring up Corazon in such a crass fucking manner.

"Is there a reason you chose to bring an omega to this meeting? Not worried about her safety?" Ford asked, his hand still tightly holding onto Cohl's shoulder.

Julian shrugged up a shoulder. "She's a needy bitch. She likes to ride her alphas' dicks as often as possible."

My eyes darted to the blonde, expecting a look of repulsion or at least anger. But she looked...dazed. Her eyes were somewhat glassy, her pupils barely pinpoints instead of the dilated pupils of an omega in heat or even aroused by her pack.

Had they drugged this poor woman? Was she some ploy to distract us? They couldn't possibly think we gave a single fuck that they'd claimed another omega when we had someone as amazing and sexy and strong as Corazon back at home.

The longer I watched her, the more my anger grew. She definitely didn't look as though she was there of her own accord. She'd willingly lowered herself onto Leo's lap, but he'd clamped an arm around her shoulders and talked about another omega right in front her and not once had she reacted. If nothing else, her instincts should have caused her to become possessive over her alphas mentioning being with or desiring another omega.

Not to mention they were speaking about her as though she was nothing more than a toy, a plaything, a warm body to slake their baser needs.

Turning to look at our pack lead, I almost recoiled at the murderous look in his icy blue eyes. His shoulders were tense, his jaw was set, and his scent had turned bitter with his growing rage.

"We're willing to settle for sixty percent. You pull your men back behind the city line," Bain said.

To anyone on the outside, my packmate was the epitome of cool, calm, and collected. But Bain was barely hanging on by a thread. It wouldn't take much more for him to lunge at the throat of any of the three fuckers sitting across from us with smirks on their faces.

They could pretend all they wanted. They'd brought as many men as they had because they knew they would lose if they had to go against the four of us. They'd been raised to believe the world revolved around them due to the power and money possessed by each of their families.

My pack, on the other hand, had clawed our way to the top, taking out anyone who stood in our way with our bare fucking hands.

Roman barked out a laugh. "You seem to forget you're not going up against only the three of us. Not only are you dealing with our pack, but the packs of each of our families. And then there's the pack you stole from. The Alvarez codgers haven't exactly forgiven you for stealing their daughter."

"Like they give a shit," Cohl gritted out. "They ran like a bunch of little bitches at the first sign of trouble. And I don't remember seeing any of you attempting to intervene."

Leo's shoulders shrugged up again. "Like I've said a few times – too many fucking fish in the sea to give a shit about one slicked pussy."

"You mother fucker–" Cohl roared, shoving to his feet and shoving Ford's hand away when he tried to restrain our packmate.

Garcia's guards moved forward. And so did ours.

"You should have your omega escorted out," Bain warned, though his tone was even and conversational, regardless of the hefty rush of alpha power bursting from him. He was like a coiled snake waiting to strike at the first chance.

At the mention of her exit, the omega whined, sending the hair at the back of my neck on end while my alpha fought the urge to protect this unknown woman. I had no desire to fuck her or mark her. But I couldn't fight my own biology when it came to an omega in distress, regardless of whom she was bonded to.

A snarl tore from Cohl. Ford struggled to restrain him.

And then Roman reached over and tugged at the omega's top as though to pull it down and reveal her breasts to the room.

"The fuck are you doing?" I barked out, moving forward as though to cover the woman.

And that was exactly what these fuckers had been hoping for. To anyone on the outside, it looked as though I'd attempted to either attack or steal their omega…again. When all I'd wanted was to protect her dignity when she looked like she was barely aware of her surroundings or the tension sucking the oxygen from the room.

The omega was practically tossed to the ground as Leo lunged to his feet, pulling his pistol from under his suit jacket. That did nothing but urge the four of us to follow suit. Now, seven guns were being waved around while the guards eyed each other and us, their own firearms in their grip but pointed to the ground.

The first shot would end up in pure chaos and someone would end up dead.

My eyes darted to the woman on the ground who was climbing to her feet in slow, clumsy, sluggish moves.

"Did you drug your fucking omega?" I bit out. When her shirt shifted, there were several bruises and bites along her shoulder, her neck, and her upper arms, as though these cocksuckers hadn't been satisfied with marking her once, but rather had tortured her.

Another of those infuriating shrugs from Leo. "Keeps them docile. Makes them more…compliant."

A new rush of rage and absolute terror tore through my system. That's what they would have done to Corazon. They would have drugged her. She would have been covered in dark red and swollen bites. Her beautifully soft flesh would have been riddled with bruises that did not look like the kind that were achieved from a passionate night of fucking.

The omega swayed on her feet, her eyes narrowed on me. An animalistic screech tore from her lips a second before she lunged at me, her hands curled as she scratched at my face, my neck, anywhere she could touch. I did what I could to restrain her without hurting her or accidentally firing off a round.

But Pack Garcia had exactly what they wanted. It looked as though I was attacking their omega. In the eyes of the law, they had every right to take whatever measures needed to stop me from hurting, killing, or stealing their mate away.

* * *

Now

CORAZON'S SCENT filled the shower stall, but was no longer the sweet, floral scent we'd all grown obsessed with. It was bitter and a little rotten with her anger.

Once I was cleaned of the blood, I wrapped my arms around her, tightening my hold when she tried to shove me away.

"Why the fuck are there scratches on your chest, Valen? Why did you all smell so…wrong when you came home?"

I was surprised she could smell anything past the metallic scent of blood, the anger tainting our scents, or the gunpowder from so many rounds fired.

One look at Corazon and I realized our night was far from over. She'd stripped to climb in after me, her concern for her alphas causing her to chase us upstairs instead of waiting for us like we'd asked.

"Pack Garcia," I growled out.

Her dark brows lowered over her brown eyes that held so much venom and suspicion. "What about them?"

"We went to meet with them. We'd hoped for a…truce of some form. A compromise."

Her frown grew deeper until a little crease formed between her perfectly arched brows.

"What kind of compromise? Was an omega part of that compromise?"

"For fuck's sake, sweetheart," I said, reaching back to end the spray and stretching past her for a towel. "You think we're shopping for another mate? Or that we would ever allow anyone to come near you again? You're ours. We don't want anyone else."

We'd done our best to shield her from the less savory side of our business, but the more we hid from her, the more she would come up with her own conclusions and the crazier the scenarios her imagination would conjure.

"You come home covered in blood, scratched up like you were in a cat fight and carrying an omega's scent, and I *still* don't carry your fucking mark. Not to mention no one will tell me shit about where you go or what you're doing. You just lock me in the house with your employees or Bain's brother."

I still don't carry your fucking mark.

Out of everything she'd just said, the cutest growl vibrating from her chest, that was the one thing my brain decided to latch onto.

"We don't tell you because we don't want you to worry. That's not the kind of shit an omega should have to deal with…ever. The fact your family–" I cut myself off and dragged in a deep breath as I scrubbed the towel against my skin a little too roughly.

She was standing in front of me, completely naked, water rolling down her beautiful curves and it was growing hard to think straight as my cock took notice and rose as my knot began to throb.

"Here," I said, handing her a towel. I hadn't meant for the word to come out so gruffly, but I was still riding the adrenaline from the past hour. "We were trying to squash this shit between us and Pack Garcia. They've been attacking our warehouses and killing our men. We'd hoped to be able to come to an agreement that would make everyone happy."

That was a bit of a lie. I'd known damn well those cock suckers would never be happy with thirty percent of their own operation.

"They brought their new omega." I winced internally, but she didn't so much as bat an eye to that news. Why the hell would she care whether they had an omega when she hadn't chosen them to begin with? No. She'd chosen us. Even after the way we'd started, she had chosen us.

The crease between her brows smoothed a little and her lips parted. "What do you mean they brought their new omega? Did she... what happened?"

So, I told her the entire story, about the number of guards we all brought, about how Leo had tossed the small woman to the ground when he'd thought there would be gunfire instead of protecting her or ordering one of his men to get her out of the restaurant. I told her about the omega appearing drugged, about how she'd attacked me when I'd tried to protect her honor.

Then I told her about the men that had been cut down by gunfire, about how the three alphas who led Pack Garcia fled without their omega, barely sparing a glance at her lifeless body as she'd laid bleeding out on the restaurant floor. A stray bullet had sliced right through her throat. There hadn't been a chance to save her.

"Oh my god," she whispered, covering her mouth with both hands. "They...she's dead?"

As would she have been had she been bonded to that pack, had she been dragged into that same situation. I could tell she'd come to the same conclusion as though I could see the thoughts and emotions flashing through her beautiful eyes that were now glimmering with unshed tears.

I nodded, reaching forward to wrap the towel around her shoulders and tugging her to my chest, wrapping my arms around her back and resting my cheek on top of her head.

"This is the kind of shit we want to protect you from. We don't withhold anything because we don't trust you. We just...your happiness is more important than anything other than your safety. If we could convince you the world was nothing but sunshine and rainbows and shit, we would."

"I grew up in the criminal world. Pretty hard to convince me evil no longer exists," she said, her voice muffled against my chest.

"And as far as not marking you, I wanted to give you time. Cohl... after that day in the yard, I wanted you to decide when each of us left our mark on you. We all want you to decide who, when, and where you want us to bond you."

"I want it now, Valen. Cohl locked the bond down until I could barely feel him. Do you have any idea how scary that is? To not have a clue whether you're in danger? To not know whether or not I'll ever see you again?"

Cupping her face in both hands, I so badly wanted to promise her that we would always return to her. But that would have been a blatant lie. Because the truth was, we didn't know each time we left the pack house whether it would be the last time we laid eyes on our beautiful omega.

CHAPTER TWENTY-EIGHT

<u>Corazon</u>

It didn't take a rocket scientist to read between the lines.

Had I been bonded to Pack Garcia they would have treated me as dismissively and horrifically as they'd treated the omega who was now dead.

Had my fathers known what kind of men they were giving me to… and would they have actually cared if I had been killed?

I still wasn't thrilled by the claw marks on Valen's chest; that odd possessive instinct demanded I rub myself along every inch of his body until he was smothered in my scent. But the omega wasn't a threat. She had never been a threat.

They'd drugged her. To keep her docile and compliant. I had no doubt they would have done the same thing to me the second they realized I wouldn't simply sit around and let them treat me however they pleased.

My heart hurt for so many reasons. My instincts were all over the place. My mind and body were constantly warring for control.

Valen's warm hands cupped my face as his gaze bounced between my eyes before he gently pressed his lips to mine. As soft as it was, it held so many emotions, so many thoughts and feelings he didn't need to voice for me to understand.

Love. In the few weeks since I'd been forced into this house with this pack, we had grown to love each other. Sure, maybe the whole thing was a little unorthodox, but what part of my life had ever been normal?

The words were on the tip of my tongue, but I was terrified to say them aloud, terrified letting them free might change things or tempt the universe to take one or all of them away from me.

"I need my pack," I whispered against his lips.

"Give us a few minutes. Get ready for bed and we'll be in there as soon as possible."

He wrapped his hand around mine and led me from the bathroom, guiding me to his bed while he started pulling clothes free and pulling a pair of sweats over his legs.

I could stare at Valen all day, stare at the planes of his chest, the muscles bunching in his back with every move, the delicious V of his hips that dipped down below his pants, even the scar that crossed over his side.

"Wait...why am I going to get ready for bed and wait for you guys? I just said I was tired of being kept out of the loop. I'm tired of the secrets."

He glanced at me over his shoulder as his pumpkin scent turned sharper.

With a sigh, he nodded. "At least get dressed. Cohl might kill Enzo and the others if you walk downstairs in that towel," he said, his lips pulling up in a forced smile that didn't reach his eyes.

"If I leave this room, are you going to rush out and make sure you boys talk about shit you don't want me to hear?"

That at least got a real smile. With a chuckle, he wrapped his hand around mine again and led me from his room, down the hall, and into my bedroom. He waited patiently as I pulled panties, sweatpants, and a t-shirt from the dresser drawers, tugging them on quickly. My hair was damp and a little knotted, but I didn't care much about that right now.

"You might want to put on a bra," he said with a raised brow.

I glanced down and sighed at the way my nipples were pebbled and straining against the fabric. I swore my body was primed and ready for my alphas at all times of the day lately. Especially since the moment Cohl's teeth had penetrated the skin of my shoulder.

With a huff, I grabbed a hoodie that sat on the back of the couch and tugged it over my head, sweeping my hair from the collar to settle down my back.

"Happy?"

"Much better," he teased, twining his fingers through mine and leading me through the house to where my pack sat in the living room with Enzo, Ax, and Cyrus.

Instead of tempting my alphas' possessiveness, I sat next to Cohl, nuzzling my head under his chin when his arm draped around my shoulders and tugged me closer. Valen sat on the other side. Ford and Bain each sat in winged back chairs across from us until the whole group sat in a conversational circle.

Bain cocked a brow at Valen.

"She doesn't want to be left out. No point in hiding shit from her anymore. Not like she's not used to this kind of life."

"She has a name," I ground out, frowning at Valen beside me.

Enzo smirked. Ax chuckled as though nothing bothered the big alpha. Something like respect shone in Cyrus's green eyes.

"Where's the omega? Please tell me you didn't leave her laying on the floor in her own blood."

Growls erupted and a whimper tore from my chest before I could swallow it back. I knew they weren't angry at me, but that didn't stop that part of me from wanting to cower from so much alpha anger and power.

"*We* didn't leave her," Ford growled.

"Her alphas left her there?" A miasma of emotions ripped through me, making my blood go from ice to lava within a span of seconds.

"She'll get a proper burial. We contacted her family, but they weren't interested. She's been...delivered to a funeral home," Bain said.

Every single alpha in the room was emitting so many hormones that the small hairs on my arms and the back of my neck stood on end.

I'd grown up around powerful men. But I'd never been in a room with so many strong alphas, men who actually cared about what happened to innocent people, innocent omegas. Their rage for the treatment of the omega whose name I would never know warmed my heart while awakening a new sense of betrayal toward my family.

They had sold me to the same assholes who'd put that woman in a dangerous situation. They'd allowed her to be killed, left her there as though she was nothing more than roadkill on the side of the highway. And I knew without a doubt I would have received the same treatment.

Taking a deep breath to settle myself before I sent Cohl or one of the others into rut and caused them to attack Enzo and his pack, I asked, "So what happens now?"

I nuzzled into Cohl's arms as I listened to my alphas discuss their plans. They had every intention of punishing Pack Garcia for their actions, and I was totally behind that.

What I didn't approve of were the risks to my alphas. They could have easily ended up dead, just like guards from both sides had.

Of course, Leo, Julian, and Roman had run the moment bullets had started flying, leaving their omega behind as a distraction and using her as a shield so they could flee without having to actually fight.

Cowards. My family had sold me to fucking cowards.

As the conversation began to die down, as plans were put into place without anything being hidden from me, I decided I was ready to speak up.

"I want to be bonded to the whole pack. And I'm tired of being locked up in the house."

A soft rumble vibrated against me from where Cohl held me, but the others went silent.

"It's not safe for an omega of your standing–" Enzo started, but I cut him off.

"There are plenty of people who work for my alphas that wouldn't let anything happen to me. I'm right back to being a prisoner all because of my fucking family. I won't let them destroy everything we're building. I won't let them control my life anymore."

"You want to be bonded to us?" Ford asked, his brows lowered a touch, but his scent lifted on the air and slick coated my pussy and thighs at the warm saffron essence teasing my nose.

"Every time you guys leave, all I can do is wait. I can feel Cohl, but today..." I turned a glare up at him. "Why did you shut me out?"

"He gets too distracted," Bain answered for him.

A distraction in their line of business could end in blood shed. As in *his* blood being shed.

"Okay. Forgiven. But next time, open it back up when you're safe. I hate sitting here like the kept omega, waiting to see whether or not the loves of my life–" The words dried up in my throat as I realized what I'd just said.

"Welp. That's our cue," Enzo said, slapping his knees as he pushed to his feet.

The three alphas hurried from the room without another word, the front door opening and closing loudly.

I had more or less just admitted what I'd only begun to realize. And yeah...I was still a little pissed at Bain. But I was tired of denying what was right there in my face – these alphas were mine. They were my pack. They were my family. They were the family I'd never dreamed I could have but had always wanted.

It wasn't a second after the front door closed that Valen dragged me from Cohl, lifted me into his arms, and was sprinting through the house and up the stairs, kicking the door to my bedroom open fully until he was dropping me onto the huge pack bed.

Feet thundered behind us. Scents wrapped around me, teasing against my flesh like fingers stroking me. Hands frantically tugged and pulled, removing my hoodie, my sweats, dragging my panties down my legs, and removing my t-shirt.

I laid naked and spread out on the bed like an offering to this pack.

But wasn't I? Wasn't I offering myself to them, my body, my mind, my heart and soul to these men who had showed me that I could matter to another person for reasons other than my designation?

My thighs were parted with rough hands, fingers digging into the soft flesh. A tongue swiped through my folds, tearing a moan from my lips that was swallowed by Valen's mouth as he kissed me in a bruising kiss.

Fingers toyed with one of my nipples while lips wrapped around the other. My alphas were everywhere, toying with me, pushing me higher and higher as pressure built low in my belly until I was ready to beg for release, beg to be fucked, beg for a knot.

I was so wet. When a finger was pushed into my cunt, the vulgar squelch of my slick was nothing short of erotic, especially when that finger began to thrust into me, rubbing that perfect spot deep inside, until a second digit was added to the first.

"Please," I whined against Valen's mouth. "I need…"

"Tell us, sweetheart. Tell me. What do you need? I want to hear the words come out of your beautiful mouth," Valen said, his lips brushing against mine, his taste landing on my tongue until I was drowning in spicy pumpkin.

"I need to come. I need to feel you inside me. I need a knot. I need your mark. Please. I need to feel all of you." And I literally meant every part of all four of them but didn't have the mental bandwidth to articulate my needs.

It didn't matter. They'd all become so attuned to me that they kicked into action within a half second of the words leaving my mouth.

Clothes were removed, skin was hot against mine, hormones flooded my senses and mixed with my omega pheromones. Slick pooled beneath me, soaking the mattress as someone continued to feast on my core even as Valen rested on his knees beside my head and tapped the head of his thick cock against my lips.

I opened eagerly, swiping my tongue along his slit and basking in the sweet warmth of his precum. I was addicted to the taste of my pack, the feel of their hands, to the way they stretched me so perfectly.

But it wasn't enough. I needed to carry all their marks. I wanted my neck and shoulders to be a necklace of silver scars so everyone would know I'd claimed and had been claimed by Pack Rivera.

Valen's fingers tightened in my hair, guiding me down his length. The tongue and fingers toying with my clit and entrance was pushing me closer and closer to the edge of the cliff, but I desperately wanted to come on one of my alpha's dicks. And as much as I wanted to be knotted by each and every one of them, we would have to wait for their knots to deflate before the next could take me. I only had three holes to be used and four alphas to enjoy.

"Fuck. I need to feel her cunt," Ford growled out.

Cohl was primal, liked to chase me and tackle me so he could fuck me like a rabid animal. But Ford and Bain...they were so dominant and verbal and made my omega want to bare my neck and submit in the most tantalizing way.

Valen pulled his cock from my mouth. The tongue and fingers were removed. And then I was lifted and set on top of Ford until I was straddling his waist. His hands dug into my waist and he urged me to rock so his shaft was rubbing along my clit and covering him in my slick.

"You want our marks, omega?" he asked, his eyes full of so much heat, the gray of his irises nearly invisible with his blown pupils.

"Yes. Please, alpha. I need to feel your bite. I need to feel you. I'm yours," I said, not giving a shit how needy I sounded. I was theirs as much as they were mine.

A rumble lifted on the air as he helped me get settled until the head of his cock teased my entrance. I didn't want a tease. I wanted to feel him inside of me. I wanted to be filled and stretched. I wanted to feel their teeth sinking into my flesh as their cocks filled every part of me. I wanted to be covered in their scents, their sweat, their cum.

"Please, alpha," I whined.

Ford's nostrils flared, his growl grew louder, then he thrust his hips up hard and fast, filling me in one stroke until his knot pushed against my opening, teasing and stretching.

My head fell back on a cry as that one stroke inside me sent me careening over the edge I'd been balancing on like walking a tightwire.

"Fuck, you're so beautiful," Cohl muttered as he leaned forward and sucked one of my nipples into his mouth.

"I'm going to take your ass," Bain said from behind me, his hands smoothing across my shoulders until one hand cupped my throat and tilted my head to the side.

His lips and teeth grazed my skin, nipping and nuzzling and promising nothing but pleasure.

"Yes. All of you. Please."

A dark chuckle shook against my back from where Bain was settling behind me and between Ford's spread knees. "As much as we want to take you at once, I don't think your tight little pussy is ready for more than one dick at a time."

Oh, but the temptation was there. Definitely something I wanted to try at another time.

But for now, I needed this connection. I needed them inside me while they marked my flesh, while they tied me to them permanently, making us a completed pack, a real family.

Bain's finger moved to my core where he used my slick to lube the tight ring of muscles of my ass, probing inside before adding a second, stretching me and getting my back hole ready for him.

This wasn't the first time I'd taken two or more of them at once. But I still needed time for the size of each of my alphas. All four of them were long and thick, although Bain was probably the bigger of the four.

The hair was pushed away from my shoulder as the crown of Bain's cock nudged against me. He peppered kisses along my bare shoulder as he slowly pushed forward, his moan mixing with mine while Ford held still below me.

I needed him to move. I needed him to fuck me. I needed them both to take me. I needed...so much more.

Once Bain was fully sheathed inside my ass, his arms circled around my waist and his fingers toyed with my hard nipples. "Fuck, you're so tight. Your ass is gripping my cock like a vise."

"Yes. Fuck me. Please," I begged, attempting to rock to take them both.

Cohl had surprisingly settled against the headboard to watch, fucking his own hand as he watched his packmates take me. Valen pushed to his feet until his cock was at the perfect level for my mouth.

As though they'd planned it, Bain, Ford, and Valen all pushed forward until I was drunk on dick. I was full, stretched, and already on the verge of another release within seconds of their hips pumping into me from every direction.

"I'm going to fill your ass, then clamp my teeth onto your throat. I'm going to tie you to me forever. I'm going to make you my queen," Bain grunted as he picked up his rhythm until his hips slapped against my ass while Ford thrust from below.

I moaned around Valen's cock. His eyes squeezed shut and he threw his head back at the vibrations from the sound. "Fuck. I'm going to come down your throat, sweetheart. Can you swallow it all?"

"Mmhm," was all I could mutter with how far he was pushing into my mouth until the flared head hit the back of my throat, almost triggering my gag reflex.

But I was an omega. I was built to take an alpha dick. I was built to please and to receive pleasure over and over again.

"Fuuuck," he groaned out, his fingers tightening in my hair to hold me still as he did exactly as he'd promised and shot his load to the back of my throat and across my tongue. I swallowed greedily, not wanting to lose a single drop.

The sounds of us fucking were obscene and vulgar and so fucking sexy. The wet sounds of my pussy being pounded by Ford, the grunts and curses from Bain, even the way Cohl shoved Valen away so he could shove his cock into my mouth and fuck my throat until his sweet vanilla frosting cum filled my mouth, some dribbling down my chin before I could drink it all down.

"You ready for my bite, omega?" Bain asked, his hips stuttering as his dick twitched inside me.

With Cohl still holding my mouth hostage, all I could do was moan my approval.

As hot jets filled my ass, Bain's teeth sank into the flesh along the left side of my throat, sending me spiraling again. I pulled my mouth from Cohl as a scream tore from me as wave after wave crashed over me, pulling me under, stealing the oxygen from my lungs and squeezing my heart.

I felt Bain's presence explode inside my chest as he filled my back hole.

"Fuck," Ford said, sitting up and clamping his teeth around my breast, circling my nipple with his mark so every time anything brushed across it my body would react.

Ford and Bain felt so similar through their individual threads, both powerful and dominant. But there was more. I could feel their absolute adoration and love for me. And it stole my breath for a whole other reason.

One more. I had three bites, but I was still lacking Valen's.

Tears burned my eyes before I could stop them or even understand them. It felt like a rejection that Valen hadn't marked me, but I knew that was stupid. He was waiting, biding his time. He couldn't exactly shove everyone out of the way or crowd me. My sweet alpha might be strong and beastly when it came to the enemy, but he would always be careful and gentle with me.

Bain pulled away and left the room. Water turned on in the bathroom and he returned with a wet washcloth and a soft towel.

Cohl helped me lift from Ford and laid me on my back so Bain could gently clean me up.

Valen's face hovered over mine. "Why the tears?" he asked, the pads of his fingers so soft as he wiped them away.

"My omega feels rejected. You didn't bite me. I know it's stupid. I can't seem to control my emotions lately." I'd never been bonded before. I'd never been in love. I simply assumed this was normal for any omega who found her true mates, her scent match, the alphas meant solely for her.

My alphas exchanged a look, but I couldn't decipher it, nor did I have the energy to question it.

"Where do you want to wear my mark, sweetheart?" he asked, feathering kisses along my forehead, my cheeks, even my nose.

I pointed directly over my throat, front and center. All but Ford's marks would be visible. I had meant to tell them all I wanted a necklace of their bites, but we'd gotten lost in the moment.

Besides, it was kind of sexy and a little naughty to think that every time my bra or a shirt brushed along my breast, my body would instantly react and I would grow aroused, craving my blond alpha.

Valen settled between my thighs, kissing a path from my breasts to my throat as he slowly entered me. My head tilted back and to the side, both in pleasure and pure submission. Finally. I would finally and proudly wear the bonding marks of the pack I hadn't wanted but had chosen whole heartedly.

He kept fucking into me, slowly at first, until I felt his knot swell and nudge against me. "I want to knot you when I bite you, sweetheart. Then you're ours. Forever."

"Yes. Please," I cried out. Literally cried, tears streaking down my temples to soak into my hair.

His thrusts grew harder, faster, more frenzied, until he pushed hard into me, his knot stretching me and settling behind my pubic bone, locking us together as his dick twitched and painted my inner walls with his hot release. His teeth slowly sank into my skin around my throat, like the most perfect adornment, more beautiful than any diamond or rare gem.

A silent scream tore from me as my body spasmed around him, our release and my slick locked inside by his knot as he exploded within my chest with the others.

And just like my other three alphas, I didn't feel a hint of regret, not a moment of hesitation.

"Fuck," he ground out, rutting into me in short thrusts. "I love you, Corazon. I love you. Fuck, I love you," he grunted over and over.

I wasn't surprised Valen had been the first to say the words. What surprised me was when I wrapped my arms and legs around him to hold him closer, and said, "I love you, too. I love all of you so much."

CHAPTER TWENTY-NINE

Corazon

It had been three weeks since all four of my alphas had officially marked me and claimed me as theirs. Their omega.

Their mate.

Since that night, each of them had found little ways to show me exactly what I meant to them. Bain could still be an asshole at times, still verbally lash out when he was frustrated, but he was my asshole and I'd learned how to deal with him – by telling him he was being a dick before he went too far and hurt my feelings again.

Today was the first day since I'd demanded to be let in the loop about their business and where they were going each time they'd left the house that we were all leaving the house together. I was finally leaving these four fucking walls.

It had been close to three months since I'd seen anything but this house and the property or anyone other than my pack, their guards, and Enzo and his pack.

We were going out for dinner and possibly a little shopping if the guys didn't go all possessive alpha while we were in public.

I could feel their anxiety through our bond like someone was strumming a guitar that had been strung too tightly and was one pluck away from snapping.

The downside of our outing was the number of guards Bain and Ford insisted join us. Keller, one of the pack's longest employed guards, was under strict instructions to keep me in his sight at all times, and if anything were to go down while we were in public to get me to safety.

I paraphrased all that, of course. What they'd actually said was to keep me safe or he would die in a slow and painful manner.

To the alpha's defense, he'd had a sense of humor about it and smiled with a nod as he'd received his instructions.

Bain's brother and his packmates were meeting us at one of a few local restaurants not owned by my alphas. On paper, my pack looked like businessmen, but after growing up with Pack Alvarez, I knew the restaurants, clubs, and other businesses were nothing more than fronts and the easiest way to launder the money they earned from black market sales of weapons and such.

I was mildly surprised they'd agreed to my leaving the safety of the house being as the nonsense between them, my family's pack, and the assholes of Pack Garcia hadn't slowed. In fact, from what I'd gathered, it was amping. There had been losses on all sides. Including quite a few guards that had worked for my alphas since the beginning.

Keller and four others rode in an SUV behind us, and three more guards rode in an SUV ahead of us, sandwiching my pack between them like we were royalty.

Or rather like I was royalty.

Bain hadn't lied when he'd said he would make me his queen. Like Valen had done in the beginning, Bain was constantly ordering me new clothes, new stuff for my nest, perfume, jewelry, anything he thought I might like.

Honestly, I was happiest when we were all in a puppy pile on the couch or the pack bed. When I knew they were all home and safe and could inhale the combination of their scents.

"You look really pretty," Valen said from my right.

I was wedged between him and Cohl in the back seat, while Ford drove and Bain rode shotgun.

Since this was my first time in public in close to three months, I'd taken my time to dry and curl my hair, worn makeup, even picked out one of the pretty dresses and heels Valen had ordered in the beginning.

I'd been so tempted to forgo panties to tease my pack the whole day but was worried I'd end up aroused and would embarrass myself with a slick spot on the chair at the restaurant.

"Thank you," I said, tilting my head to give him access as he trailed his lips along my throat, his breath warm against his mark and instantly making my body react.

I'd gained a couple pounds over the past few weeks, but my alphas loved it. According to Cohl, a fat ass was better to grab onto. Not that I liked having my ass referred to as fat, but hey, if it kept their attention, I was fine with the weight change.

Cohl's hand was wrapped around mine, his thigh lined along mine, and he purred lightly. The atmosphere in the cab of the SUV was tense, but happy. I'd fallen in love with these four without being officially courted. It almost felt like we were going on our first date, except without the awkward small talk crap.

Not that I had much experience in the dating scene. My fathers had set up any and every meeting I'd ever had with an alpha or pack. Any time I'd actually gotten laid had been when I was able to sneak away from my guards for a one-night-stand.

I craned my neck to see through the windshield and through both side windows as the scenery passed. And then it hit me.

"We were less than thirty minutes from my family's estate," I blurted as a familiar area came into view.

The tension grew so thick in the vehicle you could cut it with a knife as a fresh wave of anxiety trickled through the bond.

"Oh, calm down. I think it's obvious by now I'm not going

anywhere. You four are stuck with me." Because fuck my fathers. Fuck my family pack. Fuck that whole crew.

Yep. I was still angry over the fact they'd sold me to a pack of underhanded cowards and had so easily thrown me away when Bain and Ford had attempted to use their rare gem of an omega daughter as a negotiation tool. To this day, none of them had bothered to offer up any form of a truce in exchange for my safe return.

Wouldn't matter if they did. I wasn't going anywhere. I was sure my family would accuse me of being a victim of some kind of Stockholm syndrome, but this was my pack, these were my alphas.

This was my true family and where I belonged.

Valen chuckled and pressed a kiss to my temple. Cohl tightened his grip on my hand and tugged it until our entwined hands rested on his thigh. Ford and Bain physically relaxed, as though they'd blown out a synchronized breath of relief.

After another fifteen minutes, the black SUV ahead of us pulled along the curb of a restaurant, the guards immediately climbing from the front and back seats to wait for us to park behind them.

My pack didn't even bother heading into the parking lot. I supposed being the powerful and well connected alphas, they could do whatever the hell they wanted.

"Wait…this isn't the same place where that omega…" I let the words trail off, unable to complete the sentence. No way would I go in there if that poor woman had been killed.

"No. Why would we bring you there?" Bain said, turning his upper half in his seat to shoot me a disgruntled look.

My alphas climbed through their doors. Valen extended his hand and waited for me to carefully scoot across the seat and swing my legs out to avoid flashing anyone on the street a view of the thong I'd chosen for the night. I had very intentionally chosen every single thing I wore – the dress and heels as well as the lingerie beneath – to tease my pack while we were in public. I wanted them nearly insane with need and lust by the time we stepped through the door to the pack house.

Valen's hand was warm and I giggled the girliest sound when he bowed at the waist and pressed a kiss to my knuckles. New love was so…butterfly in the stomach, girly sighs, and giggle inducing.

But I knew this feeling wouldn't fade over time. In the past three weeks, it almost felt as though the guys were all trying to one up each other on how to make me blush, smile, or moan the most.

And I was so silently cheering them on since I was the one reaping the benefits of this little competition.

The sun was setting, casting everything in a pretty warm, orange glow. Valen tucked my hand under his elbow while Cohl damned near shoved Bain out of the way to get to my free side so he would wrap one of his strong arms around my waist.

I still couldn't believe it had only been three months since that first day we'd met, when I'd feared they would kill me, when I'd hated them and sought a way out of the house and away from them.

There was nothing that could pull me away from this pack short of death.

Man, I was being dramatic today. But it was the truth. I felt stronger with them by my side. I felt seen, heard. Not like I was nothing more than a decoration on their arm or a pawn in whatever games they played.

And they were honest with me about their business, even going so far as telling me they would never promise me anything they weren't sure they could follow through on, and that included returning home to me whenever they left for business. Bain and Ford took turns keeping the bond open enough for me to know they were safe when they left, but that was only after a colossal meltdown two days after they'd all bonded me to them.

Every time they left, Enzo and his pack stayed with me while Keller and a few other guards stood sentry at every entry into the house, regardless of the weather or how often I invited them inside and out of the rain.

As we neared the front door, it swung open to reveal none other than the brother of one of my mates. Enzo's eyes did a quick scan of the area, darted toward me before darting away just as quickly, then zeroed in on his brother.

"Checked the place. Got someone watching the kitchen and back exit. All's good in here," he said, extending his hand and clasping Bain's before pulling his big brother in for one of those manly back slapping hugs.

Ax and Cyrus were waiting near a closed door as we passed through the bustling dining area. Eyes lifted to watch us. There were whispers, as though my pack was known. But I was used to this kind of attention during the times I'd gone out with my family. Hell. They might even recognize me, might have already heard the rumors of the Alvarez omega bonding with a pack not chosen by her fathers.

Cohl snarled at a table as we passed. Nudging my elbow into his ribs, I shook my head with a smile when he frowned down at me in confusion. "Leave them alone," I whispered only loud enough for my alpha to hear.

It wasn't surprising that Cohl was being overly protective and overly possessive during our first outing. But it wasn't necessary. Not with so many alphas and the guards watching every single person coming and going into the place.

A waiter in an expensive, tailored suit pulled open the door to the VIP area and stepped out of the way. There were only a few tables occupied. I recognized a few of the packs, but merely dipped my head in greeting when their attention fell on me.

There was obvious surprise on a few faces, but no one outwardly said anything or came over to speak to me. I was pretty sure none of my alphas or even Enzo and his pack would have allowed anyone in this place to approach me, anyway.

Didn't matter. There wasn't a single person in this place I wanted to speak to, none I would have considered even acquaintances. They were people my fathers knew or had worked with at some point.

Valen released my arm and pulled out a chair before the maître d could reach for it. Cohl winked at me as I lowered and stepped away so Valen could push my chair in while the others took their place around the large table.

And of course, Enzo, Ax, and Cyrus sat at the opposite end of where I'd been settled while my pack circled me with my back to a wall. I was so used to my fathers always taking a seat facing the door to ensure they could see who was coming and going while my mother and I remained exposed.

Just another reminder of how different this pack was from the cowards who'd raised me. My pack was keeping my back to the wall, keeping their bodies between mine and anyone who might enter, shielding me from any danger from the outside world.

Warmth rushed through my chest and I glanced up to find all four of my alphas smiling softly at me. They'd felt my emotions, felt the swell of love I felt for them and were silently telling me how important I was to them, as well.

Everyone settled in, ordering drinks and appetizers, soft conversation rising around me. And, unlike my family, they included me in everything, even when the topics required them to keep their voices low enough the surrounding tables wouldn't overhear.

I didn't trust anyone in this room other than the men at this table. The people in here weren't loyal to anyone other than themselves and would easily sell out my pack if they thought it would benefit them in some way.

Lifting my dirty martini to my lips, I took a sip and smiled as Bain and Enzo exchanged insults, teasing in a way only brothers could do. My brother-in-law and his pack might keep me at arm's length to avoid my pack from going all possessive alpha, but I'd grown to like all three of them. They were loyal, if not a bit strange and unorthodox at times.

The door to the private dining area opened and a scent blew in, causing every muscle in my body to tense. The grip on my martini tightened and the vodka drink sloshed over the shallow edge as tremors began to rattle me from head to toe.

My eyes rose slowly, just in time to see one of my fathers step inside, then another, until all five of my fathers, my mother, and my sister and her alpha filed into the room.

Their eyes moved around the room, inventorying the people present until all eyes landed on me.

"Oh shit," I breathed out, slowly setting my glass down before I spilled it everywhere.

Valen noticed my reaction first, frowning, then glancing to the side to follow my line of sight. A soft growl rumbled from his chest. Then, one by one, all the alphas at the table growled until the hair on my body stood on end from the excessive level of alpha power and hormones was enough to steal the air from my lungs.

All five of my fathers froze, their eyes narrowing on me. I lifted my chin, proudly displaying my bonding marks, and held their gaze. They could kiss my ass. They'd tried to sell me to a bunch of assholes who would have willingly – and probably happily – sacrificed me.

Reaching over, I laid a hand on Cohl's, hoping my touch would settle my less controlled alpha before he pushed to his feet and lunged at a member of my family.

"Corazon?" my mother's soft voice broke through the growls, the hint of her Sicilian accent making her voice sound like poetry.

Ignoring my fathers who attempted to stop her, my mother surprised the shit out of me and made a beeline for where I sat with my new pack.

I pushed to my feet and intercepted her before my alphas could react and attempt to stop her. My mother wasn't a risk. She had never so much as spanked me or any of my siblings.

She'd also never been affectionate or loving. So imagine my surprise when she lifted her arms and wrapped them around my shoulders, pulling me tightly to her as she nuzzled her cheek against mine.

"I've been worried sick," she whispered into my ear.

She…what?

"Are you okay?" She finally pulled away and cupped my cheeks, looking into my eyes like I had always wished she would when I was growing up.

"I'm great, actually. Do you…um. Do you want to meet my pack?"

Her eyes left my face and moved around the table. "You bonded with seven alphas?" Her eyes were wide as she asked, but, unlike my fathers, she wasn't staring at the alphas behind me as though they were a pile of dog shit she'd just stepped in.

"What? No. Oh my gosh. No. Um…" I turned, pulling away from my mom's soft embrace, still shocked by both the appearance of my family and the way my mom was treating me. Most by the latter. "This is Cohl," I said, pointing to my sexy redheaded alpha who was glaring at my fathers. "Valen," I said, smiling when he stood and offered a hand to my mom. That, of course, earned growls from my family, but whatever. "That's Ford. And Bain, my pack lead. The other three are Bain's brother and his pack. This is…Mom, this is my pack. My family."

"Pack Garcia was chosen for you," Vance, my family's pack lead and one of my least favorite – if that was possible – fathers, said.

Another round of growls erupted.

"The same pack who brought their new omega to a negotiation and left her dead on the restaurant floor?" Bain asked, so much growl wrapped around his words, nothing short of hate and rage burning bright in his icy blue eyes.

Vance barely graced Bain with a glance before returning his attention to me.

Mom tensed but didn't turn back to her alphas or my sister. I was mildly shocked to see Isabelle out with my family, and even more shocked to see Antonio with her. Of her two mates, the alpha was the biggest piece of shit and had treated Issa like an afterthought from the moment they'd met. Not met. *Arranged.* Just like me, my fathers had arranged the bonding mates of all their children, making sure the families tied to ours held power and some form of influence in order to increase the size of their reach in politics, business, and the criminal world.

When Antonio leaned to whisper into Vance's ear, it all made sense. He was trying to move up the ladder in the Alvarez empire, hoping to be the next in line since my fathers hadn't birthed any alphas and their only omega child had defected.

"Nice to meet you, Omega Alvarez," Valen said, raising one brow at me as though to tell me to end our little chat.

But this was the first and only time in my life that my mom had treated me like...well, like her daughter. Her eyes looked clearer, instead of the emotionless mask she'd worn my whole life. In fact, there seemed to be a touch of anger in the brown depths of her eyes that I'd inherited.

"It was nice to meet you all." She lowered her voice to a whisper that was barely above a breath. "Please take care of my daughter."

Then she smiled sadly at me and turned to join the rest of my fathers.

I took a deep, shaky breath and lowered into my chair as Vance wrapped a hand tightly around my mom's bicep and led her to a table on the other side of the room. I could still see them all clearly, but at least they couldn't eavesdrop on us, and I could easily move to the side and block their sight of me behind one of my alphas if I was tired of the glares they all constantly shot my way.

Or maybe they were glaring at my pack. I didn't know, and honestly, wasn't sure I cared.

Issa had only looked in my direction when she'd first stepped into the room and had looked damned near shell shocked, her face paling as though she'd seen a ghost. Had my fathers told her and my siblings I'd been killed during the ambush?

Valen wrapped a hand around mine and squeezed, dragging my attention back to him. "You okay?" he whispered.

I forced a smile and nodded. "Yeah. Eventually running into them was inevitable. The city is only so big, right?"

My sweet alpha didn't return my smile, just kept his hand around mine. I felt his concern through our bond. I also felt strong surges of anger coming through the bond from my other three alphas who were steadily glaring in the direction of my fathers.

I wished they would stop. I wanted to return to our easy dinner, the banter and laughing. I wanted this to be a fun day out with my family.

Tears burned the backs of my eyes; I blinked rapidly to keep them from spilling over. For one thing, I didn't want my fathers to see an ounce of weakness from me. That kind of thing had been drilled into all of us since birth. But…I also didn't want to ruin my makeup after carefully applying it and making myself pretty for my first true pack date.

"Excuse me," I said, pushing my chair back again and climbing to my feet.

"What are you doing?" Cohl asked, rising from his chair.

I held out a hand to stop him. "I'm just heading to the lady's room. I'll be right back."

"Let me text Keller," Bain said, pulling his phone out.

"Seriously?" I said, stopping beside him to nuzzle my cheek against his. What can I say? I needed more of his scent on me. "I can use the bathroom all by myself. I'll be back in a minute."

Besides, the only possible threat would be in the same room with my pack. They would see if any single person at that table stood and tried to follow me. I was safe here.

Trailing my fingertips over my alphas, I kept my chin raised and my eyes forward as my heels sank into the thick carpet of the private dining area.

As I pushed the door open to head into the main part of the restaurant, the conversations from the packs dining mixed with the scents of so many different meals until I grew overwhelmed.

Bullshit. I'd become overwhelmed the moment I'd caught my families' scents of ash, stale bread, old, sticky beer, latex paint, oysters, and my mom's sweet magnolia. My senses were on overload, and I needed a second to clear my mind.

I refused to let my fathers ruin what was supposed to be fun day for us, the first time I had the opportunity to show off the marks left by my pack, to let the whole world know I was claimed and had claimed my four alphas.

Eyes followed my path to the hall leading to the restrooms, but I ignored them, keeping my head held high and shoulders pushed back. I might be Omega Rivera now, but I was still the same bad ass woman I was before and would never let anyone see what was going on inside my head and heart.

Once the bathroom door closed behind me, I stopped in front of the sinks and stared at my reflection.

Please take care of my daughter. I wasn't sure whether it had been my mom's actions or her words that confused me the most. That was the most love she had shown me as far back as I could remember.

What had changed?

And if I wasn't mistaken, she looked mildly pleased to meet my alphas. Unlike my fathers. But my bond with Pack Rivera didn't benefit them so why the hell would they be happy? Fuck the fact these alphas treated me like royalty, that they put my safety and happiness above their own, or that we were all crazy about each other. None of that had ever or would ever matter to the men who'd fathered me and my siblings.

Maybe she was actually happy for me. Maybe my mom was overjoyed that at least one of her children had found freedom away from a life dictated by my fathers.

Or…maybe I was simply reading into things and she was relieved I was still alive and in one piece.

Since I didn't really need to use the restroom, but only needed a moment to myself, I turned the water on and washed my hands, dried them, then checked my reflection, fluffing my hair. The door swung open and a wave of fresh linen preceded my sister, her face devoid of any hint of emotion, her eyes dull and so much like our mother's had been our whole lives.

"Hey," I said, a slight crease forming between my brows as she continued to walk straight for me.

The confusion fell away and was replaced by trepidation when Antonio stepped in behind her. He turned, as though to lock the door behind him, but thankfully, he couldn't. I still had a route of escape for whatever the fuck these two thought they were doing.

"Save your bullshit for someone else," I said to Antonio. I knew this hadn't been Issa's idea. The way she was watching me was as though she was seeing through me. She no longer looked shell shocked, but her skin was still a little too pale.

When I tried to step around the two of them to rejoin my pack,

Antonio blocked my path and stalked toward me until I was forced to either retreat or bump into him.

"What the fuck, Tony?" I had never been close to any of my siblings' mates, but I had never worried that one of them would corner me in a bathroom, either. Any encounter had been cordial at best, and those of us with vaginas were always dismissed from the room whenever the big, strong men decided to discuss business matters.

"You're going to go out there, tell those mother fuckers you changed your mind, and go home," he growled out, crowding me until my back hit the far wall.

"And again I ask, what the fuck? As in, what the fuck are you talking about and who the fuck do you think you are?"

Craning my neck, I sought help from my sister, but her eyes were downcast, her hands gripped in front of her as she squeezed her fingers and fidgeted.

"Issa. Could you get your mate, please?"

A gasp tore from my lips when Tony's hand shot forward and wrapped around my throat, slamming me backward until my head hit the wall. His other hand slipped into his pocket and withdrew a gaudy knife that looked as though it had been purchased for show more than use.

The sound of him flicking it open was way too loud in the silence of the bathroom. And Issa still didn't move from her spot near the door, still didn't speak up on my behalf or tell her mate to leave me alone.

"Issa! The fuck?!" I wrapped one hand around Tony's wrist in an attempt to pull him away from my throat while the other shoved at the hand holding the knife when he held it up in front of my face.

When the tip touched my throat, I stopped struggling and stared wide-eyed into the alpha's face. I didn't really know Antonio, no more than I knew any of my siblings' mates, but I would have never thought he would not only be cold enough or stupid enough to threaten me with my pack just in the other room.

"You will leave that pack. You will do as your fathers say. I refuse to lose my place in line because you're thinking with your cunt. I'll personally mow the entire group down myself if that's what it takes."

Oh, *hell* no. It was one thing to threaten me. It was a totally other to threaten my alphas.

Taking a deep breath, I opened my mouth and screamed as loud as I could, ignoring the prick of the knife against my throat when I startled Tony.

"Fucking bitch!" he roared, slamming me against the wall, turning, and grabbing my sister before dragging her from the bathroom behind him.

Nope. Not happening. Not only would I not stand there and watch that asshole manhandle my sister who looked as though she'd either had her spirit ripped away or had been doped to the gills, but he wasn't getting away after threatening to kill my alphas if I didn't obey him or my fathers.

Slapping a hand over the nick on my skin, I stumbled and nearly fell over my heels as I sprinted for the door, jumping back with a shriek when it crashed open and Keller filled the frame, his gun sweeping around the room as he sought who had caused my reaction.

"Tony. Antonio. My sister's mate," I rambled out as quickly as possible.

His fingers dug into my arm as he dragged me to the dining room and practically threw me inside before taking off through the public area, his gun held by his side, in search for my assailant.

My pack and my brothers-in-law lunged to their feet at my hurried and frazzled appearance, growls and snarls erupting as their alpha hormones filled the room until I was nearly choking on the smokey, heady scents.

Our fun pack date just went from wonderful to awkward to dangerous within a blink of an eye.

And all because of the assholes who stood glaring at me, ushering my mom from the table as though they knew exactly what had just transpired and wanted to be gone before my pack was made aware that they'd allowed someone to put their hands on me.

CHAPTER THIRTY

<u>Bain</u>

Our omega was shoved in the room by Keller, who then slammed the door shut behind him. His gun had been in his hand.

And there was a bloody mark on Corazon's throat that she kept dabbing at, pulling her fingers away to check them.

"What the fuck happened?" I bellowed, rushing to her side and turning to her fathers. They merely glared back as they casually stood, tugged her mother to her feet, and began ushering her toward the door. "What did you do?"

"We've been right here in the same room with you, pup," Vance said.

Of the four, he was the most verbal, the only one who'd bother saying a word since they'd walked through the door.

My eyes scanned the table. There were two people missing from the group. A female who'd resembled Corazon with dark hair and dark eyes who I could only assume to be my omega's sister, and the alpha who'd escorted her from the room minutes ago.

Growls erupted until all ambient noise was drowned out by the sound. The scents of my pack turned bitter and smokey as their rage rose to match my own.

Cohl darted toward the door, snarling at Pack Alvarez as he passed, and ripped the door open so hard it slammed against the far wall and left a divot from the handle.

I wanted to follow suit, to chase after the cock sucker who'd dared touch our omega, to put my gun to his head and pull the trigger. I would revel in the sight and scent of his blood spilling across the restaurant floor and didn't give a fuck how many witnesses there would be.

But I needed to check on my omega, make sure she wasn't hurt.

Glancing at Enzo, I jerked my head toward the fleeing alphas with a silent order to not only ensure they left the building, but the parking lot. I knew they would also be on the hunt for the fucker who'd followed my princess from the room.

Taking her by her shoulders, I turned her toward me as my brother and his pack followed Pack Alvarez so closely I was sure they could feel the anger radiating from their big bodies. Corazon was our omega, but they would always protect a member of our family.

"What happened?" I asked, pulling her hand away and tilting her chin up so I could figure out where the blood was coming from and determine whether she needed medical attention.

"I went to the bathroom. Issa...my sister Isabelle came in. Her alpha mate, Antonio, followed her in. He tried to tell me I had to leave you guys and go back to my parents. And then the asshole threatened to kill you. *To kill my pack*. That was when I screamed. And he jumped and...did this," she said, waving at her neck.

"*How* did he do that?"

She blinked a few times and her bottom lip quivered. "He was holding a knife to my neck. To my throat."

Another growl tore from me and she whined at the sound, sagging toward me slightly as her omega instincts forced her to submit to my alpha's possession.

There was only a nick, but the fact he'd not only threatened her, but had dared to touch her sent a white-hot rage burning through my system until I was having trouble seeing straight.

There was still food and drinks on the table, but I wanted my omega out of this building and back home where it was safe. I still couldn't believe I'd let her talk us into taking her into public.

And why the fuck hadn't one of us followed her from the private lounge? I should have known those Alvarez fucks would try something, even in a crowded public place. I wouldn't have been surprised if the Garcia cowards were still in their pocket, simply waiting for us to be out of the way so they could claim Corazon as they'd originally been promised.

After a few seconds of me examining her, running my hands over nearly every part of her I could, she batted my hands away.

"I want to go home," she said, her bottom lip still trembling, and fuck if that didn't make me want to beat every one of her fathers to a pulp. Hopefully, Keller had been able to catch up with that Antonio fucker.

At least he better hope it was Keller who caught him and not Cohl. The redheaded alpha was unhinged at the best of times. The fact the alpha had dared to touch our omega...Cohl would tear him to pieces like a rabid fucking animal.

My hopes were dashed when Cohl came barreling back into the private area, snarling at the diners who watched him with varying looks of confusion to fear to outright disapproval.

"Who was the motherfucker?" Cohl growled, pulling Corazon to his side and hugging her tightly, rubbing his chin along the top of her head to scent mark her.

"Brother-in-law. That was my sister and her alpha, one of her mates."

She kept her head high, barely glancing in the direction of the diners as we escorted her from the room, flanking her on all sides. Two of my guards waited outside the room and walked ahead of us, stepping outside and giving the all-clear for us to step out of the restaurant and onto the sidewalk.

Cohl kept our omega close to his side, his arm draped around her shoulders until she was almost stumbling over her feet to keep up. But she didn't complain. In fact, other than the quivering of her bottom lip, she was cool as a fucking cucumber on the outside. She refused to allow anyone to see how rattled she was.

What really pissed me off was not only the fact some cock sucker had the nerve to touch my omega, but she'd taken a risk with a knife so close to her throat. Yeah, I was glad she'd screamed and alerted Keller to the danger she was in, but it would have been so easy for that Antonio fuck to have taken her life. She would have been dead on the floor before any of us could have gotten to her.

Instead of climbing into the driver or passenger seat, I climbed in beside Corazon with Cohl scooting in on the other side. Ford climbed behind the wheel with Valen taking the passenger's seat. He glanced back with his brows raised.

"You okay, sweetheart?"

"I'm pissed," she said, crossing her arms over her chest after Cohl stretched the seatbelt over her and clicked it into place as though she were a child. More like precious cargo.

"I should have known that fucker would be upset that his place was at risk."

"I'm confused. How does your bonding with us have any effect on his place in your fathers' business?" Valen asked. He was belted in, but kept his upper half turned so he could look at Corazon as though afraid to pull his eyes away from her.

With the tiny cut on her throat, the blood smeared and dried, I could totally understand. Our first pack outing together, and she'd come so close to being killed.

I supposed I should be thankful it wasn't completely because of us, although it was because she'd chosen us rather than fighting to return to her family or demanding she be united with Pack Garcia.

"Power. It's all about power. Every single one of my siblings are bonded to packs that had been chosen by my fathers. My sister, Issa, is only bonded to a beta and that one alpha. She's the only one with the one alpha."

I watched her profile and waited for more of the story. Because so far, nothing she said explained why the hell her personal life had anything to do with Antonio or any of her other siblings.

"I'm the youngest, not just the only omega. Until I fall in line, everything is put on hold. My fathers maintain their death grip on the business. I know damn well they planned this shit to keep us all in line, to keep *me* in line. Until every one of us is bonded to the pack of their choice, none of us gets even a whiff of their fortune or power. Not that my sister, brothers, or I would have reaped any of the benefits. It would have all gone to our packs, our alphas. And since Issa only has one alpha, he would be in charge of a larger hold than someone like me who would have had three. Does that make sense?"

A growl rumbled from Cohl, but he kept his mouth shut and his hold tight around Corazon's shoulders.

"So, they not only handpicked the people you each would be bound to for life, they dangled carrots in front of the alphas you were bonded to," I growled.

Isabelle had strongly resembled Corazon. They both strongly resembled their mother. But being as all five of their fathers looked so similar with their dark Sicilian traits, it would have been impossible to pinpoint who was each of their biological fathers without a DNA test.

My omega's beta sister had looked as though she were sleepwalking. Her eyes were as dim and dazed looking as the omega's the Garcia fucks had dragged into our meeting.

Was she being drugged by her alpha? Did the alphas chosen by the Alvarez men keep their mates doped to keep them compliant while they waited for their share from the empire built on blood?

From the research we'd done, Corazon's brothers and one sister were all betas. Had her fathers forced even her beta brothers into packs of alphas?

Honestly, the only thing I cared about at the moment was getting my omega home. I wanted her in the safety of our house, behind the locked and guarded gates of our estate.

"Did Keller catch up to that fucker?" I asked Cohl since he'd been the one to chase our guard through the door.

I knew the answer but needed my brain to focus on something other than the fear I still felt at how close we'd come to losing our omega after such a short amount of time together.

Who the fuck was I trying to fool? It didn't matter if we had a hundred years together. I would never get enough of Corazon.

Twining my fingers through hers, I pulled her hand to my mouth and pressed my lips to her knuckles, breathing in her scent that was still tainted with a bitter hint of fear and anger.

Once the rage and residual terror wore off, I knew I would feel nothing short of overwhelming pride for my girl. She hadn't wilted under stress, hadn't cowered when she'd been cornered. She'd alerted one of our guards that she was in danger only after that asshole had threatened us, threatened her pack, her alphas.

My girl was so fucking strong. From the moment she'd woken in our house, she'd fought. She'd kept her wits about her, had been defiant, had even attempted to seduce Cohl in hopes of finding an ally to let her go. That little moment had backfired and started something deeper.

And now? Now, she was the absolute love of our lives. I would willingly walk away from everything we'd built if she'd asked, would hand over every bit of power and wealth we'd grown if it would keep her safe.

But, as long as her fathers were still in the scene, she might never be safe. And the fact I might have to kill her parents didn't sit well with me. While Corazon might understand the whys, that didn't mean she wouldn't feel a touch of guilt that she was the reason her family had been slaughtered.

The first SUV pulled through the gate with guards standing nearby to ensure no others could follow our small caravan down the driveway. We hadn't been alerted that we'd been followed, but I was on edge as were the rest of the pack.

Since the moment Ford, Valen, Cohl, and I had fully bonded Corazon to us, every single emotion of my packmates had flashed in my chest as though they were my own, even stronger than before we'd met our omega.

The rumbling of Harleys echoed across the area as my brother and his two packmates followed the last SUV and idled along the driveway until they'd parked in the grass. Assholes. We weren't exactly the *get off my lawn* type of people, but they could have at least parked on the blacktop like normal fucking human beings.

Cohl stepped from vehicle and pulled Corazon along with him, tugging her away from me before ushering her up the stairs and into the house. The increase in his alpha hormones was enough warning that he would have her bent over the first surface he could find, knotting her and covering her in his scent as his baser side demanded. Of the four of us, he was the most likely to go feral and the only way to keep that from happening was his omega's touch, her warmth, her scent, and her body wrapped around his.

"She okay?" Enzo asked as we watched Ford and Valen follow our packmates into the house.

"She's strong. I'm sure she's shaken up, but she'll be okay. I appreciate your help."

Enzo took my offered hand and squeezed. "Never have to thank us for protecting family. She's your omega. That makes her our sister."

I ignored the rush of lust and rage pouring through the pack bonds so I could focus on my conversation with my brother. Last thing I needed was a boner while we figured out how to go about ending any risk to my mate or any members of our pack.

Then there were the fuckers from Garcia who were attacking our warehouses and taking out guards left and right. Sure, we were still stronger than they were, but that wouldn't last if I couldn't end this bullshit as soon as possible.

I really didn't want to force Corazon to spend the rest of her life locked in the house. And I knew she would fucking hate that. She'd been so excited to finally get out, had spent extra time doing her hair and makeup until she felt pretty. None of that shit mattered to us – all four of us saw her as the most beautiful woman we'd ever laid eyes on and, personally, I still couldn't believe she was ours.

All the preparation and excitement and we'd had to cut our date short because of her fucking family.

Something else was niggling at the back of my brain – the way she'd reacted to her mother when she'd approached. Her mom had touched her, hugged her, whispered something in her ear, had even paid attention as we were each introduced. From what Cohl had reported, her mom was very hands off with the entire family and behaved like…

Fuck. The way he'd described it, she'd behaved the way Isabelle and that other omega had. And the question of whether those assholes were doing something or giving their omegas some kind of drug to keep them complacent and docile bounced around in my head again. Was the woman we'd met a stranger to Corazon because her alphas had forgotten to dose her?

Or had it been an act to disarm her daughter in hopes of learning something to take back to Pack Alvarez as ammunition against us?

I fucking hated all these unknowns, all these unanswered questions. It caused far too much risk for my princess.

My princess. Mild amusement touched my heart. I'd used that as an insult in the beginning when I'd seen her as nothing more than another of those spoiled ass omegas who lived off her alphas' money, who demanded to be spoiled and pampered.

Corazon was nothing like that. Sure, she appreciated the things Valen had purchased for her, but the only thing she'd ever asked from us was our time. She wanted to know when we would return only because she worried about us, not because she felt as though she had any power over us.

Little did she know she held our entire world and our hearts in her soft little hands.

CHAPTER THIRTY-ONE

<u>Corazon</u>

A week after our botched pack date, and I was back to being a prisoner in the house. At least I was no longer staring at the four walls of my bedroom.

However, as time stretched on and my pack started closing the bonds down more and more…depression was settling in. I knew they were doing it to protect me. My rational, logical side was aware of that. My omega instincts, however, were all over the place. Rejection burned my heart every time they'd left me here with Enzo and his pack.

At least the three alphas no longer ran away from me any time I entered the room. Didn't matter if they did. I'd been spending more and more time in my nest any time my pack was gone. That was where I felt safest, where it smelled most heavily of my pack.

I'd also noticed that my body…well, I felt as though I couldn't get enough of my alphas, their cocks, or their knots. I swore I was constantly wet, my panties and thighs damp with slick nearly twenty-four/seven and I had no explanation for it. Not like my mom or even the teachers at boarding school had explained the details of life with a pack you actually cared about. Probably because so many of us rarely found someone we loved who loved us back.

At the moment, I was curled under a mound of blankets in my nest with my laptop open while Enzo, Ax, and Cyrus sat on the couch in my quarters shouting at some game playing on the huge screen. Apparently, being in the same house wasn't enough after our run in with my family.

There wasn't a chance in hell any of the three alphas would dare to venture into my nest without permission. Not only was every omega possessive as hell over their space, but my alphas would beat the shit out of them if they muddied it with their scents.

Pulling a blanket around me until I looked like a villain from some sci fi movie, I started typing keywords and questions into the search bar. I wasn't even sure how to word it other than *why are my emotions all over the place* or *why am I so horny all the time?*

The first few articles were obvious propaganda written by alphas trying to convince omegas of their roles in society.

But then a few popped up and certain words stood out like neon lights. My heart began to race and my palms were clammy.

No way. It couldn't be possible…could it?

With shaky legs, I stumbled from the nest and stared at the backs of the three alphas' heads, struggling to form words or force them from my throat.

"Um, Enzo?"

He turned and glanced at me over his shoulder then frowned. "What's wrong? Do you need me to call your pack?"

The moment he mentioned my alphas a whine tore from me. But that wasn't exactly what I needed at the moment. Or I did. But not for the reason he thought I did.

"I think I need a favor. But I don't want you to tell your brother or my packmates."

Enzo turned to look at Ax and Cyrus. Ax shook his head. "Nope.

I'm out. She asked you. If anyone's getting the shit beat out of them it's you."

"Asshole," Enzo muttered before pushing to his feet and approaching me.

He stopped several feet away, keeping enough distance neither of us would carry the other's scents and make my alphas go all possessive and violent.

"I need to go to the store. To get something. Something very personal."

"Nope. No way am I taking you anywhere. I don't feel like getting my throat slit today."

Cyrus muted the TV and frowned at me. "What do you need? One of us can get it."

"Not one of us. One of *you*. She just said she doesn't want her pack to know and I'm not about to keep secrets that will end up with me buried in some shallow grave in the woods," Ax said with a smirk.

I wanted to tell him he was being dramatic, but if my pack was anything at all like my family pack, there might very well be a bunch of unmarked graves in the city and state that were filled with their enemies.

For the first time in as long as I could remember, I felt shy. Awkward. I really, *really* didn't want to have to ask one of these guys to go into the store and buy a pregnancy test. What if someone saw them and recognized them? What if someone knew Enzo was my mate's brother? What if someone called one of my packmates and told them what they'd seen?

It wasn't that I thought any of them would be upset if the test happened to be positive – I wanted to be the one to tell them. And…I wasn't sure how *I* would feel about being pregnant after such a short period of time with my alphas.

We'd only spent one cycle together. The odds of getting pregnant outside of my heat were pretty slim, but it wasn't completely impossible.

Enzo tilted his head and narrowed his eyes. "You think you're pregnant," he said.

My lips popped open as my eyes widened. "How did you…"

"I mentioned to your pack there was a chance. You've been a little…needier. And your scent is off. I'm not sure whether they noticed it or chalked it up to one emotion or another."

"Yeah. I mean, I don't think I am, I just…I don't know. But my hormones, emotions, and instincts are all over the place. I have never been an overly emotional woman, but I keep feeling like I'm on the verge of crying. And every time the pack leaves, the fear of rejection makes me almost fucking dizzy."

Ax snorted. "Those suckers would never reject you. I don't think I've ever seen anyone as pussy whipped as those four alphas."

Cyrus cuffed his packmate against the back of his head. "Don't say pussy in front of the omega."

"Why not? She said fuck."

I ignored their bickering and refocused on Enzo, nothing short of a silent plea in my glassy eyes as I fought a fresh wave of tears.

Enzo growled a frustrated sound on a heavy exhale. "I'll go get it. You…wait here and do whatever you were doing before. Relax or something."

"Relax?" I huffed out. How the hell was I supposed to relax when there was a chance I was carrying a child while my pack was constantly at war with both my family and the fuckers who were supposed to have bonded me a couple months ago?

At any point, one or all of my alphas could be killed. And the odds of an omega being allowed to raise her child alone were not in my favor.

Would Enzo and his pack protect me if my alphas were killed? Surely, they would at least protect a child that might very well be Bain's.

Tears rolled over my lashes no matter how hard I tried to keep them at bay.

"Fuck. She's crying," Ax said, his discomfort more than obvious in his tone, on his face, and in his changing scent. "Go get her whatever the fuck she wants. Do you want some ice cream or something while he's gone? Or...what the fuck do omegas need when they're...like that?" he said, waving a hand in the direction of my face.

His panic actually worked to quell some of the emotional roller-coaster and put a smile on my face.

"Calm down. Go in your nest. I'll go get the pee stick thing. But if my brother gets pissed you better tell him this whole thing was your idea."

I just really didn't want to get anyone's hopes up. Or worse, find out they weren't quite ready for children. Any disappointment from them would feed directly through the bond to settle in my heart.

But what if it was positive and one or all of them weren't happy? What if I wasn't pregnant and they were disappointed and saw me as defunct?

"Dude. You seriously don't have a poker face. I can practically hear your thoughts just by watching your face. Everything is cool. It'll be fine one way or another. Go chill in your nest. Or hang out here with us and watch the game," Ax said, patting the cushion Enzo had vacated.

I looked at the TV through watery eyes and curled my nose. "No thanks."

"We can turn on whatever you want," Cyrus said.

"No, we can't. We're in the fourth quarter."

Cyrus's nostrils flared with his frustrated or maybe exasperated sigh.

"Will you be okay until I get back? Or are you going to have a meltdown?" Enzo said, shoving his big feet in the shoes that sat on the floor by the couch.

"I'll be fine," I lied. Or half lied. Not like I would die from waiting. But I couldn't promise my emotions wouldn't be all over the place.

Were Enzo's packmates not staying behind, I might have crawled into one of my alpha's beds and gotten myself off while covering my skin in their scents. Because of course I was horny. It was like my body no longer had an off button.

* * *

IT DIDN'T MATTER how many times I opened or closed my eyes, the results never changed. I'd done my best to shut down the bond so my pack wouldn't feel my nerves, anxiety, and panic and think I was in danger. If they were in the middle of some kind of issue, the last thing they needed was to be distracted by me.

I had taken a shower, slathered lotion on every inch of my body, blow dried my hair, and was currently dressed in a soft pair of pajamas and bundled under about ten blankets in my nest.

My pack still wasn't home and it was driving me crazy. I'd taken a few peeks into the bond just to ensure myself they were okay, but I refused to be the reason I lost one of them.

When my stomach grumbled, I wasn't sure whether I was nauseous, hungry, or simply nervous. Maybe all three. Because holy shit...I was pregnant.

I had dreaded the day I would see those results on one of those damn pee sticks, but that had been when I'd been forced to bond with alphas I didn't love or even really like. But now...

What if they weren't happy? What if it was too early to start a family? What if only one of them was happy? What if they wanted a DNA test to discover who the biological father was? What if the others didn't accept our child?

Tears burned the backs of my eyes as so many freaking worst-case scenarios played through my head.

There was also the whole families at war thing, meaning my child wouldn't have any relationship with my family pack, wouldn't have a grandma or grandpa Alvarez, no aunts or uncles from my side who would love and dote on my son or daughter?

And what if my child presented as an omega? Would my mates treat them the way I was treated and use them to draw more power from other packs? After the way they'd treated me like royalty, I couldn't see them doing something like that, but thinking a thing and experiencing it in the future were two different situations.

A dull throb started behind my eyes as my brain refused to stop focusing on every possible negative outcome of my pack learning that I was carrying a child by one of them. I could picture Cohl being over the moon – my first official alpha was like walking sunshine, beautiful and cheery but could easily cause a painful burn.

Valen would be supportive even if he wasn't thrilled about us adding a pup to the family. But what about Ford and Bain? The two were broody and sometimes surly. And Bain had issues with keeping his mouth shut when he was angry and had verbally lashed out at me during our first few weeks together when he was frustrated or his feelings were hurt.

A keening whine tore from my lips before I could stop it as tears welled in my eyes and fell over my bottom lashes.

The door to my nest slammed open and Enzo's large body was backlit as he stood in the frame. "What? What's wrong?"

"What if they don't want a baby?" I whispered as emotion clogged my throat.

He lowered to his haunches, not daring to enter the room to get closer to me. "It was positive?"

I nodded.

A heavy sigh left his mouth, but I couldn't see his face from where he stood, and his scent didn't change enough for me to deduce anything about his emotions.

"How do *you* feel about it?" Enzo asked, his voice low and careful.

After sniffling, I swiped the tears away with one of the blankets and shrugged. "I want to be happy. I didn't really want to have kids before, but that was when I thought my life would be controlled by… well, everyone else. But I want to be happy. I want *them* to be happy."

"Are *you* happy about it?"

"I am," I whispered. "But if they're not…what if they don't want a baby? What if I end up being thrown out? I'll be on my own with a pup with nowhere to go and–"

He stood abruptly and marched forward, surprising me when he bent and lifted me from the padded nest floor and carried me from the room.

"Bain's going to kick your ass when he gets home," Ax said as Enzo carried me into the living quarters and lowered onto the couch with me cradled in his arms.

"Look at me," Enzo said as the tears began to flow freely. I blinked them away and tried to focus on the face that was so similar to one of my alphas. "They might be shocked that it happened so early. They might even be nervous about being fathers. But I've seen them with you. I've seen how my brother has literally changed from a complete asshole to a true alpha and a good mate. There isn't a chance in hell any of them would ever willingly let you go."

A sob caught in my chest and I hiccupped.

He didn't release his hold on me, and I didn't want him to. There wasn't an ounce of attraction to him or his two packmates, but he was family. They were my brothers-in-law. And...damn it, I needed the touch to keep from spiraling.

Cyrus pushed to his feet and left the room. My eyes began to droop until I heard his feet thudding through the hall. In one hand was a box of tissues and in the other was a mug.

"Hot chocolate," he said as he offered it to me, somewhat of a sheepish look on his face as he held both hands out.

"Thank you," I muttered between sniffles.

Even wrapped like a burrito in a bunch of blankets and held against an alpha's chest – one I trusted – I still couldn't keep the fear and anxiety at bay. Tears would well and trail down my cheek and then I would start to doze off. I wasn't sure how long that cycle continued, but eventually, my body relaxed against Enzo's body as three rusty purrs rumbled through the room, calming my omega enough to get a little rest before I had to face my pack with news that very well could irreversibly change our lives...

Or only mine.

CHAPTER THIRTY-TWO

<u>Cohl</u>

It felt like we were finally making some headway with all this bullshit lately. No one had mentioned it to Corazon, but Bain had received an odd text from a blocked number, warning us of an upcoming attack on one of our warehouses. We were able to put enough guards in place to head it off and avoid losing any of our own men.

We were also able to get some information from one of the fuckers who apparently wasn't exactly loyal to Pack Garcia but simply enjoyed the paycheck. Not exactly the type of person we would ever allow on our team – if he could so easily roll over on his employers, he would do the same fucking thing to us if he was ever cornered by an enemy.

Unfortunately, we also couldn't let him run back to the Garcia fucks with any information about us. So, once we got what we needed from him, I personally put a bullet in his brain pan.

We'd been gone for far too long, away from my omega for way

longer than I would like. I'd peeked in on her through the bond a few times, but she'd shut it down on her side. That didn't bode well with me.

There were not only our guards on the property, but Enzo, Ax, and Cyrus were there as they often were when we had something that required us to leave the estate.

It was my job to protect Cora. Our job. We were her pack, her alphas. Every second spent away from her sent my instincts into a tailspin until it was a feat to keep from mowing through anyone and everyone who stood in the way of me getting back home.

At least we weren't returning to our omega covered in blood. There was a small smatter on my shoes and pants, but other than that, we wouldn't require showers immediately upon walking through the door before I could hold my sweet girl.

Leaning my head against the rest, I checked on the invisible thread that tied us together and found something, but it was weak. It was a touch of anxiety, but it felt as though she was asleep. Maybe she was having a nightmare.

"Fuck. Can you drive faster?" I growled out to Ford as he navigated the highway and side roads that would lead to our somewhat secluded estate. It was close enough we didn't have to stock up on groceries and essentials but far enough away that there were no busy bodies to see us coming and going loaded down with weapons at all hours of the day and night.

Ford didn't answer. But he also didn't shove his foot against the gas pedal. I was pretty much forbidden to drive the pack to and from jobs because of my tendency toward treating the speed limit as more of a suggestion than the law. And I might have cost our pack some money in lawyer fees when I accrued a few speeding tickets.

"We're only about ten or fifteen minutes away," Valen muttered. But I could feel him in the bond through Corazon, could feel he was just as anxious to get home as I was. He just didn't tend to speak out like me. That day he'd attacked Bain was the most anger I'd ever seen him display. He was more like the dog that stalked silently before attacking.

After what felt like way too long, the SUV stopped at the gate and waited for the guard to hit the button to open it before Ford could pull forward.

I didn't bother waiting for the others, didn't wait for the engine to shut off. I wasn't even sure it was in park before I'd shoved from my seat and began to jog toward the front steps.

The door swung open and Cyrus stepped out, pulling the huge door shut behind him and heading me off before I could rush inside.

"Get the fuck out of the way," I said, stepping to the side and growling when he matched me step for step.

Bain, Ford, and Valen joined me.

"The fuck is going on?" Bain asked. "Where's Corazon? Where's my brother?"

"Before you go in there and go full possessive alpha, you need to know your omega had a fucked up night. Enzo had to comfort her. And before you start growling and charging inside, she's currently asleep in his lap."

A growl ripped from my throat before I could even contemplate swallowing it back.

"Why the fuck is Enzo touching my omega?"

"Did you hear a word I just fucking said? She needs to talk to you about something that she's terrified will…she's scared you'll kick her out. She was spiraling so Enzo made her sit with us. The only way to calm her was with touch. She's asleep right now. But…fuck, I know she's your omega, but if you make that girl cry, I might take it upon myself to challenge every single fucking one of you."

"What happened? Why is she so upset?" Valen asked.

More importantly, how could she think there was anything she could possibly do or say that would make any of us send her away? She was mine. She was ours. She was literally a part of me, and I could no more tear a piece of my soul away than I could let her go.

"Talk to her. She's not hurt or anything like that. But it's something that *she* needs to tell you, not me. Not my pack. It's between her and your pack," Cyrus said to Bain.

He finally moved out of the way and I rushed through the front door, through the foyer, took the stairs two at a time, and skidded to a stop inside Corazon's room.

Just as Cyrus had warned, she was wrapped in so many blankets she looked like a big puff ball on Enzo's lap. He raised one brow and shook his head in warning. Not that his little warning stopped the possessive growl from bursting up my chest. I didn't like to see another alpha touching my omega, and he was full on holding her on his lap with his arms tightly wrapped around her back. Her head rested on his shoulder, her lips parted as she breathed slowly in her sleep.

Ax stood and made room for the four of us to get closer.

"Is she okay?" Valen asked, taking a seat on the coffee table across from her while I sat directly beside Enzo and reached for my omega.

It was a struggle, but we were able to transfer Corazon from Enzo's lap to mine without waking her. Although I wanted to shake her until she opened her eyes and told us whatever secret she was carrying that made her think we wouldn't want her anymore.

A stuttering purr rumbled from my chest when she turned her face into my neck as though seeking my scent.

Bain waited for Enzo by the door. Their heads bowed close together as they whispered, but my sole focus was on the beautiful woman in my arms. I'd noted her pink nose and her slightly swollen eyes that were obvious even in her sleep. She'd been crying and I wanted to know who I needed to kill for causing her to become so emotional that she sought comfort from Bain's brother.

After a few nods, Bain shook his brother's hand and closed the door when Enzo and Ax stepped through, leaving our pack with our omega to wait for her to wake. The unknowns were fucking killing me. What if someone hurt her? Bain had received an anonymous text – what if someone was fucking with her?

Or could she simply have been upset by the separation from her pack? She'd been a little more emotional since the other three had marked her and made her our pack's omega. I supposed it could have been that.

But...that wouldn't convince her we would no longer want her.

I hadn't realized I'd fallen asleep with my head leaned back against the couch cushion until Cora stirred on my lap, her floral scent spiking before taking on a bitter scent.

My head shot up to find Bain, Ford, and Valen watching her closely.

Her head raised and she groggily looked around the room, settling on each of us before her eyes became glassy and her bottom lip quivered.

"What happened? Did someone hurt you? Is something wrong with you?" I blurted out, taking her face in both my hands so she had to look me directly in the eye.

The first few times she'd tried to speak, her voice came out more of a squeak. On the third try, she cleared her throat, pulled my hands away from her face, and whispered, "I'm pregnant."

I swore it felt like the air had been sucked from the room and like someone had reached into my chest and put a death grip on my heart.

"What did you say?" Ford said, shifting to sit on the coffee table across from us.

She looked at him over her shoulder with tear stains on her cheeks and fresh tears welling in those beautiful brown eyes I'd been obsessed with for months.

"I'm pregnant. I guess…maybe during my heat? I mean, it could have happened outside of my heat, but that's not as common. I took a test. Enzo went to get one for me since you guys don't want me to leave the house. And…I'm pregnant. With a baby. And I'm so scared." Her words were distorted through her emotion as those tears continued to stream down her beautiful olive complected cheeks.

"Holy shit," I breathed out.

She turned to look at me, a look of pure fear and desperation pulling her brows up and her kissable looks into a pout.

"Holy shit," I said louder.

Lunging to my feet with her still in my arms, my eyes went wide as my brain finally kicked into gear and caught up to what she'd said.

"I'm going to be a dad?"

"*We're* going to be dads," Valen said.

I glanced at where he still sat on the couch, a small smile pulling up the corners of his lips.

Ford and Bain looked as though they were still in shock, but surely, they had to be as happy as I was. I didn't even give a fuck which of us actually knocked her up – our beautiful omega would grow a big round belly and birth our first child, the first offspring of Pack Rivera.

Hugging her tightly, I leaned my head down and kissed her until we were breathless.

Then pulled away and frowned down at her.

"Wait – is that why you've been crying? You thought we wouldn't want a baby with you? You really fucking thought we would throw you out for carrying our child?"

A lone tear rolled down her left cheek and I couldn't help but lean forward and kiss it away.

"You could cut off one of my big toes and I still wouldn't let you go, omega. You're mine. Forever and ever. And even after we die, I'll make sure we haunt people together."

"Idiot," Ford muttered.

I turned a glare on the two who had yet to show any emotion one way or another. If either of them made my girl cry again, I'd drag them into the back yard and beat them both to a pulp.

"You're having a baby?" Bain asked, his face and voice completely devoid of emotion.

Cora bit her lip and nodded. "I'm sorry. I know we should have used…I didn't think about it then. And my parents wouldn't let me get on birth control because of–"

A growl burst from Bain's chest, cutting off her words. "Let's not bring up those fuckers or any former relationships."

The room went quiet for a few more seconds.

"We're going to be fucking fathers," Ford said as though thinking out loud. His head lifted and he looked to each of us. "We need to hire more guards. And start interviewing nannies. Shit. We need to set up a nursery. What about the security alarms and cameras? Are there enough?"

"We've got a few months," Bain said, raising a hand and rubbing the back of his neck. "Holy shit. We're going to have a kid. I'm going to be a dad. There's going to be a little girl or little boy running these halls."

"You're not mad?" she whispered.

I turned a look on her that hopefully told her exactly how absurd her question was. "Why the fuck would we be mad? You're going to make us a family."

"We got to start cleaning up our language," Valen said as though adding things to Ford's list of preparations.

"We run guns and drugs and dodge bullets on a regular basis and our language is what you're focusing on?" Bain grumbled.

His words set Cora off again. She huffed out a sob as fresh tears streamed down her cheeks.

"Oh my god. You guys could be killed and leave me alone with the baby? Or they could come after him…or her."

"We would never let anyone hurt you or our baby," I said, hugging her tighter.

I lowered onto the couch again, draping her legs over mine so she was sitting sideways, and pulled her head against my chest, tucking her under my chin so I could scent mark her. A purr that rattled to life was from pure joy and excitement. We did have a lot to do in a relatively short amount of time, but we had plenty of resources to help with all that shit, especially the security side.

"We're going to have a baby," I whispered, pressing a kiss to her temple then the top of her head. "You're going to be so fucking sexy with a big belly, round ass, and huge tits."

Her giggle shook against me. I rested my cheek on top of her head and sighed. Holy shit. It didn't matter how many times I said or thought those two words…it would take me a minute to fully grasp the fact that the most beautiful woman in the world had not only accepted us as her alphas, as her pack, but she was gifting us with a child.

And fuck…we had a lot to do yet I couldn't wait to start the preparations and start ordering anything and everything our first child could ever need or want.

"Do you think we have a big enough yard for a pony?" I asked. Because yeah, I would totally be that parent who would give my son or daughter anything they asked for the moment they could speak.

CHAPTER THIRTY-THREE

<u>Valen</u>

My head rested on Cora's belly. It was still way too early, but there was a part of me that desperately wanted to hear our baby's heartbeat or maybe feel it move. That would be months from now, but that didn't stop me from daydreaming and fantasizing.

It really didn't matter to me which of us fathered our son or daughter; all that mattered was my omega was carrying the newest member of our family in her beautiful little body.

"What if we have a daughter? What if she presents as an omega?" she asked softly.

Bain, Cohl, and Ford were out checking inventory and making sure one of our shipments went smoothly. No one wanted to leave our omega, even with Enzo, Ax, and Cyrus currently sitting downstairs, but we couldn't provide for her and our pup if our business went belly up. And that was exactly what would happen if the Garcia or Alvarez assholes continued to fuck with our exports.

It had come down to Corazon. We'd let her follow her omega instincts. When she'd asked me to stay, I could have dropped to my knees and kissed her feet.

"What do you mean?" I asked, rolling my head to look at her face.

We were on the pack bed with a movie playing softly in the background. Her fingers toyed with my hair, her nails gently scraping against my scalp.

"As a big, bad alpha, you don't know how fucked up it can be for my designation, especially growing up in a powerful family."

"If you're worried we would ever do to our child what your parents did, I'm going to have to put you over my knee and spank your ass. You should know better by now."

She smiled at me. "Spank my ass, huh? Threat or promise?"

Reaching under her, I pinched her ass, causing her to jerk and giggle.

We both went quiet again. I kept my head on her belly, closing my eyes and dreaming of the day her belly would be round and I could feel the little pup kick against the side of my head. Her fingers continued their slow comb through my hair, nearly lulling me to sleep as her Lily of the Valley scent wrapped around me.

A purr rumbled from my chest at how perfect the moment felt. I knew she would have preferred all four of her alphas be here, wouldn't grow fully settled until the pack was all back together, but at least she was calm for now.

"You think I should call my parents and tell them? Or at least my mom?"

My eyes flew open and landed on her face. "Why would you do that?"

Her shoulders shrugged awkwardly as she laid against the pillows keeping her shoulders and head raised. "My mom seemed…I don't know. At the restaurant that day, she actually acted like she'd missed me, like she'd been worried about me. I always thought I was nothing more than a means to an end to all of them. My sister and brothers were all but forgotten because of their designation, but none of us were exactly treated as though we were wanted or loved. But…maybe my mom was just going through the motions because of my dads. You know?"

I pushed up onto my elbow and looked at her. "Do you want to call your mom? You know we'd support you if you wanted to try to open the line of communication with her." Not that we would ever allow her out of our sight without a heavy presence of our guards.

Her hand smoothed over her flat stomach. She would only be a few weeks along and we'd yet to set an appointment with a doctor, but that needed to happen sooner rather than later. I knew I wanted to see physical evidence of the life we'd created with our omega. I couldn't wait to hear the little heartbeat, to see her belly grow, to watch as our child prepared to join our lives.

We also needed to make sure the little bean in there was healthy. Cohl had waited all of a day before he'd hired someone to work on the room we'd designated as the nursery and was already filling it with furniture and ordering clothes before we knew whether a son or daughter would join our pack.

She worried her bottom lip between her teeth, her eyes on the path her hand made on her stomach. "I wish..."

When she didn't finish, I sat up and scooted so I could pull her onto my lap and wrap my body around her as much as possible.

"What, sweetheart?"

"I wish my dads were more like you guys. I mean the loving part." Because, business-wise, we *were* like her fathers. Both their pack and ours earned our fortune through...unsavory means. The only thing we refused to have any part in was the trafficking of humans. That shit was disgusting and, to me, was one of the purest forms of evil out there.

Rubbing my chin along the top of her head, I let a purr rumble up again as I hugged her tightly against my chest, bracketing her body with both my legs.

"I'm sorry, sweetheart. I wish it had been different for you, too. Although...don't get pissed at me for saying this, but had you been gifted with parents who actually gave a shit, we might never have met."

"Meaning I would never have been sold to alphas I didn't know, and you never would have ambushed the convoy and kidnapped me?"

I would have worried if I hadn't heard the humor in her voice or felt her body shake lightly with her chuckle.

Lowering my head, I rested my chin on her shoulder and turned to press a kiss to her cheek. "I hate that our first memories of each other are..." I didn't really want to say the words, remind her of the blood and brain bits that had covered her, or that she'd been so fucking terrified of us.

I hated that our beginning had been wrought with fear and danger.

But really, in our world, that was a given. She'd grown up with men in our line of work and had seen the uglier side of society. That didn't mean I couldn't wish we hadn't met like normal alphas and their omega, that we hadn't courted her properly, taken her on dates and lavished her with expensive, pretty shit.

Cora dropped her head against my shoulder and turned so she could reach my lips. The kiss was slow and gentle before she pulled back to look into my eyes. "Our start was fucked up; I'll give you that. But I'm a firm believer that everything in this life happens for a reason. I think my omega knew you were mine from that first night I caught all your scents, regardless of how close my heat was. You were always meant to be mine, Valen. All four of you were. Even Enzo and his pack were meant to be in my life."

A low growl trickled from my chest as a touch of possessiveness turned my stomach.

She gave me a look and raised one brow. "Oh, please. I don't want them. They're like brothers. I guess they kind of are now being as Enzo is the brother to one of my mates."

"You better not want them. I'd hate to have to kill Bain's brother."

A wry smirk quirked up one side of her pillowy lips. "Hmm. You're kind of sexy when you get all jealous, alpha."

There would come a time when we would have to be gentler with Corazon, when we would have to be careful of her belly and the child she was carrying.

But that time was not now.

Arms tight around her, I lifted and turned her so she was on her back with me hovering over her. "You want me to be jealous?"

Her chest rose and fell in rapid breaths, her pupils were blown, and her perfume lifted on the air in a burst of floral sweetness. "Maybe I'll go flirt with Ax, ask him to show me one of those dances."

I knew what she was doing. Knew she was goading me. Didn't mean my alpha didn't instantly push forward and demand I claim her body, cover her in my scent, and make sure any fucker who came within twenty feet of her knew she was mine.

"How much do you like your clothes?"

Her dark brows puckered for a brief second before my meaning became clear.

"I'm sure Ax could show me how to–" Her words were cut off with a gasp as I grabbed her shirt and ripped it down the center, exposing her tits to me.

Her shorts and panties suffered the same fate as I tore them and tossed them over my shoulder.

I wanted to taste her, run my tongue along every dip and valley of her body, to taste every inch of her. But my little omega had decided to play with fire tonight. Of the four of us, I'd always been the most even keeled...until it came to my omega.

Running my fingers through her folds, a pleased growl left my lips at how wet she was, her sweet slick drenching her pussy and thighs. Lifting my hand, I sucked her arousal from my fingers, my eyes nearly rolling in my head at the addictive sweetness that burst across my tongue.

A needy whine lifted on the air a second before I pushed her thighs open and shoved her knees to her chest, opening her for me so I could slam my dick hard and deep inside of her. I wanted to coat her inner walls with my cum. After that, I would fuck her again and again, leaving my release on her tits, her stomach, her face until she carried my spiced pumpkin scent for days.

She cried out as I began a hard and fast rhythm, her hands reaching for me. "No. Hands above your head. I'm going to make sure

Ax and every other fucker on this planet knows exactly who you belong to."

That whine grew louder as her need swelled, sending a burst of her perfume into the air until I could taste it on my tongue, until I swore it was sinking into my pores.

"I'm yours, alpha. I'm all yours," she repeated over and over like a mantra.

"Mine," I growled out, fucking into her slicked cunt so hard the headboard smacked against the wall, the sound warring with the slapping of our bodies.

Would I ever get enough of this feeling, of the way Corazon felt under me, the way her body felt wrapped around me, of the sounds she made in the throes of passion and pleasure?

"I can feel you clenching my cock," I growled out. Her breathing was heavy, her moans lifting as her inner walls pulsed around me. My omega was so fucking close. And I would make sure she shattered around me.

"I'm going to...fuck, alpha. I'm coming," she cried out, throwing her head back, her arms still above her head like I'd demanded, her fingers clenching the pillow under her head.

Releasing her thighs, I leaned over her and kissed her, a deep, licking kiss so I could swallow her moans, claim them as my own, own them.

My balls tightened, tingles rippled up my spine, then I pulled my mouth away from hers and buried my face against her neck, licking at the mark I'd left on her as I filled her, my dick twitching and sending wave after wave of soul shattering release.

Her pussy still fluttered around me when a whimper tugged at my heart. Pulling back, I looked down into glassy brown eyes and trembling lower lip.

"What? Did I hurt you?" Panic rippled through me as I moved to pull out of her.

But she hooked her feet around my back. "You didn't knot me. And now my omega is all over the place. It's the fucking hormones, but...it feels like rejection."

It took a few seconds to catch up, or maybe catch on, but a smile tugged at my lips before I lowered to press soft kisses to her cheeks, the tip of her nose, then her lips. "I didn't knot you because I'm not done with you yet, omega. You wanted to see how far you could push me, how jealous you could make me. By the time we leave this room, you're going to have a hard time walking and those three fuckers downstairs will choke on my scent all over you."

A fresh wave of slick coated my dick, mixing with her release and mine. The tears were still there, but her increased perfume nearly drove me insane with need. Again.

I had no idea when our packmates planned to return. But I had every intention of fucking my omega over and over until her other alphas demanded her attention. Only then would I stop filling and covering her with my cum.

CHAPTER THIRTY-FOUR

<u>Corazon</u>

*L*ast night, Valen had kept his promise about making sure I had a hard time walking on my own and covering me in his scent. After the first round, he'd pulled out twice to cover my tits and stomach, before fucking me the fourth time and finally giving me his knot. Only after he'd locked us together did my damn emotions cease to make me feel as though I was losing my mind.

This was a moment in time I wished I had someone to talk to about my pregnancy. My mother sure as hell hadn't bothered talking to me or my sister, Issa, about what we could expect if or when we got knocked up. But, being of the same designation, Mom could have at least warned me that not only would the emotional rollercoaster be even worse than during my heat, but I would feel almost as insatiable as when my body needed to breed with my alphas.

Luckily, my three alphas noted how rubbery my limbs were and how utterly – and beautifully – exhausted I was and simply stripped and climbed into the pack bed to hold me through the night.

And then I'd woken alone.

I really had no attraction toward Enzo or his two packmates, but teasing Valen sure had been worth it. He'd become so dominant, something I rarely saw in my sweet giant of an alpha. Bain and Ford were always a little on the dominant side. Cohl was very primal and aggressive. But Valen always watched for any and every little reaction from me as though making sure he wasn't being too rough, regardless of how many times I reminded him that, as an omega, my body was made to take my alphas in any way we could dream of, including but not limited to having three of them knot my pussy, ass, and mouth at once.

Pulling my arms over my head, I stretched from my fingertips to my toes and rolled from the bed. I'd intended to shower before seeking my alphas…until I found a hastily written note on the mirror with my lipstick.

You better still smell like me.

I bit my bottom lip as a grin stretched across my lips. Valen. He was still teasing me, testing me. He wanted me covered in his scent when I'd acted as though I would seek Ax for a little private dance. Little had I known I'd awakened a possessive beast inside of him. And hell yes, I loved it. It was just another layer of my alpha that I'd successfully unwrapped.

The five of us had only had a few months together, but it sure as hell felt longer. At times, it felt as though we'd had a lifetime together, as though there had been no awkward time, as though there wasn't a time when I fought my mind and body against hating or fucking Bain. Oftentimes, the two were the same when he would hurt my feelings or piss me off and my omega would demand I remind him and myself that we were meant to be tied together for life.

Skipping my morning shower – for now – I brushed my teeth, ran a brush through my waist length hair, then pulled it into a bun on the top of my head to keep it out of my face.

I was half tempted to walk through the house and downstairs naked in case there were others still here, simply to make my alphas possessive, even if it felt a little petty. Would all four claim me the way

Valen had last night? Would all four demand they leave me covered in their scents and marks from their hands and fingers?

"Get it together," I whispered to myself.

I really shouldn't have been so fucking horny first thing in the morning after how many orgasms Valen had wrung from my body last night, but...all I could do was chalk it up to pregnancy hormones.

As I pulled a pair of leggings and a sweater from the closet, I thought about calling my mom again. She might not have been the mother of the year when I was growing up, but she really had acted as though she cared that day at the restaurant. She'd asked my pack to take care of me.

And she was the only omega in my life. The only person I could call for some answers about the way my body was behaving. I knew I could call the Omega Center, but I really had no desire to talk to complete strangers about why I was so horny all day.

It had only been three days since I'd discovered I was carrying my first child, three days since I'd told my pack and Cohl had immediately started making plans about the nursery. I needed to find a good OB/GYN and get my first checkup scheduled. I didn't care how my child presented later; I just wanted to make sure my little one was happy and healthy and knew how much he or she was loved.

The voices of my pack and a few guards I'd finally gotten to know a little filtered up the stairs. When I heard Enzo's voice, I hesitated on the stairs, my hand gripping the railing.

Damn it. They were talking too low for me to catch the words, but the change in the scents floated on the air, telling me I wouldn't be walking into a pack of happy alphas. Something was definitely up. And if Enzo was here, I wondered if that meant my pack would be leaving me alone again.

I hated when they were all four gone. It was bad enough with the new rush of hormones constantly making me feel like a stereotypical needy omega. But when they were all gone, a sense of abandonment and rejection constantly made me feel as though I could burst into tears at any moment. The only thing that distracted me were the few times Enzo and his packmates would hang out with me and play cards or a board game.

At least they were no longer fleeing the room as soon as I stepped in anymore.

When Enzo had held me the night I'd fallen apart after seeing those two lines on the pregnancy test was the day our relationship had shifted the tiniest bit. He no longer saw me as a claimed omega, but rather a member of his family, his sister-in-law, and I was carrying his first niece or nephew.

Giving up on eavesdropping, I jogged down the remaining steps and followed the voices to the kitchen. It wasn't early, but I was still surprised to see everyone showered, dressed, and fully alert. Bain, Ford, and Cohl had gotten in after three last night. Meaning Enzo and his pack either went home late and came back this morning or they'd crashed in one of the guest rooms.

Everyone went quiet the second I stepped into the room.

"What's up?" I asked, heading for the coffee.

Of course, Bain stepped in my way with a shake of his head. "No caffeine. Sorry, Princess."

I grumbled a curse under my breath and grabbed a bottle of juice from the fridge instead. "You realize I'm going to have withdrawal headaches? And I plan to make your life a living hell until they stop," I said to him with a glare as I poured a glass while Valen made me plate.

Settling down at the table, I lifted a piece of bacon and searched the faces watching me closely. "Okay, seriously. What's up? Why did you stop talking when I walked in here?"

When the seven alphas exchanged a look as though having a silent conversation, I shook my head. "Uh uh. Nope. Not doing the secret keeping shit again. We all agreed to that months ago. What's going on now?"

"Someone has been feeding us inside information. Someone...in your family pack's inner circle," Ford said, his thick arms crossed over his chest. His gray eyes were smokier than normal, closer to gunmetal than the storm cloud gray I'd fallen in love with.

"How do you know they're in my family's inner circle?"

"Because the information they've been sending us could only be gleaned by either sitting in on meetings, or…"

"Or…what?" I asked when Ford didn't finish his sentence.

"Or overhearing it from one of their mates," Valen said.

"You think it's one of my siblings?"

"Either one of your siblings or one of your family's guards. They've been able to report to us any time Pack Garcia has planned to attack one of our warehouses or exports. That's why we had to leave last night. I received a text about a possible threat," Bain said, running a hand across my belly almost absentmindedly.

"You said you needed to check inventory." I raised an eyebrow.

"Wasn't a lie. We needed to make sure nothing had been stolen or destroyed. I'm not sure whether your family has a mole working with the Garcia bunch, whether your fathers are more in the know with their activity than they would ever admit, or maybe someone on the Garcia side is feeding information to your fathers' men," Bain said.

I narrowed my eyes as each new piece of information began to feel like a weight around my neck. "Why would anyone from either pack help you?"

"Because of you?" Enzo offered. "Were you close to any of your fathers' employees? Maybe the guards?"

"No. Not really. They were polite and protective, but I wasn't close with anyone in the house. Out of my siblings, Issa was the only one who didn't treat me like I was a threat to their very existence."

Because, while I wasn't exactly treated with love, my parents at least acknowledged my existence because of my designation. My beta siblings were solely raised by nannies before they were sent off to boarding school or college.

Issa and I had never had the sisterly bond that I'd always wanted, but she at least talked to me and would check on me when I'd had a bad day or our fathers were hard on me.

I really had no idea who the hell would benefit from helping me or my pack.

Bain sat on my right. Cohl sat on my left. The moment Bain pulled his hand away from my flat belly, Cohl's hand took its place. There was absolutely nothing to feel yet, but the fact my alphas were so head over heels happy and already in love with our child filled me with a warm and fuzzy sensation and caused tears to well in my eyes.

"Shit. What's wrong?" Cohl asked, turning in his chair and turning my face toward him in his big, warm hands.

"Nothing," I said through a watery smile, waving his concern off. "It's my emotions. I was just thinking...I'm happy. And apparently, omega pregnancy hormones are more potent than heat hormones."

"She definitely smells different," Enzo said.

"Stop sniffing my mate," Cohl growled.

"Don't have to sniff her. Her perfume is following her like a fucking cloud," Ax said with an unrepentant grin. Of the three, Ax was so similar to Cohl with his *don't give a fuck* attitude.

Matching growls lifted on the air, but I ignored them.

As though my emotions wanted to enforce my earlier statement about being all over the place, my happiness quickly bled into anger. "Wait. You said someone has been feeding you information. For how long? And why the hell are you just now telling me?"

At least my vision was no longer blurred by the tears. Nope. Now, my heart thumped with anger that they were still keeping me in the dark about something as important as someone having my alpha's phone number and sending tips. Tips that could very well end up being nothing more than a trap.

What would happen if my alphas were mowed down when they checked out one of those so-called tips, especially now that I was carrying a child by one of them?

Yeah. Anger. Or rage. Maybe fear?

I really needed to talk to someone about all this before I drove myself insane. And dragged my pack along for the ride.

CHAPTER THIRTY-FIVE

<u>Ford</u>

Enzo, Ax, and Cyrus finally went home a few hours ago. They'd been here for two fucking days. Not that their presence kept us from burying ourselves in our omega every chance we got. Like Ax had pointed out, her perfume was constantly lifted on the air and kept my dick hard whether I was awake or not.

And my girl sure as hell wasn't complaining about all the dick or attention. She'd told us she thought her increased need and scent was due to pregnancy hormones, but we wouldn't know for sure until her doctor's appointment next week.

What did it say about me that I couldn't wait for the baby to be born so we could try for another? That primal need deep inside of me wanted to breed my omega as often as possible. Even if she wasn't amenable to having another child right away – or at all – we could still have fun practicing. We'd just make sure she found a safe birth control so there wouldn't be anything between us. I would never grow tired of her tight, slicked pussy wrapped around my cock, squeezing as she fell apart.

A text came through from a guard at the gate that yet another delivery was in route to the door. Fucking Cohl. We had at least seven or eight months, yet the crazy bastard was already going overboard. And I knew he wouldn't care whether that child came out with a head full of red hair or not – he would be the most protective, overbearing father to the first child of Pack Rivera.

Holy shit. We'd found out just over a week ago, yet the fact we were going to be fathers, *I* was going to be a father, still shocked the shit out of me. We'd given up searching for an omega to add to the pack years ago, figuring if we met the right person…

Apparently, fate or destiny or whoever the fuck decided this shit knew better than us and knew the only omega who could ever make us feel so fucking complete was the daughter of our enemy. Only Corazon could have so utterly wrecked us and became the center of our universe.

The sounds of Corazon's giggles from the living room tugged at my heart and elicited a small smile as I headed to the front door to intercept whatever bullshit the ginger alpha had ordered this time.

A phone rang in the other room as I signed for at least ten boxes and started hauling them inside.

It didn't take but a few seconds for me to feel the shift in the air, the way my omega's perfume had taken on a slightly bitter hint behind the floral signature.

Abandoning the boxes on the foyer – Cohl could put away all this shit – I headed for the living room where Corazon was hanging out with Valen and Cohl while Bain and I had gone into the office to work for a few hours.

"Hey," Corazon's soft voice said as I turned the corner.

I frowned at Valen, but he shrugged and shook his head.

"No. I'm glad you called. I just…I didn't want to tell you over text. I'm, um…Mom, I'm pregnant."

Mom. Her mom had called. Valen had told me about their conversation while the three of us had headed out to check out the newest tip that had been texted to Bain's phone. We all supported anything she could ever want, but no way in hell would she be meeting with any member of her past without all four of us as well as a decent number of guards there to keep her safe. Especially after that fucker had held a knife to her throat and threatened her life.

Leaning my hip against the end of the couch, I crossed my arms and watched her face for any tells, then swallowed back a growl when her eyes grew glassy with tears before one spilled over her bottom lashes and a wobbly smile tugged at her lips.

"Yeah. Only a few weeks, I think, but I have a doctor's appointment next week."

It was a struggle to keep my face emotionless. I really did not want anyone knowing her schedule. It would be too easy for someone to set some kind of trap or ambush against her to get to us...

Like we had done that first day. Cohl had watched her long enough to learn her routines and patterns, had been able to find out the exact time and date of the bonding ceremony, even got his hands on the route they would take.

Anyone could do the exact same thing. Only we sure as fuck wouldn't take off at the first hint of danger. Anyone who thought to so much as breathe in her direction would immediately forfeit their lives.

Corazon looked up at me with raised brows. "I...can't remember the doctor's name off the top of my head."

I emphatically shook my head in an exaggerated motion. No fucking way. With the level of power her family had, they might very well convince someone at the office to tell them exactly when her appointment was.

"Maybe we can set up a day for the two of us to catch up." She went quiet as she listened to her mom. "I mean, I kind of just wanted the first ultrasound to be the pack. I'm sure you can understand that after having six of us." She laughed and anyone who'd known her for more than five minutes could tell how uncomfortable she was and how forced that laugh was. "Maybe the next one, though. How's Issa?" she asked, obviously trying to change the subject.

After a few quiet moments, her eyes flew to mine before darting to Cohl and Valen.

Cohl tensed and tugged her roughly onto his lap, wrapping his arms around her as though there was a threat in our living room and only he could protect her.

"That's…yeah. I guess. You know, I, uh, I'm really not feeling well." Her eyes found me again. "Yeah. Morning sickness, I guess. Can I call you tomorrow? Thanks, Mom."

She didn't say love you, too, meaning her mother hadn't bothered saying it. And then I wondered whether anyone had ever said those words to her before us. Had she ever felt appreciated, adored, cherished the way anyone should experience, especially an omega before we'd all accepted our scent match and began to build our pack bonds?

"My sister is missing," she said, and I hated how hollow her voice sounded or the spike in bitterness in her scent.

"What do you mean? How is she missing?" Valen asked.

She blinked a few times as new tears welled in her pretty chocolate brown eyes. "Mom said Antonio and her beta mate haven't seen her since the day after our date, that day at the restaurant. Mom said supposedly Issa went shopping and no one has heard from her."

Rage bubbled up in my chest and made my blood feel molten in my veins. How the fuck were her packmates not out there tearing the city – or even state – apart searching for her? Hell, they hadn't contacted us. If Corazon had disappeared, her family would be the first people we would have contacted followed by the Garcias. And we wouldn't have stopped with simple phone calls. I knew Cohl alone would have kicked down doors and demanded he personally search every inch of their homes until we found our omega.

But Isabelle wasn't an omega. And I highly doubted her pack gave two shits about her. Those type of men, those type of alphas only cared about power and money, and Isabelle was a beta. For men like Antonio, she was interchangeable.

She was also their only link to the Alvarez empire. Without her, why the fuck would Corazon or Isabelle's fathers give two shits about him or the rest of his pack? I knew literally nothing about her siblings other than their designations. I wasn't sure I could even tell you her brothers' names. I only knew her sister's because she'd been at the restaurant that day; it had been her alpha who'd followed Corazon into the bathroom and threatened her.

"Mom didn't even seem concerned," Corazon said, sadness in her voice and on her face as a single tear trailed down her cheek before she swiped it away. "I'm so tired of crying. I swear I cry over everything these days."

"Your sister missing is a legitimate reason to cry, sweetheart," Valen said, scooting closer so he could touch her.

"Is it common for her to disappear?" I asked, my brows furrowed. I still couldn't believe her sister was missing and, according to Corazon, their mother didn't seem the least bit phased by it.

"Honestly, I don't know," she said, angrily swiping at another rogue tear with the pads of her fingers. "We were never close and she packed up when I was a teenager. My parents arranged her bonding barely a month after she graduated high school."

I already hated the Alvarez fucks, but the more I learned, the more I despised them. They didn't give two shits about any of their children. At the least, they should have protected their daughter; regardless of their designations, females were always at risk of one sick asshole or another.

"Do you want us to look for her? We've got connections. Resources. We can put the word out to watch for her," Valen offered.

"Unless her alpha is full of shit and is keeping her locked up," I muttered.

A pitiful whimper tore from Corazon and I could have punched myself in the dick for causing that sound.

"Sorry, omega. I'll make some calls. Someone had to have seen her if she managed to slip away from her pack." Or was trafficked by her own fucking alpha. "Tell me what you want me to do when we find her. You want her to disappear? Find her somewhere safe where your family can't find her?"

She sniffled and shrugged. "If she's still alive, leave that to her. I can promise you there's no love lost between her and her two mates. I doubt she'll want to return to them. If she was taken and not sold off by Antonio."

"How would that benefit him, though?" Valen asked, taking her hand into his and toying with her fingers. With our omega's emotions unsteady, touch and our purrs would be the best way to keep her calm. Cohl was still wrapped around her from behind, his cheek nuzzling against hers and marking her over and over with his scent.

But even the two alphas didn't appear to be enough, not with the new information.

"I'll make some calls. Figure this shit out. For now, hang out with these two idiots. We'll order in for dinner tonight."

She sighed dramatically. "We order in a lot. I wish we could just be normal and go out to eat."

I opened my mouth to list every reason I – and the others – refused to take her into public. But she held up her hand and shook her head.

"I know. It's not safe. And I would never put myself at risk now." She pressed a hand to her belly as though to protect our child. "I'm just bored. It needs to get warmer faster so we could at least hang out by the pool."

The temps had begun to change with the season, but it hadn't gotten warm enough to officially open the pool for use. Even if she were to take a dip, the evenings were still cold enough the water would feel like an ice bath.

"Not much longer and you'll be laying out by the pool with your manservants bringing you drinks and snacks," Enzo said as he walked through the living room.

"The fuck are you doing here?" Cohl growled.

"Bain called," Ax said as he sauntered in behind his packmate followed by Cyrus.

I frowned and pushed to my feet, following them to where our pack lead was staring at his laptop.

"You called your brother in? Something up?" I asked as I settled behind my own desk instead of the chair in front of us.

For alphas whose business wasn't exactly on the books nor taxed, we'd made sure to have a space where we could work that was separate from the rest of the house with desks, computers, and even comfy chairs.

"Another text," he said, tossing me his phone for me to read over.

"This doesn't make sense," I said, rereading the words.

"Same thread as the others, but it reads like someone was trying to text in a hurry. Can't make sense of what the hell they were trying to say. I was hoping you might catch on to something."

I shook my head.

> Missing with inventory lost night careful of watching

I HANDED the phone to Enzo, who bent his head to read the absolute shit show of word usage.

"No fucking idea. I would assume they were using predictive text, but that would at least form a coherent sentence," I said.

"I want to check out an import arriving today but I'm not leaving Corazon unguarded," Bain said, leaning back in his chair.

"Want us to check out the inventory so you four can stay with your omega?" Cyrus offered.

I jabbed a finger in his direction. "I like that idea."

But the fucking asshole shook his head. "No. This is our deal. They don't know our men, they don't know the business. They'll stay with Corazon. I've also made sure there are a few extra guards arriving before we head out."

"She's not going to be happy." Ax chuckled and shook his head.

"Let her know what's going on. If she freaks out again, give her the choice of which of us hangs back," Bain said.

Last time, she'd asked for Valen and we'd come home to a slick and cum covered omega snuggled beside her fully satiated and satisfied giant alpha. As much as I wanted to find out what that fucking text meant, I really hoped this time she requested I stay with her, if only to make sure I kept her safe from any possible threat.

I knew Enzo and his pack would guard her with their lives, but she was my omega. She was my responsibility. And she was carrying a child fathered by one of my pack. I hated handing her over to another alpha to protect. Hated any time we had to leave her, regardless of how short the time of separation.

"She talked to her mom," I told Bain as Enzo, Ax, and Cyrus left the office, presumably to raid our kitchen as usual.

"How'd that go?"

I shrugged, turning my seat to fully face him. "She asked for the doctor's name and asked to attend the ultrasound. Corazon shut that down. Diplomatically, of course. But our girl obviously doesn't trust her mom any more than her fathers."

"I wouldn't either."

"And her sister's missing. The one that was at the restaurant. Said her mom didn't seem the least bit worried that her two-man pack hadn't seen her since that day."

Bain's brows slammed together. "That was weeks ago. How the fuck has no one found her? That fucker Antonio probably has her locked in the basement or some shit."

I huffed a dark laugh. "That was exactly what I was thinking. But I told her I'd make some calls and have our connections and people watching for her."

Bain's head wagged up and down slowly as his eyes stared toward the door as though he could see our omega from here. "Make the calls. Once the others arrive to keep an eye on the place, we'll head out to intercept the delivery. Then, I'm calling in one of our tech guys, see if they can't track this fucking anonymous number. I want to know who were dealing with before our kid is born."

And there went the excitement tickling my stomach and squeezing my heart. We had a few months to prepare, then we would have a tiny little human to protect, to love, to cherish as much as we did their mother.

CHAPTER THIRTY-SIX

<u>Corazon</u>

Bain was settled behind me on the bed, his knees on either side of my hips, his arms wrapped around my middle, his chin on my shoulder. Cohl's head rested on my stomach. Valen and Ford were struggling to get closer to get a peek at the black and white photos I held in my hand.

"How can they even tell that's a baby?" Cohl said, moving my hand so he could stare at the images for the fiftieth time since the technician handed it to us.

I ran my finger along the shadowed little bean growing in my belly. A smile stretched on my face at the nickname Valen had given our child and it stuck. We wouldn't know whether I was carrying a boy or girl for a few months yet. And I was doing my best to convince my alphas to refrain from learning so it would be a surprise.

I didn't care what we had, didn't care how they presented as they matured. I was already head over heels in love with my baby. And he or she had four big, burly daddies to keep them safe for the rest of our lives.

"If we don't find out the sex, how will we know what color to buy for the room and the clothes and all that shit?" Cohl asked, finally releasing the ultrasound when Ford tugged it closer to him.

"First of all – now might be a good time for us all to start breaking the cursing habit. Kids pick that stuff up fast," I said. And yeah, that went for me, too, since I wasn't exactly known for my prim and proper speech. "And it's easy to decorate in neutral colors. We can buy all the pink or blue crap after. But yellow, green, orange…there are so many colors that work for either."

"How will anyone know whether we have a son or daughter if they're wearing orange?" Cohl said with a curl of his nose.

I tilted my chin down and raised my brows. "You plan on letting anyone near our child for the first ten years of their life?"

He actually looked as though he was thinking about my question before he shook his head, the back of his skull rolling on my belly. "Nah. And make it the first twenty-five."

I giggled as a fresh wave of joy washed over me. I was head over heels with the little person growing inside of me and I was head over heels in love with all four men crowding me and the ultrasound. I think I fell a little harder at the look of awe and happiness on each of their faces when that first rapid *thump, thump, thump* of the baby's heartbeat filled the room. Valen's eyes actually went glassy as he stared at the grainy image on the screen while the doctor ran the little paddle thing over my stomach in search of the baby growing inside of me. According to her, I was about eight weeks along, further than I'd originally thought.

And she also confirmed that I could very well have gotten pregnant outside of my heat – although the time lined up with my cycle – and that my emotional rollercoaster and increased libido were both directly related to the extra onslaught of hormones brought on by pregnancy.

My phone vibrated on the nightstand, but none of us even glanced in that direction. We were too enthralled staring at the little being we created, the little human growing inside of me.

I hadn't had a drop of caffeine since the day Bain had taken the coffee mug from my hand. And yeah, that withdrawal shit had sucked. But I'd gotten used to it, had been making sure to eat my veggies, and we were currently waiting on the super-duper headphone Cohl had ordered. Because, according to him, I needed to wrap the set around my belly and play classical music, something about a study he'd read about classical music and brain development.

Within seconds of the vibrating ending, it started up again.

Valen sighed and lifted it, checking the caller ID. "It's your mom. You want to talk to her or do you want me to tell her you're busy?"

I'd promised to call her as soon as I was done with my appointment, but I'd been too busy celebrating with my alphas.

"I'll take it," I said, handing the long sheet of pictures to Bain when he reached around me for it. "Hey," I said as a greeting.

It was still odd that my mom actually gave two shits that I was pregnant. Especially since I was pregnant by alphas my family had considered their enemy and not the pack my fathers had chosen for me.

"Well? Am I going to have a granddaughter or a grandson? Is everything okay? Is this a healthy pregnancy?"

I turned my head to glance at Bain over my shoulder with wide eyes. Part of me wanted to ask her who she was and what she'd done with my mother. But the other part of me was simply happy that she was at least pretending like she gave a shit about me or my child.

"It's way too early to know the sex. But everything looks good. I'm healthy. The little bean is healthy."

Valen smiled up at me, his straight, white teeth on full display at my use of his nickname.

"Do you need anything?"

"Like what?" This was uncharted territory for me. I can't remember a single time my mom had asked about my mental, emotional, or physical health growing up.

"Clothes? Maternity clothes for you? Baby furniture? That kind of stuff," Mom said.

As much as I liked the idea of having a real mom, of having a grandma for our child, I was growing a tad leery. It all felt almost over the top, like she'd had a personality implant. She'd always been cold, aloof, indifferent, and not just to us but anyone she'd met. I still wondered whether she'd been drugged our whole life after my alphas had mentioned the behavior of the omega Pack Garcia had brought to the meeting.

"I'm okay for now. Cohl – he's one of my alphas – he's been shopping like crazy. And I'm not really showing so no need for maternity clothes yet."

I sat forward, earning a soft growl from Bain, and switched the phone to my other ear.

"Did the doctor say how far along you are?"

"Approximately eight weeks," I answered.

"I know you wanted your pack with you at the first, but I would really love to be there for at least one of the ultrasounds. One of my daughters is finally having a child."

Turning, I looked at Bain, then Ford, to Valen, then finally glanced down at where Cohl was watching me closely. This whole conversation felt...I don't know, forced. It felt as though she'd watched a movie and taken notes on how to interact with her pregnant omega daughter.

But what could she possibly get out of it? What could a relationship with me or my pack offer her?

Unless my fathers finally came to the conclusion it was better to keep their enemies close since it was obvious they were no match for Pack Rivera.

Would that be a good thing or a bad thing? I knew the reason behind the original attack was to coerce my fathers and possibly Pack Garcia into some kind of agreement that would result in my current pack holding a majority of control of the import and export of various merchandise. But I also knew my pack was completely against the human trafficking the Garcia family operated.

"I haven't scheduled the next appointment, but I'll let you know when I do."

"How about lunch this week? Give us some time to catch up," Mom said, and I swore warning bells clanged like crazy in my head.

My alphas couldn't hear her side of the conversation, but I knew they would be shaking their heads in unison if they'd heard her question. "We've been so busy lately. I'll have to check our schedules and see when the pack is free."

"We can meet somewhere just you and me. Give us some time to catch up. I feel like I haven't seen you in ages."

Yep. Warning bells. They sounded like my head was in the center of a church bell while someone hit it with a sledgehammer.

"Uh oh," I said, forcing my voice to sound pathetic. "I need to throw up. Can I call you back?"

"Of course. I'll talk to you–"

I hung up before she could finish her sentence.

"Are you sick?" Valen asked at the same time Cohl asked, "What did she want?"

He pushed off my stomach and held his head propped on his hand.

"She wants to attend an ultrasound and asked if she and I could have lunch. As in just the two of us."

"Absolutely not."

"Fuck no."

"You're not leaving the house without us."

"Is she fucking nuts?"

All four alphas spoke over each other until I held up my hand to stop them. "That's why I acted like I was sick, so I could hang up and talk to you guys about it."

"It's not happening," Bain said, wrapping his arms around my waist to tug me back to his chest.

He was so warm and firm against me, his arms so thick with muscles, so strong. All of my alphas were big and strong and loyal.

And so damn sexy.

No. Keep your thoughts straight. Can't focus on the ready supply of cocks when there are other issues to deal with.

I couldn't believe I was not only arguing with my omega instincts to rip the clothing from my alphas and spend the rest of the day in a tangle of arms and legs, but that I had to literally talk myself out of doing exactly that when we had no idea what was going on, when there were so many unanswered questions floating in the air.

The day Bain had received yet another anonymous – albeit unintelligible – text, he, Valen, and Ford had headed out to check on their most recent delivery of goods. Nothing had been amiss, no one had attacked the shipment, no one had shot at my alphas or the guards.

I'd immediately begun to panic when they mentioned leaving, even though Enzo and his pack would remain behind with me, but they'd done as they had the last time and let me choose who stayed back with me.

Cohl had been more than overjoyed and had lifted me into his arms and run upstairs with me where we stayed locked in the omega quarters until the rest of the pack had returned. In his words, if Valen could cover me with his scent, then he should have the same opportunity.

That was also the same night I'd wandered downstairs for a drink when my pack had fallen asleep and discovered that Enzo and his pack were more than friends.

"What did you expect with your pheromones drowning us and all that grunting and moaning upstairs?" Ax had chuckled when I'd gasped at the sight of Cyrus practically swallowing his cock.

I hadn't said a word about that to Bain or the others. I had no idea whether my pack knew the three alphas were romantically involved and it wasn't my place to say a damn thing about it. Their business, not mine.

There was some stranger texting my alpha with tips to protect the business, my mom had suddenly taken in an interest in my wellbeing, my sister was missing yet no one seemed to give a fuck, and I was eight weeks pregnant. I was probably forgetting something or there was bound to be yet another clusterfuck to arise, but for now...I really needed to figure out a way to reduce my stress.

With knots.

I sighed audibly when those two words immediately entered my chronically sex obsessed brain.

"Do you boys have plans today? Tonight? The rest of the year?" I asked, dropping my head against Bain's chest.

A soft purr rumbled against my back, easing my omega and filling me with peace.

Valen chuckled.

Ford sat at the end of the bed. "You're not going anywhere alone with your mother."

"No shit, Sherlock."

"What happened to the new no cussing rule?" Cohl muttered.

"I was going to ask if we could just...I don't know. Veg. Bed rot. Order a bunch of greasy food, binge watch some TV, maybe get naked. All the fun stuff."

Cohl's hand shot straight in the air like an overly excited kid in school. "I vote to get naked."

Ford shoved his shoulder, but he couldn't hide the smile.

"Anything you want, omega," Bain muttered in my ear, his lips brushing against the outer shell and his breath warming my neck, sending a shiver down my spine and slick weeping from me.

"Greasy food isn't exactly pregnancy approved," Ford teased.

"I'm eight weeks along. I wouldn't have even known if my emotions and libido hadn't been all over the place. I want to eat so many egg rolls I have to be rolled to bed, watch some unrealistic action or cheesy horror movies, then fuck until none of us can keep our eyes open."

Because there would come a day when our time would be occupied with caring for a newborn. Not that being a parent would stop me from wanting my alphas as much as I did at this very moment. And we could always hire a nanny. To help, of course. Unlike my mother, I couldn't wait to actually raise my child.

Since that first time Valen had told me he loved me, the night I admitted to loving all of them, none of us had exchanged the words again. Yet I still felt them in my chest, through the bond. I knew how much they loved me, how important I was to each and every one of them. I just hoped they could feel how deep my love ran for them.

CHAPTER THIRTY-SEVEN

Ford

$\mathcal{W}$e had been arguing for the past fucking hour, but no matter how loud each of us got, we couldn't figure out how the fuck to spread ourselves to be everywhere at the same time.

Another mysterious text had found its way to Bain's phone, another warning. Another *vague* fucking warning. We only had one shipment due this week and it just happened to be the same mother fucking day our omega was scheduled for her second ultrasound to ensure the pregnancy was still going well.

Our girl hadn't had much in the way of morning sickness, but her libido and emotions were still off the damn charts. Not that I was complaining about the latter. It was the former that was tearing us all apart. We tried our best to anticipate Corazon's needs, but sometimes even *she* didn't know what was making her cry, what she needed for comfort, or even something as trivial as what she was craving.

Right now, this very moment was another of those moments when I would have gladly torn open my chest, ripped my heart from my chest, and handed it to her if it would make those tears glistening in her eyes go away and that pillowy bottom lip stop quivering.

She got mad every time she cried, but we all knew she had no control over it.

"I'm not comfortable with her going to the doctor with her mom alone," Bain said for the tenth time.

"*Her* is standing right here and can make *her* own decisions," Corazon said, rubbing her eyes with the heels of both hands.

"We can go with her," Enzo offered, earning a chorus of growls from the pack. Bain's brother held up his hands and stepped back, smirking at his own packmates as we continued to squabble.

We needed men at the delivery, someone to be with Corazon since she'd agreed to allow her mom to join her, and someone needed to remain behind because Cohl's dumbass wouldn't stop ordering shit.

To top it all off, we had yet to receive a single whisper about Corazon's sister, as in none of our connections, contacts, or employees had seen her out with her tiny pack. The alpha and beta men had been seen with the Alvarez elders, but no Isabelle. That shit was suspicious as fuck.

"Why doesn't Cohl come with me, you three go check on the delivery, and Enzo's pack can stay here and sign for…whatever was ordered?" All eyes turned to Cohl for a second, although Corazon was the only one who looked amused by his constant shopping.

"I still don't like it. Your fathers could easily try to fuck with you," Bain said.

"You think I can't protect my omega?" Cohl growled.

"I think you could easily be outnumbered, especially if they start shooting and you're busy being filled with holes while trying to shield our omega and our child," Bain shot back.

"So send Keller. And a couple other guards. They can do a quick check before we pull into the lot, then check inside and outside before and after the appointment," she offered.

Bain looked to me. It was the best any of us had come up with since all this shit started over an hour ago. And she needed to leave soon if she was going to be on time. We could always reschedule it to a day and time when we could all four be with her, but our lives weren't exactly predictable. We didn't clock in and out at regular business hours. No nine to five, Monday through Friday for us.

With a shrug, I swallowed back the growl that had been filling my chest since we started talking about all this. Honestly, the growl had built until I feared I would explode since the moment Corazon announced her mother was joining her for her appointment. I didn't want any member of that family anywhere near my omega.

"It's the best one so far. At least there will be plenty of eyes on her. And someone to get all the fucking shit Cohl keeps ordering."

"Language," Corazon said, rubbing her slightly rounded belly. Her already full tits were swelling as was her ass, and fuck me if she wasn't the sexiest person to have ever walked the planet.

"Fine. Cohl, text Keller and tell him to get at least six guards ready. Send three ahead to check the area for any Alvarez or Garcia assholes. The three of us will oversee the merchandise delivery. Enzo, you cool with the three of you housesitting for a few hours? How much shit is coming, Cohl?"

The asshole shrugged.

Bain shook his head and turned back to his brother.

"We're good. We'll just wait 'til you all get back. Let us know if you need us to meet you at the drop location."

"You're taking extra men with you, right?" Corazon asked.

When those cursed tears welled in her eyes again, I spoke up.

"There will be our guys waiting there already. We'll be fine. All that matters is your safety. And call us as soon as you're done with any updates," I said, crossing the space between us to pull her into my arms.

"I don't want to distract you. I need you boys to stay sharp."

Lowering my head until my lips were right against her ear, I whispered, "Keep calling us boys and I might have to prove otherwise."

She shivered but pulled away. "And I might start calling you boys just to test that threat."

After a sharp swat on her ass – and an adorable squeal from her – we all split off to get ready. Cohl walked through the front door to speak with Keller and the other guards. I texted our guys onsite to alert them of a possible threat. I didn't bother telling them we were coming; I still wasn't convinced that we didn't have our own mole. It was better if we showed up unannounced.

Bain, Valen, and I double checked our sidearms then grabbed a couple long-range rifles to load into the SUV. In our line of work, we could never be too careful and there was no such thing as too much firepower.

Cohl and Keller better make damn sure both vehicles were loaded and armed for bear before taking our omega into public and to meet with her mother. *Her fucking mother.* The same woman who sat by and did absolutely nothing when her mates sold her to a pack of assholes. The same woman who apparently wasn't bothering to look for one of her daughters.

The same woman who was seen enjoying time with the mother fucker who'd put a knife to my omega's throat – her *daughter's* throat – and threatened her. That alone should have ended Antonio's life. I would swear on everything, including my own life, that if any cock sucker dared to threaten or scare my child, I would end their life myself.

AN HOUR AND A HALF LATER, we all headed out the door and to the garage together. After I pressed a long, lingering kiss to Corazon's lips, Bain and Valen did the same. The giant alpha held onto the back of her neck, pressing his forehead to hers.

"Be safe and call us the second you're back home," he whispered.

"I'll text you. That way you won't be distracted. But you guys call me as soon as you're done so I'm not freaking out all day."

Valen pressed one more kiss to her lips, bent to kiss her belly, then joined me and Bain at the vehicle we would be driving.

She climbed into the backseat with Cohl and one of our guards flanking her on either side and another climbing behind the wheel. I was surprised Cohl wasn't snarling at the man on our omega's left, but he did wrap an arm around her shoulders and tug her closer until she was practically sitting on his lap.

Corazon leaned forward, put her palm to her lips, and blew a kiss at us as the SUV pulled from the garage and slowly rolled down the driveway toward the gate manned by several more of our men.

I should have told Keller to ride with her. Of all the guards, he'd been with us the longest. He was the one I trusted implicitly.

But Ford and I had ensured we had vetted every single person who worked for us. They each knew we wouldn't hesitate to rip their hearts out through their throats if they stabbed us in the back or endangered our omega in any way.

"This is fucked," I grumbled, dropping my head against the rest and watching the SUV with the most important person in our life drive away. Fuck. The two most important people. Because there was nothing that mattered more to the four of us than Corazon and the little bean she was carrying.

Fucking Valen. His stupid nickname had stuck. But it was cute. Even I could admit that. Although, with the way her belly was growing, I was sure the baby was bigger than the bean we'd seen on that first ultrasound.

I wanted to be there. I wanted to be with my pack surrounding the bed as the doctor squirted that gel shit on Corazon's belly and smoothed the wand back and forth until something appeared on the screen.

Surely, we still wouldn't find out whether we were having a son or a daughter and Corazon was adamant we wait and be surprised. Didn't matter. We would love our child no matter what. And I would destroy anyone who dared to come for him. Or her.

CHAPTER THIRTY-EIGHT

<u>Enzo</u>

I would have loved to complain about hanging around and waiting for a bunch of baby shit to be delivered, but honestly, I was a little excited. Maybe not about the waiting around or the deliveries, but the baby stuff was for my first niece or nephew. And nah, I didn't really give a fuck which of the alphas impregnated Corazon.

She was my sister-in-law, mate and omega to my brother and his pack. Therefore, any and every child she birthed would be my niece and nephew and would be protected with my last dying breath. He or she wouldn't only have four overprotective daddies but three over-protective uncles, as well.

Someday, the three of us would find our mate. I wanted an omega because I wanted the guarantee of children, but one of us could succeed in knocking up a female beta, too. And yeah, that was the end goal for the three of us, to one day have a family of our own.

Just not yet. The three of us were in our mid-twenties, ran a successful club, and were having entirely too much fun to willingly tie ourselves down just yet.

Ax and Cyrus were stretched out on the couch, their booted feet resting on the coffee table in front of them while I lounged on the recliner that I'd decided was my favorite chair in the world. I definitely needed to order one for our place because this fucking thing was by far the most comfortable chair I'd ever sat on.

Ax and Cyrus were on the very couch where they'd released some pent up sexual frustration when Corazon had wandered downstairs and caught them. I had no idea whether my brother knew we were beyond simply packmates, but lovers. As in, I loved these fuckers and would lay my life down for them. Yeah, we'd love to add a beta or an omega to the mix, but we were just as content as a trio.

Nah. Content wasn't the right word. We were all three insanely in love with each other. And anyone we added would not only need to be okay with sharing all of us with each other, but we would need to feel as deeply for them as we did for each other.

Corazon had looked shocked when she'd caught Cyrus swallowing Ax's cock while I'd rubbed one off on this very recliner. When Ax reminded her of the constant barrage of omega pheromones and their constant fucking around while we were here, she'd lifted her chin, erased the shocked look, then hurried to the kitchen and back up the stairs.

Whether she'd told my brother or not, I didn't know. Nor did I care. No one had said shit to us, nor would they have any right. It was our life, not theirs.

"They could have at least left us the tracking info so we'd know how long we'd be here. I wanted to take a shift tonight," Ax said, stretching his arms over his head before slumping further into the cushions.

We had plenty of employees, plenty of bouncers, servers, bartenders, and dancers, but Ax had a long background in several styles of dance. Being on stage was an outlet for him since there weren't many chances for him to show off his ballet or lyrical skills.

It had been two hours since we'd all made our plans for the day and the three of us had volunteered to intercept the deliveries from Cohl's excessive online shopping. I didn't blame him; I would have totally gone overboard if it was my first child, too.

Shit. I would go overboard if we ever found our omega.

My lids lowered as boredom turned to sleepiness. A nap would make the time go by faster.

I was in one of those in between stages of dreaming where I was partially conscious, enough to hear the sounds of the TV, but my dreams were morphing around whatever movie my mates were watching.

CRASH!

Until it sounded like a bomb had gone off somewhere on the property.

I was on my feet and sprinting toward the door before my eyes were fully open, only a half second behind Ax and Cyrus.

Cyrus threw the door open and stormed outside. Then the three of us stared at what looked to be a newer model Benz. At least it used to be before it smashed into the tall, stone pillars on either side of the iron gate.

Guards were running from every direction, all racing toward whoever had dared to try to crash through the gate and onto the property.

Ax darted back inside then reemerged with pistols for the three of us, passing them out as we jogged in that direction.

"Necks on a fucking swivel," I ordered.

We might not have been official members of Bain's empire, but we'd been on enough assignments with him, his pack, or his guards to know there could always be danger waiting, that any and every single incident could be a trap, an ambush waiting for enough of us to be near before we were all taken out by explosives or gunfire.

Men clad in all black surrounded the vehicle, their rifles pointed at the driver's side.

My socks were soaked from the damp grass, water and mud squishing through and between my toes as I ran with my mates until we were close enough to see which asshole had been stupid enough to fuck with my brother's pack.

Just because Bain wasn't here didn't mean they wouldn't die for their offense. I had no problem playing judge, jury, and executioner.

Until my eyes landed on a petite woman with chin length dark hair, and a face sporting bruises that were absolutely not caused by the crash.

"That's Corazon's sister," Ax said, pushing through the throng of guards to get closer.

They all still had their rifles aimed at her while watching for any other incoming threats.

I was focused on the way the woman could barely keep her head up. One of her eyes looked almost swollen shut, and there were bruises ranging from purple to that sickly yellowish green that looked older.

This woman had been abused. A lot.

I jerked on the handle, but it was locked.

Rapping my knuckles against the glass, something twisted in my gut when she started hard and turned unfocused eyes in my direction.

"Open the door." Isabelle. Wasn't that her name? I could have sworn I'd heard Corazon refer to her only sister as Isabelle. "You need medical attention, Isabelle. Open the door so we can help you."

And find out why she'd not only rushed here so frantically that she'd slammed into the damn gates, but why she looked as though she'd been going ten rounds with a professional boxer.

It took a few seconds of her blinking at me before she reached down and hit the button to unlock the doors.

As I yanked the door open, Cyrus moved forward, dropping to his knees and running his hands along her face, her head, and down her neck. "Is anything broken?"

"What?" she asked. Her voice was a little raspier than Corazon's, the one eye not swollen almost shut a lighter brown, almost a honey color, and her pupils were pinpoints.

"Can you tell me if anything's broken? Do you have a headache? Any dizziness?"

She continued to stare at him as though she couldn't make sense of his questions until she tried to push him away so she could climb out of the car.

When she stumbled into him, Cyrus scooped her into his arms and started carrying her to the house.

"Call Bain," he ordered, but Ax already had the phone to his ear, either to call an ambulance – something none of us would encourage since that would mean the police – or to call my brother.

"Can you tell us why you're here? Who hurt you, Isabelle?" I asked. From what we'd learned from that day at the restaurant when the beta sister's mate had dared to threaten Corazon, she only had two mates, one was an alpha, the other a beta, and both chosen by her fathers.

"Corazon," Isabelle said on a groan.

"She's not here," Cyrus said as he carried her into the house. "Call a doctor. Is Henderson still working for Bain?"

"No idea. And Bain's not answering his phone."

My stomach twisted. The fucker better not have gotten himself hurt or killed. Especially since three of the pack were in the same location and Corazon was expecting in just a few more months.

"I'll contact the doctor," one of the guards said. The only one I was familiar with was a blonde brute named Keller. He'd been with Bain and the pack from the start. I didn't know this guard as he held his phone was to his ear and stepped through the front door, leaving my pack alone with Isabelle.

Cyrus set her on the couch he and Ax had vacated upon the beta's arrival.

Ax jogged from the room and returned with a wet dish cloth and a glass of water. "Here," he said, handing her the glass before dabbing at a bloody cut along her hairline just above her left eyebrow.

"Tell Corazon," she said, wrapping her hand around Ax's wrist.

His brows lowered and he looked from her to me then back again. "What do you want me to tell her? You want her to know you're here?"

Her head wagged side to side then she listed to the side from the movement. Cyrus kept her upright with his hands on her shoulders.

"Not mom," she slurred.

She was way too damn close to passing out and we still didn't have a fucking clue what the hell was going on.

"Not mom. Not your mom?" Cyrus asked, cupping her face in both hands to keep her steady.

"She's lying. Mom...my mom. Tell Corazon."

Cyrus raised his brows at me in question and all I could do was shrug.

"Your mom is with Corazon today. Did you want us to call her?"

Her one good eye went wide. "Stop her. Tell Corazon. Mom...the baby." Every word was garbled and slurred. "She'll hurt Cora."

Fuck. Her mom was with Corazon. Her mom was going to hurt my brother's omega.

Instead of calling Bain, I hit Cohl's number since he was the alpha with her at the appointment today. I really hoped he was in the room with his omega at all times, but just in case, he needed to know something was up, and, until we knew exactly what the fuck Isabelle was trying to warn us about, the omega needed a wall of bodies around her.

Isabelle's eyes finally rolled shut and her head slumped forward. Cyrus cursed and laid her along the couch, draping a blanket over her while we waited for the doctor to show up.

Cohl's phone rang twice before he answered. "'Sup?" he said.

"Are you in the room with your omega?" I asked, getting straight to the point.

"I'm looking right at her and our son," he said, a smile evident in his voice. It appeared Corazon had lost the battle of waiting to find out the sex of their baby. "If the wiener is anything to go by, he's definitely not my–"

"Is her mom there?" I asked.

"Yeah...why?" His playful tone immediately changed as his voice went deeper, deadlier.

"Stay with your omega. Do not let her out of your sight. Something's up. Her sister just showed up here beaten pretty badly.

Crashed into the gate. She's not making sense but keeps saying something about their mom and warning Cora."

"Get the fuck out!" Cohl barked.

"Excuse me?" a female said in the background.

"You heard me. Out! Now!" A door slammed in the background. "I'm texting the guards outside and in the hall. Keep the sister there and let Bain know something's up."

"We can't get a hold of him," I said.

Cohl muttered another curse under his breath. "Keep trying. We'll be home as soon as Cora's done here."

I'd noticed Cohl was the only one – other than her sister, apparently – who shortened Corazon's name. The fact her name translated to heart seemed appropriate – because she'd absolutely become the heart of Pack Rivera in the months since their fucked up meeting.

And if anything happened to the heart of the pack, Bain, Valen, Ford, and Cohl would leave a trail of blood behind them as they punished any and every single mother fucker who'd had any part in it.

CHAPTER THIRTY-NINE

<u>Corazon</u>

I hadn't meant to discover whether I was carrying a boy or a girl, but when Cohl damned near pressed his nose to the monitor and pointed out what was either a little weewee or a third leg...the secret was out of the bag.

"It's a boy!" he'd yelled. "We're having a son!"

My mother was on the side of my bed, her eyes on my face, a forced smile on her lips. There was something odd about her eyes, that hazy look I remembered throughout my childhood there. She'd congratulated me, had smiled at Cohl when he continued to celebrate the fact our first child was a son, but it all felt so...weird. Like her smile, her sweet words had felt forced.

Cohl's phone rang in his pocket. Eyes still on the screen, he pulled it from his pocket and answered it. "'Sup?" he said.

His beautiful brown eyes swung to me, that grin still wide on his face as he listened to the other line. "I'm looking right at her and our son. If the wiener is anything to go by, he's definitely not my–"

The smile faltered as his eyes moved to my mom, who was watching him closely.

"Yeah...why?"

A few seconds later, his expression turned dangerous, deadly, and he moved toward my mom.

"Get the fuck out!" Cohl barked.

"Excuse me?" Mom said, moving closer to the bed as though I would contradict my alpha.

"You heard me. Out! Now!" He followed her to the door with the doctor watching wide eyed and slammed it behind her. "I'm texting the guards outside and in the hall. Keep the sister there and let Bain know something's up."

Another few seconds of him silently listening before a soft growl rumbled from his chest.

"Fuck," he muttered softly. "Keep trying. We'll be home as soon as Cora's done here."

Pocketing his phone, he turned to the doctor. "Is she done here?"

"Yes, sir," the doctor responded, hitting buttons to print out the newest ultrasound images.

"What's going on, Cohl? Who was that?"

"Enzo. Your sister showed up at the house." He gave me a pointed look that said the details would wait until we didn't have an audience.

"Issa showed up at our house? Why?"

Once the printout was practically shoved into my palm, the doctor handed me a towel to wipe the gel off my belly and excused herself.

"She crashed into the gate. Enzo said she looked like she was beat up or some shit. Your sister kept saying something about your mom and you. They couldn't make sense of it but said to keep an eye on you. They're trying to get a hold of Bain and the others so they can meet us at home."

"Why would Issa warn me about anything? Mom was with us for the past two hours."

But it had been weeks since the last time I'd seen her face to face. Months since I'd resided under the same roof. And I knew how much control my fathers had over every single person in their lives; if even one of them gave her an order, even if it was to hurt me, she would follow their instructions without a single complaint.

Her eyes. She'd had that same faraway look, the one that had been missing at the restaurant. I remembered thinking she looked like a different person than the one who'd raised me. Or rather the person who'd paid nannies to raise me.

"Wait…you said Issa had been beat up?" Mom had said she'd been missing. Had I been correct that Antonio had locked her up? Had he been the one to hurt her? Why? What was the point of abusing my sister?

And did my parents know he'd been hurting her? Did my mom? I still wasn't over the fact Mom had been so blasé over the fact her oldest daughter had been missing for weeks, but now I wondered if she'd known where she was the whole time.

"That's what Enzo said. And you and I know damn well it was that piece of shit who threatened you who hurt your sister."

"She has to stay with us, Cohl. She can't go back there."

He shook his head as he helped me to my feet and guided me to the door with a hand on the small of my back. "We'll take care of her. I agree. She can't go back there. Fuck her alpha. Fuck her pack. Fuck your parents for allowing that shit."

His voice was deep, the soft growl growing when he opened the door to find my mom standing in the hallway, her purse in her hands, a look of confusion on her face.

"I don't understand what's going on," she said.

I looked at her, really looked into my mom's eyes. Her pupils were small, too small to be normal. And her voice was a little different than it was each time we'd spoken on the phone, too.

"Mom?" I asked softly, resting a hand on the side of her arm. "Are you…do they dope you?"

"What?"

"Are you on something?"

She made a sound in the back of her throat, like my question was ridiculous. But if they were doping her, forcing her to bend to their will, she couldn't go back to my fathers, either. I wasn't sure how my alphas would feel about having not only my big sister but my mom staying with us, as well, but if Mom was being mistreated…I couldn't turn my back on her. Regardless of how dismissive and distant she was to me while I was growing up.

"Don't be ridiculous. I'm just excited! This is my first grandchild." Her smile was lopsided, kind of crooked, and very forced.

Something was definitely off, but, short of forcing her to get a drug test, there wasn't anything I could do to confirm my suspicion.

Cohl put himself between my mom and me and ushered me toward the elevator. There were two more guards walking closely behind us, their holstered guns on full display on their hips. They weren't even bothering to conceal that they were armed bodyguards for the pregnant omega.

Mom wedged herself between Keller and the wall. *I really should make a point to learn all the guards' names.*

Being as I'd grown up with guards coming and going, it had never made sense to get to know anyone in my father's employ. The only long-term employees had been killed while protecting me on the way to my bonding ceremony.

Wow. That day seemed like ages ago yet was only months. My life had become so different. *I* had become so different. I was happy now. I was free, or at least as free as someone with so many people who wanted to use me to punish my alphas could be. I had to believe there would come a day when I could actually go to a store with only one of my alphas or one guard tagging along.

The ding alerted us to the main floor. The two guards stepped out first, waited for my mom to step out, then flanked Cohl and me as we walked through the fancy foyer and toward the waiting SUVs that had been driven around to the back. Less eyes on the vehicles meant less people to know where I was and would, hopefully, eliminate any further threat on one of my few outings into the public.

"I'm so ready for all this to be over." I sighed as a guard pushed the door open and waited for me to step through.

"It'll never be over for omegas like us," my mom muttered. And something in her tone made me turn to look at her profile.

Her eyes moved across the back lot, to the few cars parked back here, to the random person entering or leaving the various buildings.

There was no one here for her, no one here protecting my mom. She was past childbearing age, so there was no reason to snatch her for breeding. But wasn't she still at risk because of her connection to my fathers?

We stopped near the hood of the second SUV where I would be riding back with my mate and my personal bodyguards.

"Mom, are you safe at home?"

The look on her face reminded me of the kind you would give someone who'd said something absolutely ridiculous or absurd.

"Why wouldn't I be? I have everything I could ever want." Her eyes went over my shoulder.

I glanced back to see the guards and Cohl talking discreetly, their attention partially on me as though ready to jump in front of a bullet at any time.

"You still have a choice," Mom whispered, dragging my focus back on her. "You're not that far along. The Garcias are still amenable to taking you as their omega after you've terminated..." She waved her hand toward my belly.

"You said...I thought you were excited about your first grandchild."

A smile stretched on her face that sent ice to my heart and chilled me to the bone. When she took a step closer to me, I reflexively took a step back, cradling my arms around my baby bump.

"Is that a no?"

"What?"

"I'm supposed to take an answer back to your fathers. Is that a no to the Garcias?"

"Mom. What the hell is wrong with you? I have a pack. I have alphas. I'm having a baby in four or five months–"

Anything else I might have said was cut off when her hands landed on my shoulders and she shoved me past the protection of the two vehicles, causing me to lose my balance and land hard on my butt and elbows.

And then it felt as though I'd left my body and entered a damn action movie.

Men emerged from around corners, from behind parked cars, some even appearing as though they'd exited from inside some of the businesses.

"Fuck! Cora!" Cohl bellowed, diving forward and covering me with his own body.

Voices raised. Growls erupted. The pop of a firearms echoed off the asphalt and concrete.

"Fuck! Fuck!" Cohl repeated, his hands smoothing across the back of my head. "Are you hit? Are you hurt?" His voice raised over the sound of constant gunfire.

He was still hovering over me as he shuffled me toward one of our SUVs, planting me behind one of the wheels and keeping his body between me and the side where the guards were firing at our assailants.

"My mom!" I yelled over the sound.

He glanced over his shoulder, but didn't say anything, simply pulled his phone from his pocket and held it to his ear.

After a few seconds, he cursed. "Everyone's been trying to get a hold of you, asshole…" He cursed again, his eyes slicing to me then away. "At the doc's building. We're pinned down. We're being fired on. Get your asses here and send anyone close enough." Then he ended the call and tossed the phone to me.

What the hell was I supposed to do with it?

Shoving it into my bra, I made myself as small as possible, hugging my arms around my belly in hopes of adding another layer of protection to my son.

Keller planted himself on my other side, peering over the hood with his gun raised. A growl burst from his lips before he lowered and turned his head toward Cohl. "The fucking Garcias," he ground out.

"Give me a gun," I called out over the sound of bullets flying, of cars being hit, of growls from alphas. It was only a matter of time before someone called the police. At least we could say we were simply protecting ourselves.

Though I doubted the cops would be cool with the use of semi-automatic rifles being fired in a public place where there was risk of an innocent person being struck.

Keller glanced in Cohl's direction, then pulled a handgun from the holster, holding it toward me handle first.

Turning it over, I popped the magazine, checked the ammunition, then pulled the slide to chamber a round. I shrugged when Keller raised his brows at me. I'd grown up around criminals. I knew my way around a gun.

How far were we from the back door of the medical building and what was the chance I could dart toward it without being struck?

This was a full-on assault, and it was more than obvious by my mom's actions that they didn't care whether I was hit or not. Why? Was this a punishment for refusing to bond with the Garcia jerks? Was this revenge on my pack?

No fucking way would I let anyone hurt my son because of some stupid ass vendetta.

My heart hurt that my mother had not only been pretending to care, but that she was more than willing to see me and my unborn child mowed down by gunfire. She didn't give a shit about me. She never had. She'd been putting on a show to get close, to get me to lower my guard, to let her into my life.

Good thing my pack and I were all suspicious of everyone and I hadn't gone to my ultrasound alone with her. Who knew what might have happened?

Actually, pretty sure I knew exactly what would have happened – either my parents would have forced an abortion on me and I would have been locked away by the Garcias, or I would have been executed the moment I was away from my pack.

Anger mixed with fear as those fucking pops continued to echo around me, around us, dinging and ricocheting off vehicles and the asphalt.

I wasn't a violent person. I didn't revel in the pain of others. But at that moment, I wanted nothing more than to ensure every single person who was involved in this attack was punished – with a bullet directly between their eyes.

Because not only were they risking my life and the life of my alpha and our guards, they were risking the life of my unborn son. And I would destroy anyone who even contemplated hurting my family.

CHAPTER FORTY

<u>Cohl</u>

I didn't do fear. Didn't feel that useless emotion. I didn't do panic.

Past tense. I didn't feel those things before. As in, before my beautiful omega had come into our lives, until she'd accepted my bonding mark, until she'd become mine.

The look on her face, the way her eyes had widened the second her mom had shoved her shoulders and pushed her before the telltale sounds of gunfire had exploded around us…that shit would live with me for the rest of my life.

I had never felt the insane level of panic that I had the moment I'd seen her falling backward as though I'd been watching in slow motion. I was on the move from the second her mom had taken a step closer, her arms raising, but hadn't been fast enough to stop my sweet Cora from being hurt.

She wasn't hurt. I needed to remind myself that she wasn't hurt. She hadn't been hit by any of the bullets whizzing by like bees.

Fuck. We'd brought guards with us, but it felt as though the gunfire was coming from every direction. Glancing over my shoulder, I tried to gauge the distance between us and the door we'd stepped out from. Maybe the guards could circle Cora and get her inside.

Too far. Too risky. Even if we tried to get in the SUVs and speed away, the fuckers firing on us could easily shoot out the tires, send bullets piercing through the doors, the windows…

And my sweet omega could be hit. Unlike the day we'd brought her into our lives, these assholes wouldn't be careful to avoid hitting her. Especially when this felt like a full-on assassination attempt on not just me, not just our pack, but our omega, as well.

Her mother. Her fucking mother had shoved her into the path of those bullets. Luckily, the extra weight from our child had sent her to the ground instead of out in the opening. Otherwise, she would be dead on the pavement.

Another wave of absolute terror sent ice through my veins, mixing with the inferno of rage. One way or another, I would make every single person out here pay.

Then I would track down her family and take them out one by one, taking my time so they would suffer as long as possible before ending their lives.

Where the fuck was my pack? Where the fuck was our backup? Yeah. It had only been minutes since I'd finally gotten through to Bain, but it sure as fuck felt like hours as we stayed pinned down behind the SUV.

Checking on Cora, I huffed a surprised laugh. She was holding a pistol in her hands, an angry frown drawing her dark brows together as she kept her knees up to protect our son.

Keller was on her other side, protecting that side of her with his own body. Another reason the alpha was our most trusted employee. He had become loyal to Cora the moment she'd become our omega and would sacrifice his own life for her. Dude definitely deserved a raise after today.

Tires squealed in the distance. Sirens howled, the sound faint.

Maybe we'd get lucky and the cops would show up before we all ended up full of fucking holes and bleeding out on the back lot.

An older red truck drove through the lot, slamming hood first into a vehicle. Two guards poured from the driver and passenger seats, immediately firing the moment their doors were open. They were firing on the enemy. Bain had sent some backup.

The two fuckers had literally driven straight into the fray, creating another barrier between the enemy and Cora. Still wasn't enough to either get her back into the building or tucked into the back seat of one of the SUVs and on the road to safety.

"Mother fucker," Keller growled out.

I turned my head to look in his direction. He'd risen to his knees and was looking through the back windows of the SUV. "All three of those fuckers are out there."

We'd known it was the Garcias. And yeah, that shit pissed me off, but this felt more like a gift wrapped in a pretty bow. Because we could take all three of those cocksuckers out in one day. As long as my other three packmates were able to send enough reinforcements to even out this fight.

For now, I would keep my ass parked directly beside my omega to ensure no one got anywhere near her.

The two of us only had handguns. Scanning the area for our guards, I waved my hand to get the attention of one of the betas firing at the enemy from behind the hood of the second SUV.

"Hey!" I bellowed. It took three more attempts before he caught on, lowered behind the protection of the engine, and turned his eyes to me. "Take the Garcias out. I want all three of those cocksuckers dead." The guards all carried long-range, high-powered rifles. It would be easier for them to hit their mark from this distance than for Keller or me.

He nodded, then pushed back to his knees, staring down the scope as he scanned the area for his intended targets. No way would Leo, Julian, or Roman put themselves out in the open. I was actually shocked as shit they were even here. The fuckers weren't exactly the epitome of alphas and normally had their lackeys do their dirty work.

The pops had slowed but not stopped. We were still pinned behind the SUV. I would have loved to climb from behind the vehicle and throttle each of the Garcia fucks but refused to leave my omega's side. Maybe when our packmates arrived, I could let my alpha beast loose, quench the thirst for blood that seemed to arise the moment I felt my omega was at risk.

No way had her mother acted on behalf of the Garcias. This was her fathers' doing. And as soon as I had her safely behind the gates and walls of our house, I was going hunting. I would find out which of them had a hand in this and personally rip them to pieces.

* * *

Valen

BAIN'S PHONE had been blowing up, but it had taken a while before we could draw our attention from the shitshow that had been playing out in front of us to answer the phone. We'd checked in on our connection to Corazon to ensure she was safe, then fought our way through the fucking ambush.

We'd once again lost some of our men, but the enemy was finally down. All three of us looked like shit. Ford had a bullet hole in his shoulder. Bain had a knife slash across his chest and blood was seeping steadily from the cut and soaking his shirt. I was pretty sure I had broken ribs.

But none of our injuries were life-threatening. The moment Bain answered the phone and we'd all caught the panicked yelling from Cohl over the line, we'd raced for the vehicle and sped toward downtown.

Ford and Bain were making phone calls, sending anyone and everyone they could contact to the area while I slammed the gas pedal to the floor to get to our omega before it was too late. If my sweetheart was hurt...

304

Fuck. Fuck fuck fuck. Panic caused a tremble to rattle through my body. My fingers clenched tightly around the wheel, making my knuckles white. Horns blared at me as I darted through traffic, cutting people off and coming close to sideswiping a few drivers.

I didn't care. I didn't give a fuck about anything but getting to my omega, to our pup. They were under attack.

And it was our fucking fault.

We should have left her alone. We should have gone after the alphas of Packs Garcia and Alvarez and left the omega alone. Instead, we'd fallen in love with her and bonded her.

Now, she was under fire simply because of us, because of her connection to us, because we'd claimed her and filled her with our child.

The SUV bounced as I hopped the curb to go around a vehicle and get to the back lot, stopping directly in front of the vehicle where I'd seen Cohl and Keller protecting Corazon.

Bain climbed over the center console and exited the driver's side the moment I was clear while Ford lunged from the backseat. Our rifles were raised the moment our feet hit the ground and we began firing.

There was an old red truck near the enemy, two of our men firing off round after round.

I paused, pulling my finger from the trigger. "Hold your fire!" I yelled out as I realized a majority – if not all – the gunfire was coming from our side.

One by one, the few guards who'd escorted Corazon and the two who'd been close enough to arrive before us ceased fire.

I lowered behind the wheel well and turned toward where I'd seen our omega. "Is she okay?" I yelled.

Cohl's auburn hair appeared as he peeked over the side. "She's okay."

"She has a name!" Corazon yelled back, one of her go-to lines that would normally amuse me squeezing my heart instead. She sounded terrified. The source of that fear needed to be punished. And I desperately wanted to be the one to dole out that fucking punishment.

Cohl crouched low and jogged toward us. "It's the fucking Garcias. Did you see them when you pulled in? All three are here."

"Leo's down," one of the men near the old truck yelled back. There was a feral smile on his face as he pointed toward the east side of the lot. I didn't know this particular beta well, but he'd been with us for a few years. And the fact he'd put himself directly between the enemy and our omega just earned him a spot high on my list of trusted guards.

Without letting my brain catch up to my actions, I left the safety of the SUV and stormed toward where the alpha was pointing. Blood was pooling from behind a vehicle. I wasn't sure whether they had any more men left, if they'd run, or if Julian and Roman were still here. Didn't matter. They would all die whether in the next few minutes or after we tracked them down. Each and every single person who'd had a hand in attacking my omega, in risking the life of my sweetheart and my child would fucking die.

CHAPTER FORTY-ONE

<u>Ford</u>

$\mathcal{E}$ven after getting Corazon checked over by the doctors then getting her behind the safety of our gates, inside our home, and surrounded by anyone we could spare – including Bain's brother and his pack – we'd gone hunting.

And it had been far too easy to take out the guards protecting Corazon's fathers and infiltrate their ugly ass mini mansion.

Maybe we should have felt a certain way about the fact we were minutes away from ending the lives of our in-laws. Killing a woman had never set well with me. But as Corazon's mother knelt beside her alphas, I couldn't drum up an ounce of regret or empathy for the woman who'd intentionally pushed my omega into the path of dozens of gunmen.

"I'd wanted to peel the skin from your flesh. Let you die slowly. You can thank your daughter for the swift death," Cohl said as he stood in front of the alpha, Vance, who'd demanded she return to the men he and the others had chosen for her.

"Fuck you," Vance said before spitting at Cohl.

Corazon's five alpha fathers and her mother all stared up at us with varying expressions of hate and disgust. It pissed me off that none of them looked afraid. I wanted them to feel the same terror my girl had felt as she'd huddled behind the SUV, praying none of those bullets ended her life or our son's life.

"I still vote for slow and painful," I said as I stared down at Miguel Alvarez.

We'd brought Keller with us for this particular mission. One of us would have the privilege of killing two of these assholes, but I didn't give a fuck who earned that kill, as long as none of them were breathing by the time we walked back through the doors of this house.

Our omega told us there wasn't anything in the house she wanted when we told her we planned to burn it to the ground after executing her parents. She'd looked mildly upset that the people who'd brought her into the world would die...until we reminded her they'd been the ones to order the hit on her.

All because she refused to fall in line, because she refused to kill our son and obey their orders to join Pack Garcia to be their fuck toy. And that was all she would be to them. Those assholes who we'd left dead on the back lot of the doctor's office would never have treated her the way she deserved. They would have used and abused her, beat her the way her sister's alpha had beat her.

Yep. We'd learned Isabelle was the one behind all the anonymous tips. And when her alpha, Antonio, had learned about it, he'd beaten her to within an inch of her life and locked her up. She'd barely escaped and run straight to our estate to warn her sister of their mother's plans. And had almost been too late.

That Antonio fucker was in the wind, but we'd find him. And he would earn the same fate as these fuckers kneeling in front of me.

Bain turned toward me, a brow cocked. "I'm bored," he said.

I huffed a humorless laugh.

"Is this where you ask us if we have any last words? Expect us to apologize? Fuck–"

I didn't bother waiting for the last of Vance's tirade. I pulled the trigger, as did the others, and smiled as each of them fell backward, their eyes wide open and staring sightlessly at the ceiling.

Walking closer, I looked down into Corazon's mother's face and searched for the guilt. Nope. Nothing. Not a single ounce of remorse. The bitch deserved death. All six of them deserved something more than the quick deaths we'd delivered.

Too late now.

One of our guards waited at the front door, gas cans lined up at his feet. We each took a container and started splashing gasoline everywhere, including along the corpses coating the floor with blood and brain matter. I, for one, wanted to make sure there wasn't much to identify when the fire was finally put out.

We sat in the SUV, watching the smoke billow from the broken windows as the fire licked along the walls and crept outside. It would only be a matter of minutes before the place was engulfed and we needed to make sure we were long gone before any passersby caught sight and called nine-one-one.

"I want to go home. I need my omega," Cohl said from the backseat.

Our omega. The love of our life. The mother of our son.

And we'd come way too fucking close to losing her.

I knew she wanted to return to a semblance of a normal life, but I couldn't imagine a day when any of us would be comfortable letting her out of the house without an army of guards surrounding her and our child. We might have eliminated two of our greatest enemies, but there would always be more. There would always be packs who wanted our power, our control, our wealth.

Our omega. There would be assholes who would target her or our child to get to us, to punish us, to weaken us.

Valen put the SUV in gear and rolled forward. We would have to keep to the speed limit to keep attention off us. We would always have authorities who would accept money under the table to keep the focus away from us, but there were a lot of others who would love nothing more than to see our empire fall.

As we pulled to the gate, I bit back a chuckle. From the size of security at the gate and around the house, it looked as though the president of the United States was inside instead of our beautiful, pregnant omega.

We'd lost a lot of men through the last few months, but we still had plenty who were loyal to us and now loyal to our growing family. There would come a day when we'd need to start seeking new employees, vetting alphas or betas to ensure they would sacrifice their own safety or lives for Corazon.

The front door opened and Enzo stepped out before Corazon. He kept a few feet away from her but was close enough to protect her if needed.

"Your brother might be my new favorite alpha," Cohl said as Valen pulled the vehicle along the circle drive and stopped it at the base of the stairs.

Enzo and his pack had proven over the past few months that they were not only good men but had more than earned the money they pocketed from the club we'd helped them purchase and grow.

They'd also earned their title of uncles.

Her arms were wrapped around her belly, her brows pulled together as she watched us climb from our seats and approach her. "Is it done?"

I pulled her into my arms, rubbing my chin across the top of her head before lowering to taste her lips in a quick kiss. "They'll never hurt you again."

Isabelle stepped out with Ax and Cyrus, the bruising and swelling on her face finally beginning to fade enough that her natural beauty shone through. The sisters held a few similarities but were different in their own way.

"Did you make them cry? Did you make it hurt?" Isabelle asked. Her chin was jutted forward but her bottom lip trembled and tears welled in her eyes.

My brows rose up my forehead when Cyrus wrapped an arm

around her shoulders and pulled her close to his side in a comforting gesture.

"It's over," Bain said. He tugged Corazon from my hold and hugged her as tightly as he could without squishing her belly. "You're safe."

"For now," she said against his chest, her thin arms sliding around his waist to hug him closer.

After each of us took a moment to touch her, to leave our scents on her, to ease the instinctual need to reassure ourselves she was still safe, we all filed into the house.

For now. She'd mirrored my thoughts almost exactly. The current threat was over, but we would always need to ensure our family was heavily guarded and protected. And the moment our son was old enough, I would be the first one to teach him how to handle his first firearm.

CHAPTER FORTY-TWO

Six months later

<u>Corazon</u>

When Pietro was born with a thick head of dark blond hair, I thought Ford was going to hire a damn marching band. I didn't have the heart to tell him our son's hair color could change, or that I was sure I saw hints of auburn in certain light.

Honestly, each of my alphas had stood around the bed trying to find hints of themselves in our son. And all four treated Pietro as though he was theirs. They were all four the fathers to our son and I had no doubt they would continue to love him regardless of how he presented later in life.

"He's so perfect," Valen said, craning his neck to look into our son's face as Cohl held him tightly, snarling when any of the other alphas came near. "You have to share, ass—jerk."

I chuckled softly at how quickly the giant alpha corrected himself before cursing in front of our newborn.

Bain brushed the hair from my face. "You are so amazing," he said with a purr, leaning over the bed to press his lips to my forehead.

After a thirteen hour labor, our first son had been born at two thirty-two in the morning. My pack had made sure we were in a private room that had spaces for them to rest during the labor and as I recuperated after delivery.

And of course, there was a ridiculous number of guards posted outside my room and around the hospital. I was mildly surprised Bain and Ford hadn't demanded I have a home birth and called in a midwife so I wouldn't have to leave the house.

The main threat was over, but my sister's asshole alpha had disappeared into thin air. I knew my alphas wouldn't rest until he was eliminated, as well. But for now, we were all over the moon with the tiny bundle who'd barely made a peep when he'd entered the world, instead, blinking unfocused eyes as though checking out his environment.

"I swear he just smiled at me," Cohl said.

"He's probably just gassy," Ford teased.

He approached the other side of my bed and pressed a kiss to my lips. "Are you hungry? Thirsty? Want me to run down to the cafeteria and get you anything?"

"I would kill for a soda. Or a cup of coffee," I teased.

"You can't–"

I waved Bain off before he could finish his protest. "Yes. I'm aware I still can't drink caffeine until after I'm done breast feeding."

We could have always chosen to use formula, but I wanted the closeness feeding our son would provide. We might have hired a nanny to help, especially during my cycle, but *I* would be raising our son. *We* would be raising him.

✳ ✳ ✳

Ten months later

. . .

We were all making preparations while the nanny kept our son occupied. My preheat had hit a few days ago and the fever had started to take root. We were hours away from being locked in my nest while Enzo, Ax, and Cyrus helped Issa take care of their nephew, giving our beta nanny the week off.

It had been Issa's idea, an excuse to spend as much time with her nephew as possible. And Enzo wanted to be there to watch over his nephew while we were completely lost to our hindbrain.

At least that was his excuse. Once Issa's injuries had fully healed, she'd been too afraid to move out on her own. My pack and I had told her she could stay with us for as long as she needed, but Enzo, Ax, and Cyrus had welcomed her into their home as a roommate, giving her the fully finished attic for her own private quarters.

Valen set a box of condoms on the floor of the nest. I hadn't had a chance to get a birth control implant, so the guys had volunteered to use protection. My omega had whined at the thought of not feeling the softness of their cocks deep inside, of not feeling the heat of their release coating my inner walls.

I wasn't sure whether my hormones were taking over and controlling my brain, but my mouth opened and the words poured out before I could stop them.

"I want another baby," I said as the guys filled the mini fridge with bottled water and easy to eat snacks packed away in containers.

All movement ceased. Four sets of eyes turned toward me.

"Are you sure?" Valen asked. "Pietro isn't even a year old yet."

I nodded.

"Omega, we should probably wait until after your heat to discuss this. We don't want you to regret the decision," Ford said.

A sense of rejection hit hard as my emotions rode that stupid ass rollercoaster. "Do you not want to have another child with me?"

Cohl lunged forward, scooping me into his arms. "I told you I wanted to keep your belly filled with my babies. If these assholes want to wear rubbers, that just means I'll know damn sure who knocked you up."

"Fuck off. I get her pussy first," Bain said.

"Nope." Cohl leaned forward and licked a path from my shoulder to my temple, causing me to giggle and squirmed. "I licked her, I claimed her."

My heat hadn't fully hit yet and we still weren't done filling the nest with bottled water or snacks, but I was beyond ready to feel Cohl's wickedly talented tongue in more places than my damn shoulder.

"Fuck them. I'm going to breed you so hard. Want me to kick them out? I can lock the door," he teased, one brow raised as a smile quirked up one corner of his sexy as sin mouth.

"Nah. They can watch," I teased back.

A not-so-serious growl rumbled up from Bain's chest. "Watch? You think I'm going to sit here with my cock in my hand while this asshole has all the fun?"

He shoved Cohl out of the way and started tearing my clothes from my body. Literally tore them from my body, sending the ripped pieces of fabric fluttering to the ground.

"Damn it. You boys keep ruining my clothes," I said with a huff.

"We'll buy you more," Cohl said as he shoved his sweats down his legs and kicked them away.

"I'm pretty sure I warned you about what would happen if you called us boys," Ford faux threatened as he slowly removed his clothes in sexy yet intimidating movements.

He stalked toward me and I stumbled back, my feet sinking into the cushioned floor. My back bumped against a hard, warm body, and thick arms wrapped around me as lips lowered to my ear.

"Where you think you're going, omega? Seems to me like you need to be reminded that your alphas aren't boys," Bain growled in my ear.

A shiver traveled down my spine and my pussy instantly grew wet with slick, the fluid dampening my thighs as my perfume lifted on the air.

My first heat with these four men had been out of my control. I'd been put in a situation I hadn't asked for. And then I'd fallen in love. I'd found my scent matches. I had claimed each of them before I ever allowed them to leave their bonding marks on my flesh.

"I love you," I whispered to Ford even as he continued stalking toward me.

"You trying to earn favor now? Talk your way out of a spanking?"

A flirty smile pulled up my lips. "Oh, alpha. I would beg for that. I just wanted to say the words before I lose all coherent thought. I love all four of you. You've given me a life I didn't know was possible."

"Well, shit. We can't spank her now," Cohl said, sticking his bottom lip out in a pout.

Oh, but I wanted them to spank me. I wanted them all naked and touching me. I wanted to feel their hands and lips and tongues on me.

And then, I wanted all four of them to take turns knotting me over the next week.

I couldn't help but wonder whether our next child would be another son or a daughter. And which of my alphas would get the most use of my pussy and father our next child.

FROM THE AUTHOR

If you loved Corazon's story of discovering her inner strength, finding her pack, and building a loving family, I would love if you could take the time to leave a review on your favorite site.

For cover reveals, early sneak peeks, and free novellas, make sure to subscribe to my newsletter here.

www.ingramcontent.com/pod-product-compliance
Lightning Source LLC
Chambersburg PA
CBHW061639190726

48289CB00006B/1660